Praise for

ROBIN D. OWENS

"[A] multi-faceted, fast paced gem of a book."
—*The Best Reviews* on *Guardian of Honor*,
book one of The Summoning series

"Owens takes...elements that made
Marion Zimmer Bradley's *Darkover* stories popular...
and turns out a romance that draws you in."
—*Locus* magazine

"Lladrana seems like a genuine place
even with monsters and mages. The story line
is action-packed but also contains terrific characters....
Robin D. Owens enchants her readers."
—*Affaire de Coeur* on *Guardian of Honor*

"Owens excels at evocative, sensual writing."
—*Romantic Times BOOKreviews*

"As have others before her (e.g. Anne McCaffrey,
Marion Zimmer Bradley), Owens has penned a stunning
futuristic tale that reads like a fantasy and is sure to have
crossover appeal to both sf and fantasy fans."
—*Library Journal* on *Heart Duel*

ROBIN D. OWENS

PROTECTOR OF THE FLIGHT

LUNA™
www.LUNA-Books.com

LUNA™

PROTECTOR OF THE FLIGHT

ISBN-13: 978-0-373-80264-7
ISBN-10:   0-373-80264-1

Copyright © 2007 by Robin D. Owens

First printing: February 2007

Author Photo by: Rose Beetem

This edition published by arrangement with Harlequin Books S.A.

® and TM are trademarks of Harlequin Books S.A., used under license. Trademarks indicated with ® are registered in the United States Patent and Trademark Office, the Canadian Trade Marks Office and in other countries.

www.LUNA-Books.com

Printed in U.S.A.

To My Critique Group,
a better bunch of writers I've never met.
Don't think you'll ever get rid of me,
because I can't do this without you.

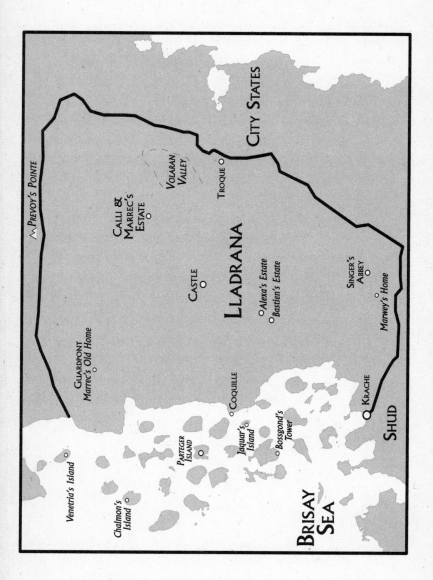

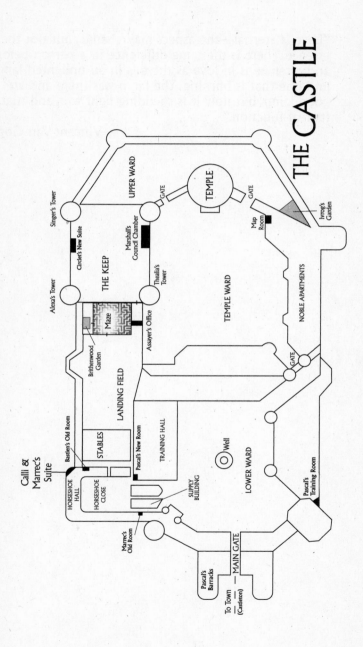

THE CASTLE

"Love is eternal—the aspect may change, but not the essence. There is the same difference in a person before and after he is in love as there is in an unlighted lamp and one that is burning. The lamp was there and was a good lamp, but now it is shedding light too, and that is its real function."

—Vincent Van Gogh

I

Colorado Mountains
Summer, Morning

Since her fall in the National Finals Rodeo, pain had been a daily enemy. Calli Torcher hesitated at the top of the steep stairs from her attic bedroom to the first floor, took a breath, braced a hand against the wall and gritted her teeth at the prospect of pain. No matter how carefully she set her feet, she'd jar herself, then stop and pant through the agony. Or she might fall and end up in the hospital. Again.

Recovering from a broken pelvis took time. The bad dreams that peppered her sleep didn't help matters. She'd dreamt of people lost in a winter blizzard. Cries for help. Short notes of doom from a clock gong or the ranch's iron triangle or a siren…

She shook her head to clear her mind and concentrate on navigating the stairs. It happened the third stair from the top, just a tiny misstep and she was leaning against the wall, trying to shut out waves of agony. When she recovered, she went on and made it to the ground floor with no other problems.

As she rested against the wall at the bottom landing, she wondered if she should ask her dad if she could use the downstairs storeroom as a bedroom until she fully healed. But things hadn't been right between her and her father for months, ever since she'd fallen and lost the barrel-racing championship, ending her career at twenty-five.

That was the past. She could—and *would*—still train horses, take a more active role in the ranch now that she wasn't on the road all the time, traveling the rodeo circuit.

Her nose twitched at the smell of strong coffee and frying bacon. Dad was up and fixing his own breakfast. Since he'd started without her, she decided she'd get some air, clear the images and sounds of the dream—the string of bad dreams—from her head and replace them with the beauty of the Rocking Bar T Ranch in their mountain valley.

Calli limped to the corral, breathing deeply, feeling the tingle of the breeze on her face, the softness of worn flannel and denim from her shirt and jeans on her skin. The ball of the sun shot yellow streaks of light into the sky.

She reached the corral fence and leaned against it, breathing fast, still weak from her last surgery. Still, if she continued to work hard, in another few months she'd be able to start training horses.

No whicker of greeting came from her gelding. Calli whistled. Nothing. He *always* greeted her. A twinge of alarm ruptured her calm. "Spark! Spark, here!" She called as if her horse was a young, heedless colt.

Her dad strode up, a lean tough man with a weathered face and hard lines carved from the rigors of cattle ranching. He leaned on the fence to her right. "The gelding ain't here."

She looked at him from the corner of her eye. Bristly gray whiskers sprouted from his jaw. He could speak well if he wanted, if he respected the person he was talking to.

She wet her lips. "What do you mean, Spark isn't here?"

His hat shadowed the eyes as blue as her own, but he squinted down at her all the same. Hard as the distant mountains. "He's a highly trained rodeo horse, worth a lotta money. Couldn't expect me to keep him 'round when you can't ride him anymore and a profit can be made. Your last doctor's appointment made me realize that."

Calli pivoted so quickly it wrenched her hip. She ignored the pain in her body, so much less than the anguish in her heart. She spoke through the shock. "Spark is *my* horse. I gave you the money for him."

Her dad shrugged. "I bought the gelding from the racetrack. The horse was registered in my name. I'm the owner of Rocking Bar T and everything on it."

"Except for Spark. *I* paid for him," Calli said through clenched teeth.

His stance was still casual. "Huh. My name is on the papers. And who paid for that horse's keep when it was young? I did."

Money wasn't the issue. Love was. Giving and receiving love was everything. She'd needed something to love and return that love in her life. "How could you do this? I love him."

He faced her now, as impassive as always, as if nothing

touched him, not even a hint of irritation in his eyes. He looked her up and down as if judging a heifer, not as if he saw his daughter. "You should know better than that. Stupid to love an animal. Stupid to love at all. Love ain't nothin' that gets a return. A profit could be made, and Spark wasn't no use to me. I sold him to Bill Morsey."

Usefulness had always been Dad's bottom line.

Her insides clenched, the pressure of hard tears backed behind her eyes. She couldn't stop the question. "What about *me?* What about *my* usefulness?"

He grunted. "You can do your chores and stay. Do the cookin' and cleanin.' But I went to the bank. Since the ranch is paid for, I set up a reverse mortgage. The money'll last long as I do, then you'll have to find another place."

Shock and nausea rolled through her. "I'd planned on training horses."

"This is a *cattle ranch.*"

"We could build up a fine reputation—"

"No. We run cattle."

She went to the bottom line. "You aren't leaving the ranch to me?" Ever since she'd gone on the circuit, she'd always thought of the ranch as her future. Working hard, she'd sent money back for expenses. She'd thought she and her dad were partners.

His gaze fastened on her middle as if he could see her abdominal scars. "No reason to. Ain't as if you can gimme a grandson, even." Without another word he sauntered back to the house, leaving Calli's world broken.

A noise tore from her, some animalistic cry of pain. Blindly she gripped the top fence rail, splinters lanced her hand.

All her life she'd shut out the knowledge of what her father was. Instead, she'd woven illusions that he cared about her. False, lying illusions that had been so comforting and that she'd held so long that she couldn't see reality.

Her mother had abandoned them, then died. If her father had loved Calli before, he'd shut off his emotions afterward. As long as she proved useful, she was tolerated.

He might have enjoyed the reflected glory of her rodeo wins and liked the big bucks of the prizes. He'd taken care of her in the hospital and later when she was healing. But now that it was obvious she wouldn't return to the rodeo she was nothing more than a woman to cook and clean.

She glanced around but refused to see past the surface beauty of the day. This place wasn't her home anymore. She couldn't afford the wrenching sense of loss.

Blood pounded in her ears and with it came the sounds of chimes and singing. Tinnitus, ringing in the ears, the doctors had said, and that it should go away soon. The illusory sounds might pass, but the very real loss of the ranch would always shadow her. More bad dreams.

Her white-knuckled hand on the wooden rail hurt from splinters, rough wood impressed hard on her palm, the ache of her stretched tendons. She let go.

She had to escape, allow emotions to surge through her— her grief for the loss of Spark, the destruction of her dreams. She'd plan later. This heartache she'd brought on herself for not letting herself see what the man who fathered her was—hard and bitter, guarding his heart from everyone, including her.

She limped, stumbled, caught herself, limped a few more steps—and found that she did so in rhythm to the reverberating rise and fall of melodic voices. Her foot brushed a fallen branch and she picked it up and used it as a walking staff.

By the time her eyes cleared from tears, she'd passed the edge of the ranch yard and was on her way to the sandstone rocks and the wide ledge on a hill that had always been her refuge. She needed air to breathe.

When she reached the ledge, her pelvis ached all the way up to her teeth. She hobbled past the huge sheered-off crystal face of the hill to solid rock and gingerly lowered herself to sit. She leaned against the hillside, her legs straight, and set the stick beside her. Then she wiped the sweat from her face, wrinkling her nose at the brown and red dirt smears on her bandana.

Her breath came fast with exertion. Her teeth hurt from gritting them when she'd negotiated her way up the rocky path. Up here, the wind blew and she heard a tinkle of chimes rushing around her.

She closed her eyes and whirls of bright colors streaked inside of her eyelids. The spots would fade as she rested.

Her heartbeat decreased to normal. Too much emotion and exertion in such a short amount of time had drained her.

Time seemed to slow until one moment was everything. The scent of rock and pine, the faint tumble of a distant stream, the cool wind, all etched on her memory.

She opened her lashes and looked out over the ranch, the kitchen gardens, the sprawling house, the land that stretched to the mountains, higher than this backyard hill. So beautiful. The stream was full—no drought this year.

For a while, Calli just sat and enjoyed the calm of her emotions. Too many problems had pressed down on her lately, flattening her spirits. For this one moment she could be quiet and enjoy life, let thoughts drift through her mind without jabbing at her heart.

Did she love the ranch?

No. It had always reflected what her dad wanted, not the kind of ranch she wanted, a horse ranch.

But she loved the land. And she loved the potential of a horse ranch. She wanted the land, wanted to shape that potential.

The rock was cold and hard against her back as her head throbbed with equally hard thoughts. She'd been a fool.

Well, that was the past. Maybe only the recent past, but time to wake up and fix her mistakes.

Spark was gone. Her heart twinged, jerking her body. She could barely stand that thought. Bill Morsey was a good horseman, and his daughter would be thrilled to have Spark. Calli's lips turned down. Her father had probably done the best thing for Spark. The horse loved to run, delighted in an audience. Calli gulped and blew her nose on the corner of her bandana.

Now that she knew she'd have to fight Dad for her vision of the ranch, or walk away, she must make some decisions.

Should she fight for the land or get a check for her share and leave? She had a chance of winning—never Dad's respect or love, she finally realized that, but she might be able to prove her contribution to the ranch, her vision was more profitable than his. In any event, she'd go to the bank and straighten them out about the equity she had in this place. She had records. There would be deposits, bills paid, after she'd sent money back, and everyone in town knew of her triumphs.

Fighting would take a lot of energy—physical and emotional, and that was a rare commodity for her during her recovery. And it would be bitter, turn her father against her forever.

But she loved the land and he already had no affection for her. How much did *he* love the ranch, the land? Would he hate her for fighting?

She didn't think so. She loved. He didn't.

He could take his share of the ranch money and walk away. It would be tough on her own at first, but she was confident she could make a name for the ranch, for herself, by horse training. She'd be well in a few months. Or after one more surgery.

Calli glanced at the smooth plane of crystal that was the face of the hillside beside her. Milky white with tints of green, the sheer face of the glassy rock stood taller and wider than herself. A small rim framed it, protecting it from the weather.

She hadn't been able to look at the faint image of herself in the crystal for a long time.

A while back, she'd done a little research and discovered it was a fine piece of microcline. Devil's Hole wasn't too far away, and it had had even bigger crystals.

When she'd first found the path and the crystal when she was six years old, she'd been a little afraid of it. The green had tinged into dark shadows inside that reminded her of the tiny, dark bedroom her mom had locked her in when she'd left the ranch as evening fell—walked away from the land and her husband and her daughter forever. A memory Calli suppressed as much as possible.

Years later, sunlight had danced on the face of the crystal

and lit the angles deep inside. Then she pretended she saw a different world dimly through the crystal, a place with flying horses and those who rode them lifting flashing swords. Later still, she just saw herself in the shadows.

She'd faced disillusionment today, maybe it was time to face herself again—then she'd know she was strong and able to deal with the future on her own. She'd never ride the rodeo circuit again, but she'd come to terms with that. She'd never have her father's love, and that left a bitter taste in her mouth.

Levering herself up the wall slowly, she rose from the ledge and balanced on the stick.

She stared into the crystal and the shadows beyond the smooth outside plane. Her image was wavery, her blond hair a shade of yellow on the milkiness. She made out the curve of breast and hip.

But besides herself, she once again saw an imaginary vision of otherwhere. This time a section of a great, circular stone wall, and flickers of colorfully robed figures. Once again the strange sounds the doctors had called tinnitus plagued her. Chimes. A gong. The chanting of many voices in words she couldn't seem to grasp. Gregorian chants, maybe.

Bong!

The sound came next to her ear, louder and more vibrant than ever. She pivoted, lost her balance and fell. Ah, shit, she was going to hit her head on the damn crystal.

But she fell *through* it, into a blank whiteness so pervasive she couldn't tell if her eyes were open. She choked on a scream. All the emotions that had calmed as she sat on the ledge jammed into her. Fear. Despair. Most of all, a great longing for someone to love. Someone to love her back. A partner.

It lasted instants. It lasted an eternity. Then bright colors whirled in her sight—patterns, stained glass! She glimpsed pillars around the curved walls of a circular room, and rafters with huge crystal ends.

Pain shot up her hip, stealing breath. Calli didn't believe this. Her throat closed with fear. She must have hit her head on the rock and was dreaming. She rubbed her head, but didn't feel any bumps. Dazed, she examined her surroundings. A big round stone room with an altar and colored goblets. A gong. A circle of people.

Calli sucked in air. It didn't smell anything like a hill in Colorado. It smelled like incense in a church. She gulped and shivering seized her.

A small woman with white hair and a young face, green eyes and a long scar along her cheek caught Calli's attention. The lady wore a long velvet robe with silver threaded designs. "Hi, I'm Alexa Fitzwalter. Welcome to Lladrana," she said.

This couldn't be happening! But she wouldn't take it lying down. When Calli awkwardly sat up, pain lancing low in her torso, the singing stopped.

Alexa stepped forward into the center of the star, compassion in her eyes. "It's a rough trip." She held out her hands.

Calli stared at her, touched her fingers. They felt solid and warm! Another moment passed and Calli realized that Alexa wouldn't push. The dream woman was courteous. Alexa would let Calli make her own choices. A hard knot in her chest loosened, she was in charge of the dream. She put her hands in Alexa's and was drawn to her feet with surprising ease and strength.

Alexa kept an arm around Calli as if to steady her and Calli was grateful for the physical and emotional support. Her gaze swept the circle of people, pausing at the men and women who were dressed more roughly than those in velvet robes.

When Alexa looked up at Calli, her expression was haunted. "We need you really, really bad." Alexa licked her lips. "Do you know anything about horses?"

Clang! An alarm shrilled. Everyone in the room tensed.

Alexa cocked her head, her hands fisting. "We have no volarans," her voice broke. "We can't fly to battle."

Stranger and stranger. Calli shot glances around the room, wanted to run, didn't think she could hobble fast enough to escape...what?

"How good are you with horses?" Alexa demanded again, squeezing her arm.

Calli knew she flushed but shot up her chin. "Excellent. I'm an excellent horse trainer and one of the top barrel racers—"

People ran to the great door, flung it open, sending in bright summer-morning sunlight. A whir of wings rushed into the room.

Cheers rose outside. A young man shouted something.

"They came back," Alexa whispered. Tears ran down her face. "The volarans have returned." She looked up at Calli, sniffed. "I knew it was right to continue with the Summoning."

Hooves hit the stone courtyard. The next moment people were spreading out in the room, making way for...for a winged horse.

Calli blinked. Blinked again. The pegasus didn't vanish. In fact, *more* swept into the room. Ten. With dozens outside. Chestnuts, roans, piebalds, even a palomino or two. She caught her breath in sheer wonder and thought the top of her head would explode with this huge wave of horse-thoughts and horse-love radiating from them, inundating her.

A gray clopped up, stretched his wings, forcing people aside. Her mind spun. Her mouth dropped open.

The stallion's large dark gaze fixed on her. *We love you. You are the Volaran Exotique.* She heard the words in her head.

Then chimes clashed and she *felt* the sound storm through her, plucking at muscle and bone and nerve. She cried out, arching away from Alexa, escaping the woman's grip. Reached for the winged horse, missed. Calli landed on the floor again on her butt and shrieked with the pain radiating through her pelvis.

Only agony existed. Everything else around her dimmed—she couldn't see. Again and again the chimes rippled, but they sounded muffled as she grimly fought through the pain and hung on to the edge of consciousness.

Then someone struck the gong. Once. Twice.

She only heard a part of the third beat. Sweet darkness descended.

2

"She's hurt!" Alexa Fitzwalter, once of Denver, now a Swordmarshall of Lladrana, whirled to face the Marshalls and Chevaliers.

Few were paying attention to her or the new Exotique. They were herding the newly arrived volarans out the door, the gray stallion grumbling, then taking off. People ran with unseemly haste to find their own winged companions.

The defection of the flying horses ten days ago had devastated the Chevaliers and Marshalls. A black pall of despair had filled the Castle. Calls to battle had been blessedly few— only three—but fighting without the flying horses was nearly impossible. Lladrana would be lost to the invading monsters without volarans. Dread had circled the Castle like a vulture.

They'd been desperate when they'd worked the ritual,

praying the one they Summoned would somehow lure the volarans back.

A medica strode forward and crouched by the woman on the floor. Alexa turned back to watch the examination. She didn't even know the woman's name yet, but Alexa feared for her. She and the Marshalls had Summoned this woman from Colorado, away from Earth to this world, so Alexa was responsible for her until she made her own place on Lladrana. Biting her lip, Alexa shifted from foot to foot, grateful when her husband, Bastien, joined her.

He cocked his head, as if he listened to the mind-Song of a volaran—or many. His nostrils flared, then he grinned. He grabbed Alexa and spun her around and around, then placed her gently on her feet. Holding hands, they looked down where the medica sat next to the new Exotique, smoothing blond strands of hair away from a pale forehead.

"The volarans came back," Bastien said. "For *their* Exotique."

Alexa leaned against him in relief.

The medica said, "The Lady's pelvis has recently been broken in three places."

Alexa winced.

Glancing up at them, the medica said, "I suggest we all join together to do a healing spell."

Alexa said, "I'll call Marian, the Exotique Circlet Sorceress. She can help, too." The community of Sorcerers had had Marian Summoned from Boulder, Colorado, just a few weeks ago.

"Good idea." The medica hummed a slow lilting spellsong that settled the woman deeper into a healthful sleep.

* * *

Marrec watched as Lady Hallard closed the door of the healing room behind her, muting the continuous lilting of a healing Song. Hallard, the noble he swore loyalty to, ran her fingers through her hair.

He pushed from the wall where he'd stood, guarding the corridor for the last hour. "How's it going?" he asked.

"Good," Lady Hallard rasped. She rubbed her throat. "She might not be able to ride long hours horseback, but flying a volaran will be possible."

"She's the right one?"

Hallard shrugged. "Has to be, if you believe in the Song and the Marshalls' Summoning."

Amusement unfurled inside him, mixing with deep gratitude that his volaran had returned. He'd never prayed so hard as he had the last ten days, wanting Dark Lance back. Marrec was a poor man with only the one treasure—his volaran—to his name.

But he answered his liege-woman. "I don't dare disbelieve in the Marshalls' Power."

She grunted, pulled out the gloves tucked in her belt and put them on. "Think I'll take a late-afternoon ride—if my lady volaran will deign to do as I say." There was irritation in Hallard's tone. Like all the rest of them, they'd thought of the flying horses as their property. They'd never been so shocked in their lives as when the volarans—even those born and bred in noble stables—had all deserted to the wild herds and the legendary Volaran Valley. It had never happened before.

All the Chevaliers—and the Marshalls—would be uneasy for some time.

Looking at him from under lowered brows, Hallard said, "You're one of those who can hear and talk with the volarans mentally, right?"

He kept an easy smile on his face, though all the muscles of his body had tensed. Now that their special gift was known, those like him could be either prized or destroyed by the rest of the Chevaliers, and everyone knew it. A delicate situation. A balancing act. He ducked his head. "Yes, my lady."

"Huh. Your volaran say anything to you?"

"No."

"I asked Bastien, he says they aren't talkin' to him, either. Says they want to talk to the new Exotique first."

Marrec lifted and dropped a shoulder. "Bastien's the best with the winged steeds."

Without another word, the Lady strode away. Marrec exhaled a sigh and rubbed his forehead. Lady Hallard was rich, had six volarans and fifty Chevaliers who'd sworn fealty to her.

He had one volaran, Dark Lance, that he couldn't even consider his anymore. He shuddered. He wasn't getting any younger. Time to seriously think about making his fortune, taking risks on the battlefield for booty. He'd have to give the Lady thirty percent of what he earned, but somehow he must come up with a stake to buy a small parcel of land where he could retire and ranch. He didn't want to spend his older days as a pensioner in Lady Hallard's castle. *If* he lived that long.

The Chevaliers were hoping that the new Exotique would participate in a Choosing and Bonding ritual for a mate. Marrec hoped, too, that she might choose him.

Fast footsteps approached. Marrec moved to stand in front of the door, listening to the stride. A tall man, rich because he had good, hard leather for the heels and soles of his boots. Arrogant. Probably a nobleman.

Even before the man turned the corner so Marrec could see him, Marrec sensed it was Faucon Creusse. A nobleman with many Chevaliers, wealthier than most Marshalls, and nearly of equal status. Attractive to the ladies.

Faucon glanced at the door behind Marrec, probably didn't even notice Marrec.

Faucon would want the woman. Marrec had heard that Faucon was one of those men who was innately drawn to Exotiques. Something in their mental Song or their strangeness or even their otherworldly scent, drew Faucon like light drew moths. He'd sniffed around Alexa until Bastien, and Bastien's brother, Luthan, had interfered.

He'd met the Circlet Sorceress Marian and given her expensive gifts. Marrec had heard the nobleman had become close friends with the Lladranan-Who-Was-Now-Exotique, Marian's brother, the Chevalier Koz who had a Lladranan body and Exotique mind.

The new female Exotique behind the door had been expressly Summoned for the Chevaliers, would bond better with the knights than any other segment of Lladranan society. All the more exciting for Faucon. Yes, he'd want her.

Any smart Chevalier would want a Powerful, rich, volaran-beloved woman.

Marrec wanted her, too.

Faucon's expression was pleasant, but his body tense with need. His eyes burned. A smile formed on his lips, but he didn't meet Marrec's gaze. "Lady Hallard asked me to relieve you or join the healing circle."

Marrec knew which one Faucon preferred, but the man was being courteous to him, lesser Chevalier, giving Marrec the choice. He didn't particularly want to take part in the healing, his Power was only fair, but he wanted Faucon near the Exotique even less. The nobleman already had too many advantages and would no doubt charm the lady out of her senses…when she came to them.

"I'll go in," Marrec said. He opened the door and entered, shutting it behind him.

He'd never been in the Marshalls' Healing Room before and hesitated on the threshold. For a stone room inside a stone tower in a stone Keep, it looked unexpectedly…soft. The curved room was paneled with wainscoting along the lower wall. Plaster above it was painted warm tones of some pinky-yellow-peach colors that seemed to shift in the light from the fat pillar candles of dark green and the sunlight. A row of pointed windows showed a summer-blue sky. The healing dais was set on richly layered rugs with long gold fringe. Atop the dais was a thick mattress, from the looks of it, made of pure down. The injured woman lay on her stomach, still fully dressed.

The rhythm of the chant did not break, though several gazes fixed on him. The circle was a mixture of Chevaliers and Marshalls—with two Circlets, mages of the highest degree—the Exotique Circlet Marian, who held the yellow-haired woman's right hand, and her own husband, Jaquar.

Alexa was on the opposite side of the prone woman and held the new Exotique's left hand and was linked to Bastien.

Marrec could *see* the strong aura of Power rippling the air from the magical and prayerful Singing. He stiffened his spine. He didn't care for linking with others, but he was needed. "I've come to replace Lady Hallard," he said.

Two people raised their connected hands, indicating he should insert himself between them. Marrec sucked in a big breath. He'd be between the Circlet Sorcerer Jaquar and the leader of the Marshalls, Swordmarshall Thealia Germaine. The Power that cycled through the group was strong indeed. Flying out of his class. Too bad.

Moving as smoothly as he could, he walked around the foot of the dais and the people there, then stood in front of a plush chair and slowly insinuated himself into the circle, disturbing the flow of magic as little as possible. The medica at the foot of the table handled the uneven stream as he joined the group.

The force of Power rushed through him, the Singing whipping his blood, flooding his every cell, even as he passed most of it from Jaquar to Thealia, sending it around and on.

His hands heated to unbearable tenderness. He held on. The Power threatened to rock his balance. He hunkered down. His chest constricted. He opened his mouth to breathe and when he could, he added his voice to the Song.

It was an intricately layered Song, blended of voices from bass to soprano, harmonizing, hypnotic, healing. After a few minutes, Marrec became accustomed enough to the huge energy pouring through him to sink into the deep softness of the chair. He was aware of every nerve of his body, every pulse of his blood, every hair on his head—and some of those were turning silver with the Power he handled—

making his own gift stronger, opening up rivers in his mind that had been trickles before.

Wondrous.

He wouldn't walk away from this place the same man he'd been when he entered the door. The thought scared him, but he squeezed the fear into a tiny ball and hid it from the others.

His throat cleared, and he sent strength to his voice, to his words, full of Power. Gazes flew to him. He inclined his head. He knew he had a good voice, clear and true, he just hadn't been able to use it fully until now.

A whispered murmur came to his mind. *You add beauty and Power to our healing. Our thanks.* Swordmarshall Thealia on his left dipped her head to him. The compliment surprised him, but he kept his Song steady.

Now that he was linked, he could see the green energy web they spun, blanketing it over the lady, subtly shifting it into her, healing as it went.

The lilting melody swept him along and now he *felt* the traces of the others—the steely bond between all the Marshalls at the table, forged time and time again as they linked during battle; the sizzling might of the Circlets, with hints of wind and wave and lightning—and an additional strange tang of *other* from Marian. *Exotique.*

Another taste of spice and blood and *alien* from Swordmarshall Alexa. *Exotique.*

And a fabulous, poignant sweetness that cycled several times before he realized where it originated. The lady on the mattress. *Exotique.*

She would never go unnoticed in Lladrana, this woman

Summoned for the Chevaliers. Her hair was filaments of light, a color he'd never seen, never imagined. As golden as freshly minted jent coins. For long moments he stared at her hair, wondering at its fineness, pondering the texture.

Her face was turned toward him. Her skin was not as fair as Marian's, slightly more tanned than Alexa's. The woman worked outdoors, and for longer than Alexa had, but Alexa had come to Lladrana in the early spring and it was now late summer. Still, the new lady's skin was not the color of a Lladranan's and here and there he could see the interesting blueness of her veins.

Her brows were golden, too, her lashes a shade darker.

Her features were...not what he thought of noble. Surreptitiously, he studied Alexa and Marian. Of the three Exotiques, he'd have said that Marian looked the most "noble" with straight nose and comely eyes and lips, though her hair was that odd shade of dark red.

The light flickering on the golden hair caught him again, brought him back to the woman. Her energy was stronger now, more mixed with theirs. A new pitch had been added to the Song through her, vibrant, potent—pure, raw Power.

Marrec swallowed. All three of the ladies were Powerful, though their magic took different aspects, and the new one contained a greatness that matched the other two. She was for the Chevaliers, his portion of Lladranan society, the knights. He couldn't see her in battle. He shook the thought away. Anticipating too much.

She whimpered. Marrec flinched. Thealia squeezed his fingers, reminding him to keep the Power flow even.

Their healing net had penetrated the woman's body, was

working on her broken bones. Marrec sensed this wasn't the first time the procedure had been done in the hours since she'd arrived, but the fifth or sixth. Everyone had taken shifts of Singing except the Circlets and Alexa and Bastien, who had stayed the entire time. But then Bastien carried the wild magic of a black-and-white.

Marrec wasn't tired at all, in fact he was still a little jittery from joining the circle, but he could tell others were at the last of their strength.

He glanced around, some looked worn and weary, gray-faced. Everyone here was of higher rank than he. It was not his place to tell them when to leave.

Projecting his voice, he added more Power so some could relax.

Eyes met his, and thanks were nodded.

As the Song swept him away, he studied the woman they healed again. A redness had come to her cheeks. He stared—of course Lladranans flushed, but it wasn't nearly as noticeable as this. Her lips had parted and he saw even white teeth, but her mouth attracted his gaze. It was a deep pink. He'd never seen lips that color. A wash of heat slipped along his blood as he considered what the rest of her would look like.

Her breasts were flattened on the mattress, but they looked round and full. He eyed her butt and legs, muscular, like a rider's would be.

He'd heard there were no volarans in the Exotique Land, but that there were horses. She had the tone of horsewoman.

A frisson of awareness raised the hair on the nape of his neck. He lifted his gaze from the woman to find four beady eyes fixed on him. Marrec tilted his chin at the two beings who hunched on either side of the injured woman's head, still staring at him.

Then Marrec realized what they were—magical shape-shifting beings called fey-coo-cus. One had become Alexa's companion after she arrived, the other had originally come from Exotique Terre with Marian. Today they appeared as foot-long rabbits, brown and white with dark patches over their eyes and noses as pink as the horsewoman's lips.

They should have looked harmless, fluffy. They looked dangerous and threatening.

The door opened and several Chevaliers walked in, including Faucon and Lady Hallard.

"This is a good time to switch singers," the medica rasped. "We have lowered the web through our patient and it is below her. We can swap people, then raise it one final time through her body. That should be enough."

The rabbits turned their combined gazes to Faucon. He stopped under the weight of their scrutiny, then nodded. "Salutations, feycoocus."

The magical beings twitched their ears, radiating welcome. Even they wanted Faucon for the woman. What chance did Marrec have?

3

Calli woke to foreign singing. Muzzy-headed, she didn't know where the sound came from, but it was a lot better than the chanting of her tinnitus. She felt *good*, except a little cramped, and her face was squashed into something so soft she had trouble breathing.

She stretched, long and slow. Her mind caught up with her body. No pain! She rolled over to her back, eyes wide open…

And saw a bunch of strangely dressed people standing around her whispering, and not in English. Her insides clutched and she was suddenly afraid to move. These folks were armed. Those who wore richly colored poncho-like robes had chain mail underneath and a sheath on each hip. The people in leathers had swords at their sides.

She gulped, realizing they looked a lot like the people she'd glimpsed in the crystal on the hill for years. Riding flying horses—like those winged horses who'd come to look at her, *speak* to her in her *mind*.

She remembered falling through the face of the hillside—how could she do *that?*—and…and…being greeted by someone.

Glancing around, she saw that same someone, a small woman with silver hair, smiling at her from the right side of her bed.

"Hi, welcome to Lladrana." Her face clouded. "It would have been better if you'd *told* us you were hurt as soon as you came."

"Urgh," was all Calli could manage.

A woman's laugh came. "Give her a break, Alexa. Don't you remember how it was?"

Calli struggled to sit up, strong hands grasped her shoulders from behind and lifted her easily. She heard a tinkling song. She eyed the people around her. They were all tall and beautiful, with golden skin and dark hair and eyes, not quite Asian looking. *Other.*

"You're not in Kansas—well, Colorado—anymore," the other woman said.

Alexa chuckled and patted Calli's hand. "You're not in Oz, either. This is Lladrana, another dimension and I'm Alexa Fitzwalter." She beamed.

Calli must be dreaming.

A tall, auburn-haired woman, plump and pretty, came to stand next to Alexa, the second woman who'd spoken in English. "Hi, I'm Marian Dumont, late of Boulder, now a Circlet of Lladrana." She touched a golden band she wore around her forehead. The hammered design showed clouds and lightning.

Sticking out a hand, Alexa said, "I came from Denver in the spring. Pleased to meet you, Ms.—"

Letting her gaze roam, Calli figured out that the rest of the folks were watching intently and not talking because they didn't understand English. She wondered what language they spoke. She looked at Alexa's hand, put her own in it and received a surge of warmth that flooded her and left her fingers tingling. She licked her lips and tried her voice. "I'm Callista Torcher. Calli."

The redhead jostled Alexa aside in a teasing manner and held out her hand. There was something about the gesture, maybe the way Alexa and Marian stood, that warned Calli that she was being tested somehow. Besides the incredible little surge of...*something*...she'd felt from Alexa, the smaller woman's grip had been firm and strong, her hand callused.

Calli shivered and slid her fingers against Marian's. This time she felt a heady zip that made her head buzz. She shook her head to clear it. Marian released her fingers and chuckled, a richer sound than Alexa's.

Large hands squeezed her shoulders, making her aware of them once more. Man's hands. Thumbs brushed her shoulder blades, then the hands vanished as a man to her left circled the bed she was on. He wore leathers the color of butterscotch that were obviously expensive. He made a flourishing bow to her. "Faucon Creusse," he said, and she decided that was his name.

Never in her life had a guy bowed to Calli. She nodded at him, but too-handsome men made her a little wary. They usually had great expectations of a woman and didn't return much. At least the rodeo cowboys she'd known tended to be that way.

"So, how much French do you know?" Alexa asked briskly, drawing Calli's attention back to her right.

"Uh, none," Calli said.

Marian nodded. "How good are you at languages?"

Calli shrugged. "Pretty fair. I have quite a bit of Spanish."

Alexa made a face. "I'm terrible. I'll have a bad accent for the rest of my life. I chose to stay here on Lladrana."

Calli froze. She wasn't ready to accept she was in a different place—who would? And if, by some impossible chance, she *was* somewhere else, she wasn't ready to cope with that, either. The hurt of her father's rejection still shadowed her heart, echoed in her mind.

An older lady spoke, and the language was French sounding, for sure. This woman wore tough, dark brown leathers. She walked up the right side of the bed to stand next to Alexa and did a half bow. "Nuaj Hallard," the woman said.

Again Calli nodded. Who knew what they did as greeting here? From the long robe with no armor that Marian wore, they might even curtsey. Like bowing, curtseying had never been an item in Calli's life.

"Lady Hallard's right," Alexa said. "Callista doesn't need to know Lladranan to get a tour of the Castle."

Lady? Castle? Uh-oh. Sure didn't sound like Colorado.

With glee in her eyes, Alexa smiled at Calli, and Calli braced herself for a zinger. "How would you like to see the winged horses again?"

The flying steeds couldn't be real, could they? She just

stared at the grinning Alexa, the smiling Marian and the serious Lady Hallard. After a minute, Calli said, "Say again?"

"Winged horses," Alexa said.

"Flying horses," Marian said.

The words rang in Calli's ears, but she could almost see a big question mark hovering above her head with the word *duh?*

"It's true," Alexa assured. "We have flying horses here, called volarans."

"From the French word *fly,*" Marian said.

"Uh," Calli said. She *did* want to see them again.

"So," Alexa said, "do you want to humor our madness?"

Once more, Calli scanned the room full of men and women—some in robes and armor, some in leathers that looked to be for fighting. Caution, deep and strong, swept her. Weapons. Armor. These people were at war. If they were being nice to her, it was because they wanted something.

If they were really here at all and she wasn't crumpled on the ledge of the hillside from cracking her head hard—having a dream more imaginative than ever before.

A man said something and Lady Hallard withdrew and Alexa and Marian stepped aside. Another guy, this one not as tall but more solid and with a gleam of devil-may-care that Calli knew all too well from her rodeo days, bowed in front of her and offered his arm. Alexa circled his other biceps with her fingers. "My husband, Bastien Vauxveau."

He was married. Good. But to Alexa? She'd *married* a guy here? Then Calli noticed a strange thing. They both had a golden color pulsing around them, merging where they touched, sparkling with glitter. Wow. And they looked really good together. Happy.

A bolt of yearning for such love struck Calli so hard she nearly doubled over. She'd thought she and her dad were partners. She'd loved him, ignoring some of the offers for sex and a serious relationship with rodeo men. She'd had her plans to build up the Rocking Bar T to a fine horse-training ranch with Dad and when she was successful look around for a man.

All gone.

Bastien quirked a brow at her, wiggled his elbow. Alexa grinned. Yep, a happy couple. Partners. Calli turned wide eyes to Marian.

"Yes, I'm married, too. To a sexy Sorcerer. A Circlet like myself." Marian answered Calli's unspoken question.

Oh, wow. The back of her neck tingled. Slowly she turned her head to see Faucon Creusse smiling at her.

"He's unmarried and available," Alexa provided. "But we need to talk a little."

"We need to talk *a lot*." If she weren't dreaming. From the corner of her eye, she saw a woman bobbing her head.

"She's available and unpaired, too," Marian said. "This culture has no bias against homosexuality. There are different levels of commitment, here, too."

"I'm straight," Calli said absently, doing another scan of the people in the room—different colored and worn leathers—some people wore bands around their arms. Did that mean anything? From the gazes she met, she thought about a third in the room were "available."

"Marian's right," Alexa said. "She and her husband were married in a formal, long, magical ceremony that bound them together, hearts, minds and souls."

"Not to mention bodies," Marian murmured.

"Bastien and I haven't done that yet. But we're Paired. The guy, here—" Alexa poked him gently in the chest "—is commitment shy." Bastien winced as if he got the gist of Alexa's words. Calli didn't doubt the statement.

"I see," she lied, turning back to the women and Bastien. She looked at Marian, dressed in a long linen dress of beige with a deep over-robe of dark blue, remembering her words. "You're a Circlet, a Sorceress?"

"Yes," Marian said. "I'm only visiting the Marshalls' Castle, to help in the healing spell and to aid you in adjusting to Lladrana. Alexa called me by crystal ball," she ended blandly.

Calli let that one go. She stared at Alexa, who wore a blue-green robe over chain mail, had a sword at one hip and a short, cylindrical sheath at the other—and a nasty scar on her face. "You're a…" Calli didn't know what.

Alexa dipped her head. "I'm a Marshall." She tapped the short sheath. "This is my Marshall's baton."

Calli vaguely remembered the words from long-ago history lessons, but the concept still eluded her. "And that means?"

"She's the crème de la crème of magical warriors in this society," Marian said.

So Alexa had landed on her feet. Calli wasn't surprised. The woman had an air of complete competence about her. Calli gestured to Lady Hallard. "She doesn't wear the same sort of clothes, so she's a…"

"Very observant," Marian said.

Calli didn't think so. It was just natural curiosity.

"She's a Chevalier," Alexa said.

Now, *that* word Calli knew. "French for horseman."

"Right," Marian said. "In this instance it translates to 'Knight,' and in this culture, it means those who ride volarans or, if no volarans are around, horses. Lady Hallard is the leader of the Chevaliers, with men and women under her." Marian gestured to a tall, lean man who wore the same yellow and green as the Lady. At Marian's wave, he nodded, unsmiling, to them.

Again a tinge of wariness slithered up Calli's spine. Warriors. Knights. She sensed there was a lot no one was telling her, even these seemingly welcoming women who said they were from Colorado. What *was* going on?

Bastien joggled his still-extended elbow. "Ven?"

"What could a tour hurt?" asked Alexa.

"You will certainly confirm that you aren't in Colorado anymore. And once you see the volarans—"

"You'll know you aren't even on Earth," Alexa said cheerfully.

Calli shuddered.

Marian touched her shoulder. "It takes some getting used to."

Ignoring the banter, Calli swung her legs around, pushed off from the high bed and jarred to her feet. Bastien caught her hand in his and placed it on his arm, steadying her balance. There was a faint spurt of warmth from his touch but it felt unlike the women's.

She should have shrieked in pain at the combination of movements. Instead, she felt almost as good as new. There was still a tenseness about her muscles, a sense of the fragility of her mended pelvis, something she didn't think would ever go away, but she moved as if the fall had been a year ago, not months. That, more than anything, scared her into believing she was "somewhere else." She didn't want to think about that, though. She cleared her throat. "What did you do to me?"

"We healed you," Alexa said.

Marian said, "We have magic. *All* of us have magic, and you do, too. It's called Power here, and the culture is an aural one—more based on sound than vision. They call the Supreme Being 'the Song,' and use singing to channel their magic."

Yeah. Right. Calli narrowed her eyes. Marian looked like a woman who would call the Supreme Being "Goddess." Calli hadn't often run into that religion, except the time when a pagan group held some sort of retreat on a campground near town.

She licked her lips.

"Want some water?" Marian asked. She went to an elegantly carved wooden corner table topped with marble and poured water from a pitcher into a heavy glass goblet, then brought it to Calli.

Calli sniffed, it smelled minty.

"Only water with peppermint," Marian said.

Calli didn't drink.

Alexa heaved a sigh. "On my word of honor, only minty water." She touched her baton sheath.

Marian nodded. "On my word of honor."

Alexa was from Denver and Marian from Boulder. Both city types. Would their words be good? Calli considered them and decided to trust them. It might just be a dream, after all.

As the water slid down her throat, leaving a tang of peppermint on her tongue, Calli thought it tasted awfully good and was pretty damn wet for a dream. She finished the glass and handed it to Marian, who put it back on the table.

"First things first," Alexa said, starting toward the door. Bastien tucked Calli's hand in his elbow and he and Calli followed Alexa.

Alexa continued. "This is the main healing room in the Keep of the Castle."

"Keep?" asked Calli. That didn't sound too familiar.

"Uh, the Marshalls' Headquarters," Alexa said. They exited into a wide hallway made of gray stone. Rustling behind her told Calli that others would be leaving, too. Now that they'd healed her. Huh. She wondered who would accompany her on the "tour." She had an idea Marian and Faucon would come along.

"We're on the second story of a five-story building, near the front that faces the Temple Ward. A 'ward' is a courtyard, and this one has a big, round Temple at the end. That's where we Summoned you and where you came through the dimensional corridor this morning," Alexa said.

They turned left and walked to the end of the hallway to a set of stairs.

"We'll give you a map," Alexa said.

"When we brief you later," Marian said. "In private."

That might be good. So many new faces were a little intimidating. Calli really hadn't believed she had such an imagination to populate this dream. All of her other dreams—until recently—had been of simple stuff.

She suddenly recalled the dream that had woken her that morning. Alarms. People needing help...like several she'd had lately.

They tromped down the stairs and sounded like a bunch of people clattering down a stone staircase. The floor was hard under the soles of her boots, too.

"My tower's diagonally behind us." A smile flickered over Alexa's face. "I have a whole tower to myself, here at the Marshalls' Castle. I also have an estate of my own. You'll get one, too."

"A spread of my own?" Calli pounced on the statement.

"Yes."

"Are there mountains?" Even walking down the large hallway, Calli could tell the air was more humid, felt different in her nose and on her tongue than the air she was used to. All her senses fed her unfamiliar information. She had to be dreaming, or there was a really big catch.

A shadow passed over Alexa's face and for the first time she answered hesitantly. "There are mountains, but I don't think you should live in them."

"I can handle anything the mountains throw at me," Calli said. She'd been through blizzard and fire and drought. But that was Colorado. If she was in some other dangerous place, she didn't want to stay. She wanted her land, her ranch.

They reached a door. Alexa threw it open.

And Calli saw dozens of winged horses. Once again a flood of affection came from them.

Bastien urged her forward, but as soon as she took a step outside into the yard, the horses trumpeted in greeting.

She couldn't help herself. Fascination at their beauty mesmerized her. She threw off Bastien's hold and strode into the yard and was immediately surrounded by horseflesh. No, *volaran* flesh. Warm and fragrant and strong and just completely marvelous.

They pushed against her, noses snuffling at her hair, her shoulders, everywhere.

She was buffeted and…passed around.

What was even more fabulous was that she heard—whisperings—brushing her mind.

Our Exotique.

Our Calli.

Our friend.

She reached out and stroked a neck, patted a nose and finally touched the wing of the dappled gray stallion.

The volarans moved several lengths away from her and the gray. The courtyard fell silent. Quietly, with infinite grace, the gray stretched out his wing for her to study.

It was simply the most beautiful thing Calli had ever seen. Huge and soft with feathers. But this was a big horse. She didn't know how it could fly.

Magic. She heard the word clearly in her mind. *And our bones are strong but hollow.*

She swallowed.

Quick, small footsteps advanced and Alexa joined her. The woman's face was alight with wonder.

"They love you," Alexa said. "You've only just met them and they all love you."

Once more Calli became aware of the delight emanating from them. This time it wasn't words or just a feeling. This time it was a Song of welcome, blended of harmonies that sang of wild flight with the wind, of running, of pirouetting and playing in the air.

Like the sound that she had heard as a child when riding free and fast across a mountain meadow. A sound so sweet it made tears sting her eyes.

There were quick notes that skipped like her pulse before a barrel-riding competition.

The tune changed, became a song of fighting in battle.

An alarm clanged, echoing around the stone castle walls, pounding danger into the silence, breaking the mental song into a hundred fragments.

"Horrors invading through Arde Pass!" Alexa shouted.

Suddenly Bastien was there, running past them and grabbing Alexa. Saddles appeared on the backs of many volarans. Calli goggled. Had to be magic.

Bastien flung Alexa up onto the back of a big, black volaran, sprang into the saddle behind her and they rose in an upward spiral.

Calli's breath caught as feathered wings swept the sky, flashing all colors against a bright blue. There was *nothing* so beautiful as a volaran in flight. The loveliness tightened her stomach.

Others ran and claimed their mounts. Calli saw Lady Hallard, Faucon, a man in pristine white leathers. Chevaliers in riding garb and Marshalls in their armor, all rose on a flurry of wings.

Two hawks bulleted from the Castle walls and flew beside Alexa. Soon, only a few volarans remained in the courtyard, including the gray and a mare with her young filly. Marian, a tall man with startling blue eyes and a golden headband standing next to her and some soldiers were the only people around.

Slowly Calli turned to the Circlets—Marian and her husband. A question she didn't want answered tore from her throat. "Where did they go?"

"They go to fight the invading monsters. To live or die," Marian said, face white and strained.

It *had* to be a dream.

4

Calli ran her fingers all along her skull, paying attention to her temples, and the side of her head that would have hit the crystal. No cracks, no breaks. No pain.

She pressed a hand to her chest, felt the *thump-thump-thump* of her heart. Hearing it in her temples, it was slightly loud, slightly fast.

"You really are in a different world," Marian said. Her gaze swept the empty ward, her smile forced. "Well, it looks as if the briefing is up to me." Her hand reached out for the man's next to her and was immediately clasped and squeezed.

Another woman who'd found love on Lladrana.

After a deep breath, Marian said, "We have several choices as to where to go. Alexa's tower guest suite is open. The Chevaliers, of course, prepared a suite in Horseshoe Hall and Jaquar and I are living in the Sorcerers' guest rooms. We'll have tea."

Calli stared at her. "Tea! What about beer? Better yet, whiskey."

The man snorted. He appeared totally masculine in the long robe. A thought struck Calli.

"Shouldn't he *not* understand us?"

Marian flushed, but answered with more grace than Calli might have managed. "We've developed a potion that helps with language comprehension. Naturally, we needed a test subject. Jaquar volunteered. He's the only Lladranan who understands contemporary American usage."

"You said you were from Boulder. The university, right? What were you, a prof?" Calli asked.

"Close, a grad student on the way to a professorship and a nice tenure track."

"I might understand the words, but the concept of that last sentence eluded me," Jaquar said in English. He bowed. "My pleasure to meet you, Lady Callista Torcher."

"Boy, you catch on fast." Calli stared at him. His words had a definite lilt, especially when pronouncing her name, but were perfectly understandable.

Since Calli wasn't wearing a dress, and wasn't sure how to curtsey anyway, she inclined her torso. Without pain. *That* notion still amazed her.

"Though drink sounds good, I think it might be most illuminating for Calli to visit the Map Room," Jaquar said.

"I don't know—" Calli started.

The little filly danced up to Calli, butted her. *I am here and wanted you here and we all wanted you here and you came! Love us.*

Another hard shot to the heart. How could she *not* love

this dainty…what? Tentatively she stretched out her hand and stroked the little hor—volaran top to toe.

The dappled gray crowded close. *Except for this one, I am the best at talking to humans. So I am yours to partner with.* He nickered, then sniffed at her. *You are healed and well. Want to fly?*

Her hand went to her throat, clogged with turbulent emotions. Would they *ever* calm down and sort out? What a day! "I…I don't know how."

The volaran blinked. She'd spoken English. But it had spoken…what? Pressing her lips together in concentration, she sent her wide-eyed amazement at a flying horse to the volaran, with the image of a lot of horses—a herd of horses, and no volarans.

Horses only? His mental voice held disbelief.

She nodded. *Yes.* Nibbling her bottom lip, she considered what to do. Just the offer by the gray volaran was a challenge.

Marian and Jaquar stared at her, muttering to each other, faces set in fascinated expressions.

"You're talking to the volaran?" asked Jaquar.

"Did he speak telepathically to you?" Marian said at the same time.

Calli rolled her eyes. "Shit, you two."

Marian chuckled. "Yes, we're endlessly interested in everything. I saw you nod. A nod means agreement, just like in the States."

Practicality surfaced. Calli'd never ridden a strange horse without playing games on the ground with it first. She sent an image of her favorite game, followed by *Play first?*

Snorting, the volaran said, *I am not a horse. Volarans are much superior.* He paused and she realized that he wasn't speaking English or—or that other language. He was speaking horse-volaran-equine.

And she was understanding, in her mind and by watching him—eyes, ears, mouth and feet.

We play games in the air.

Well, that let her out. Volaran or not, she'd bet that, like horses, these equines tested their leaders. She may have been welcomed by them, felt that wave of love, but that didn't mean they'd automatically elect her leader.

My back is broad and I will be careful. Just a short ride...I will use no distance magic.

I will be in charge, Calli replied, lifting her chin, getting the hang of the talking. She felt she spoke horse better than any other language.

Of course. Was there a hint of slyness in that reply, in the dapple's eyes?

It didn't matter. Anything other than a flying horse, Calli could have resisted. But if this was a dream, she didn't want to wake before she'd flown on a winged horse.

Me, too. Me, too. Me! The filly gamboled about. Tossed her head, then blew out a little breath and continued, *My Dam will fly with me. We will all fly together.*

The gray's back rippled and a saddle appeared on it. Calli went up and checked the tack. It was harsher on horse—volaran—than the bits and bridles and saddle she usually used.

That would change if she stayed...if she awoke and it wasn't a dream.

No, said the mare to her filly. *Thunder and the Lady will fly high and fast and far. We will stay here.*

The filly huffed and circled the courtyard.

Smiling, Calli unsaddled and unbridled the volaran, leaving the equipment on the ground. He watched her with an astonished gaze. So did the Circlets. Marian's mouth had fallen open. Calli sensed that both she and her husband rode horses and flew volarans.

She'd like a hackamore, but if she was going to impress the stallion, she'd go all the way bareback. Hey, if it was a dream, all she'd do was wake up if she fell, and if it wasn't, well, maybe her life wasn't too much to pay for a ride on a flying horse.

Don't you humans need those things? The stallion still looked at the saddle.

Trying to talk in her head and aloud, Calli said. "I didn't like the tack I saw."

"Oh," Marian said.

Calli smiled. "Ever hear of natural horsemanship?"

Marian relaxed and smiled, too. "Of course. I saw a few demonstrations." Her face clouded. "I never learned and my mother's polo ponies—" She stopped.

"Polo." Calli huffed a breath. Were they from different backgrounds or what?

With a determined nod, Marian strode to face the gray stallion. "Listen here." She gestured to Calli. "This is *your* Exotique. If you lose her, you will have to explain to the Chevaliers why. *And* those who brought her here will re-consider Summoning someone else if you have no respect for her."

Calli could have told Marian that she was wasting her breath. The volaran was paying more attention to Calli stroking his ears than Marian's words. A shadow in his mind did hint at a concern of losing her and explaining that to the alphas in Volaran Valley.

As she continued caressing his ears, he relaxed, just as the horses she knew did, lowering his head.

Smiling, she relaxed, too, relieved. She *did* have knowledge that could apply to volarans. She ran her hand from neck to shoulder, shoulder to withers and barrel, again and again. His coat was silkier, softer than horsehair, as if each individual piece was not a hair strand but a minute feather. He stood quiet under her hands, yet pleasure emanated from him. Occasionally she sensed a "nudge" to rub or scratch him in a particular spot.

Cautiously, she set her hand on the upper edge of the muscular ridge where his wings attached to his body, marveling again at them—their softness, the coloring that complemented his coat. All the equine cues she'd read showed respect. With a deep breath and a prayer in her heart, she set one hand in the dark mane, the other in the small of his back and hauled herself up—nearly *flew* onto him. Something inside her sprang open, imbuing her with energy and grace and…and…magic?

She rubbed up his neck, all the while realizing that he was extraordinary, felt *more* than horselike. His wings fluttered against the back of her calves, causing an amazing feeling to well up inside her. As if here, on the back of this volaran, was her true destiny. For a moment she just sat, eyes closed. He didn't smell horselike, but sweet and musky, like some crumbling amber she'd once had.

Interesting, he said. The neck muscles under her hand moved and she opened her eyes to see him staring at her.

He whinnied. *You feel good, you have great Power. Let's go.* He lifted his wings.

Calli's stomach dipped. *One moment.* She scanned the area. The courtyard was huge.

Now she'd see if he'd obey her. *Back for a running start.*

Don't need a running start.

Again she stilled, let the beginning of her day rerun in her head, how she'd risen with pain, negotiated the steps, called for her horse...the emptiness she'd felt for months at not riding. Then she settled back, brought her legs forward slightly, squeezed and released. *Back.*

The volaran backed, she even turned him so they had all the courtyard ahead of them. Her mind seemed to touch his and it was almost as if they were one creature and not two. He was calm and a little amused.

"Good going!" Marian called. She and Jaquar had stayed near the door of the big square building with the large round corner towers. All along the courtyard people showed up in the walks to watch. Calli thought she saw money changing hands. She chuckled. Maybe not too different from Ea— Colorado after all. For a dream.

Finally, they stopped in the shadow of the huge white round temple behind them. At the opposite end of the courtyard was a three-story building with two small towers.

Another big breath. Soon she'd find out just how well she'd healed. The courtyard was paved with large gray stones. She leaned forward, whispering in the volaran's ear and in its mind. *Ready to run?*

Yes.

Go!

He ran. Elation flooded her. No pain! More, the volaran's gait was smooth, his body powerful under her. Strength and vitality flowed from hindquarters to neck, sifting down to his wingtips. She *felt* his energy mingling with her new extra sense. Before they were halfway down the courtyard his wings lifted, caught the air and they were soaring!

Calli gasped as they cleared the buildings, gasped again as she saw an additional courtyard beyond the one that held the temple. They flew high, angling toward the sun, and the moment was so huge, so incredible that it sank into her forever like she'd been gilded with sunlight.

Once again that day she lived in a moment of exquisite awareness, of total brilliance. The blue bowl of the sky dusted with clouds whirled around her and her mount. The entire universe centered around her and every wonderful thing in it focused on *her.*

She was life.

She was Power.

She flew.

Song filled her ears—wispy airs from the clouds, a hollow gonglike reverberation pulsing from the sky, a small, erratic Song radiating from the eart—planet below.

The planet is named Amee, said the volaran.

His Song enveloped them, laughing, exhilarated. He swept through a cloud and tiny particles shivered over her skin and cooled her.

She laughed to herself.

I am Gray-Clouds-That-May-Rain-Or-Thunder-Or-Clear.

The English name sounded awkward in her head—the name was more than an image, it was active motion. A sky billowing with gray clouds of infinite possibilities which might change any moment. A future of many paths hung on that name. She'd call him Thunder.

"Callista" meant "most beautiful" and until now she'd never felt she'd lived up to that name.

But now, now, as they rode through the sunlight and shadow, wind tearing her hair back from her face, caressing her body, atop the volaran, Calli was the most beautiful woman in two worlds.

Finally she looked down and her gut clenched. She held tight to Thunder's mane. The world below was green and fertile. And a long, long, *long* way down. What had possessed her to fly without tack? Yes, she, a wingless human *did* need something familiar to hang on to, even if it wasn't as horse-friendly as it should have been.

She could almost hear herself go *splat*. Then she *saw* what she was flying over. Rolling green land. Fields. Woods. Manor houses. Villages. She thought a couple of towers and spires on the horizon to her left might be a small city. Land like this on Earth would be crowded with people.

Scents rose to her—rich and summer and humid, lush with verdant plant life. Not Colorado.

Was she dreaming? Or had she really fallen through that crystal to another world and was finally *living* the life always destined for her?

Too much. Far too many exotic, exciting experiences today. She nudged Thunder to circle and return to the Castle. He ignored her.

Panic twinged each nerve, though she kept an easy, calm and confident posture.

Thunder chuckled in her mind and she realized that flying on a volaran would take different skills. She was used to thinking through any demonstration of horse fears, staying positive. She wasn't accustomed to some damn horse rustling around in her mind. With a couple of breaths, she settled herself completely. She *was* sure that she was the alpha in this situation, despite what Thunder thought.

With her legs, hands *and* mind, she concentrated on the pressure points of the horse/volaran's body. Horses were prey animals, always aware of their surroundings. Calli didn't sense that volarans here were as preyed upon as horses had been on Earth, but they would have prey instincts.

Humans were predators. She didn't want to remind Thunder of that, she just wanted him to accept her as the alpha of the herd. The herd of two here in the sky. She kept her own concerns tightly reined. He might sense them, but he'd also see that she did not allow them to control her.

She reached out and touched the wing ridge of the side she wanted to turn.

He dipped.

She hung on and asked again for a turn.

He glanced back, lowered his head, licked his lips and made a wonderful, sweeping turn.

"Yee-ha!" she shouted into the blue, rubbing Thunder's neck.

His mind melded with hers. *You are most beautiful.*

Soon a rocky promontory was in sight, and upon it, the Castle. She sighed, definitely ready to return. Calli noted how big the Castle was, larger than she'd thought. Frowning, she understood that there must be even more to it than the two courtyards she'd seen. On the land below it—what direction?—was a large town.

South of the Castle is Castleton.

Castleton, huh? Well, that made sense. And if Castleton was south, that meant they were flying east toward the Castle and had been flying west to the...great lake? Sea? Ocean?

The Circlets have Towers on the islands off the west coast of Lladrana in the Sea of Brisay.

Thunder seemed eager to please, now. His mind was completely unruffled, and completely accepting of her.

Calli tried more telepathy. *I saw no one else flying.*

The horrors invade from the north. Thunder tensed under her. He flew faster, tucked his legs close to his body. A prey animal making himself a smaller target. Whatever these horrors were, Calli got the idea that they ate volarans. Predators.

You will see, Thunder said. He quivered and his thoughts disintegrated into images and shapes and tones she couldn't understand. True equinespeak that she could feel but not completely understand.

The Castle loomed bigger and bigger, with a wall about three stories high and the square building with four towers rising an extra two.

Awesome.

Most of it was gray stone, though part was of yellow, and she could discern the round white building of the great Temple.

There is a Landing Field. Thunder's ears flicked. It was more a question than statement.

We will land from where we took off. I'm sure Marian and Jaquar are waiting for us. Now she thought of them, she could *feel* them, as if they'd connected with her some way.

During the healing? Probably. Wouldn't folks who healed you with magic from the inside be connected with you afterward? Made sense. She might have a lot of bonds already, then. Huh.

More than feeling them, she could hear Songs. An interesting, intricate Song with echoes of Earth rhythms from Marian, an equally complicated, more masculine bass and brass from Jaquar. And a powerful twining Song greater-than-its-parts from them as a couple.

She saw them in the courtyard, sitting and observing her, leaning together. A brief spurt of envy held her still.

Thunder zoomed down, turned. The wind caught his wings and he tipped sideways. Calli's fingers slipped from his mane and she fell right off him. She screamed and plummeted. A whisk of air surrounded her, spun her like she was trapped in a gentle whirlwind, then she was righted and set onto her feet before Marian and Jaquar.

Marian's eyes were huge, her hands to her throat. Jaquar's right arm was outstretched. Calli stared at it. It had been *he,* the Sorcerer, who'd caught her and brought her down safely.

Magic.

She really needed that whiskey.

Marrec could hardly believe Dark Lance was back and they were flying to battle, just as they had for many years. He swallowed hard. The cool wind stung his eyes. He blinked and looked around him, awed by the sight of all the Marshalls and Chevaliers streaming to the battlefield at the same time. Bright colors, shining armor and gleaming volaran coats flowed like banners against the summer blue sky.

Usually there'd be fighters caught elsewhere when the alarm rang, who'd arrive later, but all the Chevaliers of the Castle had been near the Keep, or lounging in Temple Ward, to glimpse the new Exotique.

So they flew together and Marrec's heart lifted. The Castle alarm was connected to the magical fence posts along the north border of Lladrana. When it rang, the pattern of the notes and the stridency alerted them to the place where the monsters invaded and the number of horrors to expect. Experience had taught him to understand the alarm. They flew to the northeast.

As he watched, opaque bubbles formed around volarans and riders, masking the bold heraldic colors and gleam of mail. "Distance magic," spells that increased the distance a volaran flew with every beat of its wings. Warriors could fly immense distances and engage the enemy near the border instead of dealing with monsters deep in Lladrana.

Need Power for Distance Spell, said Dark Lance.

5

Marrec sent Power to his volaran. Together they curved the distance-magic spell around them. With every beat of wings, leagues were covered.

Dark Lance whinnied in surprise. *More Power.*

It was his first real mental communication since he'd returned.

Yes, Marrec said. *I linked with others, with the Marshalls and stronger Chevaliers to heal the new Exotique. The pathways in my mind that channel Power opened more.*

Good, Dark Lance said, then fell silent. The volaran had never been one to speak while flying unless it was urgent. Their few real conversations had taken place in the stables. Marrec ached to question Dark Lance on the disappearance but had to put his curiosity aside to prepare for battle.

When the bubble of distance magic popped, Marrec rose

from a light trance and watched the ground near. They descended to a large clearing in the shadow of the mountains. Dark Lance was following Lady Hallard's volaran down to the west side of the battle. The Marshalls were already down and fighting as the incredible team they were—fifty linked minds decimated the monsters.

With a clutch of his gut, Marrec saw there were plenty of foes still available. This was one of the largest attacks he'd ever seen. Had the Dark taken note that they'd struggled to repel the last few incursions—and on horseback, not volarans? He was all too sure of that.

Not one slayer, render or soul-sucker could be allowed to escape into the interior of Lladrana.

He slipped his shield onto his right arm, unsheathed his broadsword.

"Marrec!" Two volarans and riders were at his left, Chevaliers sworn to Lady Hallard, a man and a woman with whom he usually teamed. All of them could speak with their volarans. He hesitated.

Dark Lance didn't, and Marrec was pulled into a loose connection of minds. The other volarans were mere murmurs.

That mixed bunch, left! cried Sharmane, diving toward a group of ten.

Renders are mine! Jon shouted, heading for a massive black-furred beast with razor-sharp claws.

Soul-suckers! Marrec called. Dark Lance trembled, but Marrec was determined and urged his mount toward the two soul-suckers on the fringes. Soul-suckers rated the best bounty and he wanted some hides.

I will Shield you both, Sharmane yelled.

Dark Lance caught a soul-sucker with one hoof in its nose hole, smashing the gray head apart with a killing blow. The three tentacles at its right shoulder writhed, one whipping across Marrec's waist. A yellow slayer spine shot to him. He deflected the poisonous arrow with his shield, swung his sword and decapitated another soul-sucker, continued his blow to slash the back of the yellow-furred slayer. The thing shrieked and turned, spines shooting from its arm straight to Dark Lance.

Terror flooded Dark Lance. He reared. Spines struck, bounced off the protective shield both Marrec and Sharmane had slapped over the volaran. Marrec pulled the fear from his steed's mind, using the emotion to drive his own Power, making his strikes harder, faster. He sent iron calm and fierce determination to the volaran. *We shield. You live.*

Only the moments mattered, the next blow, ducking, turning, spearing. Slashing, kicking, cleaving. His mind held the volaran's, refusing to let the winged horse panic, bolstering its innate courage. Imposing his will for the duration of the fight.

He caught sight of the bright blue line of energy from a newly raised fence post. In a fury of fighting, he forced a render and a soul-sucker onto the border line and killed them. The energy field flared high and secure at that point and Marrec grinned, a rictus of triumph.

Done! came the loud shout of the Marshalls, rushing from mind to mind to the Chevaliers. The battle was over, all the horrors destroyed.

He panted a spell over his blade to clean it, ordered Dark Lance to the ground. Marrec wiped his forehead with his arm, winced as he finally felt the sting of two sucker rounds that had raised bumps on his cheek. His muscles were tired, aching, but his blood still sang with the aftermath of victory. He grinned at Sharmane and Jon and went to count his booty.

He found six soul-sucker bodies with his killing mark, three renders and a couple of slayers. A third of his kill went to Sharmane who'd acted as his Shield. He gave his tally to Lady Hallard and she took her third, choosing to keep the two headless soul-suckers with most of their hide and tentacles. Soul-sucker was now in demand for hats ever since Bastien Vauxveau had shown how well they protected a person from the frink-worms that fell with the rain.

When Marrec piled his prize in the spell-net, ready to take to an assayer, Dark Lance lifted his lip. *Nasty smell.*

"Yes, but I made some decisions when you were gone. From now on we'll be taking all our kill."

The volaran shuddered. *Uses more Power to fly back.*

"From both of us." He attached two long lines to rings on both sides of Dark Lance's saddle to the net. "I promise this catch will feel no heavier than a pouch of silver coins. And I'll buy a better net. There's zhiv to be made in selling hides. The demand for slayer and render hide has gone up from the City States and Shud."

Dark Lance snorted, then looked away. *We last.*

Marrec looked around. His volaran was right. Everyone else was gone. An atavistic tingle slithered down his spine. The sun was setting and they'd be lucky to be back at the Castle before dark. He tested his reserves and found them acceptable for the flight. That was a relief. Not everyone had taken their kills. The Marshalls and wealthier nobles who had paying estates didn't need the extra zhiv and only claimed trophies they wanted mounted. A whole soul-sucker was a few strides away.... He snorted in disgust at the idea of becoming a scavenger...but he wanted to better his lot in life. Still, his net was full and his Power limited.

And night threatened. There was no local landowner so far north to offer hospitality. Died out long ago, just as had Marrec's parents and the rest of his village. His memories of that massacre were blessedly vague. Again he shivered, then the light dimmed just enough for the boundary line to brighten the evening and he was comforted.

The ancient fence posts that had begun failing a couple of years ago were now being replaced. Everyone now knew how, and how to energize the boundary line from one fence post to the next. This bit of land was secure.

That didn't mean he wanted to hang around. "Let's go home."

Home, echoed Dark Lance wistfully. To Marrec's relief he saw the image of the Castle stables in the volaran's mind, instead of Volaran Valley. Thank the Song.

An embarrassed Thunder took off, with a brief telepathic, *I must report on our ride together.* Huh. Calli rolled her shoulders and fell into a standard analysis of her performance. The flight had been magnificent. She'd bonded with the volaran more than with the simple empathy she'd felt for her lost Spark. They'd been partners, but with her in the lead. She sensed a volaran's threshold of going "right brain," acting in panic, was far higher than a horse's. They must not have had many predators, probably not for a long time.

Marian and Jaquar took Calli to the Map Room on the other side of the courtyard. Something in the way people referred to the room jittered her nerves so she thought of it in capital letters. When they reached the door, she noted incised golden letters in curlicued words which she couldn't read. More and more this was seeming less a dream, more like an alternate reality, but how *could* she believe that?

Jaquar opened the door and held it. She stepped in to see a topographical map as large as a California king bedsheet angled before her, looking like no country she'd ever seen before. And it was animated. Bright yellow-white dots pulsed fast, other dots, smaller and yellower, blinked slower.

Marian marched up to the map and touched the largest island off the western coast. "This is where Jaquar and I, and my mentor, Bossgond, live." She indicated a small castle in the middle of the map. "This is where we are now."

Calli gulped.

Jaquar pointed to the lights Calli had noticed. "This is the magical northern boundary, Power strung between the fence posts—" he tapped the lights "—to keep the horrors out."

Nape prickling, Calli took a few steps closer. Her mouth had dried. She swept a tongue over her lips. "There are gaps."

"Indeed," Jaquar said. "The old fence posts are failing. Only recently have we been able to replace them—"

"Alexa's task," Marian interrupted, her dark blue eyes serious.

"Alexa's task." Calli cleared her throat. "And yours?"

Marian shrugged. "I had a couple. The Marshalls hid the fact that the fence posts were failing and the monsters were invading easily and in greater numbers. This splintered already distant communities within the culture." She gestured to herself and Jaquar, indicating their golden headbands. "Such as the Circlets of the Tower Community."

"And most especially divided the Chevaliers from the Marshalls," Jaquar said. "Alexa was Summoned for the Marshalls, Marian for the Sorcerers and Sorceresses, and you for the Chevaliers." He took his wife's hand and kissed her fingers. "Marian has done a brilliant job of mending the breach between the Marshalls and Tower…as well as being an ambassador from the Tower Community to others. They trust us now."

"As much as less magical people trust the most magical," Marian said with a wry smile.

A hum came from the map and both Marian and Jaquar turned back to it. "Ah," said Jaquar. He tapped a spot on the border where bright flashes came. "The battle is over and the Marshalls and Chevaliers are returning." He let out a big sigh. "We lost no one and there's a new fence post. The border is strengthened to the next post, so we killed some horrors." He eyed the map critically. "No larger monsters made it very far into Lladrana."

That was the second time Calli had heard "monsters." She straightened her shoulders. "Guess that's what I'm supposed to do, right, kill monsters? Maybe stop the invasion?"

Marian's forehead creased. "Since the volarans disappeared and only returned after you were Summoned, it can be extrapolated that not only will you mend the divisiveness within the Chevalier community, and their distrust of the Marshalls, but also—um—speak on behalf of the volarans to everyone, particularly those who fly on—*with*—them."

Calli blinked as she unraveled that sentence. She wished Marian had spoon-fed it to her in little bites.

But maybe she was just in an elaborate dream. Maybe a coma. Damn! Not more medical bills.

Jaquar's penetrating stare pulled her from her thoughts. "But the Chevaliers fly to battle. They are our—" he frowned as if searching for a word "—knights. They would expect you to fly, train and fight with them."

Marian put an arm around her and squeezed, a small smile on her lips as they met each other's gaze. "I know it's difficult to believe you're on another world, let alone understand what's going on in a few short hours."

Rubbing her temples, Calli didn't answer—but something else was telling her she might not be in a dream. "Is there a toilet around here?"

The Circlets smiled. Marian said, "We don't know the Castle well, there's one in Alexa's guest suite and in the Circlets' Apartments, both in the Keep." She cleared her throat. "You'll be staying there tonight. The medica recommended you be close, and both Alexa and I would like to talk to you."

Indoctrinate her. "I'm not staying." If she was really here. Still, her bladder was full...but she'd had dreams about that, too.

"It took all the Marshalls and the Chevaliers to bring you here. How do you think you'll get back?" asked Jaquar.

Calli could feel her expression set into pure stubbornness. She didn't care.

What could these dream people do to hurt her? She shifted. She didn't want to know, but confidence and fearlessness were as important in relation to people as they were to horses. "I don't know, but I'll think of something." A thought struck and her smile widened. Horses didn't lie in any of their body language and she believed volarans couldn't either. "And I can double-check anything you tell me with the volarans, can't I?"

Jaquar's eyes twinkled. "That you can."

"I promise you I won't ever lie to you," Marian said. Her aura throbbed with what Calli sensed was pure truth.

"Okay," Calli said.

"On my word of honor," Marian said.

Calli nodded. "Right." She turned to the door.

"One moment," Jaquar said. An extra lilt in his voice caught Calli's attention. He sure was learning English quickly. She glanced at him.

"Behold," he said.

Marian coughed.

He waved and huge chunks of the map went golden yellow. "These are the unoccupied and unclaimed estates of Lladrana. Many are very prosperous. You will be allowed your choice."

Breath caught in her chest, Calli stared. Land of her own. Everything in the mountains of the north seemed empty, but so did a bunch of other places in the real "green" part of the land. *Big* pieces of land.

Walking to the map, Marian pointed. "This is where Alexa and Bastien live. Her estate was vacant. She's very wealthy now. As am I."

"Money's not everything," Calli muttered.

"Alexa wanted a real home. She has that, and a man she loves. I have a husband and a tower I built myself with magic. I have great magical ability—Power. I'm free to research whatever I want, whenever I want and I'll be founding a school in the future.

"What do *you* want? I'm sure whatever it is, we can accommodate you," Marian asked.

They couldn't give her children. No one could do that. Calli wanted to whirl on her heel and walk away, but her gaze was still stuck to the map. She wanted a spread of her own...and look at all that land! Part of her dream could come true. But land was the least of what she truly wanted. She wanted family. And her family, what there was of it, was back on Earth and had rejected her.

Now the watery gob in her throat was more from sadness than surprise and dazzled greed. "I gotta pee," she said. She headed out the door and across the courtyard to the keep building. The Circlets paced her.

"What's your vocation?" Marian asked and Calli knew she meant it in the widest sense of the word, what job really drew her.

With a lift of her chin, she replied, "I'm a horse trainer." She'd meant to be. When she returned to Colorado, she would find a way to make that dream come true.

Marian smiled. "I bet you're more of a 'horse whisperer.' But you can do that here. And I'm sure volarans need to be trained, too." Marian waved a hand. "Or people and volarans need to learn how to partner each other better." She glanced back at the Map Room. "To better vanquish the Dark. The Marshalls and Chevaliers and Circlets are working on that." Marian looked at Jaquar. He lifted and dropped a shoulder. Calli smiled. Obviously academics. Didn't look at all like

nerds or geeks or whatever, but they sure were more interested in more brainy things than physical.

"The volarans talk to some others, too, most primarily
Bastien. He'll know what Chevalier-Volaran needs are,"
Marian said.

A few minutes later, Calli was checking out the large
round guest suite in Alexa's tower. There was a toilet, one
of the old kind with the tank on the top, and a shower. She
yearned for the shower but wasn't about to take her clothes
off. The way this day was going, anything could happen and
she wasn't about to be naked and vulnerable if it did.

When she returned to the main room, the Circlets smiled
at her with identical gleams in their eyes and Calli didn't like
it. Especially when she saw Jaquar shaking a dark purple
bottle about two inches high. "What's that?"

"The language potion," they said in unison.

"Nope."

Jaquar sent her a winning smile. "You see how it
worked for me."

"Like a charm," Marian said.

"Nope." Calli wanted to slip her hands in her pockets but
thought she should keep her hands free.

"You could try just one drop," Marian said. "That would
be temporary."

Again shaking the bottle, Jaquar said, "There's about three
months' worth of potion in here. The magical properties fade
with time, so you learn the language gradually. After three
months, you should know Lladranan."

"So you know English now, but if you don't use the
language every day, it will fade away?" asked Calli, intrigued.

Jaquar frowned as if he didn't like the idea of losing a skill. "True."

"Pillow talk," Marian said. "And if you marry a Lladra-nan and bond with him mind to mind, you also learn the language, the more, ah, intimate you are."

"Many pathways are opened during sex." Jaquar grinned again.

That sounded even more frightening. "Absolutely not." Calli smiled herself. "I'm not convinced this isn't a dream." She looked around at the color of the furnishings. "Though there's more purple than usual in my dreams."

"That's the heraldic color assigned to Exotiques, especially Marshalls. Alexa's suite was mostly purple, she's switched out a lot of furniture from there to here."

"Purple is *not* my color," Calli said.

At that moment a triangle rang. Calli sensed an inrush of bright and healthy volaran minds.

"The Marshalls and Chevaliers have returned!" Marian said. Jaquar stood and pocketed the bottle.

Calli ran to the window where she'd caught sight of beating wings. The whole army swooped down to the landing field out of her sight.

I am here, too, Thunder called.

Calli exited the opulent rooms without a backward look, running down the tower stairs to the outside door. She flung it open only to face the tall hedges of a maze.

6

A young woman in her mid-twenties, dressed in buff-colored Chevalier leathers, but obviously not a fighter, hovered between the hedges. Shifting from foot to foot, she smiled and bowed to Calli, then pressing her fingers to her chest, she said, "Seeva Hallard."

Calli nodded, probably a relation to Lady Hallard, daughter maybe. "Hey, Seeva."

Seeva swept a hand toward the interior of the maze and said something in the French-like language. Once again the strangeness of this place struck Calli, but when the woman took off through the maze, Calli followed. It took longer to wend their way through than Calli anticipated. Impatience to see a *lot* of volarans again nibbled at her. She let her mind *reach* and knew all the winged horses were fine. Thank God.

Finally she and Seeva made it to the field, and all the

volarans, even those being led away by grooms, stopped and turned to Calli.

Thunder pranced up to her. His hide rippled. *Grooming time.* The strong scent of amber rose from him. Volaran sweat, Calli guessed.

I'm sure, she replied to him.

I would like a rubdown.

He was demanding, but Calli felt indulgent. "I can do that," Calli said, sending images of standard grooming. He whickered.

Three people separated themselves from the rest and walked toward her—Alexa, Bastien and the older Chevalier who Calli had heard was the "representative to the Marshalls." She wore yellow and gray. Her tunic, which Calli recalled as being pristine, was stained and torn. Yeah, she'd been fighting.

Against monsters that Calli hadn't seen. Yet.

The woman shot orders to Seeva, who ran across the landing field. Calli recalled the older woman's name was Hallard. *Lady* Hallard. If Calli remained in this dream, would she get a title, too?

"Exotique," Lady Hallard said with a little bow.

Oh, she already had a sort of title. Exotique Calli. Exotique Alexa. Exotique Marian—Calli had heard all three of them called that. Women from Earth.

Lady Hallard sent a stream of rapid-fire words to Alexa, who winced and kept nodding, a pained smile on her face. Then Alexa bowed to Lady Hallard, answered in a mild voice and talked a while.

After she ended, Lady Hallard nodded, bowed again to

Calli and strode away, leaving her volaran to grooms. Calli saw several people who wore her colors on an armband bow to her. The older woman waved casually to them.

Bastien shook his head. Alexa sighed. "She said that she was told Thunder gave you a good report and she wants you to be integrated into the Chevaliers' ranks as soon as possible. And you shouldn't be up at the Marshalls' keep." Now Alexa's smile-grimace was aimed at Calli, who wanted to pay more attention to all the volarans inching closer to ring them. The flying horses still seemed as fascinated with her as she was with them.

"I insisted that you stay in my tower tonight," Alexa said.

"All right. I need to groom Thunder," Calli said.

"Fine." Alexa rubbed her gauntleted hands together. "Calli, do you want Marian and me to lay all this out at once or drop it on you in little bits?"

Calli sent Alexa a crooked smile as she stroked the exquisite softness of Thunder's near wing. "I think this is all a dream and I'll wake up in my own bed tomorrow morning."

"Not going to happen," Alexa said.

Bastien spoke and Alexa nodded again, this time with enthusiasm. "The more you bond with the volarans, the more you are physically aware of this world—like by grooming Thunder—the more you'll believe you're here. So Bastien'll take you to the stables and teach you. Later we'll eat in my tower with Marian and Jaquar."

"Jaquar speaks English."

"*What?*"

"They made a potion—"

"Of course they did," Alexa said.

"—and he tried it out. So he can speak English."

Alexa looked up at Calli. "Wonder how that works."

"Me, too."

Bastien gently jostled Alexa aside and offered his arm to Calli. She didn't need it this time. She made a lead-the-way gesture.

He grabbed Alexa and kissed her hard, patted her butt and sent her off toward the maze. Apparently she didn't groom volarans. But then, she didn't ride them by herself, either. Interesting.

Bastien sent a loud mental message that showed the stables. Once again the volarans began to move to the large building at the opposite end of the Landing Field. Calli blinked. Was that really the stables? It was huge. Big enough to house every volaran here, for sure.

They walked through a corridor of volarans, with people standing behind the winged horses, staring. The folks wore a mixture of expressions. Everything from irritation and resentment to...awe? She didn't want to be awe inspiring.

As Calli passed, she felt soft muzzles sliding against her, sniffing. Once again overwhelming approval came as she sensed the volarans' feelings. She smelled *wonderful*. Different. She'd flown with Thunder and smelled of him, too, and the mixture was lovely. She smelled sweet.

Calli stopped. Sweet?

Bastien chuckled, as if he heard the volarans. "Ayes," he said, nodding. "Doose."

She didn't think of herself as sweet. Tough, practical, with horse sense, but not sweet.

Sweet. Thunder pranced by her side. *I will get the best stall, with plenty of wing space.*

She stared at him, turned to Bastien. Thunder turned his head, too, and squinted at Bastien.

Bastien grinned, showing flashing white teeth. Though he smelled of man and volaran sweat, he looked none the worse for battle…except there was dark, nasty goo on his right sleeve. He nodded. "Ayes." He held up one index finger. "Calli." Then he held up the other forefinger. "Thunder." He linked them.

Calli frowned and used wide hand gestures. "Why does Thunder get the best stall?" She said it loudly and flushed. As if speaking loudly would make someone understand your language. She lifted her shoulders high and spread her palms up.

Bastien just winked and kept walking. Thunder said, *Because I partner with you, I am the most important volaran.*

That was a little scary. She caught up with Bastien and entered the most luxurious stables she'd ever seen, but didn't have time to linger because of the press of volarans and Chevaliers behind her.

Babble and grooming sounds rose throughout the stables as the Marshalls and Chevaliers spent time with their volarans. Great waves of relief and love blanketed the big building. No sooner had Calli entered the large stall with Thunder and Bastien than the strikingly handsome Chevalier she'd seen during her healing leaned over the stall's half door.

"Salut, Bastien," he said, looking at her.

Bastien snorted. "Salut, Faucon."

Smiling, Faucon said, "Prie introd moi?"

With a tilt of his head, Bastien replied. To her surprise, Calli found a wash of brotherly love coming her way from him. It startled and touched her. How could he like her so soon?

Because Thunder told Alexa and me of your flight and Alexa likes you. Bastien spoke more in Equine and images—Thunder's idea of their flight, Alexa with her arm around Calli—but Calli got it. She turned to the back of the stall and blinked rapidly. The outpouring of feeling toward her today was nothing she'd ever experienced. Even when her fans at the rodeo yelled or clapped, it was nothing compared to this. This warmth sent to her was *personal,* based more on who she was than what she was…an Exotique. The Chevalier Exotique.

There was a brief conversation, with Bastien smiling but contrary, and the handsome man moved on with irritation in his eyes and a smile on his lips.

Then Bastien and Calli worked together. She had no trouble recognizing the standard implements hanging from the stall sides, but when she took them down, she found them a little different. The brushes were made of something she didn't recognize—something for the feather-hide of the volarans. There was also a faint sheen on the fine bristles—oil for the feathers. Furthermore, the tools tingled in her hands. Magic.

Grooming the horse part of Thunder went easily. They paid special attention to the hide under the wings. Thunder's mind lightly touched both hers and Bastien's and he helped her.

The stall was much wider than usual and she found out why when Thunder moved to one side and stretched out a wing. Calli looked at it nervously. Shouldn't he be able to clean them himself?

Thunder snorted. *You.*

Bastien took down a couple of fancy brushes and they flared in his hands—more magic. With exaggerated motions he taught Calli to groom the wings. He started with the undersides and moved with incredible gentleness from where the wings attached, outward to the tips of the feathers. Watching closely, Calli wasn't sure that the brush actually touched the feathers at all, more like some sort of aura or field. Or something. She saw, she *felt*, but she didn't have the words to describe.

Yet there was a connection here, mind to mind with Thunder. Working with her hands, the brush, stroking the winged horse, made this dream seem all too real. Thunder's muscles flexed under her fingers. The stable was full of odors—volaran sweat, human sweat and an occasional whiff of something Calli thought might be volaran shit. Not too smelly for her, but then, horse shit didn't bother her much, either.

By the time Marrec had sold his kill to an assayer south of Castleton and flown back to the Castle, he and Dark Lance were exhausted.

Don't like this long day. Dark Lance blew out a breath.

"I don't, either, but we must plan for the future." If he lived long enough to have a future. One thing was certain, his bargaining skills were too damn rusty. He should have gotten more for his haul.

He'd been stuck in a rut, living the life of a soldier attached to a Lady, with no home, no land of his own. Had somehow lost that dream. Had been spending his pay and not always collecting his kills, and taking those he had claimed to the

Castle Assayer who paid a lower price. "We'll fight until we have a stake good enough for land of our own. You'd like your own land, right?"

Yes, but Castle is good. Walking toward the stables, Dark Lance whuffled in Marrec's hair. *Back.*

"Yes," Marrec said. "Thank you for coming back."

Warm. Good food. My place low in Volaran Valley herd. Mares no look at me. My place with you high.

"The highest. And I'll find a mare in season for you." Any vow was worth having his volaran stay. Dark Lance had become his highest priority.

Too big and ugly in Volaran Valley herd.

Surprised, Marrec stopped and looked at his steed. He was large for a volaran, but any human would consider him a good-looking flying horse. His hide and wings were solid black, with each wing feather outlined in silver. He stroked Dark Lance's neck. "You *are* beautiful."

Humans think so. Not volarans. He rolled his dark eyes and they looked sly. *You will show me to the lady of volarans and she will think me beautiful. Then I will get higher place here. And a mare.*

Marrec laughed shortly. Like master, like volaran. He was considering ways to gain status and wealth himself. "I'll do that." He inhaled deeply. "I'll introduce you to the Exotique, but she will be fighting, too." If she really was for the Chevaliers.

Lady inside stables with Thunder and Bastien. Show me now! Dark Lance's tone had taken on a weary stubbornness, warning Marrec it would be wise to agree.

He wanted another look at her anyway, that incredible

hair, those blue eyes. Two of the Exotiques had blue eyes. How common was that? Faint curiosity about the Exotique Terre tickled his mind. "Very well." But he needed to press his point one more time. "The best way for us to get you a mare is to take more chances for honor on the battlefield."

Dark Lance shivered, but finally said, *I trust you. We fight well. We will get higher place.*

So it hadn't escaped the volaran's notice that Marrec wasn't exactly the alpha of *his* herd, either.

"Yes." Somehow, yes.

Clop, clop, clop.

Latecomers were entering the stable. When they reached Thunder's stall, a volaran stopped and a beautiful horse head looked at her. He lifted a wing and Calli's breath caught at his loveliness. He appeared to be night made tangible—midnight dark edged with moonlight.

Thunder whickered. *Dark Lance.* An image of a sword blade etched with a streaking volaran came to Calli's mind.

Dark Lance whinnied and dipped his head to her. *Come see me.* His voice was deeper than Thunder's.

Though Thunder's mind hummed with a little irritation, he sidestepped so Calli had room enough to pass him and Bastien. Gently she touched the soft nose, stroked Dark Lance.

Beautiful Lady. The volaran's deep voice resonated in her mind.

"Ayes," said the man who joined the winged horse, his large, callused hand resting on Dark Lance's neck.

"Salut, Marrec," Bastien said, moving to stand beside Calli.

"Salut, Bastien." His gaze went to her. "Salut, Dama." He nodded.

She recognized another Chevalier who'd been in the healing room when she'd awakened. His leathers were old, with fine cracks and several stains. He wore an armband of yellow and gray—Lady Hallard's colors. His face was bony, with deep-set eyes, a strong jaw and firm lips. Beneath his golden complexion was a gray tinge that spoke of exhaustion, though nothing else did about this tough, lean man. He was taller than Bastien and the other man who'd visited.

"Salut," she said.

He turned his head fully to her and she saw more than weariness. Two round circles of red raised bumps showed on his far cheek.

Bastien whistled, reached into his pocket and pulled out a tube, offered it to Marrec.

For a moment, he seemed to hesitate, then his scarred fingers took the tube. He ducked his head to Bastien. "Merci."

Beautiful Lady. Dark Lance tossed his head. *Beautiful Dark Lance.*

Calli and Bastien laughed and Marrec's smile was quick and easy, lighting his serious expression. He ran a hand down his volaran's neck in a loving stroke that Calli knew was habitual.

Avanser. He gestured to the end of the stables. Calli heard the instruction to Dark Lance easily. The mind-tone was as caring as his fingers had been. Man and volaran moved down the stable corridor.

Calli frowned. She'd noticed that the stalls got incrementally smaller down the line and Dark Lance was larger than

Thunder. She asked Thunder a question in Equine that was becoming easier with each use.

Low status, replied Thunder with a hint of arrogance.

Since he included both man and volaran in the image, Calli figured the term applied to both.

Bastien tapped her on the shoulder and indicated feed sacks and a trough at the back of the stall. As she helped him mix Thunder's dinner, Calli wondered about rank and status and contrasted the clothing and bearing of Marrec with Faucon.

Faucon was a noble, she was sure. He'd worn finer-grained leathers that looked newer, and heavier chain mail. His leathers had been dyed, Marrec's had just been cured. Faucon had not walked with a winged horse. Probably had someone else tending it. Calli smiled. His mistake.

A small whirlwind entered the stable, Alexa, followed by the two amused Circlets. The little Marshall stomped up to the stall door. "What's keeping you?" she asked, and repeated it in Lladranan.

Bastien started to answer, but she cut him off, addressing Calli. "We have a lot to cover, especially since Lady Hallard insists that we tell you they want you married tomorrow evening."

The lulling comfort of being around volarans vanished in an instant. Warning bells rang in Calli's head. "What did you say?"

7

Marian stepped up to the stall door, tsking at Alexa. "Well, that's crude."

Alexa flushed. "I could've been cruder."

"Yes," said Jaquar. "Why don't you be? I think I'd like to know some *exotique* words that might excite my wife."

Bastien made a protest that included the word *Lladranan*, and Calli thought he was demanding they speak so he could understand.

Jaquar whipped out the small bottle of language potion he'd offered Calli, jiggled it. Expressions flowed across Bastien's face: wariness, unwilling fascination. He held up one finger.

More discussion—and negotiating. Calli knew horse trading when she heard it, despite the language. Finally Jaquar frowned, pulled out some big coins—they looked like real gold—and handed them to Bastien. Bastien pocketed the money and stuck out his tongue.

The tiny cork lifted with a little pop. A thread of lavender smoke puffed from the bottle. Bastien's eyes widened, Alexa stepped closer, and Calli sidled next to Thunder, feeling better with strong, warm hors—volaran flesh at her side.

Jaquar tipped the bottle and a drop of liquid hit Bastien's tongue. The cork popped back into the bottle. Bastien swallowed.

He slid down against the stall side onto the floor, grabbed his head and moaned.

Calli and Thunder stepped back. She was glad she hadn't tried the stuff.

Alexa was suddenly in the stall with them, crouched over Bastien. Calli hadn't seen her move. Had she jumped? The stall door came nearly to Alexa's shoulders. Surely not.

Jaquar looked at Calli and Thunder. "I'm opening the door to retrieve and examine Bastien."

Keeping a hand on Thunder, who was only slightly disturbed, Calli nodded. Her mind was with Thunder's. She could keep him from fear.

The door opened soundlessly, and Jaquar, Alexa and Marian dragged Bastien out. He tried to move himself.

With a whoosh, a large hawk swooped into the stables. It lit on Bastien's head.

"She says it's his wild magic that makes him react so," Alexa said.

She? Who?

Thunder stepped forward until he was nearly out of his stall and into the crowded corridor. *Feycoocu.*

"Feycoocu?" Calli asked.

"A magical shape-shifting being," Marian said absently.

Oh. Of course.

The hawk pecked Bastien on the head. He yelped and grabbed at it. It flew away. Thunder followed it with his gaze. *I would like to talk to the feycoocu.*

Calli decided she wouldn't. The day was rapidly becoming overwhelming with the huge input of information.

Bastien shook his head and stood, helped by the other three. "Gonna lie down," he said in heavily slurred English. "Bed."

"Let's get you there," Jaquar said.

Bastien rubbed his temples. "Horrible headache. When did you say this would wear off?"

"Always too reckless for your own good," Alexa scolded.

He closed his eyes. "Oh, that's bad. Can be nagged at in two languages. No. I don't like this."

Jaquar said, "I'll get him back to your suite, Alexa. You two should brief Calli on what she needs to know about the Summoning, the Choosing and Bonding ceremony, and the Snap."

None of that sounded good to Calli. But one thing she knew, she wasn't drinking any potion.

We made good impression, Dark Lance said smugly.

Marrec had used the last of his energy and Power to groom every inch of his volaran, murmuring compliments with each stroke. He didn't want Dark Lance to ever leave again. Now he leaned against his mount, breathing in musky fragrance and thanking the Song that Dark Lance was back.

All around him other Chevaliers, even Marshalls, lingered, spending more time with their volarans. Especially those who could mind-speak with their mounts, even if only a few images. Especially those who only had one volaran. Those like him.

He shuddered again at the remembrance of loss. Not just of his best companion, but of his entire future. He did well enough with horses, but didn't own any, didn't know if he cared to. He'd have been penniless, with no decent way to support himself, if Dark Lance hadn't returned. He hadn't truly faced that fact until the volaran was gone.

One of the female Chevaliers sobbed, and Marrec had to gulp hard.

Cheek stings.

"What!" Marrec straightened, went to Dark Lance's head.

Yours.

"Oh. Yes." He pulled out the tube Bastien had given him, opened it and dabbed healing cream on his face. He chanted one chorus of a spell and the hurt diminished. That was different, too. Usually it would have taken three verses to repair the light soul-sucker wounds. He rubbed his hand over his cheek. No bumps.

More Power.

"Yes."

More Power means more status.

"I hope so." He cleared his throat and asked what he'd heard whispered in many stalls around him. *Will you go away again?*

No. Head Stallion called. I obeyed. Back here now.

"Thank you," Marrec repeated.

We together.

"Yes." He wanted to ask why the volarans had left and why

they'd returned, hear the answers for himself, but Dark Lance's mind-tone had been forbidding.

Rustling came from several stalls. Some of the Chevaliers were going to sleep with their volarans. Because they were afraid the winged horses would fly away again? He was torn, he wanted to stay, for the sheer comfort of Dark Lance's presence. But if he did, he'd show the volaran he didn't trust him.

After one last rub, Marrec left. He had to tally up his zhiv, plan for the future. See how long it would take to accumulate enough to buy a small piece of land in the north.

The tasty dinner Calli was tucking into seemed real, too. So far the normal things her senses understood—grooming, eating, peeing, made what she was experiencing real. But the *strange* events outweighed them. Falling through the crystal, waking up healed, moving without pain after a nap, hearing folks speak a different language.

Flying on a winged horse.

That had been the best.

As the plates were whisked away by Alexa's serving woman, Calli studied her fork.

"We believe there's always been sharing between our culture and Lladrana," Marian said.

"Yes," Alexa said, wiping her mouth with her napkin. "There have been Exotiques Summoned before, but not for a century."

"I'm working on a Lorebook," Marian said. "That's what they call their reference volumes here. Lorebook on building Towers. Lorebook of Community Rules." She made a face.

"Before I started my own work, the Lorebook of Exotiques was a short one-page list."

Alexa grunted. When Calli met her eyes, the Marshall held her gaze and said, "Lorebook on Summoning. Lorebook on Monsters."

"That's why I'm here," Calli said. "To fight monsters."

"That's why we're all here," Marian said. "We were Summoned here by the Marshalls, and you by the Marshalls and Chevaliers, because the Song said we could vanquish the invading Dark. The dimensional corridor that links Earth and Lladrana is close. We deduce that there will be six of us Summoned."

"So that's the Summoning. Understand?" Alexa asked.

"Why me?" Calli asked.

Marian answered, "The Chevaliers had specifications of the qualities that they wanted in their Exotique, particularly after the volarans left. The Summoning would only be heard by a person who matched their needs—you."

Alexa said, "During the Summoning ceremony, the Song is sent back in time on Earth to find and prepare a person to come to Lladrana." She waved a hand. "Don't suppose you heard chants and chimes and a gong over the last month, did you?"

Calli fell back against the plush dining-room chair.

"Thought so." Alexa smiled.

"So you have all the qualities the Chevaliers wanted—someone the volarans would love, courage, determination." Marian waved a hand. "You're flexible in mind to accept the Summoning, probably don't have deep emotional ties to Earth—" Calli kept her mouth shut "—or would consider staying permanently in Lladrana."

"Fighting monsters, I don't think so." Calli crossed her arms. "Assuming I'm not in a coma from banging my head against that crystal."

"What crystal?" Marian started.

"Stay on topic," Alexa said.

Alexa stood. Her deliberate movements kept Calli watching her. She walked to the far corner of the room, where the wall separating the bathroom met the curving outer wall of the tower. Slowly she pulled her baton from her sheath. Green jade glowed above and below her fingers. The top of the wand had sculpted bronze flames. Nerves jittered under Calli's skin.

"Calli, call it to you."

Her breath stuck in her chest. "What?"

"Want the baton in your hand. Feel it in your hand. Reach out and say, 'Baton!'"

"I don't think—"

Coward. It came in her mind. In stereo. Alexa and Marian.

"You can do it," Marian said.

"Why would I want to?" But she rose slowly and faced Alexa.

"Why not?" Alexa's smile dared her. "Especially if it's only a coma-dream."

Marian frowned. "I'm not sure people in comas dre—"

"On topic, Marian."

The atmosphere of the room became heavy and charged. It wasn't only Alexa's and Marian's minds brushing hers, but Thunder's and other volarans', some people's linked to them, too. All added to the anticipatory pressure around her.

"Fine. Baton, *come!*" Calli ordered.

It flew across the room and slapped into her open hand, stinging. And everything took on a solid reality that she couldn't deny, as if her mind, her body, completely focused. The baton belonged to Alexa, *vibrated* like Alexa, but was real and solid in Calli's hands. And magical. There was a force within it that compelled her to believe, to face the fact that she was no longer in Colorado, on Earth, like a door slamming shut behind her.

New place, new rules.

Before her eyes the metal flames atop the stick bloomed into real fire. She dropped it. Instead of hitting the ground, it shot back to Alexa, who sheathed it at her left hip. "There, you see? You have great magic. That's another reason you're here. We all have great magic. Cool, huh?"

"Magic," Calli repeated.

Marian joined her. "Look." She pulled a finger-length wand from her sleeve. Flicked it, it became larger, flipped it in her hand and flicked it again and the wand elongated into a walking staff. Calli's mouth fell open.

"We all have magic here," Marian repeated. "We have magic on Earth, too, it's just very hard to access it. Earth is also a more visual culture. The Songs can't be heard or Sung as easily."

Alexa went to a love seat, sat and crossed her ankles. "I wouldn't know. I didn't return to Earth when the Snap came."

Calli's knees went weak and she crumpled into her chair. There was another one of those strange phrases.

At that moment a white, long-haired cat strolled in from the bathroom. Calli stared. She could have sworn the door was shut.

"A cat from my past. Actually, my magical shape-shifting feycoocu companion." Alexa grimaced. "A cat. I hate when this happens. You get nothing out of a cat."

Marian sighed.

The cat went up to Alexa, stropped her ankles and began a purr that only increased as it leaped onto Calli's lap. It turned around a few times and settled. Calli found herself petting it. Its fur was as soft as volaran feathers, and she felt oddly comforted. "The Snap?" She managed a squeak.

Drawing up a chair next to Calli, Marian said, "At some point in time, Mother Earth will call to you, strongly enough to pull you back home. You'll have a choice to stay or go."

"When?"

"No one knows," Marian said. "There isn't enough data for a hypothesis. Perhaps after you experience it…"

Alexa said, "We do know that time passes the same here as on Earth. If you're here for, say, three months, the same amount of time has transpired in Colorado."

"The ranch!" She'd lose the ranch. Her dad would think she'd just walked away. Her fingers tightened in the cat fur. The feline grumbled.

"Sorry."

The cat jumped down and went to sit in the middle of the floor and groom.

Calli wouldn't walk away from the ranch, but her dad would think her cowardly enough to do so, dammit.

Both the women appeared sympathetic.

"The shortest amount of time before the Snap came was two weeks, the longest was seven years and three months, the average is about two months," Marian said.

Two months.

Alexa smiled. "We have examples of the Bonding ceremony—" she waved at Marian "—and the Choosing and Bonding ceremony, an older Marshall Pair, coming later."

"This is the marriage thing?" Calli asked, attention diverted from her dad and the ranch.

"Yeah."

"I'd like coffee," Calli said, going to the sideboard. She made the drink dark and sweet.

Alexa cleared her throat and sat, but didn't relax. "You know that the Chevaliers want you to stay. It's easier for a person to stay if you're paired or bonded—"

"Involved with someone," Marian said, "but to be precise, they don't have just a Pairing ceremony in mind." She tilted her head. "I think a Pairing would correspond to an affair and engagement."

"Yeah," Alexa said. "They want you to agree to a *coeurde-chain*, which is like soul melding or something."

Marian chuckled and her eyes went dreamy. "It's more."

"But they want a quick marriage, and to do that, they're willing to use, uh—" She threw a look at Marian.

"Another magical ritual," Marian said. "I blood-bonded with my tutor, and also with Alexa. Then Jaquar and I decided we wanted the whole deal, minds, souls, bodies."

"Huh!" Calli said.

"The upside is that we're very close. Neither of us are lonely. We're partners in the truest sense of the word."

"The downside?" Calli asked.

"We'll die at the same time," Marian said.

Alexa stood and paced the room, hand on her baton.

Finally she turned and skewered Calli with a gaze. "You want to be a horse-volaran trainer. That's doable. You want land. That's easy, too. But there must be something more, some bigger reason that the Song resonated with you and called you and made you a perfect person for Summoning. An emotional reason. What do you *really* want, Calli?"

The demand had words slipping from her mouth, "To be loved." She had to look away from the two very beloved women while heat painted her cheeks, her neck, even her ears hidden under her hair. Hell, she hadn't blushed in a long, long time, and now she had twice in one day. She decided to continue with brutal honesty. "And to have a family of my own. Children of my own." Pretending not to see the glance exchanged between the other two, she upended her mug, drank and set the mug aside. "And even Lladrana and all its medicas can't give me children. The infection from one of the surgeries took my ovaries."

"It isn't common that Lladranan and Exotique couples produce children," Alexa said. "I don't think Bastien and I will ever have any."

Calli whipped her gaze to Alexa, then to Marian. "Your guy, Jaquar, he has blue eyes—"

"Yes," Marian said. "He has some Exotique blood in his lineage. Whose or when, we don't know." Her aura spiked green.

"Bastien and I will just have to adopt," Alexa gave Calli a direct look. "Wouldn't that be good enough for you? Or being a cowgirl you gotta have the right equipment and bloodlines and breeding and all that jazz?"

No. It was as if a note had echoed throughout her being.

She didn't *have* to give birth to children of her own. Children who loved her would be enough. Feeling uncomfortably vulnerable, Calli said, "Drop it."

"If you want pedigree—" Alexa swept a hand around them "—you're out of luck. You've landed in with a motley crew. I don't know my ancestors, grew up in foster care. Bastien's a black-and-white, which can mean mentally handicapped, and his father was an asshole."

"My mother's a bitch," said Marian. "My brother's a jewel, though." She looked thoughtful. "He came with me…sort of… If you don't reject the Choosing and Bonding ceremony, he might be right for you. The Song might have led him here for you."

"She should stick with Faucon Creusse. Noble, rich, sexy and handsome." Alexa wiggled her brows. "What's not to like?"

"Tell me about the Claiming and Bonding ceremony," demanded Calli. She'd backed up against the bar.

"That's what we were getting at. Magic…Power…the Song, choosing the right guy for you." Alexa waved her hands.

"You want love?" Marian joined Alexa to face Calli. "What if I told you there's a surefire way to find the right man for you? Your soul mate?"

Calli's heart thumped hard. A man who would love her. A man she would love. Was she really ready for that, despite what she yearned for most?

Marian spread her arms wide, and the gesture emphasized the rich robe she wore, the Circlet around her forehead, the expensive surroundings. "What do you want, Calli? True love? There are plenty of Chevaliers ready to bond with you—men and women of like mind with you. Land of your own? You'll get it." She laughed a little. "Children? Unfortunately Lladrana is like Earth...there are abandoned children you can make into a family. Volarans? I think you can have as many volarans as you want."

"They are their own," Calli protested, but vividly recalled the horse bodies pressing against her.

She'd never be lonely again.

She remembered the Map Room, the unclaimed land.

She thought of Faucon Creusse, all too willing to be her lover at any moment. Already. That was a little scary. He had to want her just because of *what* she was and not who she was. He didn't know her.

But this notion was a little tempting, too. A magical ceremony could bring her a guy? Some sort of matchmaking deal? Intriguing. Especially since after her disastrous illusions about her father, she didn't trust her own judgment worth spit.

She thought of children. With a big ranch, she could have many.

Finally, an image of a flying volaran herd circled in her mind's eye. Wings of all colors, equine faces looking to her. She could almost hear the wind rush through thousands of feathers.

When she glanced at Marian and Alexa, they were glowing with the golden aura of love. Love given and received with their men. Friendship love between them. They liked her already; could they become good friends? With these women there would be no competition between them, no moving around that meant brief and broken ties, like in the rodeo.

The room wavered before her as if behind a rich haze.

She'd be rich and valued and respected and would own land. And love would come into her life.

Grabbing her mug, she filled it again and went to a wing chair. "What about this magical ceremony?"

8

The sound of strumming strings came once. "That's the doorharp," Marian said.

Calli remembered seeing something like half an egg slicer mounted on the door.

When the door opened a huge man and much smaller woman entered. Just the sight of their strong, intertwined aura had Calli sitting down on a little sofa, blinking. They brought music with them. It was the strongest tune she'd heard from people, truly a Song with a capital S.

Alexa introduced the two Marshalls as Mace, the arms master, and his wife, Clua, who was a battle strategist.

"You know, Calli, it would be much easier if you took just a *drop* of the potion," Marian said, pulling the little bottle from her robe pocket.

Calli wondered if it was the same bottle or if she and

Jaquar had concocted a large batch. She shook her head. "I don't think so."

Silvery laughter came from Clua. Mace stroked his wife's hair. They were still holding hands. With a kiss on their linked fingers, the woman walked toward Calli, face welcoming, hands outstretched.

Their aura didn't break apart, but stretched, and in stretching, remained the same deep gold color and thickness. It was as if wherever they went singly, they would still keep the same strong and intimate connection with each other. Awesome.

Automatically, Calli took Clua's hands.

An image of a calendar flipped pages going *back*. Years. Calli was swept into the past, *experiencing* the Choosing ceremony of Clua and Mace.

The first thing she noticed was that she felt woozy, dizzy. A hand—her hand?—passed a goblet to someone and she noticed an aftertaste in her mouth. Another emotion swept her, anticipation at the Choosing, then, as she looked around a large room with stone walls—her Power amplified. Her eyes were sharper, her eardrums nearly exploding with the loud tangle of personal Songs.

She looked down at a table at a variety of items. A beret—nothing Calli had seen so far in this world, old-fashioned?—a quill pen, a book, a small carved volaran, a locket, a chain with keys, a brooch. She touched each and received impressions of the person who'd placed it on the table. Each time, she saw a colored link connecting the person to the object. Sometimes that connection was a thread, sometimes a cord. Once a chain. Just as the melodies she heard varied in strength and prettiness—a whisper of a tune too simple to please; a loud, intricately layered Song that *pulled* at her, awakened feelings deep in her core.

Her hand hovered over a locket. An oblong thing of gold, inset with black with a diamond in the center. She brushed her fingers across it and felt a surge of desire, longing, *belonging* from it. Looking up, she saw a huge young man dressed in a short velvet robe and tights, arms crossed, staring at her. She couldn't look away.

He was too big, too tough, too sophisticated for her.

Forcing herself to withdraw her fingers, she turned to the other tokens.

Nothing felt as *right* as the locket.

Time telescoped and Calli was able to distance herself a bit from the experience and feel the woman's fingers clamped over hers in the here and now.

She watched as if hovering outside of herself—like she'd done in a couple of the surgeries—while Clua tested each item time and again, then finally listened to the rush of her blood and heart and bone and took the locket.

A shout of celebration rose from many voices—her family—and Mace literally leaped over people to claim her.

Clua let go of Calli's hands. Calli staggered back to sink onto the sofa. "Oh. My. God," she said, even as she heard the Marshalls leaving, Clua chuckling.

"Wow," said Marian, sitting beside her. "Tell us what happened. Magical ritual, right? From what I can tell, I don't think Clua ever wrote down the story for the Lorebook of Choosing and Bonding. She hadn't ever met Mace before, that I *have* heard. But for the record, I'll need every detail from you!"

"Marian, shut up," said Alexa, wriggling in on Calli's other side. It was a tight fit. Alexa stroked her back and the affectionate caress seemed to draw the stunning magic from Calli until she breathed steadily again. "Calli, you need to watch out how you touch people," Alexa said.

"Tell me about it."

"Sometimes they don't mean to sucker punch you, sometimes they do, but we've all had an experience like that."

Marian said, "I still want to hear every detail. What were the circumstances? Did the Choosing work? Well, duh! Obviously. How did it work? Was the magic very strong?"

"Yeah," Calli said, shaking off the last of the weird feeling that she was living two lives in two different times. She rubbed her face, then dropped her hands and straightened to glare at Marian. "I'll be *drugged!*"

"I promise you, you'll be fine," Marian soothed. She went to a bookshelf and curved her fingers around empty air, hummed a few notes. A thin book appeared in her hands. "This is the English version of the Lorebook of Exotiques. I've got the recipe here, all herbs we know except for one." She flipped pages as she walked back. "And I've had that particular herb twice in larger amounts than you'll receive. I'm still here, alive and kicking." She found the entry and handed the book to Calli. "Look for yourself."

Calli did. "Cinnamon, nutmeg, mugwort, bay. Rose petals?" Marian nodded.

Staring at the page she saw another ingredient. "Centauriana," she murmured. Another horse word. Almost like a sign.

Calli felt as if a stampede had galloped right over her. "I need to go to bed."

"Can I tell the Chevaliers that you'll go through with the Choosing and Bonding ceremony tomorrow afternoon?" Alexa pressed.

Exhaustion dropped on Calli like a thick horse blanket, smothering logical thought. Her vision blurred. When she blinked, everything still seemed out of focus. Sounds—more, *music*—enveloped her, running through her mind, preeminent among the strains was the tune of the Marshall Pair. They'd been so obviously a couple, obviously in love, and after many years. They believed in the Ritual.

Blinking again, she stared at Alexa and Marian who waited for her decision. Tonight both of these women would go to bed with men who loved them, were committed to them.

Loneliness ate at Calli, along with envy. A matchmaking ritual. The idea tempted. Her own judgment was lousy, and Alexa and Marian had found their loves on Lladrana, so why couldn't she? What she'd seen of the couples, here… And magic *worked*. What the hell. Why not? What did she have to lose? "Sure, set it up."

They smiled and came toward her, hugged her and the three of them linked and a huge Song filled Calli's ears and traveled to her heart.

"The Song of Colorado women," Marian whispered.

"See you tomorrow morning," Alexa said. Both women left their arms around Calli's waist.

Marian said, "Remember you aren't alone. We're here to help every step of the way. Don't panic."

"Just yell and we'll come running."

"Huh. Sounds like you're trying to tell me something," Calli said.

"*I* panicked," Marian said.

"I did, too, especially when I saw my hair turned white overnight."

Sleepiness fled. Calli looked down at Alexa. "Really?"

"Yes."

Then Calli studied the wide silver streak in Marian's hair. "I suppose you didn't have that when you came, either?"

"Lladrana can be tough on hair color," Marian said.

"I like being blond."

"Hey, another reason to stay here." Alexa grinned. "No dumb-blonde jokes."

That just reminded Calli that her father thought her stupid and cowardly. She tensed. The other women noticed, of course.

"Sore spot? I'm sorry," Alexa said, squeezing her into a tighter hug. The woman's grip was like iron.

"I definitely need to get to bed," Calli said.

"Right." Alexa withdrew and marched to the door.

The short walk was silent, but the quiet between them was easy. Calli hadn't had good female friends since high school. Nice to be part of a girl crowd.

Alexa opened the outer door of Calli's suite and kissed her cheek, so did Marian.

"Thanks, guys." Calli's voice was hoarse with appreciation, weariness. She entered a narrow security corridor and turned left until she found another door, a tiny entryway and a third door, and finally got into the bedroom. Soft light glowed with the radiance of a summer evening from what looked like little suns on torches. Pulling off her boots and stripping, Calli slid into cool sheets. The lights went out and Calli fell into welcoming darkness.

She woke to hail pounding against the curved tower windows in the middle of the night and shot straight up in bed—a big four-poster bed with *curtains*. Weird.

She was still in Lladrana. Carefully, she stretched, and found her muscles in prime working order. Wiggling her hips, she tested her pelvis. Fine.

Oh, man.

Did she even want to wake up at home? At least the problems here were new, didn't seem as crushing as fighting her father for her home and her vision of the ranch. That would take a lot of money and effort to win. More money to fix up the ranch the way she wanted.

If she *was* stuck here, what had she gotten herself into with that damn Choosing and Bonding ceremony? Dare she trust the "magic" to find her a man who'd match her? What *was* she thinking. Was she totally crazy?

But those Marshalls—Mace and Clua—had been the most *married* couple she'd ever seen. Like Marian and Jaquar, they'd die together. She trembled. Could she possibly want that much connection?

That much love?

Yes.

This need to give and receive love came from deep inside. As if all the love she'd poured onto her father over the years had bounced off him and come back to her and she had this great store.

Getting up, she found her clothes washed and folded on a chest at the end of the bed and just stared at them. Someone had been in her rooms? Who had the key?

Surely it would only have been Alexa or Marian checking

on her. Still, the sooner she had her own rooms and key, the better. Next to her things was a stack of underwear. In her size. Must be magic, there, too—she touched her old clothes, noticing the texture of denim and cotton. Alien to this world.

She turned, staggered back at the sight of a small neon-blue volaran hovering near the corner of one of the bed's foot posts. The animal was only about a foot long.

She pressed a hand against her pounding heart. "My God, you startled me!" She knew this…person. The energy of the being was familiar. There was her sixth sense again and she disliked how much she was depending upon it.

I am Sinafinal, the feycoocu.

Of course she was. Staring at the creature, she realized she'd seen it before. As a hawk. As *the cat.* Calli sat on the chest.

You are not crazy. You are *on Lladrana. You* should *go through the Choosing and Bonding ceremony.*

"And I should listen to you, too, huh?"

Yes. The volaran loop-de-looped a couple of times, leaving a bright blue trail behind her.

"Why—"

You should stay here on Lladrana. Here you will have a love of your own, children, land, a home.

"Guaranteed?" Calli infused great sarcasm into the word.

Sinafinal fluttered up to within six inches of Calli's eyes and hung there. *Yes, guaranteed.*

Calli's stomach clutched.

Everyone wants to be loved. Why do you see your big heart as being a fault?

Because Dad never valued love? This introspection was

getting too damn intense. She didn't like it. She preferred action.

By this time tomorrow night you will be sharing a big bed with a lover, a man drawn particularly to you.

"Uhn." That idea was so good it hurt. Made Calli's chest ache.

When you both awake the next morning, you will choose your land. You will have enough zhiv from the land and an annuity as an Exotique that you will never want for any material thing for the rest of your life. Enough to build the perfect stables and training grounds for horses and volarans.

The little volaran was sure spinning a sweet story.

In three weeks you will have adopted a child.

Calli flopped back, banged her head on the wooden footboard behind her. "Ouch! Dammit all!"

Sinafinal zoomed over and perched on her head, Calli could feel four little hooves, and goose bumps covered her body. With two flaps of the magical being's wings, Calli's headache was gone. Oh, boy. She rubbed the back of her head anyway. "Why are you being so insistent about this?"

Because without you, the volarans will not bond as much as needed with humans. They won't be ready for the great, final fight.

Calli swallowed. "Who won't be ready? What final fight?"

There will be much more loss of life.

"I don't want to hear this."

That's why I am telling you.

I don't want to believe you. Though she hadn't said the words aloud, the feycoocu answered her anyway.

I know.

"Hell."

The neon-blue volaran examined one of her wingtips. *If you do not believe me and do not continue with the Choosing and Bonding ritual, I will convince everyone that you should consult the Singer for a Song Quest. Perhaps a strong vision direct from the Song will be powerful enough to convince you of your worth here.*

Ooooh. Zinged several hot buttons all right. "Damned if I do, damned if I don't," Calli muttered. "This had better be a dream."

It isn't. You will awake here. The little blue volaran's muzzle stretched in an unnatural smile.

"Go away. I'm planning on waking up in my own bed on the Rocking Bar T." But it sounded weaker and weaker to her.

Sinafinal circled the room. *All the Exotiques will have companions. Alexa has me. Marian has Tuckerinal. You have Thunder.*

Calli snorted. "Sidekicks. Yeah, yeah, yeah. I'm going to bed. I hope *not* to see you in my dreams."

Sinafinal dipped a wing and flew through a closed window into the night.

Calli looked out at the darkness below—no lights. She looked at the moon and star-bright sky. Not Earth's sky, not even from the southern hemisphere, too many stars for that. She shrugged. When she woke she'd either be home or not. If she was here, the day would be packed with fateful events from the moment she opened her eyes.

9

Calli woke and stretched luxuriously. The bed was wonderful, too bad she was alone in it. She must be treating herself to a good hotel near the next competition…everything rushed back.

She was in Lladrana. Or at least she *wasn't* in her own bed back at the ranch. What was written in those old-time black-and-white movies? *"Meanwhile, back at the ranch…"* A hollow laugh rasped from her. What little peace she'd felt when she woke up vanished.

But there were compensations. She walked from the bedroom to the den where she could see the Landing Field. A couple of volarans and riders were already out, lifting their wings and soaring. Her breath caught at the beauty.

That could be her…flying into the dawn. She watched until they diminished into specks and she became aware of standing naked in a strangely furnished den—with books and scrolls in an alphabet she couldn't read.

Her breath came in short bursts and she felt the way she did just before a race, scared and excited and determined. She'd get through this day and the one after that… Back in the bedroom, she dressed near the windows. The only person who'd see her would be riding volaran-back and she'd see them first.

Lladrana. Fabulous flying horses. Horrible monsters. Nobody had talked much about the monsters she'd be expected to fight. Trying to keep the really bad downside of this life low key. Her stomach clenched. As if they could. As if she hadn't seen wisps of them in Alexa's mind, in Bastien's and Jaquar's and in Marian's—a man with tentacles on his face reeking of evil power. Yeah, she had inklings. Enough that it made her pace, unready to open the door and explore on her own. Silly, but with a day full of such strange and magical experiences as the day before, she intended to be cautious.

Meanwhile, back at the ranch…what would her dad be doing? Thinking she'd run somewhere, no doubt. He wouldn't gloat. That would take too much emotion, show too much an investment in her, which he didn't have.

The doorharp rippled, and Marian's projected tones said, "Calli, ready for breakfast?"

Calli didn't answer.

"Think she'll drink a language potion this morning?" Marian asked.

"Not a chance. Besides, if she doesn't back out of that Choosing and Bonding ceremony, she'll get the language transfer in bed." There was a lilt in Alexa's voice.

Calli decided she didn't like being talked about. The two women were probably not going away. She opened the door. Standing before her, looking perfectly fresh, were Alexa and Marian; near their feet were two small greyhounds.

Salutations, Calli, said one. Sinafinal.

Salutations, Calli, said the other. *I am Tuckerinal.*

"Tuck's my ex-hamster," said Marian. "He's a feycoocu like that one." She pointed to Sinafinal.

I have given her my name so she can call on me at any time, said Sinafinal, *my mated name.*

Marian grinned and kissed Calli on the cheek. "Good morning. You should know that only a few people know Sinafinal's name. Only Alexa and Bastien of the Marshalls. Only Jaquar and I of the Circlets."

"Huh," Calli said. Two minutes on the threshold of her room and stuff was overwhelming her again. Magical hamsters. Sheesh.

"You really are in a different dimension." Alexa looked sympathetic. "You slept. Let's go eat."

"Try not to drop too many more bombs on me, huh?" Calli said. Alexa opened her mouth, closed it, but Calli figured they were probably thinking the same thing. In circumstances like these she'd be getting hit with strange problems every hour.

She ate in the richly paneled Marshalls' Dining Room, set up like one of the fanciest restaurants she'd ever seen—pastel tablecloths on round and rectangular tables, embroidered in rich colors, with matching napkins. Crystal. Fine china.

She had a great breakfast of a cheese omelette, bacon and fluffy croissants, and chuckled to herself. Something French she *was* addicted to, the cowgirl loved croissants, one of the ways she chose her restaurants on the rodeo circuit. She'd eaten everything from preprepared, frozen, grocery store-bought croissants to flaky ribbons of pastry steaming from the oven.

These were prime.

"I guess we should tell her about the men," Alexa said to Marian.

"Thank you, but I've learned about men all by myself." Calli didn't look up from her meal.

"What about men?" Marian sounded puzzled.

Calli caught Alexa's gesture from the edge of her vision. She could *feel* the Marshalls' gazes boring into her, their curiosity surging around her. The chief honcho, Thealia Germaine, sat at the long table a few chairs down from them, watching, as if trying to puzzle out their conversation. Calli knew if she bolted, Thealia would be on her and have her hog-tied in an instant. The Marshalls took a deep interest in her, the Chevalier Exotique.

"Lladranan men, like Faucon and Luthan," Alexa said.

As she recognized the handsome Chevalier's name she'd seen before, Faucon, a thrill zipped down Calli's spine. Would she be in bed with him by the time night fell? "And I think I'll know a lot about Lladranan men by tomorrow morning." Did she actually say that?

Alexa snickered. Marian touched Calli's shoulder. "This is important. A certain proportion of the Lladranan population find you—us—Exotiques, instinctively repulsive or attractive."

"Might be pheromones." Alexa bit into a slice of toast.

"Interesting idea," Marian said.

"With your coloring, blond hair and blue eyes, you're even more Exotique than either of us," Alexa said.

Calli didn't think so. Alexa was little and had green eyes, Marian auburn hair and blue eyes. "Faucon and Luthan?" Now that she recalled her meeting with Faucon last night in the stables, she remembered odd fluctuations in his aura. Was that why Bastien had moved him along, because Faucon was more blinded by her "Exotiqueness" than interested in her as a person?

"Faucon is attracted to Exotiques. Luthan, Bastien's brother, is repulsed. You'll work with both of them. They should be here this morning to meet you."

"They are," Marian murmured. She waved to three men who stood and approached.

"Who's the third?" Calli asked.

"My brother Koz." Marian hesitated. "His mind and soul and emotions are my brother Andrew in a Lladranan body."

Calli thought her mouth dropped wide open. She didn't know that she liked the idea of different bodies and souls.

Marian said, "It's a long story. We should have just given you our Lorebooks. The Lorebooks of Exotique Alexa and the Lorebook of Exotique Marian, where Alexa and I wrote down our experiences."

"Thank you, and that might have worked best for you and Alexa, but I liked, like, having things explained personally." Calli turned her gaze to Alexa. "Thank you for being here. It's been a great help."

Alexa pinkened.

At that moment the guy wearing pure white leathers stopped, held himself stiffly, shuddered, then drew a deep breath. His lips thinned as if in anger and disgust and Calli knew Alexa was right. The man didn't like that he had this response to Exotiques. That he was less than perfect? Or that he saw himself less than a normal Lladranan?

Faucon pulled ahead of the other two, a twinkle in his eye. At least he didn't have a dumb-ass stupid dazed and infatuated look on his face. So he controlled his "innate attraction" to some extent, too. Interesting.

Koz caught up with Faucon. Luthan drew near more slowly.

When he and Koz neared the table, Faucon stepped in front of the other man, bowed and said the same thing he had the night before. "Prie introd moi?"

Alexa shoved back her chair and stood. Calli figured breakfast was over and swallowed her last luscious bite of croissant. She'd have to make sure the Chevaliers' Dining Room in Horseshoe Hall had the same quality. And that idea about stopped her heart. She was planning.

For a life on Lladrana.

A teeny plan, but it had risen to her mind naturally and that was a little scary.

She put her utensils down carefully, then stood herself.

"Callista Torcher, I'd like to present Faucon Creusse, an excellent volaran rider and Chevalier. A wealthy, noble landowner and all-around great guy," Alexa said.

Faucon took one of Calli's limp hands and raised it to his lips. He brushed a kiss on the back and she felt a definite tingle and a couple of musical notes sounded in her head. Maybe things were looking up. He said something in a liquid, caressing tone. Since his eyes had heated, she thought it must be complimentary.

"Hey, ladies," Koz said in accented English, jostling Faucon down a couple of seats. The other man scowled at Koz's use of English.

Marian cleared her throat. Her aura was a little spiky. "Calli, my brother Koz Perrin, late of San Mateo, California. Koz, Calli Torcher of the Rocking Bar T Ranch, Colorado."

He grinned, showing white, even teeth, and held out his hand as if to shake. Calli grasped his and felt a tiny stirring, a little "plink" like one key struck on a piano. "When you get your ranch here, you'll have to call it the *Flying* Bar T."

She laughed and shook his hand. She liked him.

Marian rose. Koz hugged his sister, ruffled her hair. "So, what's up?"

"We're going shopping in Castleton," Alexa said. "Measuring Calli for several pair of leathers, some chain mail—it's magically light—and buying whatever else strikes our fancy."

"Man, here or there, women are all the same." Koz grimaced. When Faucon asked a question, Koz turned to him and translated. Faucon put a hand on his heart and inclined his torso, speaking.

"Girls only!" Alexa said.

Koz smiled again. "Too bad." But when he relayed the information to Faucon, that man sighed and sat at the table.

"Isn't this the *Marshalls'* Dining Room?" Calli asked, stepping into the aisle behind Alexa as she walked to the door.

"Yes, but Luthan is the representative of the Singer and wealthy. And Koz was looking for his sister, who is a Circlet and in the company of a Marshall," Alexa said.

"So, I suppose I'll also have a special dispensation to eat here, too." Calli thought of the croissants.

"For sure." Alexa smiled ironically. "I can promise you that the Marshalls will want to grill you from time to time."

"Wonderful."

Marian said, "Both Faucon and Koz will be at your Choosing."

Calli swallowed, but she listened to the women's stories of attraction/repulsion experiences and how Koz came to be Lladranan as they walked to the stables.

Calli had insisted on checking on Thunder and giving him a treat of a juicy apple. When he nuzzled her and she stroked his neck, breathing in the amber scent of volaran, ran a finger down some wing feathers, once again she thought she could accept this place.

"Shopping!" Marian called from outside the stables.

"I want to fly with you," Calli whispered to Thunder. "But I don't like the tack. I'll order something different in town."

He whickered. *I am Volaran Valley born. I do not like the tack, either. Thank you. I love you.*

With one last rub of his nose, she stepped away, blinking. Stupid tears. Her throat was tight, too. She repeated the image he'd sent to her of a beating heart. *I love you.*

Alexa kicked the dirt, sighed. "This mutual admiration society meeting done?"

Turning, Calli forced a smile and found it came easier than she'd thought at the wariness she saw on Alexa's face when she looked at Thunder. "Hey, I'm the Exotique *Summoned* for the volarans. I know and love them, and they adore me." She said it, knowing it was true.

"Yeah, yeah." Alexa waved and took off at a brisk pace.

"What do you have against volarans?" asked Calli.

"I didn't ride before I came."

"City girl."

"You got it. And since—" she scowled at the stables "—I've broken both my arms twice, I don't care for flying. I. Fall. Off."

"Oh."

"I know you're laughing."

Calli cleared her throat. "Did it occur to you that you might have better luck with different tack?"

Alexa slanted her a surprised look. "City girl. No." But she appeared to be considering, and her expression lightened.

Calli, Marian and Alexa walked from the stables through Horseshoe Close and the Chevaliers who were in the court-yard all stopped and stared at them, many bowing. Calli followed Alexa's lead and nodded to them.

The walk down to Castleton was pretty and she found the town just that, an odd little place that wasn't quite a city, definitely nothing like Old West ghost towns she'd seen, or the old center of modern Western cities.

"More like late Renaissance or early industrial age than medieval," Marian said.

"You should know. But I wasn't thinking in medieval terms, either. I want to visit a blacksmith and tack and saddle maker first," Calli said.

"Okay," said Alexa.

"Why don't you have blacksmiths and artisans up at the Castle?"

"We do." Alexa shook her head. "But the best live in the city. Don't want to be under the Marshalls' and Chevaliers' thumbs, I suppose."

"And there's the fact that until a couple of years ago the Marshalls and Chevaliers usually lived on their estates—before the fence posts began to fall and the situation became dire," Marian said.

Calli sucked in a deep breath. "You'd better tell me about these monsters."

"We'll take you to the Nom de Nom," Alexa said.

"The what?"

"The tavern where the Chevaliers hang out."

"Oh," Calli said.

"It has *trophies*…heads and other body parts," said Marian.

"Oh." The hollow tone was back in her voice, along with a nice sick feeling in her stomach. "I'm going to have to fight these things, right?"

"Right. But I think you'll find you're a natural," Alexa said. "We'll train you…and *when* you Choose and Bond with a Lladranan, you'll become a fighting pair. A Sword for offense and a Shield for defense." Alexa tapped her chest. "I'm a Sword, Bastien is my Shield. I fight with magic and magical weapons. He protects me magically. Here's the saddle maker, right next to the smithy."

Neither of those places looked like anything Calli had ever seen, though the inside of the small shop smelled like fine leather and wood. She spent some time drawing what she considered the perfect saddle, hackamore and other tack for the craftswoman who kept darting fascinated glances at her. It took twice the time it should have since neither Alexa nor Marian knew the proper Lladranan words for such specific items.

All of them watched the blacksmith for a time. Marian and

Alexa seemed to like seeing how he worked with metal and magic. The heat sizzled around them.

Squinting up at the sun, Calli wiped her sleeve across her forehead. She judged the time as late morning.

"She needs a cowboy hat. A Stetson!" Alexa cried. "We *all* need cowboy hats! Oh, yeah, I can see us now. The Exotique Gang." She did a little boogie and her boots kicked up dust. Then she lifted a foot. "And some of those excellent cowboy boots, worked in patterns and colors and stuff. We need to show these people our cultural heritage!"

Calli and Marian laughed together, and it felt really good to laugh with other women.

Marian gestured to her robe. "Can you see me in a cowboy hat and *this?*"

"Well, it can't be any worse than that hat Bastien designed, which is all the rage."

"And Jaquar wears the original all the time and looks like a dweeb. All too true." Marian shook her head.

"It's *time* you get tailored leathers, Marian. A cowboy hat and boots would complete the ensemble."

Calli nudged Alexa with her elbow. "You ever had a cowboy hat, city-girl lawyer?"

Alexa scowled. "No, but only because I could never find one to fit me."

She *was* awfully small. "You could have had one made to order." Calli didn't say she could have bought a girl's size.

"Yeah, like I had the dough." Alexa snorted, then jingled money—zhiv—in her pockets and beamed. "But I do now. I'm not leaving this place until I order a cowboy hat!" She frowned. "You have any idea how they make them or the design dimensions or what, Calli?"

"I've worn them all my life, had a few droop with rain, freeze with snow and generally get trampled under hooves. I think I can give the hatmaker a good idea of what we want."

"Good, off to the leathers tailor," Alexa said.

"Combat cuirtailleur," Marian murmured. Catching Calli's expression, she said, "The fighting-leathers tailor." Her lips quirked. "Naturally Alexa patronizes only the best."

"Oh," Calli said. She walked with them three abreast on sidewalks along a spacious street, until they reached a large shop with wide windows. There she got measured for several sets of leathers and her blood chilled as she thought of fighting. Marian stood by and translated for her.

Calli pointed to a pile of "leather" squares on the counter. "What are these?"

Alexa glanced at them, went over and inspected the stack, flipped through and shoved each square at Calli. "Soul-sucker," a thick gray lizard-like skin. "Slayer," yellow with long yellow fur and strange round bare spots. "Render," thick, tough skin with a black pelt the consistency of steel wool. "Snipper," something like Calli suspected rhinoceros hide to be. "Dreeth," a fine, thin but incredibly strong skin of fine snakelike scales "Dreeth?" Alexa looked up at the old, wizened tailor. "Where did you get dreeth? And how much do you have of it?"

He bowed deeply. "Your Shield, Bastien, brought it in. We have an understanding."

"Serves me right for not paying attention," Alexa muttered.

"I will have the Chevalier Exotique's leathers ready by this evening." He bowed again.

"Please send them to me at the Castle," Alexa said, "and put them on my account."

"I'll pay you back!" Calli said when Marian translated.

Alexa shrugged, smiled and replied in English. "A gift. Many people will be giving you gifts to get in your good graces. Expect something from the Citymasters and the Singer, too. Let's head to the Nom de Nom for lunch."

"You'll love it," Marian said and Calli couldn't tell whether that was being sarcastic or not.

10

They walked up to a shabby, narrow stone building with a sign that changed magically from black letters on a white background to white letters on a black background.

This was the place that held monster trophies. Calli didn't think she was ready, but it would be better getting used to dead monsters hanging on walls than live ones attacking.

Alexa said, "Acclimatizing you, Calli. The Nom de Nom is one of the main hangouts for the Chevaliers, so you'll probably be spending plenty of time here. The trophies are in the upper third of the room. You might want to look up after we've settled in a booth." She hesitated. "This place isn't as bad as the Assayer's Office. If you need to, uh, get more of an idea what you'll be facing, you can go there." She opened the door to the scent of smoke and food and liquor. "And there's a back room you should see."

The moment Calli walked in, conversation stopped. The place wasn't packed, but the bar on her right was full, with Chevaliers leaning or sitting on stools. Of the five booths, two were taken. Alexa scowled at the couple in the last booth against the wall and they got up and moved to one closer to the door. A waitress hurried over to wipe the table.

All the Chevaliers watched Calli with considering gazes. Well, they were getting an eyeful of the Exotique they might want to mate with. Calli wondered if she'd find more or fewer tokens on the Choosing table after this visit.

A woman at the bar flinched, slipped from her seat and left.

Feeling self-conscious and wanting to get this "trophy" ordeal over with, Calli glanced up. Time seemed to stop and fear bubbled up her throat.

The first thing she saw was the torso of a snarling beast with spines on its arms. She tried to swallow but couldn't pull her gaze away from the fierce glass eyes, the open muzzle that showed sharp, deadly teeth. Its fur was yellow, as was the underside of its digited paws. Yellow skin, yellow fur. Slayer.

Marian picked up one of Calli's hands and curved her fingers around a mug handle. Her spit had dried, so she took a gulp, and cold, yeasty ale slid down her throat. She tore her gaze away to Marian who was gesturing for her to slide into the bench opposite Alexa, who faced the room. Calli decided that having people stare into the back of her head—her blond head— would feel better than meeting a stream of brown-eyed stares. She managed to pick one foot up after the other to get to the table and slide in on what seemed to be a red leather bench. Leather made from cows or something—not monster hide.

"I ordered burgers for lunch," Alexa said.

Marian took the outside seat and Calli closed her eyes a moment in thanks that these two women were so protective.

At least for now. They seemed to think that she'd go out and fight monsters like the slayer, or the larger beast next to it. This one snarled, too, its fangs as sharp as the slayers, its black furred head more massive. On either side of the head were huge paws with long, curved, *sharply* pointed claws that looked more like blades than anything else.

"Render," Alexa said, and removed a little woven basket of tea leaves from her mug, placing it on a saucer.

Calli forced herself to savor the ale. It was perfect. Rich, mellow, just to her taste, already warming her stomach. She'd settled enough from shock to glance up at the next mounted trophy of a horror—another torso. Gray, lizard-like skin, bony head with no nose, two arms with two suckered tentacles in front and behind each arm, a soul-sucker.

When she turned her gaze back to the table, she saw the other women watching her with understanding in their eyes. "Is that it?" she croaked.

"There are dreeths," Alexa said.

"Of course, how could I forget dreeths? What are they?"

"Quetzalcoatlus," Marian said.

"The Aztec plumed-serpent god?"

Alex huffed out a breath. "According to Marian, the biggest pterodactyl-type dinosaur on Earth is called a quetzalcoatlus."

"Oh."

"It has a bigger belly, though."

"Sorta bat winged?" asked Calli, trying to imagine the thing.

"Yes. Clawed front legs and spurred, too."

"Huh."

"Marian?" Alexa held both hands out, palms up.

"Oh, very well," Marian said. She linked fingers with Alexa and to Calli's amazement a 3-D image formed above the table of a flying reptile.

"Not a dragon," Calli said, looking at the hideous thing.

"No," Marian and Alexa said in unison.

Its beak was long and curved. "More sharp teeth. Everything around here has sharp teeth except us and volarans."

"The teeth are poison, like slayer spines," Alexa said.

"Of course they are," muttered Calli. "Regular teeth would be too easy. How big?"

"About the size of a bungalow," Alexa said.

A short shriek and the clatter of plates toppling onto their table caused Marian and Alexa to break apart. They snatched two meals. Calli saw one plate overturn. "No!" The burger and bun stopped in midair, the plate turned right side up and the food slid back onto the thick pottery. Marian reached out and nabbed it, smiling at Calli. "You saved it."

She'd used magic! Instinctively she'd stopped the mouthwatering food from falling. She'd even repiled the strange white fries. She looked at one dubiously. "What are these?"

"Turnip fries," Alexa said, biting into her burger.

"*Turnip?*"

"They don't have potatoes," Marian explained sadly.

"I taught the cook burgers and buns, and they're all the rage, of course, but without fries…" Alexa shrugged.

"What kind of meat?" Calli bit off the end of a turnip fry.

Not even hot oil and salt could make it good. She dropped the fry onto the plate.

"Cow," Marian said.

"Okay," Calli said. "We got mustard and ketchup?"

"Something that might barely pass for about a gold coin more," Alexa said.

"Shoot."

"I'm working on that," Marian said.

Since she was working on so many other projects, Calli didn't think she'd be seeing the condiments soon.

"Ketchup is easier than mustard. They grow plenty of tomatoes here." Marian peeled off her bun and showed lettuce and tomato.

The burger was plump and juicy and had Calli forgetting about everything except eating. The lettuce and tomato actually had taste, unlike most of the standard stuff she'd had in diners. She bit, swallowed. Breakfast seemed days instead of hours ago.

A man cleared his throat.

Calli looked up to see a tall, somber-looking guy wearing brown cotton trousers and shirt with a sleeveless tunic of dark gray over it. His left temple showed a streak of silver—that indicated he had magical powers, she remembered.

He made a little half bow to Alexa, then Marian, addressing them by name. Alexa gestured that he could join them and scooted over so he could sit next to her. He raised a hand and the waitress hurried over. Calli heard "burger," and smiled. By the time Alexa, Marian and she were done with Lladrana, the people would sure have some Americanizations in their language.

Alexa put her sandwich down. Calli noticed she'd only eaten a couple of fries. "Calli, this is Sevair Masif, Representative of the Cities and Towns to the Marshalls."

Another new face. Another guy looking her over coolly. "Tell him I'm pleased to meet him." Though she really wasn't much, she inclined her head. "What cities?"

Marian muffled a snort beside her.

"They just aren't as urban as we are," Alexa said.

"Castleton is, like, the main city, right? And it doesn't have mustard and ketchup?"

Alexa sighed.

Marian said, "We did tell you that people would give you presents. This man did me a wonderful favor by sending my teacher and me and Jaquar an excellent cook."

"He had a spice master send me a gift of tea. Expensive here. You want to ask him for mustard?"

Marian frowned. "Have you asked about mustard, Alexa? I think the southern part of Lladrana might make it, or the country south of here."

"Haven't asked," Alexa said. "How important is mustard to you, Calli? Enough to ask for it as a gift instead of anything else? Tea's important to me."

"And let me tell you, that cook has been a lifesaver...or at least made my crotchety old mentor into a reasonable human being," Marian said.

The waitress set down Masif's plate and curtsied.

"Gifts. No strings attached?" Calli asked.

Alexa said something apologetic to Masif. He nodded and began eating, a little awkwardly, as if he wasn't used to eating with his hands, concentrating on making sure the bun's contents didn't slip. For some reason Calli found that endearing.

"No strings attached." Alexa grinned. "The thing is, everyone wants to get on our good sides, and since we're virtually inexplicable, no one expects anything in return...at least not for the first gift."

"Huh," Calli said. "No strings? Ask the guy if he intends to put something on my Choosing table."

Eyes dancing, Alexa did. All three Exotiques stared at him. A faint redness appeared on his cheekbones under his golden skin. He seemed to grit his teeth around his bite of burger. Glancing at her, then away, he swallowed and said something that sounded flowery.

Alexa coughed. Marian turned to Calli and said, "He asked if you'd be unhappy if he did so."

"Unhappy." She looked at Marian. "What's the word for 'no'?"

Alexa laughed. "I learned the word for 'no' within an hour here!"

Calli could believe that.

"Ttho," said Marian.

Stomach fluttering with butterflies, Calli met Masif's gaze and said, "Ttho."

His eyes went big and he looked as if he was having second thoughts. Since she sensed he was a very serious man, she liked the fact she made him nervous. She didn't see that they had much in common, but he looked like a stand-up guy, and the more choices she had, the better.

They all ate in silence. When they were done, Marian said, "Speaking of the Choosing and Bonding, we'd better get back."

"There're hours until evening," Alexa grumbled. "Marian—"

"Back," Marian said firmly. "You can't prepare for something this life altering too early."

Calli's burger turned to lead in her stomach.

"Just gonna dump Sevair?" asked Alexa.

"If he's going to put a token on the Choosing table, he'll have to prepare, too," Marian said. She gestured around them. "The place is almost empty. Most of the Chevaliers are probably up in Horseshoe Hall meditating and bathing and Singing."

"Singing?" asked Calli.

"Praying," Marian said.

"Oh." It would probably be a good thing to do a bit of that herself. Calli didn't consider herself a very spiritual person. Her dad certainly didn't truck with any sort of religion, so she wasn't quite sure who she'd pray to. The closest she'd come to a spiritual experience lately was flying on Thunder. That decided her. "I'd like to see the volarans again."

"Shoot," Marian said, digging into a pocket of her gown and dropping a couple of gold coins into Alexa's outstretched hand.

Alexa winked at Calli. "I won the bet that you'd want to fly again before this evening."

Calli stared at Marian. "You're the one who was there when I took off and landed yesterday. You like volarans better than Alexa, why would you think I wouldn't want to fly today?"

"You fell off yesterday. You don't have the tack you like. You should be thinking of the Choosing and Bonding ritual and preparing for it."

"I won't fall off. Thunder wouldn't let me. Bastien's

bringing a variety of tack for me to examine, so I'll find something acceptable. As for preparing for the Choosing and Bonding, I'd rather keep my mind and hands occupied. Furthermore, I think the most spiritual experience I've had in my life was on the back of that volaran yesterday."

Marian's expression softened. "I understand."

"So do I," Alexa said, smiling.

"I *am* the volarans' Exotique," Calli said.

Masif wiped his mouth and hands with a napkin, then stood. He'd eaten very efficiently. All his turnip fries were gone. Without ketchup. There was no hope they'd link up together. He stood and slid from the table, offered Alexa a hand.

Alexa opened her fingers and picked out a gold coin. Masif curled her fingers back over the money and said something. He nodded to Marian and Calli.

On the other hand, the guy was obviously treating them. A gentleman. She could go for a gentleman.

Alexa and Marian murmured thanks in Lladranan. Calli waited and said, "Thank you," matching his serious expression.

He set several gleaming silver coins on the table, bowed once more and walked away.

"Nice guy," Alexa said.

"Very serious," Marian said.

"Yes, we seem to prefer the rogue and charmer types, huh? How about you, Calli?"

"I'd like a man who'd love me."

Again those warm smiles. "That's what's important," Marian said. She stood and Calli followed her, glancing around the place, not looking at the trophies. Not many people lingered. Two gay couples, one male, one female, all of whom smiled at her, and a grizzled old man, stood at the bar. The other booths were empty.

"One moment," Alexa said. She went toward a door on the wall.

"I've never been in there," Marian said, following.

Feet slow, Calli asked, "More trophies?"

"Not exactly." Alexa pushed open the door. The room was dark but the minute she walked in, light came on. She waved to roughly faceted quartz crystals sitting in brackets.

"An older lighting system, interesting," Marian said. She stopped and looked up.

Calli entered the room and looked up, too. It wasn't a large room, but it was high-ceilinged and held hundreds of flags in several rows from the top of the room to just above a tall Lladranan man's head.

"Heraldic banners of Chevaliers and Marshalls who've died the last two and a half years fighting the Dark," Alexa said.

Looking closer, Calli saw many were ripped and torn, showed brown stains of earth and blood. A couple were burnt and eaten away as if acid had spilled on them. Other colored stains, green, yellow or black, also decorated the flags.

Calli gulped.

Alexa stared at a big maroon banner edged in gold except where a chunk was burnt. Her expression was inscrutable. "That one belonged to Lord Knight Swordmarshall Reynard Vauxveau, Bastien and Luthan's father."

Swordmarshall Thealia held that title, Calli knew, the greatest title in all the land. So the most powerful man in the country had died.

Marian said, "We must return to the Castle." She

walked back into the barroom. Alexa did, too, leaving Calli alone.

Calli stared at the flags, hanging still and solemn. Her heart tightened in awe and fear. All these people had fought against the monsters displayed in the other room, and lost. Died.

Soon Calli would bind herself to a man who'd fight. She'd be expected to fight, too. Or defend with magic, Shield to the man's Sword. Risk limb and life and volaran. Volarans must have died, too. She put a hand to her throat.

She wanted a husband and a family and a ranch and beautiful volarans.

This was the price.

11

As they were leaving town, Calli heard the worst thing in the world, horses' terrified cries. She ran in the direction—more by feel and the screeching notes of mental noise than by ears. It was farther than she expected, through the town to the outskirts. There she saw a small round pen where a man flailed at two horses, a black and a bay, with a snapping whip, raising blood.

A protective force field rippled around the man with the whip, but Calli could see his aura beneath—a nauseating yellow-green color. In the shadows of the building another chartreuse glow pulsed with meanness and excitement as he watched the abuse.

"Stop!" Calli shouted, running fast. Fury burned in her so hotly she thought her hair crackled out from her head.

The men turned to her, sneers on their face. Then they froze. The guy with the whip dropped his arm, openmouthed.

Alexa, breathing hard, caught Calli's arm. "You slow down. *Calm* down. I'll translate for you, but watch yourself. Your Power is out of control, shooting off sparks!"

Alexa's strong grip gave Calli pause. Her words penetrated the red haze. Then she blinked, seeing what Alexa said was true. Little fire-bright sparks rose from her skin.

The man in the shadows bolted.

Alexa's baton flew into her hand. She pointed it at the men and yelled, "Arret!"

This time the men really did freeze, midmotion, their eyes rolling as wildly as the horses'. Satisfaction surged in Calli. Super powers at work. Excellent. She found herself grinning and knew part of the assholes' fear was because of her. Really good.

She reached the paddock where the horses still circled in fright. "What do you think you're doing?" she said softly to the men. Alexa translated the question, her voice full of threat.

The men said nothing. Calli got the impression they couldn't speak. Alexa waved. "Parly."

Calli leaned against the wooden rail, waiting until it was safe. The man in the pen gauged the horses' gallops and ran to escape when they were on the far side of him. He scrambled over the fence.

"Well?" asked Calli, lacing menace into her tone. The guy in the shadows cringed back, tumbled into speech, gesticulating.

Alexa looked at Calli, disgust on her face. "He said the horses wouldn't go."

"They're goin' now."

"That's for sure," Marian said, joining them. She sent the men an icily aristocratic look that had them bunching together.

"What's the law about animal abuse?" Calli asked.

"Don't know," Alexa said, "but I'll find out."

"Tell 'em that I want 'em gone. Now," Calli said.

That didn't go over well. The men raised their own voices, waved their hands. Calli thought they were using the old "these animals are my property and I can do whatever I want with them" defense. Mid-tirade she swept an arm out toward them and banged them up against the outbuilding wall.

Alexa grabbed her arm. "Don't do that again. Your Power is out of control."

She was right. Calli trembled from more than her anger. Power rushed through her like a flooding river. She had to dam it, use it. For good. Not to whup some stupid asses who had skulls too thick to ever learn how to treat a horse, egos too solid to ever think that someone else could teach them. Even a lesson in fear wouldn't last with them very long.

But, oh, how she wanted to *give* them that lesson in fear. Terrify them until— Sparks jumped from her skin again, and gave her a quick, shocking backlash, sizzling a few of her nerves.

"Wow," Alexa said. "Lock it down, Calli."

Dam it. Right. She sucked in a deep lungful of summer air.

Marian had been coolly watching. "I think it would be best if we paid them off for the moment. Bought the horses. Are you all right with that, Calli?"

"Yes, but I don't have any money."

"We'll take care of it," Marian said, keeping her eye on the men. She said something, sounded like a price. The men shook their heads, their voices becoming louder again.

Marian looked down her nose, gestured to the horses, obviously telling the guys the animals weren't in good shape.

They argued more.

"Arret," Alexa said, crossed her arms and glared. "Take it or leave it, but get away from here."

The man who'd been in the ring spat in the dirt.

"Too stupid to live," Marian said in a tone of wonder. "Facing the three most Powerful women in the country and arguing over a few coins."

Calli turned to the two men, considering what else she might be able to do with magic.

Marian touched her arm. "You're very Powerful. You've proven your point, you don't need to intimidate them further." She handed Calli three small gold coins.

Sending a scalding look at Marian, Calli shook off her hand. Motioning to Alexa, she strode up to the men. "You tell these…turds…that they had better not *ever* treat another horse this way or I'll skin their hides."

With a smile that showed all her teeth, Alexa fingered her sheathed baton and repeated the words. The men paled. Calli's smile matched Alexa's.

"Bastien and I will make sure they pay," Alexa growled. The two weren't looking happy now. In fact, their eyes had gone wide and round as they looked from Calli to Alexa to Marian.

Calli threw the gold coins at the men's feet. "Go."

They scooped up the gold and scrambled away without a backward glance.

Now she was faced with the task of transporting two terrified and abused horses up to the Castle. She didn't know how she'd manage. It usually took her a minimum of two and a half hours to work a green horse into trusting her, let alone a mistreated one. "We need to get the horses to the Castle."

"Or stash them somewhere until you can come back to them," Marian said.

"That could work." Calli'd rather have them close. These animals she understood. The familiarity of horseflesh, even their scent, reassured her, reminded her that she was a damn good horsewoman.

"Try whispering to them," Alexa said.

"I'm not going near them just yet."

"With your *mind,* Calli," Alexa suggested gently.

Shit, what did Alexa think Calli could say? "Here, horsey, horsey," like some tenderfoot? Calli leaned on the rail and closed her eyes. She brought the equine language she'd learned a bit of yesterday to mind and mentally *reached* for the horses. She heard fearful shouts. Men. Will kill me. Will eat me. Run. Run. Run.

Calm, she tried radiating the feeling. *Come to me. I will help. I will protect.* She said that in her mind but kept up a flow of completely confident and serene emotions to them.

The sun bore down on her, making her shirt stick to her back. Her scalp dampened. This was hard!

The horses' hooves slowed from a gallop to a canter, then a walk. Finally they calmed and lowered their heads to sniff around the ring.

Come see me, she coaxed.

Their eyes rolled as they saw her—or maybe it was the three of them, not quite in the shades they might usually see.

But now Calli could sense their thought patterns—or equine images. Of course, they weren't intelligent like volarans. But they were curious. Especially about her smell, which was volaran and horse and different-horse. And predator, but the meat-eater was behind a fence and the bad bad-men predators were gone and the other littler predators smelled interesting, too.

Calli smiled. The work to connect lightly with their minds, to soothe them, to *hear* them paid off in joy. Here, on Lladrana, she *could* whisper to horses with more than her voice and body language. In Lladrana, horses could whisper back. And that squeezed her heart nearly as much as flying on volarans. To be appreciated and respected and someday loved by beings she'd always loved herself was another priceless gift that Lladrana had brought her.

Come see me. And they did. They walked over and when she didn't move in a threatening manner, dipped their heads to whuffle her hair. They jostled each other to get the best position to sniff her up and down.

Without looking away from the two, Calli said, "They want to look at you two. Come to the rail."

"Oh, very well," Alexa huffed and came to stand on Calli's right. The horse nearest to her, a black, whinnied a greeting. Alexa held out her hand and when the horse came near her, rubbed its neck. The black lowered its head to sniff at her baton.

Calli got the impression that the horses felt slightly reassured that the three women smelled of volaran and two of them had the scent of wondrous-magical-creature.

Marian had come to stand at Calli's left—to stand near the

newcomer instead of next to Alexa!—and the black drifted over to her. Even the roan Calli was rubbing and murmuring to turned its head to see her.

To them, she smelled of ocean. And big magic. And a little of fire, which they didn't like much.

Then they stilled. Each pricked their ears, looked past Calli...and upward. A small, foot-long volaran of a demure brown, flew to them and landed on the thick rail post of the pen.

"Feycoocu!" Alexa's face lit up. "This is *so* cool. A miniature volaran." She ran a finger down a little wing as Sinafinal preened. "Why didn't you ever turn into a bitty volaran for me?" She sniffed.

For Calli, Sinafinal broadcasted.

"Thank you," Calli said.

"Huh," said Alexa.

Calli should return to the Castle, Sinafinal said. *I will help you lead these poor creatures.* She circled over the horses' heads. They acted as if she was nothing to be feared—not even starting, as if she'd been a low-flying bird. Calli didn't know what sort of magic Sinafinal was doing, but it worked.

Then she hovered over the roan, who had the most welts. The feycoocu lit on the horse's back and burst into bright light like a small glowing sun. A loud melody fluted to Calli's ears by way of her mind, another aspect of Sinafinal's Song.

"Whoa!" Alexa said as they all turned their heads away. In a couple of minutes the bright light faded. Still blinking spots from her eyes, Calli looked back at the horses. Sinafinal lay on the black mare in her small greyhound form.

Marian and Alexa and I will ride the black and Calli can ride the roan.

"You really think this will work?" Calli said.

Yes. They are calm now.

"So," Alexa said casually. "Is that your natural feycoocu form, a sun?"

I prefer to think of it as a star form, but, no, Sinafinal smiled a doggy grin, then met Calli's stare. *You and I will keep a light touch on their minds and shield them from fear. Marian and Alexa will learn from you. This will help Alexa with volarans, too.*

"Sheesh," Alexa muttered. "Another lesson today. Another slam at my riding skills. I'm learning as fast as I can."

"We all are," Marian said as she opened the gate and entered. She took a wide-legged stance and hummed a snatch of a tune that sounded suspiciously like an old cowboy song. As Calli watched, her robe split and turned into gaucho pants. Calli blinked, but the cloth remained transformed. "Some dress."

"Marian can do a lot with her clothes. They're Circlet made." Sighing, Alexa walked through the gate. Marian mounted, and held out a hand to Alexa.

"I want a dress like that," Calli said.

"That can be arranged," Marian said. "It will cost about the same as a horse."

"Maybe not," Calli said.

Alexa took Marian's hand and with a little jump *flew* up and settled on the back of the horse.

More magic. Calli's heartbeat picked up. What she could do with horses now she had Power! Incredible stuff. Lladrana wouldn't have ever seen the like of the horses she'd train.

Grinning with the plans she had, the future that continued to open out in front of her, she swung onto the roan and rode the gelding from the pen. "You lead." She smiled at Alexa.

"I don't know this part of the town," Alexa said.

Turn left, Sinafinal said.

It was good that *someone* knew how to get back to the Castle, though when Calli looked in that direction, the fortress loomed. She'd have been able to find her way, and that made her feel good, too. So short a time on Lladrana, but as Marian said, she was learning fast. Both Marian and Alexa had found places here. Both glowed with Power, and Calli thought she might, too.

She'd carve out a life here and be just as successful as her new friends.

The ride to the Castle was quick and uneventful. Both Marian and Alexa easily learned how to cradle a horse's thoughts. And to keep tight control of the horse's emotions when they threatened to panic.

An interesting technique, but it wouldn't be good for either horse or human to rely on it solely. The horses *were* prey animals, they needed such instincts, and those instincts should not be blunted by overuse of human mental control.

Furthermore, humans needed to communicate with horses rather than relying on mind control. What happened if that control failed and the horse reverted to right-brain and the human needed to use regular methods of communication like voice and body language?

Once at the Castle, Marian excused herself and hurried off, to work on the Choosing and Bonding preparations, she said. Calli suspected she wanted to note down the lesson in mental control of horses and Calli's conclusions. Surely the Lladranans had many, many Lorebooks of Horses. Calli'd like to read them. After she learned to read Lladranan.

Alexa called a couple of female apprentice Chevaliers to help Calli, then followed Marian.

Calli supervised putting the new horses in a round pen on the Landing Field. The horses looked around and their minds hummed with animal satisfaction. Calli watched for a bit to make sure the women were caring and competent. They both sent admiration and healing through their hands and their brushes as they groomed.

Then Calli went to the tack room and chose a thin-strapped hackamore for Thunder and a barely acceptable saddle. The hackamore was dark with age and contained a faint aura of Power. When she touched it, she knew it had been crafted by a nomadic people who followed more natural training than she'd seen here.

Thunder's stall was empty. *I am in the Landing Field. We have time for a short ride before you prepare for mating.*

The reminder made her swallow hard.

When she saw him, he stared at the tack, snorted. *I don't like that.*

It's to help me hang on, also to communicate with you.

You speak Equine well, better than yesterday. Horses helped. He snorted again in pity for wingless creatures.

I don't think I can have a conversation with you and guide you at the same time with my mind.

Thunder seemed to consider that. *Very well.* He dipped his head for the halter. Shook it to settle the straps.

Feel okay?

He blew out a breath.

Just live with it.

She placed the saddle on his back and cinched it. He objected. He whuffled and sidled and stomped.

So much for her hope of seamless partnership, her idea that they'd settled who was alpha in this pairing.

12

Bastien strolled up to Calli with a bland smile, thumbs tucked into the waistband of his leather pants. "Thunder is a magnificent volaran. But time is short for a flight today, and you should fly with other winged ones, too. Why don't I bring a couple I bred and raised around for you?"

Thunder quieted. *She is* mine. *We have things to talk about before the mating.*

Bastien obviously heard the volaran. From the startled looks they got from the opposite side of the Landing Field, others had heard the flying horse, too. Bastien said, "Seems to me, right now the best reason Calli has to stay here in Lladrana is to play with volarans. You aren't in the mind to fly with her, so why not let her play with another lucky volaran and have your conversation later?" He winked at Calli.

This saddle pinches.

"I'm sorry," Calli said. "I ordered a new one just for—"

But Bastien went over to Thunder, placed his hands on either side of the saddle and yanked. Power enveloped him and Calli heard a few bars of a wild volaran flying Song. "That should do it," Bastien panted. He shook his head, then leaned against the stable wall.

Feels okay now. Thunder looked back.

Bastien flapped a hand. "Go fly. Commune. See you later."

Calli wasted no time mounting, satisfied that she'd learned a lesson in handling her volaran from Bastien.

The minute she settled, she felt connected with Thunder. Both of them eager. Thunder ran a couple of lengths, then rose into the air, opening wings that smelled of floral feather cleaner. Calli's stomach dipped, but her heart lifted. They angled upward in the blue sky. Since her throat had closed at the pure beauty of the moment, Calli mentally said, *Let's circle around Castleton and the Castle.* She'd like to see—from the air!—the layout of the town and the pen from which she'd rescued the horses.

Thunder slowed his ascent. Calli sent her energy to the left and he turned to begin a wide circle of the vicinity. *One day we will fly to Volaran Valley,* he said.

Yes.

The herd is mighty and the valley is full of Song. We hear all the Songs of Amee, of Lladrana, of the air and earth and fire and oceans. We hear the Songs from the stars. The Song—the Songs the Singer hears.

Prophetic Songs? Calli shivered and told herself it was the cool wind around her.

Yes, we hear the Song, many Songstreams, but we don't all

understand. *The alpha mare. The alpha stallion, perhaps. They don't always tell us. But they will speak to you. You are our Exotique. The Protector of the Flight.*

A zing of pure Power went through Calli…from everywhere. The sky, the sun, the stars unseen in daylight. *What…what do I protect you from?*

Thunder's muscles rippled under her. *You help us with the Chevaliers, give those who speak with us, like Bastien, more respect so they can help us with our fear. You protect us from the horrors. You protect us from a dreadful future. Protector of the Flight.*

This time the zing was more like an unpleasant shudder through every muscle in her body. She leaned forward against Thunder's neck, tangling her hands in his mane, comforted by flesh and bone and sinew and the throbbing of his pulse and sweet musky amber scent. She shut her eyes and welcomed sensation—the wind against her, the heat from the sun above and rising from the earth below. Bird cries sounded around her and she wondered if it might be Sinafinal and her mate. She hoped so. Anything to make her feel less alone.

I have a special task, then. She'd known it, felt it in her bones. More than what the Chevaliers wanted of her. More than what the Marshalls would demand of her. Expectations of the volarans. How could she fail them?

Yes, Thunder said.

What?

I was not told. The alpha mare will tell you at the right time. She got an image, then, of a small chestnut volaran, older. How old?

As old as the Singer.

Calli thought that was plenty old, but she'd have to check for sure. She decided to talk about the easiest revelation, first. *Bastien, who speaks Equine, is Alexa's.*

Grunting, Thunder said, *Yes. But there are others. We believe you will mate with one. It will be a good sign.*

Great, more pressure. Calli straightened. How would she be able to discern a Chevalier who knew how to speak with volarans? Would they have a different aura? Maybe, but she hadn't sorted out what all the aura colors meant yet. Maybe Equine-speaking Chevaliers smell more of volaran. She couldn't imagine herself sniffing them. She was supposed to rely on her Power, but that sense—whatever—was so new she didn't entirely trust it.

You must stay here. With us. A mate will help you do so when the Snap comes.

Even though she wasn't talking aloud, Calli cleared her throat. *Do you know when the Snap—*

No. I only know the alpha mare told me to fly and become your volaran. He sent love through their link and the fine tension in Calli's muscles released. Thunder hesitated. *Your primary volaran. You will get more.*

More!

Some volarans who like to live with people will be given to you when you choose your land. If your man is wealthy, he will give some volarans to you.

At least Thunder said "man." Calli got the distinct impression that others thought she might chose a woman. She had never swung that way.

And you can call wild volarans to you. People who have none and wish to become a Marshall try this. Sometimes we come, sometimes not. You will have as many as you want. It is an honor to be your volaran.

Calli sniffed, grabbed her bandana from her back pocket and blew her nose. *Thanks.*

But I talk the best.

She smiled. *I'm sure.*

Enough talk, let us fly.

So they did. Calli lifted her face to the sun and let it dry the remnants of the tears at the love pouring to her from Thunder, running along their mental connection, seeping into her through their physical contact. She breathed deeply, then relaxed in the saddle. They were over green land, they'd flown due south this time, along a low ridge of hills, and the air got warmer, the land even more verdant. *Where is Volaran Valley?*

Northwest of the Castle.

She'd have to look at a map. That brought her thoughts of the Map Room and the invading hordes.

You haven't been in battle before? she asked, touching a rein for Thunder to turn around. They headed north back to the Castle.

Not partnered with a Chevalier, Thunder said. A fear-laden memory flooded him. He tucked his legs up, and Calli saw him with a group of other volarans, more stallions than mares, young and in the shadow of mountains. Fighting horrors. Distorted images of the monsters she'd seen in the tavern attacked the volarans. Some fell. Thunder screamed as he kicked a soul-sucker's head to explode like a pumpkin, whinnied again in fear as he felt brain matter on his hooves.

Easy! She forced the memory away. Thunder's body

rippled, but he hadn't panicked and that was good. She figured he might in a real battle, though. All of the volarans had done so in that long-ago battle, flown high and fast and far back to Volaran Valley, covered in sweat.

My testing flight. Only the strong and proven can live in Volaran Valley.

Calli agreed with what she imagined Alexa saying, "Shit, does every single being in Lladrana have to be tested?"

Yes. We live in perilous times, answered Thunder. *Those of my age who did not kill a horror had to live outside the herd or fly to a human place.*

That gave Calli plenty to think of. So many of the Chevaliers' and Marshalls' mounts were culls?

Marshalls fly with volarans raised by Bastien, he teaches them to partner with people and fight when they are young.

Oh.

Easier in some ways, Thunder said as they flew over the southernmost of the three Castle courtyards. He lowered himself to a small free spot on the Landing Field packed with unbridled flying steeds. *All volarans are out here to say they love you before you go to choose a mate. They want you to choose their partner.*

Oh, boy.

They pressed against her, rubbing, whuffling at her hair, butting at her and she felt a myriad of Songs from each. *Choose mine. Choose mine. Choose mine.* But under all their pleas she felt the love with every brush of each body, warming her, reassuring her, inundating her. She was *theirs.*

"Coming through!" called Alexa, baton out and raised like a torch, flaring green light. The mass of volarans parted.

Marian, more Amazonian than Alexa, followed, smiling. When Alexa reached Calli, she grabbed Calli's left arm. "I'll have my squire care for Thunder."

"Fine," Calli said. She frowned. "Will I get a squire?"

"For sure," Alexa said. "We Exotiques are wonderful to work for, or hadn't you heard? You'll have a stampede to your door."

A loud bong echoed over the Castle. It came from the alarm tower. Calli tensed.

Marian took her other arm and patted it, but now a crease dipped between her brows. "Not a battle alarm. Just the bell marking two hours before sunset and your Choosing and Pairing. We're running late."

"Just a few minutes, chill!" said Alexa.

"It's time for the purification," Marian said, increasing their pace.

"Purification!" Calli's voice rose.

Alexa squeezed her arm. "Bath."

"Oh." Her pulse didn't slow. Everything she'd been pushing out of her mind, blocking from her own emotions, rushed back.

At Alexa's and Marian's urging, the Marshalls had partitioned a small hot-springs tub in the basement of the Keep from the rest of the room with a fancy wooden screen. Calli was allowed a private bath, but was too tense to relax and soak in the water scented with herbs. Qualms fluttered like butterflies—hell, like volarans—in her stomach. She *did* want a man and a family. Of course, that would be the most fulfilling part of her life, especially since money and a ranch of her own were guaranteed.

This whole thing was like winning the lottery. She could have it all!

Of course, there were drawbacks. Instead of taxes on the money and real estate, there were more emotional-type taxes. She was promising to train horses and work with volarans and riders. She was promising to fight the monsters.

She was promising to stay in Lladrana.

Such a *huge* decision. But she'd never been any good with letting a decision dangle, always felt better after she'd made up her mind.

She was a risk-taker. Marian and Alexa were risk-takers, too, or they wouldn't be here. So were the Marshalls and Chevaliers. Face it, everyone around her was a risk-taker, ready to egg her on.

The only person she'd met who might be the slow, deliberate type she could talk to long and hard was the Townmaster, Sevair Masif, who was waiting for her upstairs. Not exactly impartial. She didn't want to talk to a man about this either.

Splashes and laughing and waves of excited auras of red and yellow and white filtered through the screen to Calli. Yep, everyone was pushing her. Probably because it was the Lladranans' passivity that had led to this mess—now they were overreacting and going all aggressive. Which, in Calli's opinion, was the right thing to do.

More splashing from the other side of the screen. "Calli, you okay?" called Alexa.

Calli had to wet her lips before she could answer. "Feeling a little crazy."

"You don't have to do anything you don't want," Alexa said.

"We'll stand by any decision you care to make," Marian said.

She'd heard enough of Alexa's and Marian's stories on the ride back to the Castle to know they meant it. Everyone had given Marian a lot of leeway when she'd been determined to learn a cure for her brother's disease and take info back to Earth. Marian had made it clear from the start that she'd return to Earth.

Calli had already said she'd stay. "What's the worse that could happen?" she muttered, but not quietly enough.

"You could get trapped in a marriage with the wrong guy forever," Marian said, as if she, too, was considering all Calli's options. Marian, the one who was emotionally bound to her guy forever. Who'd die when he did.

"Well, if the magic goes wrong and she lands a real creep, I could kill him for ya," Alexa offered cheerfully.

Calli thought she must be joking. But that thought did lead to the question of how long her lifespan could be. Days.

Days spent with a husband, hopefully loving and…sexy. Days spent flying on volarans. That was worth any shortening of her life. A life now free of pain.

Voices murmured, then a deeper voice, Thealia, leader of the Marshalls, said something and Marian translated. "You and your mate will choose your land tomorrow morning."

Oh, yeah. That didn't settle Calli down, but it did point out another big advantage. A spread of her own that she wouldn't have to fight her dad for. That she could run the way she wanted, equip the way she wanted. Money for the ranch. Advice from everyone. She had people who were fast becoming better friends than she'd ever had.

A lighter voice came. Calli recognized it as Clua's, the Marshall who'd done the Choosing and Bonding ritual herself. Marian said, "Clua promises you the Choosing Ritual works."

Calli recalled how those two Marshalls loved each other. She *did* want love. Above all, she wanted a family and love. Soon her friends would love her like a sister, she was sure. She could make a place here where people would love her.

The volarans already loved her.

Earth seemed a very cold and lonely place.

Marrec met Seeva, Lady Hallard's daughter, a Chevalier trainee, in the corridor of Horseshoe Hall. Hands on her hips, she was chewing her lip. When she saw him, she smiled and he returned it. Unlike her mother, the lady he swore allegiance to, Seeva's manner was outgoing and generous.

"I can't decide," she said. "I've prepared the North Curved Suite on the uppermost floor in case the new Exotique wants a good view of the hills and the river and the forest, but perhaps she'd rather be in a tower—both the other Exotiques seem to like towers. But Horseshoe Hall doesn't have towers, so she'd have to bunk somewhere else and then she'd be separate from us, the Chevaliers. Mother would not be pleased."

He blinked, then remembered that Seeva had been given the job of managing the Hall—which had put a few noses out of joint. Since he was a man of low status he'd been out of that internal political skirmish.

Again she nibbled her full bottom lip. "Mother's moving from the Noble Apartments and she'll want prime space, too."

"Hmm," Marrec said. He had one small room in the least favored part of the building.

She laughed. "I'm running on. But what do you think, would the Exotique want a suite with a view or a tower or an Inner Curved Courtyard Suite on the ground level closer to the stables?"

He had no idea. Didn't care the least. Which, since he was on his way to put his token on the Choosing and Bonding table, might not be a good thing. He *should* care about the Exotique's—Calli's—quarters.

"Um," he said. "Who wouldn't want the North Curved Suite?" He thought she deserved the very best.

"But being close to the stables? She seems enamored with volarans."

Marrec shrugged. "I don't know."

Shaking her head, she said, "Well, it's too late now." She frowned. "I really wish they'd had the Choosing and Bonding Ceremony here in the Hall. If she chooses someone, they'll probably go straight to bed and it should be here with the Chevaliers instead of in the keep."

That jolted Marrec. His imagination hadn't taken him any further than putting an object in for the Choosing. And he hadn't even decided what to put there, either. He touched a polished stone in his pocket that he'd picked up from his lost farm in the mountains so many years ago. It would be the best offering, since it Sang of him since childhood, but he disliked putting it on display. No doubt Faucon would offer something gold or equally expensive. That decided him. He'd have his best chance to reach her emotionally with the stone.

The clock in the entry hall bonged the three-quarter hour, reverberating through every room.

"We'd better be going. The ritual is soon." Seeva slipped her arm in his, pulling him from his brooding.

"You're going, too?"

She patted a pocket. "I have my token right here."

He looked down at her. She was young and beautiful and he could feel the strength of her Power where their bodies met. He certainly found her attractive, why wouldn't the Exotique?

"I heard she's a manlover," he said. "And I thought you were, too." He winced. He shouldn't have said that.

With a sunny smile, Seeva patted his arm. "I like both women and men, and when Power and the Song is involved, as it is in such an ancient and significant ritual, who knows what will happen. The Exotique may find she prefers a woman after all." She shrugged and Marrec noticed how full and appealing her breasts were. Yes, there was plenty about Seeva to admire, though he hadn't seen her fight on the battlefield, so didn't know how well her mind marched with other Chevaliers.

As soon as they entered the Lower Ward and angled to the gate leading to Temple Ward and the keep, Marrec saw Lady Hallard striding ahead of them. He dropped Seeva's arm.

Seeva hurried and Marrec had to decide whether he wanted to walk with the Hallard women or not. But when Lady Hallard looked up and gestured to him, he had no choice. He lengthened his steps to meet her just as she crossed through the gate—fully guarded today—and he joined her on the other side of the security door. One step closer to the Exotique's Choosing ritual.

13

Lady Hallard jerked a nod at him. "Figured you'd be heading for the Choosing. A person must try and get ahead in life, after all." She scrutinized him. "I don't see that you have anything special for the Choosing table."

"Mo-ther, it's not supposed to be something new and *special*," Seeva said.

"It *is* supposed to be something that resonates of your personal Song," Lady Hallard contradicted. "You'll probably put that worry stone you always finger on the table, right?"

Marrec withdrew his hand from his pocket without the stone that he'd been rubbing. "Ayes." His liege-lady was more observant than he'd thought. Though she was shorter and stockier than he, she set a rapid pace across Temple Ward. "I got your message that you wanted an appointment with me," she said.

"Ayes." But not now and not with Seeva there. "A private appointment."

Lady Hallard grunted. She eyed a clump of people waiting to file into the keep, including some townsmen. "What are they doing here?"

"The Choosing and Bonding is open to all," Seeva reminded.

"But this one is *our* Exotique. We paid the Marshalls to Summon her, and took part in the Summoning ourselves."

"The Marshalls thought it best for there to be the greatest possible number of suitors," Seeva murmured.

"I wonder if the Marshalls will refund our zhiv if our Exotique chooses someone other than a Chevalier."

"Just shows how important the lady is," Marrec said, "and *we* Summoned her, so she should be more attuned to *us* and *our* needs."

"True," Lady Hallard said. "It's a compliment to us that our Exotique has a large showing today."

Marrec refrained from saying that most of the Chevaliers, including himself, hadn't believed in the old ways or in a Powerful Exotique and hadn't shown up for Alexa's Choosing and Bonding ritual. Like others, he'd wished he'd done so now.

As soon as they entered the keep he felt the hum of excitement in the air, sliding along his skin, and heard a distant rush of voices raised in anticipation.

They wound their way through the building to the far northwest corner and an old, large hall with great faded tapestries emphasizing the starkness of the gray stone walls.

After one sweeping glance around the chamber, Lady Hallard snorted. "Nothing's happening. Looks like this ritual is going to be late. The Marshalls can never get anything done on time."

They could fly and fight in unison well enough, and were usually the first at a battlefield, but Marrec didn't say so. After all, Lady Hallard was the representative of the Chevaliers to the Marshalls' Council; she interacted with them a whole lot more than he did. He wondered if they usually started those meetings on time.

"Maybe the delay is due to the Exotique—" Seeva began.

"Calli," Marrec corrected, then flushed a little when both women looked at him.

Seeva nodded. "Maybe it's Calli. Or the other Exotiques. They use a drug, you know, to heighten the victim—uh, person's Power, so she'll chose the right partner. Maybe they're having trouble with the drug, like the Marshalls did with Alyeka."

"I am perfectly aware of the procedure," Lady Hallard said, not even looking at her daughter. Hallard loosened her shoulders. "It's packed in here. I don't know why we couldn't have had this Choosing in Horseshoe Close. Bunch of nonsense, deciding to have it in the oldest room of the Castle." She started weaving through the crowd. Seeva had already slipped away to put her personal token on the Choosing table. Hallard jerked a nod to Marrec. "Let's go out onto the terrace and talk."

He didn't want to go out onto the terrace, but Lady Hallard was right. The room was crowded, and with more men than women. The atmosphere seethed with the exhilaration of competition. For an instant, Marrec wondered what Songs Calli would hear, what she would sense and feel when she entered, how the pressure of being the object of such male desire would affect her. He didn't like it much himself, how would she?

But Lady Hallard had opened the door and walked out to what the Marshalls called a terrace. It was just a bunch of flagstones surrounded by a low stone wall set on a sheer outcropping of rock, no wider than the room. No one else was there.

The lady glanced out at the beautiful prospect with a gaze that scanned more for danger than studied the pretty view. She stalked to the low wall, hitched a hip on it and said, "So what do you want?"

"Time," Thealia said in a voice that echoed around the room. Calli knew that word; she heard the older Marshall splashing from the water in the pool on the other side of the screen. Calli ducked under, bobbed up, walked from the tub and dried off briskly. "I'm ready."

"Your dress." Thealia stuck her arm around the screen with a flow of glittering royal-blue shades darker than Calli's eyes. A dress that would set off her coloring to the max.

"Mine?" It was the most beautiful fabric Calli had ever seen. She took the sleeveless dress. It didn't look like much, but she knew it would cling.

"It's magic, has a built-in bra," Marian said. "I wear them all the time."

"Is this like your dress this morning?" Calli asked.

"A little. It will mend small tears, will mask any perspiration odor with herbs."

There'd been enough herbs in the bath to plant a garden.

"Think of it as a wedding dress."

A high squeak escaped Calli. She dropped the dress, then

had to pick it up, and watched water spots on the fabric fade before her eyes. Her breath came quicker.

"Marian!" Alexa scolded.

"Sorry," said Marian.

Calli pulled the gown over her head. It slipped down her body as fluid as water, then shifted. The bodice lifted her breasts until the upper curves rounded in the square neck. Only a couple of wide straps held up the top. Killer dress, and yeah, it clung. She laughed nervously. "A *take-me* dress."

"Well, let's *see* you!" Alexa demanded.

And with that reminder of one sense, Calli became aware of the sound all around her—light ripples, deep ocean sonic-type melodies, Alexa's and Marian's unique Songs. Her skin prickled. She'd be more aware of music once she stayed.

One last chance to decide whether to trust these people or not. This was a matter of trust. She knew they wanted…everything…from her. But they also seemed to give her everything *she* wanted.

And if the whole thing went to shit there was always the Snap. The thought was a wisp in the back of her brain.

Again she felt the fabric, stroking it over one hip, though there were no wrinkles, would never be any wrinkles. No sleeves, the better to stick a tube in her wrist. She gulped.

"You sure this transfusion thing will work? What about blood types?"

Marian stuck her head around the screen, saw Calli was covered and walked in. "I've done several bloodbonds— with Jaquar to bond in marriage, the coeurdechain like you'll do. Also with Bossgond as his apprentice." She shoved her sleeve up and showed her left wrist. There was a series of tatts—two golden circlets entwined, a yellow bird and a green wand...

"We did a blood-sister thing, too," Alexa said. With a wave, the screen folded back into the wall. She displayed her own wrist with a tattoo of crossed batons and a book. "Like I said earlier, Bastien and I don't have a coeurdechain yet." She nibbled her bottom lip. "I'd like to do a blood-sister thing with you, too, Calli."

"And I," said Marian. She looked down at her wrist and grimaced.

"Good thing you have long arms. By the time we bond with all the other Exotiques, we'll have a mess of pics," Alexa said, "like program icons on a computer desktop."

"That's so...eloquent," Marian said.

"Hey, I ran the law journal, I can speak well if need be." She grinned. "And legalese."

"Just what I missed the most about Earth," Marian murmured, smiling.

The exchange relieved a mite of Calli's tension. She enjoyed these women. Then she reran the quips. "Other Exotiques?"

"You're three of six," Alexa said casually. "Dress looks great."

Marian nodded. "Your suitors will be very impressed."

Alexa grinned. "Their tongues'll roll out and they'll pant."

That wrung a little laugh from Calli.

Alexa stepped close and looked up at Calli with serious eyes. "Really, the man who gets you will be lucky beyond belief." Then her lips curved again in a lopsided smile. She winked. "Trust me, baby."

Thealia jerked her head toward the stairs leading upward.

So they left the pretty, tiled baths and walked up the stairs in pairs. Thealia first, Alexa and Clua—Calli kept her eye on the goblet full of the drink that would heighten her Power to make sure nobody slipped anything in it. Then Marian and she followed, with the rest bringing up the rear. A fine quivering trembled her insides. She felt as if she was facing the most important race of her life, a championship event—win or lose all.

With every step she took, Calli changed her mind. Stop this! No, go ahead, she had nothing to lose and everything to gain! No, look things over, check out the "suitors," make the rounds of the room, *then* decide if she liked what and who she saw, if she could live with this Lladranan man or that one... Speak to the volarans!

But she continued to walk next to Marian, who was blessedly silent. Calli didn't know if the other woman sensed her turmoil, but at least they weren't dissecting it in an academic manner, or speaking of it at all, and for that Calli was grateful.

And it wasn't as if Calli *hadn't* talked to the volarans, who were all in favor of this step, or the feycoocu, who was equally in favor. Speaking of which—or thinking of which—they reached the top of the stairs and an exotic red bird with a long tail flew in and settled on Alexa's shoulder.

A grunt came before them and Calli looked down to see a huge hamster. She thought it must be a hamster, though it was about a foot long and looked more like a prairie dog. Without breaking stride, Marian scooped it up.

"Hello, Tuck," Calli said hollowly. Couldn't they, like, take *one* step that didn't reek of magic?

Oh, yeah, she was on her way to a Choosing and Bonding ritual that was nothing *but* magic.

At that moment the red bird on Alexa's shoulder turned her head and stared, beady-eyed and *full* of magic, at Calli. *If you need our help in Choosing, we will give it. We promise you that we will not let you choose unwisely if you are guided by us. Tuckerinal still has some Exotique Terre in his soul. He will ensure the man you choose will be adaptable enough to love all of you.*

Oh, God. Calli wanted to turn and run, but they'd reached a wide hallway and a flood of excitement washed over her, rushing down every vein.

They all wait for you, came a squeaky mind-voice from her left—Tuckerinal. His eyes were equally beady and he clasped his paws together and beamed at her. *It's an adventure!*

Just what she wanted. An adventure. Ha! That's not what she wanted at all. She wanted love and a settled life, especially after all her rounds of following the rodeo circuit, of going into the hospital for yet another surgery. But here she was on Lladrana. Looked like this was one more of those situations where she'd have to live through adventure to get what she wanted. This time she hoped it worked, since her rodeo money hadn't earned her father's love or built the ranch she'd wanted.

As they turned down another corridor, the anticipation in the atmosphere fizzed along her nerves. At the far end of the hall was a clump of people hanging around a doorway. Her stomach did another nervous jump. Everyone was focused on her. For once in her life she was the center of attention, the main event. She didn't like it much. She sure wished it was over already.

The slight babble she'd heard when they entered the hallway faded; everyone watched as they walked closer and closer. Calli saw men and women dressed in their best. They were beautiful, every one, with their golden skin, brown or black eyes, shining black hair with tints of chestnut or brown or raven's-wing. Beautiful. They bowed or curtsied and their movements were full of grace. She didn't recognize anyone and was frozen inside, so all she did was nod, and received huge smiles. Their teeth were good, too.

Before they reached the door at the end of the hall, Sword-marshall Thealia flung open a door to the left. A narrow, rougher stone corridor curved in a huge arc.

"This is the northwest round tower of the keep," Marian said, "the oldest part of the Castle. It's on the same side of the keep, the west, as Alexa's tower."

"Uh-huh," Calli said, as if she cared.

They walked around nearly a good half of the tower before they came to another door, this one made of wood so old it looked like it had turned to stone itself. A pattern of iron diamonds decorated it. "The door to the anteroom of the old Great Hall," Thealia said. She hummed a couple of pretty measures and the door opened. Calli got the idea it was keyed only to her voice.

So, could Calli run if she wanted? She eyed the other women. Would they let her run? Maybe. Could she outrun them? Probably everyone except Alexa. That one was little and quick.

The room Calli entered was paneled in an aged and mellow wood. Lightballs shone like miniature suns, giving off a comforting yellow light. The very walls sent off an aura of peace. Calli began to relax.

"Yes," Clua said. "It's a lovely place to sit." She swept a hand to a cushioned seat under a window made of tiny glass diamond panes leaded together—so old they were tinted by the sun and showed a wavery view.

"Nice," Calli forced from her lips.

"Now it is definitely time for Calli to imbibe the drink." Thealia crossed her arms and nodded to Clua.

"Let's take a look." Marian drew close to Shieldmarshall Clua and peered down at the drink. So did Tuckerinal. "It's fine," Marian said.

Sit, said a serene voice in Calli's head, Sinafinal. Calli looked down to see a beautiful calico cat—one that reminded her of a barn cat who'd lived in the ranch stables when she was a child. Calli went to the window seat and sat. She glanced out and saw a terrace and people moving on it.

"The old Great Hall is crammed!" said a new voice. It was the young woman, Marwey, Alexa's assistant. "There are three long tables full of items for Calli to Choose."

Oh, God.

"Drink." Now Clua was before her, offering the goblet.

Calli looked down into the silver cup. It bubbled with more than champagne. It sparkled, too. Magic.

Alexa leaned a shoulder against the wall, eyebrows raised. "Now or never."

Marian sat beside Calli, patted her hand. "It's the best potion we could brew."

The cat Sinafinal hopped onto Calli's lap, weighing much less than a real cat. Calli tangled one hand in her soft fur. The calico's marmalade and black-and-white coat stood out against Calli's glittering dress. She drew in a deep breath, settled herself. This is what she wanted. Take a chance. Win *all*.

She grasped the goblet and drank.

14

"What do I want?" Marrec repeated Lady Hallard's question. He wanted many things. Mostly to be back in the Great Hall with all the rest of the panting crowd. He cleared his throat. "Like you said earlier, a person must try and get ahead in life. I intend to take more risks on the battlefield, claim all my kills." Negotiating with assayers' offices, hustling, hustling, hustling, like a damn shopkeeper. "With regard to the new policy, I'd like permission to fly to all the battles, not only the ones you fight."

"Hmm." She rubbed her chin. "You're talking about the new rotation the Marshalls posted. It's for everyone's own good. More likely to get yourself killed if you go out for every battle. Tired. Not paired."

He flinched. Who would pair with a penniless man?

She didn't seem to notice. "We have more Marshalls, more

Chevaliers, are training new classes all the time. A rotation is possible."

She sounded as if she'd made that very argument to the Marshalls. Who'd fought for the idea, who hadn't? He wouldn't care, but it affected him—as did all the new faces at the Castle, the new Chevaliers and Marshalls. With so many, there would certainly be more maneuvering for power.

The door to the hall opened and Marwey walked in. For a moment Marrec was distracted by the teenager. Just the sight of her made him recall something that should stay in the front of his mind: the nexus of Power would center around the Exotiques.

Lady Hallard's eyes hooded. "I value you, as you should know. My Master of the Horse is getting on in years. I don't want to see him fall on the field. I'd like to retire him and promote you."

His gut tensed and mind went a little dizzy with the opportunity spreading before him. He hadn't thought that she regarded him more than anyone else. He gulped.

"Excuse me," Marwey said. "May I have your knife?"

Absently, he unsheathed it and handed it to her, then turned back to Lady Hallard. As Master of the Horse, he would be second in command to her. He'd have to give her only a quarter of his take. He'd have his own cottage on her estate. "Shouldn't Seeva be Master of the Horse?"

Lady Hallard waved a dismissive hand and raised her brows. "She's well enough off managing Horseshoe Hall. Surely you don't think I'd put a Chevalier trainee in charge of the rest of my men and women?" Lady Hallard had used a lot of influence to have Seeva appointed to her current position. It made him wonder if she worried about her daughter fighting in the field.

"I'll think—" His words were lost as a group of Chevaliers flowed out onto the terrace. One of them was the very man Lady Hallard had been speaking of, her current Master of the Horse, Yan, followed by Seeva. The two joined them, Yan walking with a limp as if his joints had stiffened again.

Lady Hallard spoke, "Yan, I've told Marrec of our plans."

The man's face cleared. "He's willing?"

"You truly want to retire?" asked Marrec at the same time.

Yan glanced around at the increasing number of people. "The fence posts continue to fall, more horrors invade and more often, but we are building an army." He gave a little sigh. "I will miss the action, but the odds are shortening that I'd survive the next year or so." He lifted a shoulder. "We'll be going all out against the Dark, maybe even going on the offensive…"

Lady Hallard opened her mouth, but Yan's hand stopped her. Marrec envied that. Would he be able to make her listen, too?

Continuing, Yan said, "The word in the Castle is that we'll be finding the Dark and attacking." He rubbed his hands. "I'd like to be in on the planning of it, but not the fighting. Bound to be the bloodiest, hardest fighting in generations, these next years." He nodded at Marrec. "You think about it, too."

Marrec started to reply, when he felt the soft brush of fingers trail over his cock, accompanied by an alluring Song he couldn't catch but strained to hear. He shot straight from his casual stance, looked around, though no one was within reach of his groin except Hallard and Yan and their hands were in plain sight. He shrugged off the sensation, dragged his attention back to the discussion. His promotion to the top of Lady Hallard's ranks. Right.

"I'll think it over." He always did. "And I thank you for the honor and believe I'll ag—" His privates were squeezed.

He gasped.

Seeva narrowed her eyes. "It's the Choosing!"

"What?" asked Lady Hallard. She touched her pocket, swore. "Forgot to put my item on the table."

Shrugging, Seeva said, "It was obvious within a minute that the Exotique had no attraction to women's tokens. That's why most of us came out here. Still hanging around to see what happens and witness the Bonding ritual."

This time the invisible fingers were less tentative, they firmly stroked his erection. The top of his head might just blow off. He wiped an arm across his forehead. Suddenly the nice summer evening had become hot, hot. One last slide, up and down, had him staggering.

An impish smile curved Seeva's lips. "I suppose we can imagine what is happening to you. What gift did you put on the table?"

"Marwey," Marrec said, fumbling in his tight pocket for the stone he'd planned to place on the table. Too late. Too damn late!

"Breathe!" ordered Lady Hallard.

He sucked in a breath, deeper than the shallow pants he could only manage when her fingers, *the Exotique's hand,* touched… "My knife."

"Very appropriate shape, I think," Seeva choked out. All three of them, Lady Hallard, Yan and Seeva, laughed.

Lady Hallard slapped him on the shoulder. "I'll miss you, boy."

"Not Chosen yet," he mumbled.

The fingers were back, running up and down his cock...the hilt of his knife, probably. A wet tongue touched the tip of him. By. The. Song. Pure fire sizzled through him, his flesh swelling until his breeches were tight. One more long, squeezing caress, one more touch of that tongue and he'd be done for.

"Make way," Seeva called, giving him a little push between the shoulder blades. "Get *in* there, you fool." A path opened before him, more than one glance going to his flushed face, his straining trousers.

Fingers curled gently around his balls and any hint of embarrassment fled in a firestorm of need. He stumbled forward, tripped over the tiny threshold between terrace and hall and was pushed upright by rough hands. "Watch it," someone growled.

He couldn't watch anything. He bumped against the wall and leaned his shoulder on it, panting. His gaze went straight to the Exotique.

The sight of her stunned him. She glowed like the sun, her hair already the spun gold of great Power, not needing to age into that color. She set down his knife she'd been holding in front of her face and he was profoundly grateful for the relief.

The red mist of lust thinned and he saw why people had streamed onto the terrace. Three long tables held a multitude of offerings, but the Exotique—Calli!—hovered in the middle of the one closest to him, ignoring everything on the other two.

Four tokens were jumbled in front of her: his knife, some purple velvet cloth, an object he stared at but couldn't identify and a golden ring.

She blinked and blinked again, her pupils so dilated her eyes looked black with only a brilliant rim of blue. Blue eyes. Blue dress. By the Song, she looked amazing in that dress, a dress that was cut like no robe he'd ever seen. Exotique maybe, like her. So gorgeous. So stunning. So special.

He had a chance to Pairbond with her and the thought nearly stopped his heart. Surely this was the most fabulous, most fantastic experience of his life.

She swayed and he wanted to run and steady her. Protect her. He strode a few paces forward; his foot crossed a force line and he hopped back, toes curling with shock in his boots. She was well protected from her suitors. He prowled back to the side of the room.

Alexa and Marian stood on either side of Calli, steadying her. Marian indicated the knife, swept a hand toward Marrec.

"About time," Alexa said.

He showed her his teeth. More than lust boiled through him. Need. Yearning.

He glanced to a side table where there was another goblet—another aphrodisiac for her mate. Along with sharp knives and strips of pure white silk to bind arms together.

A growl snagged his attention and he looked to his right. Faucon Creusse sent him a feral glance.

Marrec's ardor cooled so fast he felt the chill of sweat on his body. Unlikely he'd be able to prevail against the rich and noble and Powerful Faucon. But Marrec stood straight, gave the man a polite nod. He'd be Master of the Horse for Lady

Hallard, then. With that, he could aspire to having his own land in a few years, if the fates were kind.

His woman whimpered. Everything else faded. The lilting Song emanating from her wrapped around him like the strongest rope, trapping him, ready to be pulled in at her whim.

Calli's fingers fumbled at the purple velvet cloth. She picked up a floppy hat, stroked it, and a groan tore from Faucon. What sort of token was a floppy hat! Some effete thing only Faucon could cherish. Marrec sneered at the man, then felt unexpected sympathy as he saw Faucon's shoulders brace against the wall. A trickle of sweat ran from the man's temple. Cords stood out in his neck. With a little approving hum, Calli rubbed the nap of the hat, lifted it to her face and stroked it against her cheek.

From the corner of his eye, Marrec saw Faucon's body ripple with shudder after shudder.

"Is that what you want, Calli?" Marian asked. Marrec didn't know how he knew the foreign words she spoke, perhaps because Calli knew them and they still had a connection, his knife was still before her, with the two other tokens.

"Maybe," Calli said, voice thin.

Now Marrec could see the toll the drug took. A faint sheen of sweat covered every inch of bare skin he could see, enhancing her glow. Her face was pinker than he recalled, her eyes blacker. Her nipples had hardened into nubs.

"Maybe," she said again. Calli held the hat in one hooked finger. Faucon had stopped shuddering, pushed against the wall he'd slid down and stood straight, shaking out his limbs. His gaze fastened on Calli.

She slipped the ring up and down her finger and a new

Chevalier Marrec had briefly met fell to the floor and arched, letting out a long moan of release. Calli stared at him, made a moue and set the ring aside.

Marrec and Faucon shared a glance. The woman wanted stamina and control. Marrec wiped sweat from his forehead with his sleeve. Faucon grinned fiercely.

"The little snot," Koz said. Marrec didn't recognize the word. One of those Exotique Terre phrases. Did Koz have all the advantage, being mostly Exotique himself? An Exotique soul in a Lladranan body? Merde.

Calli picked up a gray metallic circle that looked like steel, but finer, stronger than Marrec ever had seen. It dangled a little charm that was completely unrecognizable. She smiled, toyed with the charm. Koz jerked straight, his head knocked back as if someone had struck him in the jaw.

"Vrrrooom," she said.

Koz whimpered. Shook his head, and yelled strange words, "Put that down! I'm done for." Marrec didn't know what that meant, but she dropped the item and Koz folded to the floor in a cross-legged position, back damp and rising and falling with his panting breath. His hair had come loose from the tie and swung in front of his face. Marrec thought Koz had just forfeited his chance, too, but didn't feel too bad. The man had a huge estate and enough zhiv to last him a lifetime. He'd been rich in Exotique Terre and had brought jewels and gold to Lladrana when he came.

Two of them left. People began to filter back into the room; the noise level rose with interest. With bets. Marrec figured he was the long shot.

He and Faucon eyed each other. Faucon straightened and

Marrec realized he'd fallen into a slouch. He stiffened his spine, too, jutted his chin, tucked his thumbs into his pants, then looked back to Calli.

She stood blinking down at the last two offerings. Faucon's silly hat and Marrec's knife. Damn, he wished he would have put in his stone! That might have given him a better chance. It might be over by now with a clean win for him instead of him standing here with sweat trickling down his back, providing speculation and entertainment for an audience.

Calli stroked the hat. Faucon shoved back against the wall to brace himself, his jaw clenched. Her fingers left the purple velvet and closed around the hilt of Marrec's knife.

Song save him! Her touch was warm, caressing. Tightened around the knife, his own hard shaft. She smiled. He hoped he wouldn't disgrace himself. Then she took a stumbling step back from the table. Alexa and Marian hovered around her, questioning her in Exotique Terre language.

Calli nibbled her bottom lip, held firmer to the knife, brought Marrec to his knees.

"Yes," she slurred.

She couldn't have chosen him!

Lady Knight Swordmarshall Thealia Germaine's cool gaze snagged his. "Marrec Gardpont, arise and come here for the Binding Ceremony."

A wave of pleased shouting roared around him. Two men hauled him to his feet, slapped him on the back, hauled him toward the table. Thealia brought him behind it, where his bride waited to be blood bound with him. Forever. A coeur-dechain. What had he done?

Volaran trumpeting sounded through the room, from

Power, not equine lungs. *We did it! We did it!* Dark Lance sent to his mind, then took off to fly in exuberance. *Won the Volaran Exotique. Will be admired above all.*

Oh, yeah. That's why he did it. For glory, for zhiv, for an estate.

Calli looked into his eyes, her own so large, he thought he fell into them. Her face showed exquisite vulnerability. His heart caught.

For the woman.

He had to believe that this was right. That the Song had guided her. That her Power had led her to choose him because they were meant for each other.

Then her Song surrounded him, pulsed through him, connected from his knife to him, sifting through blood and muscle and bone and it was the most fascinating music he'd ever heard, full of brightness and shadows, unexpected twists and turns. It pulled him on a visceral level, instinctively pleasing, caressing him with the notes and chords.

"Drink," said Swordmarshall Thealia.

Riding on a wave of triumphant lust, he gulped the full goblet down. He'd been expecting something nasty, but it was rare orange juice and mead, made effervescent by Power.

The potion's effect was immediate. His vision blurred, then narrowed until all he saw was the woman. The fabulous woman. A fantasy woman.

She was frowning and wandering back down the tables. The room spun a little. His brain was slowing. What was he doing just standing here when his Pairling was getting away from him? She stopped at the last table and swayed, held on to the edge, staring at something. He tried to follow her gaze and noticed that all the objects on the tables shone with a repulsive glow.

Except one at the very last table. Some small item—a brown lock of volaran hair tied with a multicolored ribbon. The ribbon twisted and throbbed with a compelling mixture of colors— bright yellow, sickly green, orange-red, black-blue. The combination tantalized, mesmerized. Pulsed with *wrongness*.

Calli reached for it.

15

That shocked him into motion. "Ttho!"

Her hand hovered as she turned her head to him, eyes wide and uncomprehending. Surely she must know the word *no!*

"Ttho!" he shouted louder. Heard a few snickers as if he was a jealous fool overreacting. You couldn't overreact to evil. All his movements clumsy, he stumbled toward her.

She focused on him and a sweet smile lit her face. She said something and the other two Exotiques chuckled behind him.

One more long stride. Then he had her caught close against his heart, soft and warm against him. Oh, she deserved to be kissed. How had he resisted kissing her over the last interminable two days since he first saw her? He should have claimed her then, the minute she'd appeared in the Temple. He'd wanted her from then. Tipping up her chin, he lowered his mouth to hers and pressed his lips against her plump red ones and a thousand tiny explosions set him afire. No more waiting.

He traced his tongue over the junction of her lips and she opened her mouth for him and he explored it and tasted a flavor he'd never known before, a taste that became instantly addictive. Her back was bowed toward him under his hands, but he wanted her closer. Needed to be inside her, her wet heat clamping around him. Now.

Hard hands grabbed both his arms and tore her away from him. He struggled, let up a fierce cry of loss, of battle. He was slapped.

Think, man! said a cold, smooth voice from his left, his sword arm. "It is time to *bond* with her," Luthan Vauxveau said.

"Bed as soon as you do," said Bastien with a chuckle. The man holding him on his right.

Thought crept in. He wanted Calli more than anything else in his life and if he bloodbonded with a…a…whatever the word was, he'd *have* her forever.

"Mine. My woman," he said, just to make it clear. Three other women—Alexa, Marian and Thealia—had surrounded her and were herding her to the little table with the knives and strips.

Coeurdechain. That was the word he wanted. That was the *bond* he wanted. The forever bond.

"Your woman," Bastien agreed.

Marrec stopped fighting the hands that still gripped him. Caught sight of Calli's arm being washed and anointed, held out for the cuts that would make them one. He surged toward her.

Thealia stepped in front of him. "Right or left handed?" asked Thealia.

She'd never bothered to notice before. A sting of bitterness nipped at him. Then he realized his emotions were being amplified. He'd have to be careful.

"My right arm is my shield arm," he said thickly. He turned his head away. Other faces swam in his vision, watching him—Lady Hallard, Yan, Seeva. He blinked and looked for his archrival, Faucon. The man wasn't there. He'd lost the lady. Marrec grinned. He'd *won!*

Neither was the new Chevalier with the gold ring. Koz was there, though. Marrec could gloat over Koz—that Exotique-Lladranan was as rich as Faucon, had at least two estates. Marrec winked at him. Koz winked back.

Marrec laughed, paying little attention to the cool wetness on his arm, the tingling of the herbal oil. Even the slicing of his vein was no more than a sharp bite, quickly over.

"Look at your lady and say the words," pressured Luthan.

His lady. She was that—and more, and less. The passion of their entwined Songs was strong enough to last a lifetime, and the rhythms of one of the harmonies of her Song hinted at the earthiness of a woman who lived close to the land. A strong woman who could turn wild in bed. Marrec gazed at his woman, his lady. Her face was lovely, the shape of her lips and eyes, her coloring, different and perfect.

A tiny tube was inserted in her left arm. He flinched. "Don't hurt her!"

"All over now," soothed Thealia.

He growled at her. She took his right arm and connected the other end. Calli's blood pumped into him, bringing a flood of strange images—mountains, not quite as tall or as massive as Lladrana's. A yellow sun, much like their own, a cloudless day with a blue, blue sky the shade not at all like his own.

Feelings swamped him. The love for the land. Deep, abiding hurt and betrayal from a tall, lean, older man with bitter lines chiseled on his face.

"I'll kill him for you," Marrec offered.

Father, she said in his mind and he could understand her. Because of the feelings, the images, the knowledge of Equine she'd already learned.

Father. Oops. But the man had hurt her, and that was not allowed. Not allowed that anyone should hurt this person who was becoming *his.* Someone to love. After all these years. *Another person to love who would love him back.*

And he knew that thought resonated and spiraled back and forth between them.

He yearned to hold her. Looking down, he saw their arms bound together. He touched her shoulder with his free hand, curling his fingers over it. Her muscles were strong and flexible, and quivered under his touch.

His vision dimmed as images came from her of sex in darkened rooms, arousing him again, even as his memories of his own infrequent sexual encounters with tavern women or another Chevalier siphoned into her.

Calli made a rough, wanting noise, tipped forward into him...and was pulled away, to his side instead of his aching front.

"Ttho!" they cried out simultaneously. She knew "no" now.

Her Song had already captured him—bright and fierce and free, the essence of a first volaran flight, with threads of harmonies and rhythms he only half heard, like wisps of cloud against his face, the slant of warm sun against his skin.

"Vows, now!" Thealia commanded.

Bastien's hand turned Marrec's face to his. "Hold on, Marrec. You need to say the vows to complete the ritual magic. They're long, and we know you didn't have the Lorebook to memorize them like Faucon, so just repeat each phrase after me. *This is important.*"

"Important." He nodded. Calli's blood trickled into him, ebbing and flowing like a tide, as his mingled with hers. He liked the feel of it, slick and sensual, licking flames brighter and hotter within him. He straightened his shoulders.

"I, Marrec Simon Gardpont, offer my body and heart, soul and Song to you, Callista Mae Torcher," Bastien said.

Marrec rattled off the sentence, settled deeper into the Power that whirled around him, so thick he could *see* it. Streams of Power, drifts of Songs from everyone in the room. The people near him glowed with Power, especially Alexa and Marian and Calli.

"I," said Alexa.

"I," repeated Calli.

"Callista Mae Torcher," Alexa said.

"Callista Mae Torcher," parroted Calli.

"Offer," Alexa said.

"Offer."

And so it went, the whole long vows, archaic and arcane words he barely understood even when he wasn't drugged. He repeated phrases or sentences. Calli said them word by word.

The atmosphere in the room hummed with more than the Power of all who were in it. The air thickened, took on the scent of a coming thunderstorm. Night gathered and dimmed the room, adding to the mystery. Marrec thought he could hear the ultimate Song—the whispery, sliding revolution of the stars.

Every so often a different-smelling herbal strip was tied, binding their arms together, at elbow, mid-forearm, wrist. Marrec watched, noting the paleness of Calli's skin, so translucent as to show blue veins. Utterly fascinating.

He promised one last vow, desperately hoping he'd remember his oaths in the morning, and felt as if the last syllable echoed through the hall, through the sky, to far-off galaxies. A single note so pure in tone, so Powerful he would have fallen to his knees had he not been supported, so touching it brought tears to his eyes, rang in his head.

His vision cleared and he saw the woman before him, looking at him. Promises in her eyes, too, vows whispering tremulously from her lips.

They connected. Beyond blood, beyond memories, beyond anything else, their souls touched and clung together.

The hall rang with cheers and shouts and Song. The Wedding Song everyone knew by heart rose to encompass them. He found himself singing. Celebrating the joy this bonding gave him. She smiled, but didn't sing.

She didn't know the words, he realized. She didn't know him, didn't know his culture, but she was entrusting herself to him. He'd never felt so humbled. He lifted their bound arms and pressed a kiss in the hollow of her palm.

Bastien slapped him on the shoulder, and with that touch the clarity that had come to his mind dimmed once more.

"Bedtime," Bastien said, his voice still rich with humor.

"*Bedtime.*" Marrec's own whisper was hoarse, but a grin stretched his lips. Bedtime. Sex time. He was ready.

"Luthan will witness."

"Witness!" The word nearly shocked him out of his preoccupation with sex and his lady. "Ttho."

"He'll keep watch in the entryway of the tower suite. Only one door to the rooms."

"Tower suite?" Marrec mumbled. Memories of every horse Calli had ever ridden were flashing from her to him. He got the notion that she was considering him a stallion of a man, and a brief surge of wariness dulled his passion.

Bastien pulled Marrec's left arm over his shoulders. He wasn't as tall as Marrec, but his shoulders were wide and he made a good prop. "Move your feet," Bastien grunted. "You can shuffle, at least."

Behind Calli, some man put his hands on her hips to steady her. Marrec felt her instant alarm. *Not my man! Who?* He glanced to his side, the side being warmed by Calli, the side receiving tingles of attraction from her aura, and looked at the hands, then up at the face.

"Jaquar," he said, and the image of the man went from his mind to hers.

Oh. She relaxed a little. Interesting, he fumbled the thought. She trusted Jaquar.

A recollection of the man saving her from falling sped from her, and Marrec's heart jumped. She'd nearly been broken again on hard flagstones!

Didn't happen, she whispered mentally. For some reason he got an image of a big red circle with a bar slanting through it.

She leaned her head against his shoulder. *I trust you.*

And he saw himself in her memories.

Her impression of him had been of a man who was tall and broad shouldered, with a strong jaw and handsome. *Handsome!* A glimpse of him, brows lowered in concentration during the Summoning, serious when she woke up and noticed him in the Healing Room, strained after the battle.

Faucon was in more of her memories, smooth and easy and smiling…but again the red circle with the bar was laid across his image. *Not for me. Too handsome. Too charming… just* too.

Marrec's heart tumbled. He shook his head to shove aside her memories to look at her…and her drugged gaze rose to his. *Yum.*

Alexa snorted, Bastien hooted. They'd heard! But Marrec was so involved with his woman he didn't care.

"This way. A little turn, here," Bastien said, and the group of them moved to the bottom of a staircase. Marrec looked up, squinted. "Lotsa stairs."

Calli responded to this by showing a box that moved straight up and down, opening to let people in and out. Marrec jerked at the strange image. Something from her past life.

"Elevator!" she said, and he guessed she meant the box. Suddenly he had views of massive buildings spearing the sky, disgorging more people than he'd ever seen together at one time. He swayed.

"Easy." The hands on his shoulders weren't Bastien's, though he'd sensed Bastien had seen such things, too. Jaquar was speaking in his ear. "Just let the strangeness flow through you. Don't stop and look and try to question or understand the images. Let the coeurdechain bind you body and heart and soul and Song, but don't dwell on her old life. That way lies madness. Believe me, I know."

It took Marrec a moment to sort out those ideas, and by the time he did, he was marching up the stairs. He caught Jaquar's eye and nodded, then stared at the Circlet. He had blue eyes, too, a darker blue than Calli's. And didn't Marian have another shade of blue? Incredible. Many colors of blue eyes.

Bastien poked him. "You're tilting my way. Watch where you're going. Up, now."

Squinting, Marrec glanced upward. "Don't know this place."

"Knight Marshall's tower," Bastien said.

Marrec stopped. "Ttho."

"Ayes!" commanded Thealia. She was the Knight Marshall.

"Not yours." He sort of remembered that she had her own tower and hadn't moved when she'd become Knight Marshall. "Whose?"

"It used to be Reynard Vauxveau's," Thealia reminded him.

"Bastard."

Bastien gave a short laugh. "That my father was."

"Beg pardon." Marrec hazily thought Luthan must be around, too, craned his neck, found the man and repeated, "Beg pardon."

"Nice guy," Calli said happily. "Isn't he a nice guy?" She wasn't speaking Lladranan, but Marrec could understand her.

"We've redecorated the top suite for the Singer," Thealia soothed. "You can have the fourth level."

Marrec grunted. "Getting tired now." Calli's many-layered Song was in his skin, running with his blood, but her life before Lladrana also spilled from her to him, flashing images and smells and sounds and even tactile impressions that he couldn't begin to understand. The horses and ranch had been the easy part. He slowed.

Bastien poked him in the back. "Almost there."

Huh! There must be at least ten more stairs.

But his steps slowed. "Feet feel funny. A little numb."

"You'll be fine once you get horizontal," Jaquar said. "Trust me." His voice lilted. "Better than fine."

"You don't think he'll pass out before they physically mate?" Bastien asked, prodding Marrec's ego.

"Sex," said Marrec. The thought energized him. He slanted a glance at the lady by his side. The pretty Exotique lady with lighter skin than his own and golden hair and blue eyes. Whose soft arm was bound to his. Whose luscious breasts showed under the slick-looking dress that made him long to tongue and taste. He hurried up and reached the semicircular anteroom. Made straight for the large wooden and leather-trapped pointed door with an impressive doorharp on it. "Bed."

"That's the way," Bastien encouraged.

Marrec reached his right hand for the doorknob and stared at Calli's pretty fingers that found the fancily patterned brass knob and caressed it. He swallowed.

"Let me cut you out of your shirt and tunic," Luthan said matter-of-factly.

"Cut me out! They're my best," Marrec said, leaning hard on Bastien, trying to move away from the knife gleaming in Luthan's hand.

"Hold still," Bastien said. "They're your best clothes today. Tomorrow you'll get better."

That didn't make sense. "What?"

"Tonight you bond in a coeurdechain with an Exotique. Tomorrow she will be gifted with an estate—" Bastien's hand spread wide "—volarans, zhiv. You just married an heiress, boy. You're rich."

Rich. The very thought made his heart thump. Land and a home in the rolling hills, a beautiful stone house. Volarans.

Bastien pulled the shirt from him.

Cool air gave him gooseflesh, but not as much as when Calli slid her hands against his bare chest.

"Oooh," she said. *"Yum!"*

Everyone laughed and Marrec understood there were a lot more people in the room than he'd thought. He blinked around, saw faces, mostly couples. Jaquar and Marian, Thealia and Partis, Mace and Clua, Bastien and Alexa. Luthan. Koz.

"Luthan will now take you to the bedroom. Be glad we live in enlightened and trusting times, otherwise he would have had to stay to make sure you two truly bonded." Bastien wiggled his eyebrows. "Worshipping each other with your bodies."

Bastien squeezed Marrec's arm. "Sink into your balance. I'm going to let go."

Marrec grabbed the rhythm of his own innate Song, loosened his knees and centered his gravity. Bastien let go and Marrec stood alone, with Calli leaning a little against him.

Gently pulling Calli's fingers from the doorknob, Luthan unlocked the door and pushed it inward. The scent of more, fresh herbs, *expensive* herbs, wafted out. Luthan appeared pale. When he spoke, his lips didn't move much. "Follow me."

Walk? Marrec took a tentative step. Calli lurched against

him. He bent their arms behind her back to stabilize them. Looking down at her, he said, "We walk together."

She stared at him for a few seconds, then nodded. Marrec put his left foot out in a step. She did the same, then looked up at him as if for approval. He smiled. Slowly they walked into the narrow hallway, barely wide enough for them, went to the door Luthan held open, to a tiny space and another door, then sidled one by one into the bedroom.

The lights came on as they entered.

"Ohh," Calli sighed.

It was the most elegant room he'd ever seen, intimidating with its luxury.

They fell onto the bed, him on the bottom.

16

He opened his mouth to Calli's passionate kiss. Her tongue dueled with his and she moaned. Her free hand continued to pet his chest. Then she spread her legs on the other side of his and straightened, wriggling until her sweet sex was atop his. He thought she was wet, he knew she was hot.

He was hard.

With her free hand, she snapped the shoulders of her gown open. The slinky material slipped down her torso, leaving her gorgeous breasts free, creamy tipped with red nipples. He gasped.

Magic, she whispered in her mind, but he heard *Power.* She flung her head back, a laugh rippling from her that rang like chimes in her Song. A delightful, harmonizing tinkle of notes that should have reminded him of sprites and fairies, but instead brought a surge of possessiveness. This woman was *his.*

He watched his own hand tremble as he reached up to shape her right breast and wished desperately that his other hand was free so he could cherish her flesh the way he wanted. He brushed his thumb across her small, tight nipple and she arched against him and his sex swelled longer and thicker. His hips bucked, and his length slipped against her hot softness. He swore.

Breeches off! Their arms tied together hadn't seemed too awkward until now.

She blinked, pressed her hand over his on her breast. He trembled, fought for control. Any more rubbing against his cock and he'd embarrass himself. His breath came harsh to his ears. Sweat tickled his temple.

Concentrate on her. On Calli. But just looking at her made him dizzy with passion, her breast, smooth and pale in his hand, his skin several shades darker—different, except where scars showed white. Her mouth was slightly open, her lips the same color as her nipples and he thought he'd go mad seeing her so lost in her own desire.

"Please," he rasped.

Her lips curved, she looked down at him from under her lashes. *You please me.*

"Inside you!" He'd never begged. He'd never been so blunt.

She stared down at him. *Hot.*

Oh, yes, he was hot.

She took his hand from her breast and trailed it down her body. Her skin was smooth. He took as much pleasure in the feathery touch as she did. Their hands slid down and he ached to touch her, but she wore some piece of underwear covering her that rose up to her hips.

High-cut panties. The phrase made no sense. He slid a finger around the edge at her waist, but she didn't want that. She pouted. Too many clothes.

He agreed.

She lifted, slithered out of the dress and the undergarment. They crossed his body with slick caresses that sent his mind away. Then her fingers were on the buttons of his leathers, opening the fly. She stopped, head tilted, and stared and he wanted to whimper. Hesitantly her fingers touched him through his loincloth and piercing desire racked him. His own Song went rough, uneven, primal. With a twist and a wrench of cloth he freed himself.

Calli made a purring noise from the depth of her throat. Her hand swept to him. He caught her seeking fingers. His lips felt swollen, his tongue thick. "Sex. Now!" He pushed both arms behind her back, pulled her toward him and her moist folds slid over him.

"Yes!" she cried, rising, freeing her hand, impaling herself upon him.

And she rode him.

Their Songs merged, their blood pounded from one to another, they strove to completion. They reached the peak and fell, and Sang.

And flew. Together.

Long moments passed before Marrec became aware of himself as individual from the universe, mind separate but still touching Calli's sleeping one. She lay atop him, her breath tickling his throat. Images of her life still flitted before his vision—a lovely summer day riding bareback, her spirit lifted by the freedom, a dark room that held emotional tones of fear and anguish.

For the first time he wondered what memories passed from him to her. If he hadn't been so boneless from flattening sex, he'd have tensed, but he didn't think he could move a muscle. His memories. He didn't like to recall some himself, let alone burden a rare and wonderful woman like Calli with them. Probably no way to stop them, those few terrible remnants of memory of the slaughter of his village by horrors.

He still wasn't sure how he'd escaped the bloodbath, except he'd been angry with his brothers and parents and had taken an old blanket and curled up in a corner under the bed. When the door had crashed open in their cottage and renders and slayers tumbled through he'd frozen in horror. They'd dragged his family from their beds. The horrors had shrieked with glee as his parents and brothers screamed in terror, the monsters' hideous Songs engorging on the fear, as if it fueled them. Slashing, ripping. Two minutes and it was over and the horrors were gone, leaving the red shreds of blood, white shards of bone of Marrec's family behind them. He didn't know how long he huddled there, until the night fell silent, until he had to see what happened to the rest.

Calli mewled, shook her head, tears trickling down from under her closed eyes to land on his neck. His free arm wrapped around her. What was he doing, sending what he recalled to her? He hadn't thought of that day for years…but he wasn't sure how the coeurdechain worked, hadn't paid much attention to the snippets of discussion he'd heard.

That cost him now. But if they were bonded like this for a full twenty-four hours, most of what they remembered, emotions included, would cycle, he supposed.

She had no memories of the horrors. He had plenty, from that day that shattered his life, to following the trail of them, seeing the brief battle between Chevaliers and the horrors, sidling up to a young volaran with an injured wing, Dark Lance, standing next to its fallen partner. Calli shouldn't have to know of, experience what he had, of the monsters.

Except now that she was bound to him, she'd be fighting them.

His jaw clenched. He didn't want that. Didn't want her with him in battle. Didn't want her harmed. Didn't want her bright spirit tarnished.

Too late, wasn't it? What would happen if he tore off the strips binding them together, refused the full coeurdechain? His chest constricted.

They had already taken vows. The Powerful ritual had already been completed. This bloodbonding was important, but it was only part of the coeurdechain. When he thought of the oaths they'd exchanged, the words sounded like a stream of silver bell tones in his mind. The Powerful Song of the ceremony itself, their Songs intertwined with the vows, made a bond that couldn't be broken without deep cost to them both.

Their lives had changed forever.

She was in a strange land, hardly anything like what she'd previously known. Horses and ranching, that was all, he figured, but that was enough for commonality between them. So most everything here in Lladrana would be different. He promised himself to help her settle in every way he could.

So she wouldn't leave with the Snap.

Immediate anxiety spiraled through him. No. She couldn't leave. Could she?

He didn't know. He ground his teeth. He'd been too damn focused on his own life, his old plans, to listen to others chat about the coeurdechain, to look at the Lorebooks of Bonding left on the study tables in the library at Horseshoe Hall. Merde, he'd been a fool!

But he'd never thought he'd win this golden woman. Now, he'd learn everything he could. He'd read, dammit, until he understood, while they worked together.

That was the most important thing that had changed in his own life. He had a Pairling now, and they would fight as a Pair. Her Shield to his Sword, he was sure. Calli was too soft to be a Sword like Alexa, wasn't she? He reached for her memories, the fiercest ones, and found her riding fast and hard around barrels. Racing. Competing. He marveled at the speed and grace of others she watched, of the feel of her body when she…barrel raced. Yes, she'd been intense and fought in that arena and he probed a little deeper for the why.

Because she had an ambition to train horses. Because she wanted to make her ranch a center of training. Because she yearned to please her father.

A hoarse sound tore from him. An angry noise. He despised her father for treating her like a person of little import, for not recognizing her value and loving her. The man was worthless.

So Calli had fought for her father, for her vocation and if

she'd stayed on Exotique Terre, she'd have battled her father for the land. But she was on Lladrana and here she'd fly into battle against monsters.

Marrec wasn't sure what Alexa had been in a former life, but thought that she might have been some sort of warrior. Calli was horse trainer, a homemaker. Yes, she'd be Shield to his Sword, and that was a relief. She'd be out of most of the action. If he was clever he could work with Alexa and Bastien on the field, have Calli fly near Bastien, another Shield who was one of the best fighters Marrec knew. Though Alexa and Bastien were Marshalls, part of that elite team.

Marrec could become a Marshall now, if he wanted. The notion appealed, then he realized he was stroking Calli's soft hair and knew she wouldn't want to do that. She wanted a ranch, she wanted to train horses, she wanted to enhance the partnership between volaran and human. He could help her with all those goals.

Calli woke and found Marrec looking at her. Her new husband. She sat up straight, then froze.

She'd learned some of the planes of his body—the ones she could reach with her right hand—and how interesting it was that he was a southpaw—he'd been inside her. But now she wasn't drugged.

Now was the time to face the music.

The music was awesome. Her Song flowed through her like the tide and she heard much of it. She suspected others, he, heard more, nuances she didn't recognize in herself. But she heard his, the beating of his heart, now picking up pace as they locked gazes. The melody of him ran in her head and her blood, and was now a part of her.

This stranger.

What had she done?

"Shh," he said, expression serious. He reached out and smoothed her hair. She bit her lip. Her hair must be a wreck, her body...she glanced down and saw the bruises from the day before, the scars from the operations on Earth.

"Beautiful," he said, and there was a tone in his voice she'd never heard from any man, from anyone. She understood the language. Alexa and Marian had told her she would, but she hadn't really believed it. Maybe she hadn't really believed anything and now she was married! Was there any way to go on disbelieving? The steadiness of the man's eyes made her think not.

She licked her lips. "Marrec." Memories called up by that name flooded her, not her own. His mother saying it in a fretful tone, his father impatiently, his brothers teasingly. Seeva. Yan. People who she'd never met but somehow knew through him. And those she knew, Lady Hallard, Alexa, Bastien.

He inclined his head. "Callista Mae Torcher." Now his eyes shadowed as if he saw her memories.

Calli flopped back onto the bed, staring at the inside of the canopy. "What next?" she said and was surprised to hear her voice speaking Lladranan. That was really strange, too.

"Our arms are bound together until this evening. I need to pee."

Well, that was down to earth enough, and now that he mentioned it... She sat up, didn't look at him. "If this suite is arranged the same way as Alexa's, the bathroom is to my right." Meeting his gaze in a fleeting glance, she saw he still wore a sober expression, realized she'd never seen him smile.

"I smile," he said.

She looked at him. He wasn't.

"When appropriate," he said.

That made her smile.

His lips slightly curved.

This was her husband. She stared at him...rectangular face with a few lines around the eyes, respectably wide silver at both temples that denoted Power...

"These were narrow until your healing. I wasn't very Powerful until then." He touched the side of his head.

"No?" she whispered.

"No. You should understand from your memories that you Pairbonded with a penniless Chevalier, average in Power." He swept the covers off himself, turned them both until they faced the curved wall of the tower and the sec-tioned-off wedge of wall that held the bathroom.

Lifting her chin, she said, "I do not Pairbond with average men. I chose you. You have Power. You have courage. Fur-thermore, you speak Equine with your volaran. He respects you. All that means you are exceptional."

"Does it?"

"Yes."

He took the lead in getting off the bed. She admired his build, the width of his shoulders, his muscularity, though he looked a bit too thin. He stood, waiting. She took a big breath and shoved the covers aside and wished she could be more casual about nudity.

"Beautiful woman," he said and lifted their joined arms

to kiss her fingers. "Beautiful Calli." Naturally the way he said it, with his Lladranan accent, had her trembling inside, but her pleasure at the compliment rose in a hum around them. She stood still.

"Disconcerting," he said. "To hear Songs, our Songs, so strongly and with the ears and not only the mind."

"Yes," she said.

The next few minutes in the bathroom as they relieved themselves and washed their hands were horribly embarrassing to Calli, but Marrec was matter-of-fact about it.

He glanced at the wooden shower cabinet. "I prefer bathing."

She sighed. "I prefer showering."

His brows dipped. "I don't know what facilities we have in our suite at Horseshoe Hall. Probably only a shower, but the baths on the lowest level of the hall are the best in the Castle."

"Your culture bathes together, men and women."

"That's right." He paused. "I have heard that both Alexa and Marian hesitate to do this."

"We usually bathe alone in our culture. Or with lovers. Upon rare occasions we might bathe with others of our own sex." Once or twice when she'd been in Denver during the National Western Stockshow she'd gone to a bathhouse during Ladies' Day. Nudity had been no big deal there. On the other hand, there had also been a mixture of races. She was only one of three white females here in Lladrana.

"What next?"

He met her eyes. "I'm hungry. We'll probably eat with the Marshalls this morning." He frowned. "Though everyone may expect us to stay in." His gaze traveled down her and now he did smile. "We could stay in. Order breakfast in."

Her mind skittered. What would be running away? Staying here with this new man who knew a lot about her now, and intimately, and hiding from the rest of the almost-strangers she'd known for two days? Or not facing all that personal flow of emotions, memories from her to him and vice versa by distracting herself with food?

He stroked her hair. "Or we could go bathe and choose land for our descendants."

Her eyes showed dread. One of her memories cycled between them again and again. Her in a bed of white sheets, a man in a white coat. A medica. She couldn't have children anymore. Her fall and infection and surgeries had made that impossible.

His gasp was one of pain. The emotional blow was bitter. Stupid! Before last night he'd had only vague dreams of children, since he could only support himself and Dark Lance. But in the misty recesses of his mind, he'd wanted children. A boy. A girl. A family.

She got as far away from him as possible. Didn't look at him, and he finally noticed her grief. *She'd* wanted children, too. More, she'd had concrete plans for them, had ideas to change her home and her business for them. She'd thought out how to care for them and had hoped her children would love the land and horse training—and her father—as much as she. She'd painted a rosy picture of herself and her children and her father as a happy family, with her husband as an indistinct but loving figure. Yet, she'd intended her children would be her greatest comfort in life.

And now she only had him. Definitely a husband. Not indistinct, not too loving. He swallowed the bitterness. He was good at dealing with reality. "We can talk about this later."

Not looking at him, she shook her head. "I think we should discuss it now."

He gritted his teeth. He'd have liked a little time. He shrugged. "All right."

"I still want a family," she whispered, head averted. "Can't we adopt?"

The idea spun in his head like a pair of thrown dice in a game of high stakes. "Adopt?"

"On Exotique Terre there are unwanted children. Isn't that true, here?"

He'd been a refugee, tolerated as part of the staff of a large, noble estate, a lost child. He and Calli could do better in raising lost children.

"The Song," he forced the words from his mouth. He should be so grateful this morning, dreams coming true. "The Song would not have paired me with you if I couldn't accept you with all your...all of you." He needed to believe that.

She glanced up at him now, wariness in her eyes. "With all my flaws." Her fingers brushed his cheek and he felt the Power of them surge straight to his groin, deeper, sink into his bones. She was *his.*

"And the Song chose me for you, despite..." Her lips curved slightly and he realized she was teasing, and *that* slammed into him with crushing tenderness. No one had teased him since he'd been a child with his own family. After that, he'd always taken life very, very seriously and people had respected that. When he'd been noticed, as if his moods had ever been of the slightest consideration. Not often. He dropped his head to her shoulder and smelled the sweet earthiness of her, of their pairing.

"Yes," he ground out the words. "I have flaws, too. Many." Fear had driven him when he was a teen. He'd chosen to serve under Lady Hallard when she'd visited his old master and offered him a place. He'd striven to become a Chevalier instead of working in a stable all his life. That climb had taken longer than he'd anticipated, and along with the battles, had simply worn him down. For a while. But he'd taken the defection of the volarans as his own personal alarm. It had scared him to the bottom of his soul. He'd be *nothing* without Dark Lance.

Correction. He'd *have been* nothing. Now he'd risen to the heady top of the status ladder overnight. Was the fact that he'd rediscovered his ambition, his fight, one of the reasons that the Song had gifted this woman to him? He thought so.

Awkwardly, he picked up their joined hands, turned them over and pressed a kiss into her palm.

Her head lifted and she looked at him with wide eyes, as if she'd rarely received affection. Perhaps despite their appearance, they were two of a kind. "We'll adopt," he said roughly.

When she smiled, their shared Song rose inside him, beautiful and potent, and brought with it the sound of volaran wings and the whisper of long, verdant grass from a place that could be their home.

He glanced away, cleared his throat. "I think we should bathe and eat," he said.

She glanced at him and nodded. "Let's face the Marshalls and whatever else we need to do—choose the land."

"Very well." He tugged on her and started walking toward a door. "We must dress."

Calli saw the shreds of his clothes tossed around and her beautiful blue dress. She liked it, but didn't want to slither into it for breakfast.

On a chest were folded clothes; pants easy to get into, and special sleeveless shirts that buttoned on the shoulders and along the sides. They were the Exotique color of purple.

Another short interval of humiliation and they were dressed and ready to go.

She opened the door to find Alexa and Marian lounging in deep chairs set in the semicircular entryway.

"We want to bathe," Calli said.

"Where's Luthan?" Marrec asked.

Bastien strolled up the stairs and into the room. Grinning wickedly, he said, "My upright brother didn't stay long. Just long enough to hear screams of delight, by which sound—and the Bonding Song emanating from the suite—he cannily deduced that the consummation of the marriage had occurred."

Heat crawled up Calli's neck, bloomed on her cheeks. She tugged on Marrec's arm. "Let's go now."

They walked together, passing the other three to the stairs.

"Calli?" Alexa said.

Calli turned her head to look at the woman. "Ayes?"

"You walk well with Marrec. In step. You look good together."

"I always was good in a three-legged race."

"What's a three-legged race?" asked Marrec and Bastien together.

Watching her step down the long flight of stairs, Calli said, "It's a race people play during, um, picnics, holidays." She waved her free hand.

Marrec frowned a little, as if accessing her memories. That was a little creepy, so Calli said, "Let's go."

17

After a quick bath in the public pools that left Calli red from more than the heated water, she and Marrec ate a late breakfast with a few of the younger Marshalls in the fancy dining room. Everyone at the table spoke more than he, and Calli sensed he was wary of those who had had great power over him just the day before. He wasn't a talkative man, so she figured she'd be relying on the memories that continued to roll from him to try and understand him. But that was a blessing. It wasn't often that a woman had so much information about her husband. At least, that's what Calli was telling herself.

As she and Marrec walked across the courtyard to the Map Room to choose their land, a group of Marshalls and top-ranking Chevaliers surrounded them. With each step, tension built and cycled back and forth. She'd try to take an easy breath and relax and niggling anxiety from Marrec would destroy her calm. He'd shove nervousness aside, boxing it away in a safe place and the strain of the unknown would flip from her to him and pop the lid off the box.

Then they were there, standing before the great, animated map of Lladrana.

People pressed around them. Calli thought that everyone's gaze had gone to the northern border just as hers had done. The room itself wasn't large, so others must be lining the cloisters and lingering in the courtyard.

Marian and Jaquar and Bastien and Alexa were there, of course, some of the older Marshalls and the two feycoocus in the shape of red birds with long tails perched on the top frame of the map. It comforted Calli that Alexa had done this same thing.

And Calli had Marrec. His Song resounded in her head, strong with excitement. His arm against her was tense as he focused on the map. Her fingers fisted as she realized he wanted the land as much or more than she did.

Swordmarshall Thealia raised her hands and the babble died. "These are the current vacant estates." She gestured.

The map, which had been topographical, showing the greens of rich farmland and brown of mountains, turned to a dark gray background with splotches of yellow.

To Calli's way of thinking, there was far too much free land, obviously because the owners had fallen in battle and left no heirs. Chevaliers, like her; Marshalls, like Alexa; nobles, like Lady Hallard and Faucon, who winked at her.

Marrec's excitement reached a shrill pitch, subsided. She saw a real smile on his lips. He stepped forward, concentrating on one dot in particular, a place that had been in the richest green, not too far from the southern border.

He gestured. "Here—"

Ttho. Calli grabbed his arm. *Ttho.*

He looked down at her, frustration leaped from him to her, through their connecting Songs, through their blood.

Ttho? It's rich. The richest we could get. Big. Close to the Shud border and good trade. Far from the north. We'd never be in danger. Never.

I'm a mountain *girl. I want mountains.* She waved vaguely to the north.

He stiffened into rigidity. His glance flicked up and to the northwest. Where his village had once been. He had few and indistinct images of the massacre, but so terrible that Calli had locked them away. When his Song went ragged, she shoved them away from him, too.

His expression was impassive, but she knew his inner struggle.

I'm a mountain girl, she repeated, putting her free hand on their linked arms.

A neigh came from the courtyard outside. She didn't recognize it, only knew Thunder's and her horses' calls.

Volaran Valley. The equine voice came to Marrec first, then through him to her.

Dark Lance, Marrec said.

Together they stared at the map and Volaran Valley, northeast of the Marshalls' Castle. To the west of the valley the land rose.

"Topographical map, please," Calli said, a little surprised that she knew the words. But languages hadn't been too hard for her, and she could pluck phrases out of Marrec's head since they were bound so closely.

The map changed back to the blue of the sea, greens and browns, and the white of the tallest peaks in the north. Those were too dangerous, Calli knew.

Marrec pointed to where the land he wanted was. *It's perfect,* but his conviction, his lust for this particular place had slightly faded.

Near Volaran Valley! came, and it was a swell of Song so strong, from every volaran in the Castle that it staggered her. Marrec stood rocklike, absorbing the shock of her body, the volarans' minds. His lips thinned.

"May we see the free estates, please?" Calli said, and as the map faded to gray and yellow, she kept the image of the mountain ranges in her mind.

She angled her chin. *The spur from the north. Near the end of the spur, on the eastern slope, closer to Volaran Valley. See? There's a place. It would be a good place for volarans and horses, wouldn't it?*

"Must we choose now? Can't we look at the land?" Marrec asked.

Thealia frowned. Lady Hallard snorted. "Calli must be trained as soon as possible."

Calli's turn to tremble.

Marrec stared at her, this woman who had shattered his old life with her choice of him. Yet, she hadn't chosen blindly. The drugs had freed her mind, emotions, Power for the Song to guide them together. He had, quite simply, been the best fit for her. He shifted from foot to foot. She still stared at the map.

He wanted a rich estate that would always support them, their children...no children from his body, but the lost children they'd adopt. They could make a large family. A rich estate would ensure their children would never go hungry, never be poor. An estate in the south would be best.

Throaty coos impinged on his hearing. He looked at the two feycoocus who perched with curled claws around the top frame of the map. They had wanted Faucon for her. A snap of jealousy whipped through him before he recalled that Faucon, rich noble that he was, garnered much of his wealth from his seaside estates and ships.

Marrec was landless, could be more flexible in the matter of property, could give her a mountain estate. The gleam of Calli's hair tempted him, golden, like freshly minted coin. He stroked her head. Her eyes, blue as the sky, met his—filled with tears.

Merde!

She'd broken his old, grinding life, given him new hope. Through their blood flashed images of her lost home...in the mountains.

They could build a good life together. They would have to learn each other's rhythms, make adjustments, when they became a fighting team. He rubbed his chin. "We'll take the land on the east side of the Eperon range, the little circular valley."

Gratitude flooded Calli, her body softened, she folded into him. The volarans outside trumpeted.

Well done, said a voice in his head and he looked to the map—where the land had already shaded into the purple of an Exotique estate—and upward into the beady yet fathomless eyes of Alexa's feycoocu.

"Thank you," Calli said it in her own language, then set her head against his heart and looked at the map. "Merci." She sniffled, swallowed. "We must choose our colors. That purple has got to go."

"What about black edged with silver, like Dark Lance?" he said.

She smiled up at him and it was free, and easy, and nearly...loving. "Done."

Shades of gray would be good, her volaran said.

"Bo-ring," Calli said in her old tongue.

Thunder grumbled in her mind.

Calli nodded to the map. "Look."

Their land had already changed to a black shield edged with silver. "A silver-gray volaran, flying," she murmured. The shield took on that symbol. Again she looked up at him. "You agree?"

"Ayes."

Thealia clapped her hands. "It is done. The Gardpont colors and heraldry are noted. The estate will be logged in the Lorebook."

Bastien laughed, put one hand on each of their shoulders. "You do know that you've chosen colors like a black and white." He touched his striped hair that marked him as one with wild, fractured Power.

Calli frowned, glanced up at Marrec. "Perhaps one of our children will be a black and white."

That could be a real challenge. "I don't see children in our future, just yet," Marrec said gently. "We're a fighting team."

She stiffened. "Ayes."

"But someday..." he said, and sent his own Song to spiral

around her, full of the knowledge that it had just changed once more, deepened, as he'd become a landowner. If that could happen, what other miracles could occur?

Nodding decisively, she said, "Someday."

When they exited the Map Room, the courtyard was filled with all the Castle volarans again, with Thunder and Dark Lance sticking their heads through the window opening of cloister walk. Both volarans radiated smug satisfaction. Marrec noted mares next to them and behind them. "I don't think we'll have any problems with that volaran-breeding program."

A hint of pink color rose to her face, fascinating him. He touched her cheek, it was slightly warmer than usual. "What is this called?" he asked. Of course, his people occasionally showed a change of color, but it was only noticeable if you were staring at them.

"A blush or flush," she said in her own language.

"I don't think I'll ever tire of seeing it," he said.

She snorted.

Thealia stopped beside them, looked at the sea of volarans. "Is this going to happen every time you're around, Calli?"

"They all want to fly with her," Marrec said.

Calli appeared startled, then blinked, looked out at the winged steeds. "You're right." She nodded. "I can do that."

The alarm shrilled. Marrec tensed, ready to run, remembered he was literally bound to Calli and stopped. Chevaliers close to the volarans at the edge of the herd saddled and mounted, began to fly out.

"The junior Marshalls will lead and fight today!" Thealia's voice filled the courtyard.

A whoop echoed from the newest Marshalls, admitted into those ranks since Alexa was Summoned. Most of them hadn't been in the Map Room and took off in the next wave.

Calli leaned against him. He drew her into his arms and they watched the mass of volarans shift as Chevaliers and Marshalls flew to fight.

"I don't like this," she muttered.

That was an understatement. Marrec felt her deep fear and anger roil her blood, ripple through her Song until it was strident and uneven.

Thunder and Dark Lance came closer, sticking as much of themselves through the cloister opening as they could. Knowing she needed comfort, Marrec drew her forward so their volarans could nuzzle them.

I do not fly today, Dark Lance said in a superior tone. *Do not carry nets of monsters anymore for zhiv and better status. Have good stall next to Thunder's.* He whickered.

"True," Marrec said, stroking Dark Lance's neck. "But we will be in the thick of battle, always, when we fight." He didn't say that the Exotiques tended to be targeted by the Dark forces…but even though they were the focus of the invading monsters' attention, they were also well prized by the Chevaliers, Marshalls and Circlets. Marrec had no doubt that every volaran on a battlefield would die protecting Calli—and now himself. For if he died, she would, too. It was a very odd sensation to know that others would give their lives in order to save his. Something he hadn't thought of before. It humbled him.

"Marrec, Calli, you should return to the Map Room," called Thealia, steel in her voice.

He and Calli shared a look, their Songs spiked in anxiety. Returning to the room, they saw the map had reverted to the aspect of a battle map. The northern border showed the fence posts, new and dying, and the force field boundary...and the gaps.

Thealia gestured to the north, a mass of horrors trickled across the northern border. "It's a big incursion," she said. "We're going to lose some people. Perhaps we all should—"

Bastien shoved away from the wall he'd been leaning on. "Let the new Marshalls lead and fight. They need to learn the confidence of taking the field and winning without you older folks." Underlying his words was the inescapable fact that some of the older Marshalls could die at any time. His dark gaze passed over Marrec and lingered on Calli. "Everyone must move from training and practice to real battles."

Now the color in Calli's face changed again; she went very pale, paler than anyone Marrec had seen alive. He didn't like this color change. He glared at Bastien, but that man was still focused on Calli.

"I haven't even begun to train yet," she whispered.

Marrec sent her the absolute confidence he gave Dark Lance, bolstering her Song. "We are Paired. We will fight together. You will never be alone."

She lifted her chin and stared back at Bastien. "I'm used to compe—fighting."

Thealia cleared her throat. "This confrontation wasn't why I called you back in here." She pointed to the map. "Look at the point where they're invading. Lately they've been coming over the northwest border. Not today."

They were invading due north of Marrec and Calli's new estate.

Exactly.

Thealia, Alexa and the other Marshalls went to the dining hall, ready to discuss the morning's events. Calli sure wasn't interested in eating again. She didn't think that her stomach would keep much down if she thought about people and volarans fighting monsters. The few Chevaliers who weren't flying dispersed to Horseshoe Hall or the Nom de Nom for lunch.

So she talked to Marrec about her horses. They went to the small round pen on the Landing Field set near the corner of the stables and the western wall of the Castle. She greeted the horses, but they didn't come to her. So she leaned on the rail, Marrec beside her, shut her eyes and *sensed* their moods. They were a little wary of her, she smelled different than yesterday, with Marrec's blood trickling through her veins, Marrec's scent on her.

Noticing their horsey scent herself, she smiled, let the warm summer sun sink into her, existed in this moment, where she was fine, the horses were fine, the *now* which didn't include fighting.

But did include a husband. Subtly turning her head, she lifted her lashes a crack and found him looking at her, serious as always, though his mouth seemed relaxed. Then she thought about kissing that mouth, and her skin tingled.

He chuckled, squeezed her fingers.

She smiled and returned her attention to the horses. They'd stopped and were standing in the middle of the pen, ears pricked forward, curious. They'd been curious all night. They'd been able to see the volarans coming and going. Many of the volarans had come by and stuck their heads over the rails to look at the horses and the horses had liked that. They didn't understand that their circumstances had changed, of course, but had been content.

Which was probably just about as much as she could expect. She itched to get in the ring with them, she hadn't been able to work a horse since before her fall in December. But they weren't ready, and she was attached to Marrec. And from what she understood, she'd be busy the next couple of weeks from dawn to dusk learning her new craft of fighting.

Marrec kissed her cheek. She jerked.

"You tightened up. You will learn to fight well and easily. We'll be a Pair team, probably with you as the Shield—protecting me and Dark Lance—and I as the Sword. Don't worry."

"I'm going into battle against those monsters and I shouldn't worry?"

He shrugged, one corner of his mouth quirked. "Don't worry about the training, and don't ever worry about a battle until you're flying to it."

"Good advice."

He dipped his head, then angled his body and gestured to the Landing Field. They were surrounded by volarans again. "I don't know all of these, but I'd be glad to introduce you to those I do, and speak to those I don't with you."

She considered him. "You have a telepathic link with Dark Lance."

"Ayes."

"But that is rare?"

His face went blank. "About ten of us in the Chevalier and Marshall ranks who usually work from the Castle can communicate with our volarans. Another five can receive impressions."

"So that's about ten percent?"

He inclined his head.

She frowned. "We'll have to see what we can do to bring that number up."

He laughed. "Good, take charge."

Her neck heated. She shrugged. "There must be a way to teach others."

"You don't think it's a natural gift?" he asked, moving to the end of a row of volarans where Thunder stood, Dark Lance next to him. Calli understood that the winged horses had ordered themselves by status in the Castle herd.

"A natural gift," she repeated, considering. "Probably. You hear better than someone who only gains impressions, but still..." She wasn't at all sure about this magic stuff. "Most of the Chevaliers and all of the Marshalls have those streaks denoting Power." Silver for the young, golden for the old. She reached up and touched his right temple. "Everyone hears Songs." Which was damn new to her.

"And you see auras...and through my bloodbond with you, I have learned to see them, too. Perhaps you're right."

"In any event, we can teach the people to be more sensitive to hors—volarans. To speak equine with body language...and...and...by projecting feelings and wishes."

Marrec nodded. "That could work." He rubbed Thunder. *Salutations, Thunder.*

Salutations, Marrec. Salutations, Calli. It was feelings and images. Marrec was a triangle-shaped stick figure of a man, his broad shoulders emphasized because the volarans—all the volarans—saw him as someone excellent at bearing burdens and responsibilities. She was a little surprised and offended to find her own image as that of a dandelion gone to seed.

But you sparkle, the dandelion fluff is made up of magical Power, Marrec said, and that, too, was images and feeling and Song with a bit of language. *And you change colors.*

She smiled at him, stroked Thunder's forehead, and said, "We'll see how they feel about me after I start lessons between volaran and flyer. Humans aren't the only ones who need to learn partnership and respect."

They moved down the rows, from Dark Lance to Alexa's mount, then Bastien's, then Thealia's. Each volaran greeted them, flicking ears at Marrec, dipping a head to Calli and letting them both know how the flying horse wanted to be stroked—a finger trace around itching wing feathers here, a hard rub along the neck—and as Calli touched them, *she* learned.

18

She received impressions of battle, how the volaran stretched its wings, to fly high and away from a dreeth, how it plummeted to kill a slayer. How well its human partner insulated its mind from panic, urged it onward to fight, turned its fear to determination to kill the invaders, protect the herds. After she reached the end of the first row, her mind was reeling and she leaned heavily on Marrec.

"Those who have been introduced to Calli, please leave Landing Field." He projected his voice and Calli heard a bunch of her new feathered friends reluctantly clopping away, sending mental goodbyes as they returned to their stables or took off to fly and play with others.

"My God," she said weakly in English, and the words changed and resonated in her mind as "By the Song." She rubbed her temples.

"There aren't many more here right now. Do you want to finish or wait until later?" Marrec asked.

The press of volaran expectation washed over her. She straightened and shook her head, breathed in the warm summer air, glanced at the remaining ten volarans. "I can do it." Their ears flicked and heads lifted in support and pleasure.

She walked slowly with Marrec to the beginning of the next line. He said, "Most of the rest are young and haven't been much in battle."

Calli blinked and realized that the grouping of the herd had been about the status of the person, the age of the volaran, how often it had been in battle and how well it communicated with its flyer. Everything about how it fit in the herd.

Marrec nodded. "If you hadn't Paired with me, Dark Lance would have been midway down the first row. Neither I nor Dark Lance had much status before you, and he's not considered beautiful by the volarans." Marrec smiled ironically. "But we've been in plenty of battles and work well together."

"Huh," Calli said. "But Alexa's volaran was right after Dark Lance and she doesn't even ride it."

"Bright Cloud is a very impressive stallion to the rest of the herd. He was wild until a few months ago. Bastien has trained him since and ridden him often, and he sometimes flies Alexa and Bastien into battle. He has a good relationship with Bastien and would communicate better with Alexa except she's afraid of falling off him again."

"Oh." Calli grimaced. "I'll definitely work with her."

The corners of his mouth turned up slightly. "She has a hard head, Bastien has trouble making her listen."

Calli narrowed her eyes, glanced at the keep where Alexa was. "She'll learn from *me*."

Now Marrec's smile widened. "I have no doubt of that."

They spent the rest of the day becoming familiar with the remaining volarans and training her horses, in an odd way. Calli spoke to the Castle stable hands, figured out which two were the most flexible and began to teach, with words and telepathy and Power.

Finally, as the evening turned into night, they bathed again in preparation for the next ritual. By this time, they were easy with each other. Calli didn't think she'd ever be shy around him again. She donned her old jeans and another sleeveless shirt that buttoned at the shoulder and along the side. Marrec had such a shirt, too, and new black leather trousers and tunic emblazoned with their heraldry. Just the sight of him made her insides mushy.

Compared to the Choosing and Bonding ritual, the Unbinding ceremony was almost private...the inner circle of the older Marshalls, Alexa and Bastien, the representatives of the other segments of society: Lady Hallard of the Chevaliers, Sevair Masif for the Cities and Towns, Marian and Jaquar for the Circlets and Luthan Vauxveau for the Singer.

The ritual took place in a pentacle in the Great Temple, the huge round area where Calli was originally Summoned. The place Sang of a thousand Songs, imbued in the walls and ceiling and floor, quivering just under or over hearing, vibrating against her skin.

Calli and Marrec stood in a star traced on the floor, surrounded by a linked circle of the witnesses. It sure felt like a wedding to her. She smiled, looked up and met his eyes.

They were fierce and she heard his mental chant of *Mine. My woman. Mine to keep. Mine to…love.*

As soon as the bindings were dissolved, the images, the incredibly intricate connection stopped. They both took a step apart. Dizziness had Calli's world tipping. She tottered. Marrec grasped her shoulders. He took her hand, and their Song escalated between them.

The Song of the Chevalier Exotique Pair. She blinked. Her left arm felt weightless, free.

All of her felt incredibly free. She was her own self again…with additions, maybe, but her own self in her own head, no one watching. A sigh whooshed from her.

Eyes narrowed, Marrec said. "I thought we'd fly our volarans together to our land. Use distance magic to get there and back, but I don't think—"

"Dark Lance can carry us both. We can help him with the distance magic." She touched Marrec's cheek. "I don't know of anything that would please me more."

His gaze slid down her and she sensed he was thinking about sex, but he nodded. "Yes." *Dark Lance, we will fly to our new home. Prepare.*

Calli chuckled, shook her head, then instead of Equine, she sent pure feeling to the volaran. Love. Anticipation of the ride to their land. Assurance that all three of them would work as a unit.

I want to go, too! Thunder sent a visual of himself accompanying them, flying without a rider.

"Ahem." Alexa cleared her throat.

"Yes?" Marrec asked.

"I understand that you'll be flying to your new estate."

Alexa gestured to a young woman, her assistant. "Perhaps Marwey would like to ride Thunder and survey the situation. With her help, you might be able to hire household staff, maybe even some folks tonight. I know there's a village on your land."

Calli hadn't known. There must be papers or a Lorebook or something. Another thing for her to read.

Marrec arched a brow at Marwey. "What's the price?"

Well, that was blunt enough. Calli looked around to see if anyone was dismayed at this conversation taking place in the house of G—of the Song. The witnesses observed with interest and Thealia was walking toward a table where a wooden chest lay.

Marwey said, "I missed the last Chevalier training class, but Calli will be starting training by herself with the rest of you tomorrow. I'd like to train with you. My Pairling, Pascal, has already won his Chevalier reins." She lifted her chin. "We want to be Marshalls someday, but I must be a Chevalier first."

"You agree?" Marrec asked Alexa.

She sighed. "Yes. I'd rather keep Marwey safe here at the Castle, but she and Pascal are adamant in their wishes to become Marshalls. Marwey *has* 'called' a volaran from the wild herd who has agreed to partner with her."

Calli eyed the young woman, surely in her late teens. "How long have you flown with your volaran?"

A tinge of red appeared on Marwey's cheeks. "Not long, a couple of weeks before all the volarans left. Once since they came back."

Nodding, Calli said, "Good. Perhaps you'd let me see how

you work with your volaran and if I might be able to improve your partnership."

Marwey grinned. "Ayes! But I can speak to the volarans. I have strong mind-merge Power."

"Even better," Calli said.

Thealia walked up to them, accompanied by a large man carrying a heavy chest. She gestured to the box. "The taxes from your estate for the last thirteen years since the previous owner died. Also, your bonus for being Summoned."

Nice.

"Steadier?" Marrec asked.

Calli nodded. He slid his hands down her arms, squeezed her hands, then dropped his own, eyeing the chest with a glinting gaze. "I'll take that, pull out enough to pay…our people…up front for a couple of months—"

"Some for getting the house ready, too," Marwey said. "It's been deserted."

Marrec nodded. "Then I'll put it in Horseshoe Hall's vault."

"You don't need to do that," Marwey said. "I looked around your rooms—I have experience serving an Exotique—and saw a lock-cache."

"Good," Marrec said. He brushed a kiss on Calli's mouth. "Let's get going, night will fall soon enough." He strode to the door and Calli watched him. His manner had changed since she'd seen him enter the hall where she'd stood behind the Choosing table. Then his lope had been easy, but diffident. Now he was a man in charge. He'd changed, too.

Thealia handed Calli the rolled long strips of linen that had been their bonds. "You might want to keep these in a safe place, too. They sing with Power."

Calli nodded and tucked them into a pouch she carried. She'd like a little money, too. Still, there should be more courtesy. She scanned the faces of the remaining people and bowed. "Thank you for coming."

There was a round of returned bows, curtseys, nods. "May the Song fly with you always," someone said.

"And you," she replied, then spun and hurried out the door. Marrec and Marwey were already nearly beyond the keep. "Marrec!"

He stopped.

Calli ran to them, delighted she could do so, that she felt totally healed. When she reached them she wasn't even breathing hard. "When you divvy up that zhiv, keep some out for yourself and me, will you?" She handed him her pouch. "And put what's in here in the lock-cache, too."

His eyebrows went up as he weighed the little bag in his hand, felt the Power of the bonds with their blood upon them. "Ayes." Again he kissed her, this time her cheek, then started off once more at a rapid pace. Smiling, she turned to the door of the keep and wound through it to the door to the maze, then through the hedges and to Landing Field, satisfaction filling her. She knew enough to walk around on her own!

Sweet.

Thunder and Dark Lance awaited her, saddled and bridled. She frowned, wondered how soon the new tack would be delivered. The sooner, the better. Too bad she didn't know how to call down to the shop. Send a messenger? Use a crystal ball? Huh. More stuff she needed to learn.

But she grinned as she reached the volarans. She couldn't wait to learn.

* * *

They came out of the Distance Magic bubble with a little pop. Calli glanced over to see Marwey on Thunder pacing them. She and the girl exchanged grins.

Marwey said something, her words vanished with the wind. She frowned, tapped her mouth, then said something again. This time the words came clear.

"I spent time reading up on your estate. It is well able to provide for a large family." She sighed as if that was one of her long-term goals, too. "Your land is surrounded by other well-tended and productive estates. With the zhiv you have, your people will be able to buy whatever you need from your neighbors."

"Good," Marrec shouted.

Calli nodded. *Marrec, you don't know how to do that thing she did?*

No. He hesitated. *I have become stronger in my Power since you arrived. Stronger still since we bonded. There are many spells we will have to learn together.*

It will be fun.

I hope so.

As they circled down, a bell tower began to ring. "The announcement of our arrival," Marrec said in her ear. To Calli's complete surprise, a brand-new banner waved from the pole on the tower.

"The Marshalls gifted it to us, I think," Marrec said. "Sent it here by special messenger this morning to announce that the estate had been reassigned—and to the Chevalier Exotique. I'd imagine anyone within earshot of the bells who can get here fast will meet us."

Calli cleared her throat. "Our ranch had about four hands. Not many people. I watched my dad, of course—"

"His style won't be ours."

"No. And there were other ranchers, folks I admired, that I learned some from. I hope."

"We'll do it together." His statement was almost a question.

They'd have to learn how to work in harness, for sure. "Yes."

As soon as they landed and turned toward the house, Calli's breath caught. It had looked a lot smaller from the air, but it was a full three-story *mansion* made of gray stone, with columns. Behind it, peaks rose in rugged grandeur.

"Ours?" she croaked.

Marrec wrapped an arm around her waist. "Ours," he said reverently.

She glanced up at him, saw moistness in his eyes.

"The house is everything I've ever dreamed of," he murmured. Glancing down, he squeezed her and his smile was full. "We'll make a fine family here."

She turned a little to the northwest and range after range of mountains rose in ever-higher rocky waves until they took up half the sky. Again she turned, due north, and more mountains defined the horizon, the spur thickened. To the south were peaks, too. She'd wanted mountains. She'd gotten them.

"It's so beautiful." Her throat closed. This was *her* land. Not the Rocking Bar T, not ever again, but this place. She didn't have the ties to it that she'd had to her childhood home, but the tingling beneath her feet, as if she was ready to *really* plant roots, told her that it could take the place of the land she loved.

"Beautiful," Marrec said. He was looking to the east and their own lush valley, the distant roofs of village houses.

The deep green of rich fields held his gaze.

"Come along!" Marwey called from the wide porch of the house.

Marrec frowned, slid his hand down to grasp Calli's fingers and strode toward the house. At first Calli stretched her legs to keep up with him, then she discreetly tugged his hand and he slowed.

When they reached the steps leading to the porch, Calli saw about twenty people gathered there. A few were dressed in rich robes that proclaimed them the local VIPs, most wore simple work clothes.

They all stared at her, focused on her blond hair or blue eyes or pale complexion. Marrec dropped her hand to wrap his arm around her shoulders.

"Excuse!" a middle-aged woman gasped. Trembling, she bolted from the porch and disappeared. She was followed by an older man who nodded to Marrec but didn't keep his distaste hidden.

Marrec frowned.

"For those of you who do not know about Exotiques, an instinctive revulsion upon first meeting can be possible to the…less open-minded." Marwey lifted her nose. "If anyone else must leave, especially those who wished to work in the Hall, please go now."

A few more people slid away.

After that, the introductions got confusing. Since Marrec was paying attention to the nobles and richer village folk, Calli concentrated on the people who'd come to take care of her new home. The Hall. The *what* Hall. Or the Hall of *What?* She cleared her throat and everyone fell silent. "What is the name of this place?"

Thunder and Dark Lance trumpeted and sent strong mind images. *Volaran Hall!*

"Volaran Hall," Marrec repeated.

"What was it before?" asked Calli. Gazes sharpened at her accent. Calli disregarded that. She hadn't been in Lladrana very long and her accent was better than Alexa's.

"Stinton Hall," someone said. "Their line died out."

"Our line will not die," Marrec said.

People exchanged glances.

"Calli and I will be bonding with children," Marrec said. "We intend to have a large family."

There was some muttering…instinctive blessings, Calli thought, wishing them long lives. The evening seemed chill.

Marwey said, "And the Chevalier Exotique Pair's children will have the other Exotiques as godparents." She sniffed and waved to a tall, thin, older man who Calli had been told was the Hall's hereditary keeper. "I think you have the keys, please open the door."

The large wooden door opened silently into darkness.

Marrec swung Calli up into his arms and stepped over the threshold. Lights went on. Calli stared up at him, open-mouthed. His eyes glinted down at her. "Alyeka told me this was a wedding-ritual custom?"

Calli could only nod.

He turned a full circle, still holding her, nodded himself. "Good place." His approval of the house slipped through him, through them both. The last faint image of a sprawling ranch house disappeared from her brain.

Carefully, he set her on her feet, then looked at the keeper. "We wish a tour."

The man bowed low, eyes down. Then led them up an imposing staircase that dominated the middle of the hall. His voice was whispery and respectful. With each step Calli experienced an echoing tone in her mind, as Marrec *felt* the stone of this house and the land beneath and was bonding to it.

By the time they'd been shown the most important rooms, the feeling that this place was home, was *theirs forever,* had insinuated itself into her very bones. Magic, again. She'd fight for this land that would house and breed volarans…and children.

But it overwhelmed her before they even finished looking at the bedrooms on the second floor.

"Calli, Lady Gardpont, is tired," Marrec said, and handed over a clinking pouch and a small, smoky crystal ball. "We will return to the Marshalls' Castle. Clean and furnish this place, and keep me informed."

Calli wanted to see the stables, whatever setup there was for horses and volarans, but Marrec's words seemed to have sunk her into a swamp of exhaustion. Even his strong hand under her elbow and sturdy endurance couldn't keep her from swaying.

Once again he picked her up, and she was barely conscious for the ride home and the walk up to their new apartments in Horseshoe Hall.

As they walked to their new suite in Horseshoe Hall, Marrec *felt* it before he saw it, a vile, crackling, invisible spiderweb of destructive force. Everything inside him clenched. The spell spread over their door and attached to a trigger. Narrowing his eyes, he saw a small glove—almost a child-size glove—near the brown-stained wooden footboard at the threshold of the door. It looked like a worn glove, the fingers curved upward, reaching to grab them.

Danger.

An evil trap.

19

His pulse picked up pace. His breathing hitched. Sweat slithered along his back and arms.

Calli leaned heavily against him, weary and still thrumming with the exhilaration of their ride, the pleasure of their discovery of her house. No, *their* house, *their* land, *their* people.

His woman. Whom he had to protect. He didn't want her to see the trap, sense the danger.

Marrec kept his voice soft and murmured words of affection as he angled Calli's body away from the threat of the door trap, placing himself between it and her.

Suppressing a shudder, he sent a mental probe sliding around the door near the knob. It wasn't one of those evil horrors, a sangvile. The taut threads of Power held notes of a vicious human. An enemy in their midst. Wearing a pleasant mask, no doubt.

To keep her safe, and angle her farther away from the door, he drew Calli into his arms. Then he set his hands against her back and stroked her torso, enjoying the suppleness of her muscles. A few minutes ago he'd been concentrating on sex. Now he was focused on keeping her safe. He rubbed his chin against the side of her head. The silkiness of her hair, that wonderful, beautiful hair, caressed his cheek like nothing he'd ever felt before. "We'll go straight to bed."

She chuckled, an image rose in her mind—something of Exotique Terre—of herself in a long, fancy white gown and him in silly black-and-white clothes, then they were rolling naked in their bed. "Honeymooners," she said, and though he didn't know the word, he knew the concept. Newly bonded people who couldn't get enough of sex with each other. His pulse leaped, but arousal stayed a second priority behind the fierce desire to protect her.

Fear snaked down his spine, he made his voice steady. "We'll go to sleep. It's been a long day for you."

"A very long day," she sighed out. Yawned. Leaned heavier against him.

His mind went over the evil threads attached to the door. A few days ago he wouldn't have had the vision to notice the spell, wouldn't have had the Power—or the innate knowledge—to disarm it. Definitely wouldn't have had the ability to split his focus on cuddling a woman and working on tracing the lines to a knot around the latch, picking at one and pulling, slowly, slowly unraveling it.

"I'm glad it was you," Calli said. She glanced up at him, ran fingers along his tight jaw. "Always so serious. You don't need to be, with me." She kissed his jaw.

He fumbled with the web, unraveling string after strained string. Worked silently, fast, sweat coating his body.

Finally he reached the last thread, taut and straining, ready to snap and unleash a spell that would lash them with energy, straight to their minds—to the seat of their Power? *Calli's* Power? Overwhelming her? Burning her Power out? He thought that was the intention.

He let his hands wander down her, shielded her with his body. Sweat rolled down him; he followed strings, unwove. Paused. One. Last. Tiny. Tug.

The thick atmosphere around the door dissipated with a little "Pop!"

A lash of pain whipped him. His mind went gray. He struggled to stand, to force the edges of fog shrouding his vision back.

Calli tilted her head, frowning. "What was that?"

"What was what?" His tongue was thick. Second by second he fought to stay conscious.

She looked around, blinking. He hoped she couldn't see the glove. His back was to it. Should he have tried to destroy the glove, the holder of the Power? He'd have died. *They'd* have died, because Calli was bonded to him.

He must get Calli inside and in bed, asleep. *Then* he'd figure out what to do next. His fingers went to the doorknob, slid off. Too sweaty.

A deep, erotic chuckle came from Calli. "Hot and impatient, cowboy?"

That note in her voice plucked a chord directly to his groin. Concentrate! He didn't want to. Relief rushed through his veins, sweeping the fog away. Now he wanted to throw her on the bed and pound into her, explore this woman he'd just saved with his hands and body and keep her under him and safe.

This time he managed the door, shoved it open with his shoulder, scooped her up and kicked the thick slab of oak shut. He probed the room, the suite. It was free of any evil. More than that, their new home at the Castle felt like sanctuary.

Calli licked at his neck.

With quick steps he crossed into the bedroom. Calli's hands were busy, stroking his chest. He laid her on the bed and her hands went to the front of his breeches. He jerked. Maybe sex was a good notion. He'd tire her out.

"What's this?" she asked, prodding. Her fingers were a couple of inches from where he wanted them.

"What's what?" he said thickly.

She reached into his pocket and held up his worry stone.

"Mine!" She barely glanced at it before her fingers curved over it in possession. She sat up. "It feels good. Like you."

"You gonna take everything I have, woman? My knife and my stone?"

"You still have Dark Lance." Her smile was sultry. "Yeah, I'm gonna take everything you have." She wiggled her hips.

"You're welcome to everything I have," he muttered.

Now she looked at the stone, sniffed it, put it in her mouth.

Song in All! If he'd used the stone as his token on the Choosing table and she'd done that, she'd have made him climax in public! His thoughts ricocheted, then snagged on a dim recollection. Another object imbued with an evil spell.

Definitely an enemy in their midst.

That cooled his ardor enough that he went to Calli, removed her shoes, stroked her face and said, "Give me the stone."

She opened her mouth and tongued it into his palm. Now it radiated of her, smelled of her, probably tasted of her—the warm, wet places of Calli. He shuddered, made to put the stone back in his pocket and she caught his hand.

"Mine," she said, then nodded to the bedside table.

He put the worry stone on the table, lifted Calli's feet to the bed, lifted and moved her so her head sank into a pillow of the finest down. She smiled at him, lips and eyes welcoming.

Keeping his gaze locked on hers, he leaned down and swept some strands of hair from her face, feathered his fingers back over her forehead, set his index finger between her eyes and sent *Sleep!* The word had Power behind it, the calm insistence he used to settle an anxious volaran.

Her eyes closed and she dropped into sleep.

He let out a long breath. Not thinking about what he did, he stripped her. Sex must come later. Would come later. Good thing he wasn't a man who was used to getting a woman whenever he wanted. He lifted the covers, then hesitated. The summer night was warm, the room cozy.

When he returned he wanted her there, on the bed, naked and waiting for him.

With a shrug at his needy thoughts, his deep masculine yearning, he turned away. His eye caught the worry stone on the table. He didn't reach for it. It wasn't his anymore, but hers.

Lips curving, he figured she must have had something with her that she could give to him. He'd insist. This partnership already tilted one way then the other, unbalanced. Her with her incredible Power, the zhiv and land and status she brought to the pairing. Him with his knowledge of

Lladrana, volarans, experience in the culture and battle-field. They'd have to work to find a reasonable balance.

Though he'd noticed she liked leaving doors open behind her, he shut the bedroom door, ran a finger down the long crack around the door. "Keep her safe," he chanted, sending all his will along with licks of Power into that spell.

He went to the outer door, frowning. This suite was more like homey rooms than the security of a fortress like the keep's towers. There weren't enough shields between her and the outside, between whoever laid the trap, whoever walked Horseshoe Hall with malice, hiding behind illusion.

Which meant he'd have to learn how to set shields inside the rooms.

He opened the outside door, examined every inch of it, the lintel and threshold around it, then turned his attention to the glove.

Squatting, he stared at the glove, noted the faded purple patterns and embroidery.

It was Alexa's glove.

Why?

And how?

Marrec studied the glove for several minutes inside their rooms that pulsed with silence. Then he sent a mental question. *Bastien?*

A startled *Ayes?* came back to him.

Marrec had given a lot of thought as to whom he should trust. Despite the fact that he was a Chevalier and would naturally look to Lady Hallard as their representative, and as his former leader, his concerns must be understood by the greatest in Power. *I must speak to you and the Marshalls—only those who are Paired.*

Oh? When?

Now. There's danger to Calli.

Meet us in the Marshalls' Council Room.

That wasn't a room Marrec had ever entered. Hadn't ever thought to enter. His life had certainly changed. He shrugged, *Ayes.*

A tapping came at the long glass window-door of the balcony. He glanced out to see a pair of peacocks. Opening the door, he stared down at the faint auras surrounding them. He could easily distinguish which of the two feycoocus was female.

"Salutations," he said. "But I don't have time to talk to you."

We will guard Calli while you discuss the danger with the Marshalls.

He had a sudden feeling that they knew what was wrong. "Do you know who her enemy is?"

The feycoocus exchanged a look. *No. We were not here today, and yesterday we were watching you and Calli, adding our Power to the ritual.*

Marrec wanted to ask why, but from the way they held themselves, he didn't think they'd say.

May we come in?

More interest rose in him. He stared down at them. "You have to be invited in?"

They clicked their beaks in irritation. *Yes.*

"You promise no harm to Calli will ever come from you?"

We promise, the male said. *I am Tuckerinal. You may call on me for help at any time.*

Marrec raised his eyebrows. "Is that so?"

So.

He had to remember that this one was an Exotique feycoocu, come to Lladrana with Marian. The notion made his mind spin. He opened the door and stood back. "Welcome."

Thank you. Eyes bright, the female walked in first.

Marrec closed the door after them.

She flew to a chair back and perched. *My name is Sinafinal. You may call on me at need.*

He'd just been given a great gift. He didn't know how many people could call her by name. Though he sensed interaction between Calli and Sinafinal, the memory didn't come clear and mention of the feycoocu's name in Calli's thoughts were blurred.

Only the Exotiques and their mates know my name. Go now and tell the Marshalls of the danger. We will watch, Sinafinal said.

With a deep bow to the magical beings and a lighter step, he left the suite and locked it after him.

Though the summer night was warm, sweat had chilled on his body by the time he reached the Marshalls' Council Room. This was the first time he'd ever speak to the Marshalls by himself regarding his own concerns. The only person he knew halfway well was Bastien.

Yesterday morning he was a penniless Chevalier with only one volaran who had disappeared with all the rest of the winged horses and could do so again. Today he was the bondmate of an Exotique. At the door of the chamber he squared his shoulders, strummed the doorharp.

"Enter," Swordmarshall Thealia Germaine ordered.

He sucked in a deep breath and opened the door. The room was bright with two miniature suns floating near the ceiling. Absently he wondered if he and Calli had the Power for such light in their own quarters. They'd need their Power for other matters.

"Sit." Thealia gestured to a chair.

He'd rather stand, but that might make him look more like a servant. He slid into one of the chairs with a sword engraved on the back.

Frowning, Alexa shifted on a stack of pillows.

Silence reigned. He kept his face the impassive mask he'd used for years. Then he met Thealia's eyes. "I just disabled a door trap." He tossed the glove on the table.

Alexa jerked. "That's mine!"

He looked at her coolly. "I know. You wouldn't harm her." He glanced around the rest of the table...all the old Marshalls and two pairs of new ones. "We have an enemy within the Castle."

Leaning over the table, Alexa reached for the glove. Both Bastien's and Marrec's hand covered her fingertips.

The three of them *linked*. The next instant, all the rest of the Marshalls seemed to crowd like shadows in the back of Marrec's mind. Before he could explain anything, they all *shared* his memories of the trap. He exhaled raggedly.

Then everyone withdrew. He sensed them communicating among themselves. Yet a small trickle of notes ran between himself and Bastien and Alexa. He liked the feel of their hands with his. Like they were family.

"Marwey threw out the glove," Alexa said. "I thought it had plenty of use left, but..." She shrugged.

It probably had another whole year's use left before the leather split.

Bastien snorted. "It's very worn, Alexa, many of the embroidery stitches were wrecked. The dyeing has dulled. It's stained and wrinkled. Marwey was right to throw it out."

Marrec lifted his hand from atop Bastien's, met Alexa's eyes. *She had been poor, too.* Before she'd been Summoned to Lladrana, she had been even poorer than Calli. Bastien, for all the prejudice against him for being a black-and-white, for all that his father had despised him, still had owned a small, productive estate.

"As you say," Alexa said. She withdrew her glove from under Bastien's and Marrec's fingers. Holding one small edge between her thumb and forefinger, she lifted it to her nose and sniffed. Her face scrunched as if she tried to sort different smells, then she sneezed, shook her head as if to clear it. "Even scent has been hidden. Nothing of this glove resonates of me or of any other person whom I could identify." She wrinkled her nose. "It reeks of Power." Scowling at the thing, she let it drop. "Marian and Jaquar left for Alf Island as soon as the Unbinding ritual was finished."

Bastien scooped up the glove, pressed it between his hands, engulfing it. A line dug deep between his brows, then his shoulders dropped. "My wild magic finds nothing either." He set the glove down.

Marrec cleared his throat. "The feycoocus are guarding Calli. If they'd sensed anything important about the one who used this glove, they'd have told me."

A corner of Bastien's mouth turned up. He winked at Marrec. "Welcome to the club." *Of those who are "honored" by Sinafinal and Tuckerinal,* he added mentally.

Scowling, Alexa took her old glove, smoothed out the

scuffed fingers. Her eyes lit with anger. "I don't like being used."

"We will all need to watch our discards," Thealia said, her mouth thinning.

"This wasn't the first trap," Marrec said. He felt the heavy weight of their focus. "I also wanted to ask if anyone noticed the lock of volaran hair tied with a ribbon reeking of evil on the Choosing Table yesterday, and if anyone knew what happened to it."

Startled surprise swirled around the room. The Marshalls' instinctive team connection snapped their defenses into place.

"Ttho," Thealia said a few seconds later.

"I just mentally called Marwey," Alexa said. "She oversaw the Choosing Table and the tokens."

"Please explain," asked Thealia's husband.

Marrec said, "Near the end of the ceremony, I noticed a lock of brown volaran hair on the table nearest to the hallway door. Calli was drawn to it. She was too drugged, or perhaps is too new to Lladrana, to sense the harm of it, but I did." He struggled with words. "The Song rising from the ribbon was…not right. It felt like a trap."

"What kind of trap?"

"I don't know. I wasn't in the best shape to observe." He lifted and dropped a shoulder, frowned. "I'm not sure what would have happened if she'd picked it up, but I think it was dangerous." He met Alexa's eyes. "So did the feycoocus."

"The volarans are elated with the Song's choice of Calli as the Chevalier Exotique," someone said. "She must not be harmed."

Bastien said, "More than that, they believe her to be

Summoned for the *volaran* community. Thunder and Dark Lance have told them glowing stories of her. Her actions in saving the horses have made a great impression. Every winged steed in the Castle has 'spoken' to the horses about Calli. I *know* every volaran wants Calli to fly with them."

Marrec nodded. "She'll do that. I don't think she could refuse any volaran request. And she'll want to get an idea of the different feel and flight patterns of the volarans." He looked around the group that fought together in rare teamwork. "She will be able to gather and hold volaran minds in battle, communicate with them, work with them as a focal point."

Thealia grunted. "I'll make sure she takes lessons in strategy with me. You and she must practice with us. Will the Pair of you want to test for Marshall?"

Alexa's gaze seemed to pierce him, as if she, herself, tested him right now.

"Ttho," Marrec said. "Calli knows her responsibilities to the Chevaliers, but she plans to establish a volaran-partnering center and horse-training center. She wants a normal family and children very much. We'll adopt." If they lived that long.

Even as Alexa's scrutiny relaxed, Thealia's sharpened. "She must fight!"

Bastien said, "Every Exotique has a specific task." He put his hand on Alexa's. "After Calli has performed hers, we can discuss the future." He cleared his throat. "Does anyone have a glimmering of an idea as to what Calli's task *is?*"

No one answered, though a buzzing hummed in Marrec's mind. The Marshalls consulting among themselves, no doubt.

"Have you spoken to Calli about this volaran lock and ribbon business?" Alexa said.

"Ttho."

Her eyes narrowed.

Marrec lifted and dropped a shoulder. "She has endured much lately. She is nervous about training, about fighting. I wanted to spare her."

Alexa nibbled her lip. "Just for now."

The doorharp cascaded with notes.

"Enter," said Thealia.

Marwey walked in with a scroll and closed the door. She looked nervous.

"Marwey, can you tell us about the tokens on the Choosing Table yesterday?" asked Alexa. "Who offered a lock of brown volaran hair tied with a ribbon?"

Unrolling the scroll, Marwey scanned it. "No volaran hair is listed." In a stilted voice, she said, "There were one hundred and twenty-two tokens. The smallest was a ruby earring, the largest a helmet." She waved the scroll. "Every person and every token is accounted for, as well as the position of the token on the Choosing Tables. I double-checked everything myself after all the objects were on the tables and before Calli entered the room."

Marrec closed his eyes, searching his memory, delving through the haze of drugs and sexual arousal that enveloped his recall. "It was on the last table toward the east door." He frowned. "Between a fancy, engraved silver spur and a pair of black gloves."

Moving to the table to flatten out the scroll, Marwey scanned the drawing, matched the number assigned to the token to the list at the top of the scroll. She looked up, face paler than usual. "That's where Faucon Creusse's hat was."

"But Calli took the hat and other items that immediately called to her to the center of the middle table," Alexa said. "Faucon's hat was one of the first she picked up. So a space must have been left."

"And someone put the lock of volaran hair in that space," Thealia said.

Bastien said, "Perhaps the owner of the spur or the gloves noticed who put the volaran lock on the table. I know if I'd attended the Choosing and Bonding ceremony for Alexa, and placed a special token on the table, I'd have been watching it."

"Throughout the whole ritual?" asked Thealia.

"Perhaps not all the time." Bastien shrugged. "But everything on those tables was special to someone. I'd check my token now and then, to make sure it was there."

"Who's the owner of the spur and the gloves and the other items around the space where Faucon's hat was?"

"The hat was in the lower corner of the last table." Marwey flushed a little. "I, um, moved it from the center table, I wanted to give others a better chance. So it was at the edge of the table. The gloves were *sent* to us by a young sorceress who didn't attend. The spur belongs to Tristan Sebold."

"Tristan flew to the alarm today, along with some of the younger Marshalls," Bastien said.

The new Sword and Shield pair glanced at each other. The Sword said, "Sebold and his volaran both died today."

"Both?" Thealia asked sharply.

"His volaran foundered." The Shield frowned. Shields were more able to note what was going on during a battle than Swords. "I don't know why." She paled a little. "One of those new flying dreeths that breathes flames got them."

Nothing would be left of the Pair.

The Shield wet her lips. "Now that I think on it, those—" her voice broke "—those particular deaths were like none I've ever seen in battle."

Everyone at the table looked as grim as Marrec felt.

Thealia glanced at Marwey. "Please keep this confidential. You may tell your Pairling only. He can tell no one. You may go."

Marwey's eyes narrowed. She jerked a bow to Thealia, turned on her heel and left.

"It's someone in the Castle with strong Power. A Chevalier or Marshall," Bastien said.

"Not necessarily," Thealia argued. "Others attended the Choosing and Bonding, we even have some guests still staying, not leaving until tomorrow."

"But it's most likely we have an enemy inside our walls," Marrec said.

Bastien took the glove back from Alexa, ran his fingers around the seams, as if extending his senses once more to discover the culprit. "I don't like that the person used Alexa's glove, as if targeting both Exotiques. The way these traps were set…more like what a Sorcerer or Sorceress would do…more like how they'd think…than a Chevalier or Marshall."

"We had no one except Jaquar and Marian from the Tower community within our walls," said Thealia.

"They wouldn't—" Alexa hopped to her feet.

"Harm Calli," Thealia finished. "Or I should say, had they wished to harm Calli, she'd be dead by now."

"How Powerful would this person have to be to set such spells?" Marrec asked.

"Strong," Thealia said.

Alexa retrieved her glove. "I'll courier this to Marian. But I agree. We have a secret enemy among us."

20

Calli woke late the next morning. Before she opened her eyes, she knew Marrec wasn't in their rooms. She sighed and stretched. The sex had been awesome. Her body felt great…completely in tune. In fact, she'd never felt this good before, as if mind and body and…soul…Song…Magic?…were completely integrated, all harmonically balanced. And she was even thinking more in musical terms. Huh.

The first thing she saw when she sat up was a glowing white crystal ball, with streaks of milky pink and blue and brown swirling in it. Next to it was a piece of paper. She picked up the note and saw angular writing that leaned to the left… Marrec's left-handed penmanship. She couldn't read it, of course, and a little flutter of panic swept through her. She loved to read, to listen to audio books, and didn't like being somewhere she couldn't. A big disadvantage. Guess she'd better add reading and writing to her list of lessons.

She drew in a big breath, let it out noisily.

Someone cleared his throat. Calli stared around.

"Salutations, Pairling. And...uh...good morning to you—" Marrec's voice came from the crystal ball. Fascinating.

"I have gone down to fetch breakfast for us. I recall that you like croissants and scrambled eggs."

Breakfast in bed, had she chosen a winner or what?

"Please stay in the...uh...*our*...rooms. If you must go out...uh...Koz is standing guard at the door and will accompany you."

Calli's eyebrows snapped down. A guard?

"There are things we must discuss. I'll see you shortly." There was a pause, then the sound of a smooch. "Your bondmate, Marrec."

She stared at the crystal. He'd sent her a kiss? She could imagine that small gesture might have embarrassed him. Yet he'd done it anyway. The sweetie. She chuckled, and he'd "signed" the message, as if she wouldn't forever know the timbre of his voice from one word.

The crystal went dark. With a lingering smile, Calli used the bathroom, then went to the long, elegantly carved wooden wardrobe and dressed in bra, panties, a thin cotton shirt and leggings, a snug tunic and breeches. Her scarred old ankle boots detracted from the look. When she was dressed she realized that for the first time since she'd come to Lladrana, she was alone. No Marrec, no other Exotique, no Chevalier just hanging around her, no volaran eyes watching. It was a very odd feeling.

She sat on the bed and let the atmosphere sink into her. There were layers of herself and Marrec, and them together—echoes of their Songs already woven into this space which was their home here at the Castle.

A wide grin spread over her face and she flopped back on the soft bed as she thought of her new land. *Her* ranch, hers and Marrec's. It was pretty land, the house was great and the outbuildings and fenced areas could be rehabbed into exactly what she wanted. Laughter bubbled up inside her and she couldn't lie still anymore. She got up, crossed to the French doors and flung them open to the beautiful summer day, then stepped out onto the balcony.

It was sturdy stone and where the curve of the outer wall of their suite met the straight Castle wall, an enclosure, like an open horse box, had been included. A stall for a volaran. She smiled. Had she landed in clover, or what? Eyeing the bare box, she decided that she'd stock it with hay, make it ready for Thunder or Dark Lance.

This apartment was at the top of the hall and she wondered if there was a chute or something to take the volaran waste away. Would they actually expect her to dump it down the outside Castle wall?

She went to the edge of the balcony and leaned over to look.

A ball of energy struck her from the side. She stumbled sideways, jammed against harsh square edges of the wall. Another jolt hit her, this time Power that *lifted* her, spun her out over the wall. She grabbed for it, fingertips abraded the stone, slid away.

Free-falling.

Shield! someone snapped.

The volarans shoved knowledge into her mind, backed by Marrec and Bastien. Her Power whipped into a *Shield*. That wouldn't help her when she hit the ground.

Two beaks caught her wrists. She screamed. Jerked.

The sound of flapping wings, more, Songs of the feycoocu, deafened her. The Power she'd formed around herself melded with theirs, boosting all.

Her descent slowed into a controlled glide, past the five stories of the Castle, the cliff it was built upon, the rising ground of the dirt road circling it.

She bent her knees. The birds let go. As her feet touched the ground, she tucked and rolled. Then she just lay there, staring at blue sky and her heart pounding so hard she thought it would jump out of her body.

Shouts filled the air, distressed trumpeting of volarans, even frightened neighing of her horses, as if her hearing had sharpened preternaturally.

Wow.

A minute later Dark Lance and Thunder had landed near her and were standing close, heads up and watching, aggressive. A war hawk settled on each volaran back.

She figured she should sit up. Running footsteps and yelling came her way. She got the idea that *others* who were close to her had felt her peril. Marrec, the volarans, Alexa and Bastien, a Shield, some of the other Chevaliers, the feycoocus. The little magical beings had been able to act the quickest.

Well, yeah, if they were more magic than anything else, that would make sense, wouldn't it?

Nothing made sense. Her mind grappled with what had happened.

What *had* happened? Lightning from a clear sky?

Alexa was the first person to reach Calli. The little Marshall had her baton out and did a pivoting sweep of the area. "Who did it?" she demanded.

"Did what?" asked Calli.

Frowning, but not taking her eyes off the countryside, Alexa said, "Attacked you. And from where? We thought you were safe. What were you doing?"

Calli got a bad feeling about this. Her brain hadn't wanted to let her know she'd been attacked. Not in her new home. Not in the Castle. Somehow she'd accepted that her life would be in danger when she fought on a battlefield in the future, the price for everything else. She thought she was safe in the Castle.

Apparently not.

She shoved to her feet, a little shaky like after she'd had a rough tumble from a horse. Looking up, Calli saw the jutting of the balcony around the top story of Horseshoe Hall.

It looked *really* far up. She frowned, checking out the Castle wall about a story below her apartment and to the north. Didn't the wall have a walkway?

"Calli! Tell me what happened," Alexa said, following Calli's gaze upward.

"It must have come from there." Calli pointed. She rubbed her side, which felt a little singed.

"What possessed you to lean out over a wall, unprotected?" Alexa demanded.

"Why shouldn't I be able to take a damn walk on my own damn balcony?"

"Maybe because twice someone's tried to hurt you?"

"What!"

"Shit, he didn't tell you." Alexa snapped her baton in its sheath.

"Who? Tell me what?" But Calli's gut churned. "Who" was running in front of a stream of others. Marrec.

He swung her up into his arms.

"Marrec!"

"You need fuel. My wife. My woman." He held her closely.

Alexa rolled her eyes.

Sinafinal clicked her beak. *No harm done.*

Tuckerinal preened. *We saved Calli.* He shifted feet on Dark Lance. *We are the best.* Then he flew up as Marrec put Calli on Dark Lance, mounted behind her. Gestured to Alexa and Thunder. "Let's take this private. The Marshalls' Dining Room."

Alexa stared at Thunder. "I'm not getting on that volaran. He doesn't even have a saddle!"

"Good thing Bastien is right behind you," Marrec said.

Bastien grabbed Alexa and tossed her onto Thunder, jumped on behind her. "Let's go." He said it and sent it mentally to the volarans.

Thunder snorted. *You did not ask my permission to ride. I am Calli's volaran.*

You want to stand on propriety or do you want to see if we can find out who tried to harm Calli?

Thunder took off like a shot, angling up toward the wide walk on the Castle wall below Calli and Marrec's apartments. Alexa shrieked and grabbed at his mane.

Landing Field, Marrec ordered Dark Lance. He rose with more dignity.

A few minutes later they had landed and the new squires

had appeared to take care of Dark Lance. Marrec grabbed Calli's hand as if he was afraid to let her go, then strode toward the Castle keep. He flung open a door and Calli tensed. He looked down at her.

"I've never been in the Assayer's Office," she said. She'd heard the place was where Chevaliers and Marshalls brought their dead monsters to be tallied…and processed.

"You want to go through the maze?" Marrec's tone was impatient, but he didn't pull her into the room.

"No. I can do this," she said, and stepped into the charnel house.

It wasn't as bad as she'd expected. There was the smell of death, strange odors that she thought must come from the dead monsters. One flayed…something…was arranged on a long counter, and she jerked her sight from it. The room was higher than it was wide or long, and held a lot of mounted trophies, like the Nom de Nom. Render paws. Soul-sucker tentacles.

Her gut shivered, but seeing the monsters again almost calmed her. These she was preparing to face, to fight. An unknown human enemy with free rein of the Castle seemed much more threatening. Today.

"Salutations." Marrec nodded to the assayer.

He stared at Calli, a small man with a gray goatee and a round paunch. "What's she doing here?"

They didn't answer and were across the room and into a keep hallway in a couple of minutes.

"Did he seem suspicious to you?" asked Calli.

Marrec grunted. "Everyone seems suspicious to me."

Calli's blood chilled.

* * *

Breakfast wasn't in bed. It wasn't an easy meal at all. She and Marrec were surrounded by some Marshalls, Lady Hallard, Koz and Faucon. Everyone watched her like a hawk—including the two hawks—to make sure she was eating, and she managed to swallow some eggs. Even the flaky croissant didn't have much taste to her, and she caught herself peeling the layers and eating in little bites.

A grim Thealia Germaine detailed past events for her. Calli got the idea that Thealia herself had swept through the Castle, including Horseshoe Hall, the home of the Chevaliers, investigating everything, demanding answers, and nothing had shaken loose. Lady Hallard sat stiffly, radiating displeasure that the Lord Knight Swordmarshall had made this a matter for the Marshalls and not just the Chevaliers.

Looking at Calli with darkly piercing eyes, Thealia said, "We will find this miscreant and punish him." She sent a chill glance at Marrec. "Your bondmate will guard you, and everyone close to you—your new squires—and the volarans have been cautioned to keep an eye on you." Her lips thinned. "These attacks won't remain secret for long, unfortunately."

Thealia looked at Lady Hallard. "The Chevaliers insist you remain with them in the Hall."

"I'm the Chevalier Exotique," Calli said. "Of course I must live in Horseshoe Hall. I love our rooms there." Lady Hallard eased a little.

"I've called Jaquar and Marian. They'll be coming in to look for more magical traces," Alexa said.

Both Thealia and Lady Hallard looked sour.

"Those Circlets were here when Calli was Summoned, for

the Choosing and Bonding, yet they didn't notice anything, either," Hallard said.

Alexa narrowed her eyes. "None of us were looking. No one knew someone in the Castle threatened Calli."

Lady Hallard snorted.

Bastien said, "Morning's passing." He gave Calli a charming smile. "Ready for your first Chevalier training lesson?"

Calli's stomach tightened and she wished she hadn't eaten at all. What if she lost her breakfast, training?

Marrec squeezed her hand, spoke to her mentally, *You won't.*

Calli envisioned volaran quick liftoffs into the sky, steep banking, loop-de-loops. "You're sure?"

As they stood, Marrec whispered, "I'll take any nausea you have away through our link." His expression sobered. "You've already learned to Shield."

A shiver traced up her spine. She didn't want to remember the fall. Now that he mentioned it, a headache lurked, buzzing in both temples, no doubt from the forceful tweaking of her Power by the volarans. "A Shield," she said neutrally as they went to the private stairway off the room.

"You form a force shield around yourself and Thunder, Dark Lance, me." He patted her shoulder. "I can build one for me and Dark Lance when we go into battle, but lately I've been sharing a Chevalier who prefers to be a Shield with some of Lady Hallard's other Chevaliers." They climbed the stairs from the second floor to the Castle wall walkway that ran from the keep to Horseshoe Hall.

They were alone, and Marrec stopped and turned to her, stroking her hair, his serious gaze meeting hers. "You're very

Powerful. You'll have modified the Shield Song to suit yourself soon, probably by the end of the first teaching verse."

"Thank you," Calli said. She slipped her arms around his waist and hugged him. She wanted to say she loved him, but was too shy, and everything that happened that morning had reinforced that she was a stranger in a strange land. The guy was her husband, was closer to her than anyone else in the world…but they were still finding their rhythm together.

They walked to Horseshoe Hall and down the stairs near the stables. There, her squire held out a different tunic for her, this one made of padded leather.

"Thank you," Marrec said, taking the item. He frowned at all the volarans in the Landing Field, grouped according to their herd status, Dark Lance and Thunder closest. Thunder shifted. "Go to Thunder," Marrec told Calli's squire, a young man.

Marrec slipped the tunic over her head, tied the sides. "This will be all you need this morning. Your chain mail should be ready by tomorrow." His hands stroked, more the leather than her body beneath.

For the first time she noticed that he, too, wore new flying leathers. She touched his shoulder. "Nice expensive clothing."

He smiled at her. "We landed in sweet hay." She heard the end of that mental thought. *After all these years.* Dark Lance echoed agreement.

Their feelings echoed her own, and she was comforted. This was the kind of man she knew and would treasure, and the volarans were already part of her heart.

But as she strode the couple of paces to Thunder, her pulse began to beat hard in anticipation. All the volarans were here, which meant all the Marshalls and Chevaliers. Ready to watch her during her first training flight. She'd never wanted an audience less.

Thunder was still unsettled from the excitement of her fall. Calli frowned. Now that she thought of it, most of the volarans were uneasy, tense and restless. Hmm. It would be a good way to see how well the Marshalls and Chevaliers partnered the winged horses, which people she might help improve their flying skills.

And wasn't that arrogant?

It is truth, Thunder said as she gave him half a carrot to nibble. *You and I fly as if we were raised together and you are the best Chevalier I have ever seen.*

"Huh," she said and used Marrec's cupped hands to mount. She leaned down and kissed his cheek. He smiled and went to speak with their squires.

Are you sure you want to be my fighting volaran? she asked Thunder. *It means danger and death.*

He flinched. His whole body rippled under her in an equine shudder. She sensed panic and used her Power to sooth his mind. Hold it, like her own, away from paralyzing fear.

I am the best for you. It was barely a whisper, as if he doubted. She didn't know how he'd been chosen for her, but she loved him.

I love you, she said, stroking his neck. She didn't want to see him hurt or killed, and kept that notion firmly away from where their minds touched.

I love you, too. I am the best for you. His mind voice came stronger, certain now.

All right. We will fight together.

He shivered again. *Together. With Dark Lance and Marrec. Yes.*

We will probably be the Shield team, he said, sounding comforted. His natural Song took on harmonics that fear had suppressed.

So I've heard.

Dark Lance is a big volaran. He can fight. Calli almost smiled, hearing the unspoken "instead of me." But she didn't want either of them to have illusions. She'd had enough illusions in her previous life. *There will still be danger, and times we must fight and kill.*

Thunder shifted. *I have never been in a battle with someone on my back, led by humans.*

Neither have I. We'll learn together. That will make us a stronger team. She held confidence firm in her mind. Marrec's Song wisped through her and she turned to see him murmuring to Dark Lance, settling him. Marrec smiled at her. "Let's fly together. Dark Lance and Thunder did well yesterday," Marrec said. "Follow me in sky play."

Excellent idea. If these had been horses, she'd have worked with them on the ground until their fidgets had gone.

"Sky play." She grinned back. That sounded fun.

He winked.

Thealia came over, holding inch-long many-pointed starlike crystals. She placed one on Thunder's head, the other on Calli's right shoulder. "These will record your flight."

Video. Great.

Others had mounted. Alexa and Bastien on Alexa's stallion, almost as large as Dark Lance.

Bastien would be teaching Calli how to be a Shield. She'd

never seen a tougher guy, obviously Shield didn't mean *wimp*. Swordmarshall Thealia and her Shield, Lady Hallard and another man and two pairs of Chevaliers who wore her colors. People who would have worked closely with Marrec.

This time when they rose into the sky, she was very aware of others around her. Marrec sent Dark Lance into a wide curve to the left with no more than the tiniest shift of his body and aura to the left. This man could ride! He'd given no mental image to Dark Lance, Calli figured that the two were so in accord that the volaran read Marrec's intention in his mind as well as body. Yet Marrec used his body to cue the flying horse, as he would a regular horse. As she and Thunder followed Marrec and Dark Lance, she settled into her balance; more, she easily found that special place where her energies and Thunder's merged in balance.

They flew patterns, dipping and curving. The cool summer breeze lifted her hair. Her headache had dissipated, her muscles had relaxed, yet she knew from the thoughts around her that the swooping and curving, the quick, rapid lifts, all were used on the battlefield. But the pure freedom of it, of not being tied to earth, of *flying,* moving in three dimensions filled her until she felt as if she was pure joy. As if she glowed.

Yet she could feel the links between herself and everyone in the air. She was a vital part of a team, yet individual. This was what she was born to do.

She caught Marrec's smile at her reaction and grinned. With a slight finger motion, he indicated they'd get down to business. Which was doing figure eights, horizontally, vertically, at a slant. When all the volarans were in tune with their riders, Marrec began games with first one pair, then two, then added the rest. Calli smiled as she realized he used not only his sensing of the Songs, but her skill at seeing auras, to judge the moment when all the fliers were integrated with their mounts.

The sun rose higher, got hotter, but Calli kept up. When she'd mastered all the beginning moves, understood the way she needed to shift her body to cue Thunder for three-dimensional flying, she began to watch the others. It was easy to tell those who had telepathic communication with their volarans, flying horse and human auras were merged. The abundance of colors amazed her. Not only were there individual colors, but that of Pairlings, and the colors of fliers and volarans. In very well-integrated fighters, such as Swordmarshall Thealia and her Shield, all volarans' and fliers' auras were the same malachite green. She looked down at herself and blinked. She was sky blue, so was Thunder. Glancing at Marrec, who was now riding slightly in front of her, she saw he and Dark Lance were the same color.

Calli turned her aura-sight to Alexa and Bastien riding his stallion, and bit her lip. Bastien and the volaran were blue-green, Alexa was tense—and polka-dotted.

Oh, yes, she'd teach Alexa to fly.

Then Thealia and Lady Hallard were zooming straight at Marrec and her. Thealia whipped out her baton. Threatening green-black light shot out. Lady Hallard came, face fiercely smiling, sword ready.

Marrec moved to meet them, his sword out.

Shield! The order came from Bastien, with a sharp two-note whistle that pierced Calli's shock. The high-pitched sounds reverberated in her mind.

21

Calli Sang the two-note *Shield* spell echoing in her head.

An iridescent, egg-shaped soap bubble formed around Marrec and Dark Lance, around Thunder and herself.

The fliers attacked, Thealia and Lady Hallard against Marrec.

Black-green baton Power struck Marrec's bubble, hit him in the chest.

No! Fear fueled Calli's spell. *Shield!* Not whistle, *gong* tones.

The bubble flashed around Marrec—stopped Lady Hallard's sword, shoved both volaran pairs *back!*

Lady Hallard's mount tipped sideways, fliers appeared around her, manipulating the air to steady the winged horse. Thealia shot upward, her own Shield-bubble glowed milky white, strengthened by her Pairling.

You are *a Shield!* Alexa's mental shriek of glee battered Calli along with the adrenaline reaction to the attack.

A natural one, Bastien agreed.

They rode to her left.

Marrec was still ahead of her, his sword drawn, fighting another rider midair.

Calli's mouth dropped open.

The Shield of a well-matched pair does not impede the person Shielded, Bastien said.

She could see that. Her husband fought with efficient grace, face a shade more serious than usual.

Disengage! Thealia ordered, circling down to their level again. *Practice over.*

The rider fighting Marrec dropped. Marrec sheathed his sword.

Calli trembled. Everything had happened so fast! Had seemed so deadly.

We did it! Thunder trumpeted. He swung up and over, legs tucked, in a loop-de-loop.

Calli shook, clamped her legs around his barrel, grabbed her saddle, handled the loop. Dizzy-headed, she sent to Thunder, *Calm.*

His head came up, but his ears rotated, as if paying attention.

Back to the Castle, Marrec sent matter-of-factly, with pride in his undertone. He and Dark Lance turned a tight left, and Calli saw many of the Chevaliers they'd worked with streaming ahead.

They go to tell all that we were wonderful. That we will learn to fight quickly, Thunder said. If he'd been on the ground he'd have pranced.

A few minutes later, they circled down toward an open

space in the middle of Landing Field, which was flooded, as usual, by volarans. It appeared that all the humans of the Castle had turned out, too.

With the beauty of a falling leaf, they landed. Thunder lifted his head and his wings in pride...and to cool himself. Calli noticed her underwear was sticking to her.

Dark Lance spread his nostrils in greeting. Marrec dismounted, smiling faintly. *That* was like a shout of triumph from her taciturn husband—bondmate. Calli found herself grinning. When he stepped forward and put his hands on her waist, she let him lift her from Thunder and whirl her around, feeling giddy with triumph and love.

He hugged her, then let her go. "My very good Shield Pairling," he said, squinting against the sun and down at her.

"Thanks."

With one arm around her waist, he turned to the volarans. Their squires had already appeared. Marrec nodded at them. "Treat our mounts well."

The two bowed to him, then to Calli, with another to the volarans. *We will be nice to them,* projected Dark Lance.

Since it was obvious that each squire had a favorite treat for the volarans, Calli didn't doubt that.

"Good going!" Alexa yelled from a few yards away. The volarans parted as she ran toward Calli, pulling her helmet off and shaking her silver hair out, beaded with sweat at the roots. "Really excellent," Alexa puffed. Calli shook her head. She wasn't quite used to hearing Americanisms translated into Lladranan.

"You mastered the Shield spell on the first try. Oh, yeah, you'll be a good fighting pair in under a month!"

Calli's gut tensed, but she kept her smile steady. Then it became real again as she said, "And I'll teach you to be a good flier within that month, too."

Alexa narrowed her eyes. "Deal!" She flung her arms around Calli and squeezed her hard, then turned to Marrec and did the same. His eyes widened in astonishment and wariness.

Bastien joined them, looked at Marrec. "Get used to it."

Thealia Germaine, Lady Knight of the Marshalls, strode up with Lady Hallard, who plucked the crystal stars from Thunder and Calli. Lady Hallard said, "We will be reviewing this morning's training in the Noble Dining Room in Horseshoe Hall."

From Thealia's narrowed lips, Calli got the idea that she'd lost the argument.

Marrec grunted.

Calli supposed she needed to do this. It wasn't as if she'd never watched her own performances time and again to see what she could have done better in a thirteen-second ride. She'd even seen the last time, seen Spark slip, her own fall, his fall on her.

She shook off the memory.

Lady Hallard swept a gaze over the Landing Field. "Everyone who flew the figures today, please attend."

Chevaliers glanced at each other.

"Not many of us are accustomed to the Noble Dining Room," Marrec whispered as he took Calli's elbow. "Faucon and Koz, who watched from the ramparts, are coming. They're both nobles."

She sent a subtle probe through her bond with Marrec and sensed that though he'd once been a little envious of the two, a little anxious that they'd win her hand, those emotions were gone.

A greeting by Marwey pulled her from her thoughts. The young woman looked pleased with herself. Thinking back, Calli recollected that Marwey had been one of the fliers doing patterns. Seeva nodded to Calli, then linked arms with Marwey, and the two began discussing the training session in excruciating detail.

To Calli's relief, Lady Hallard kept the review quick. Seeva had progressed another level in her training. Calli and Marwey had immediately become Shields to their Sword bondmates, Marrec and Pascal. The patterns had been flown well, the teamwork between Chevaliers had been good, but she was assigning new foursomes and sextiles to ensure everyone linked with everyone else. Never knew who you'd find yourself with in a battle. She dismissed the bunch with that chilling reminder.

Just as they were about to leave the dining room a voice asked if the rumors about Calli being in danger were true. The chamber grew quiet, more, Calli sensed the question had echoed throughout Horseshoe Hall and everyone waited with held breath.

"Yes," Marrec said roughly. "Calli's in danger. Someone's trying to destroy her Power." The silence deepened. "Steps are being taken to protect her. And when I find out who harmed her, I'll strip 'em and stake them out for the horrors."

Over the next two weeks, Calli's days became structured and full…just the way she liked them. Chevalier training in the morning, then she schooled the horses a little in the afternoon, then worked with Alexa and others who aspired to flying volarans.

Alexa was a problem. Actually, she was a pistol. She Sang with strong Power, love of animals and the command of her own space. This worked with horses, so she only communicated with them—spoke Equine—in a very limited fashion. Despite her small size, they instinctively accepted and followed her lead.

This combination did not work with volarans, who wanted much more communication from her instead of statements of Power and will.

So Calli taught Alexa Equine with both horses and volarans. Asking her to open up was the greatest difficulty. Alex was a fighter, used to keeping her mental and physical shields up. Only Bastien and Marian had gotten very close to her, and the Marshalls and some Chevaliers close enough to link in teamwork. Since Calli had now read Alexa's and Marian's stories, she knew Alexa had been caught in the foster care system. So Alexa's emotional shields were even higher.

Soon Alexa worked better with volarans than horses—on all ground games. One afternoon she flung up her hands at the horses and left the pen. "No wonder they think I'm stupid! They do most stuff by body language. One strange twitch on my part and it's over."

Calli had Bastien bring a very old, very gentle volaran from his stables. Like all the Earth women, Alexa was fascinated with volarans. She *did* have the longing to fly, but that had been overlaid with her falls from volarans. Calli and Alexa worked on the ground, then no more than five feet in the air, mastering listening to volaran Song, the feel of flesh

under her, the stroke of the wings and flow of air around her.
Alexa learned, and that filled Calli with the warmth of accomplishment. She *did* have a gift of training—horses, and
horseback riding, and volaran partnering.

Calli learned, too. She took classes with Alexa's fearsome
teacher in magic, was actually taught with Alexa in reading
and writing Lladranan.

Calli's Power grew and the work she did with magic—
training and communicating, refined until she had a great
toolbox of Powerful Songs. The volarans were easy to understand, the Lladranan people a lot harder.

She, herself, was protected from "negative influence" by
layers of spells—an inner one she renewed every day, and a
bondmate shield that Marrec set in place every day. She
wore a small amulet of herbs and stones, and leathers and
chain mail that had been bespelled by Marshalls and Chevaliers in a special ritual to keep her safe.

Her flying leathers weren't dreeth, like Alexa's, because
only those who killed the dreeth could cover a great portion
of their own skin with the monster they'd slain.

The balcony now had a shimmering shield around it,
slightly distorting the view and making Calli feel like a five-
year-old. But life was going well. Sex and intimacy with
Marrec was great, and though neither of them had spoken
the L word, Calli thought they were definitely going that way.
They'd visited their home and found it being cleaned and re-
finished to fit their tastes, and that was pretty damn cool.

Neither Marrec nor she were used to servants, and had
wanted to be together privately, so they'd put off hiring
people to attend them personally.

The training she was doing was fulfilling, the flying was close to ecstatic. She practiced fighting with a grim determination she got from Marrec: learning to fly on a mock battlefield with realistic illusions of monsters. Shielding him from renders and soul-suckers in ground battles, protecting him from slayers' spines. She "killed" the monsters herself.

And seven times those two weeks her belly tightened as she watched the Marshalls and Chevaliers fly to battle the horrors, and knew that within the month, she, too, would be fighting.

Luck. There was a lot of luck in the rodeo. The luck of the draw—like pulling the right bucking horse. If a cowboy got one that refused to buck and stood stiff legged, he was out of luck. If he missed the calf's head with the rope, he was out of luck and out of prize money.

If your horse slipped rounding a barrel and both landed on you, breaking your pelvis, your luck was pretty bad that night.

There was only so much that skill, technique, practice and Power could do. If you were slightly off, the horse/volaran was off, not feeling well or not paying attention, or too jittery or too calm....

Calli figured battle would be just the same. Only with worse consequences of bad luck.

She always did her best, but in battle she'd be *exceptional*; she wouldn't lose Marrec or Thunder. Not and still live.

So she practiced her fighter training hard. One morning the patterns went quickly and easily, Calli rarely fluffed these. She noted that Marwey was nearly perfect, too, and Seeva bobbled once. Perhaps she should offer to work one-on-one with her....

The foursome of Marshalls sped toward Marrec, who flew slightly ahead of her, wavered before her eyes, then became a huge *thing*.

Dreeth! Thunder screamed, panicked.

With Power just short of force, she coated his mind with cool thought, banishing emotion, even though his wings still quivered. She shut her own emotions down, too. They had nothing to do with a competition—battle.

Stop thinking, just like she had before a race—use the anticipation, the apprehension, the edge of fear. Drawing Power from herself and Thunder and the very air stirred by wings, she snapped a Shield around Marrec as he and Dark Lance attacked the dreeth in the air.

Fire shot from the creature's mouth, battered the egg-shaped force field she'd thrown around her Pairling and his volaran. She felt the crisping heat, added a layer of air… Power shaped like a wind off cold mountain snows. Cold, impenetrable.

Thunder held steady, keeping Dark Lance in sight. Calli drew her sword.

More dreeths! shrieked Seeva. White-faced, she and her volaran whirled, sped straight to the new threat…and were blackened with flame.

They plummeted. *Illusion!* Calli screamed at them. *No dreeths so close to the Castle.* They didn't listen.

Keeping one eye on Marrec, she *reached* for the dropping volaran's mind. In one of her free hours, she'd flown with him. *Your wings are whole and strong. Feel the wind lift your feathers.* She beat back panic, sent him courage, as well as to Dark Lance.

Dark Lance's ears flicked, but he and Marrec shot to the underbelly of their dreeth, ripped it open, intestines spurted.

Above us! cried Thunder, dropping ten feet. Instinctively, Calli swung her sword. Too low to get the belly, but she cut off both deadly back feet. Green ichor gushed over her. Her own Shield deflected it.

Her dreeth screamed, banked. Marrec slashed both eyes. It fell and died.

Mind spinning, heart beating so it might burst through her chest, Calli glanced around. No more dreeths. She thought there had been four. Now she saw only three four-somes of Marshalls, and Alexa and Bastien on a stallion.

God.

Return to the Castle, Marrec said. He and Dark Lance joined her and Thunder. *Calm Thunder,* he sent to her.

Calli deliberately relaxed her body, sent a soothing energy flow around Thunder, showed him through her eyes and his own that there were no enemies anywhere. She breathed deeply, gave him the scents of summer flying, the warmth of the sun not shadowed by any monsters.

His muscles loosened under hers. His mind went from flight to acceptance of communication. His sides shuddered out a huge breath. *We did well.*

Yes, said Dark Lance. *Though those were not real dreeths, you did well. You have a good flier.*

Dark Lance, Marrec chided. His volaran put on a burst of speed, leaving them behind, ignoring the rebuke. Calli's lips curved. She glanced around for Seeva and her volaran and saw them on the ground, some distance from the Castle. Then the walls were under Thunder.

They landed. Thunder's hooves clipped the ground and he stumbled, Calli fell forward. They both righted themselves. Tucking his wings close to his barrel, Thunder galloped once around the Landing Field. He slowed and stopped beside Marrec and Dark Lance.

Calli's smile turned ironic. "We're still a little shaky."

Marrec reached out and slid a hand down her back. "Well done."

He dismounted and pulled her from Thunder, held her close. *Well done, Shield and Chevalier.*

I have won my reins? Calli asked.

Yes. Today's training must have been a final test.

"Oh." His body was all hard strength. She let herself lean against him, enjoy the warmth of him and the sun, the scent of volaran and leathers and man.

All the volarans of the Castle Sang, *Chevalier Shield Calli,* our *Exotique.* Calli raised her head to see they'd entered the Landing Field, as usual. Lady Hallard stood, hands on hips, shaking her head. "Guess we'll have to get used to this."

With one arm around her waist, Marrec turned to the volarans. "Shall we groom these two, then celebrate at the Nom de Nom?"

"Sounds good to me."

Alexa ran to them. "You did it, you helped kill two little dreeths!"

"*Little* dreeths!" They'd looked plenty big to her.

"The big ones don't shoot fire." She grinned, gestured to Marwey and Pascal. "Marwey won her reins, too." Alexa quivered with excitement. "And Bastien and I got to be one of the dreeth illusions and *I* worked with his volaran for *two* attacks. I'm learning to fly, too!"

"You certainly are," Calli said.

Bastien dipped his head at Calli. "Thank you. I have been unable to teach her. The volarans get charmed or fascinated or nervous that they'll lose her and don't partner with her well."

Alexa lifted her nose. "It's speaking in English. I understand nuances in English."

"Of course it is," Bastien said. He bent over and whispered something to Marrec that Calli heard only as a ripple of notes in her husband's personal Song. Color bloomed under the golden tone of his cheeks.

Swordmarshall Thealia strode up, smiling. "An award luncheon is already set in the Marshalls' Dining Room. Today's review will be brief."

A surge of disappointment at not celebrating with her Pairling came. Marrec's arm stiffened behind Calli's back. She sent a responding pulse of resignation to him.

Their squires showed up, beaming, congratulating her. Dark Lance and Thunder began mind speaking with the two young men, telling them all about the flight.

"I want a shower before lunch," Marrec said, heading toward their rooms at Horseshoe Hall.

"Right," Calli said, thinking of the big bed.

Thealia snorted. "Lunch in fifteen minutes. Be there." She walked away.

Alexa shook her head. "No time for fun."

"That's what you think," Bastien said, scooping her up.

A twinge of envy came from Marrec. Calli glanced at him with a puzzled look. "What?"

He opened his mouth, then shut it, walking a little faster.

"Please," said Calli.

He looked at her, then focused on the narrow passageway between Training Hall and Horseshoe Close.

"Please let me know what you are thinking when I ask," Calli said a little stiltedly. "Please help me understand Lladranans." And you.

"I wished I could be as easy with you as Bastien is with Alyeka." Marrec shrugged. "But he is a charming man and I am not. He's a nobleman and I never was."

"But they weren't always easy together," Calli said, keeping up with his stride. "It was very rocky between them at first. He—" Hell, what was the phrase for "screwed up"? She flapped her hands. "He was awkward."

"Truly?" Marrec entered the Hall and they strode through the corridor to the stairs. Everything in Horseshoe Hall was built in reasonable proportions as opposed to the keep.

"I read it in the Lorebook of Exotiques," Calli said. "Alexa's story, though she doesn't give a lot of details."

Marrec grinned, showing the long crease in his cheek. "Too bad." His eyes glinted as they took the stairs. "As far as I know, no one here has exact knowledge of when and where Alyeka and Bastien met. Can I read this Lorebook, too?"

"It's in English. But Marian said she'd made some in Lladranan. There's probably one in the Marshalls' Library."

Marrec grunted and opened the door to their suite. "I'm becoming reconciled to lunch with the Marshalls at the keep, after all." He stripped quickly and Calli followed suit. He was aroused. So was she.

He scooped her up and carried her into the large shower

stall. "We'll just be a little late." He laughed and set her on her feet, turned on the water, which was hot and steamy and smelled of mineral salts.

"What?" She closed the door behind her.

"Bastien told me that now I have a bondmate I'd often get aroused by battle."

"What does he know? He and Alexa aren't bonded."

"He's Paired with an Exotique. And so am I." Marrec's hands were slick and slippery as he soaped her, transforming the leftover fear into sexual need. Calli couldn't think, let alone reply in Lladranan, so she just melted into his embrace and let passion rule.

He was warm, she was wet and the Song between them rang loud in her ears, composed of sex and the triumph of the morning and the fantastic feeling of *rightness*. She was exactly where she was supposed to be.

Then the invasion alarm clanged.

22

The heavy clamor of the Klaxon rose over the shower. Gasping, Marrec shook his head, braced himself with an arm on the wall, shuddered once then swore.

Calli's voice rasped with fear. "I've won my reins. I'm a Chevalier now."

"Yes." With a twist of his wrists he turned the faucets off, flung the door open, grabbed a towel and dried as he jogged to the bedroom.

Calli caught up her own bath sheet and followed. "I did well this morning. The invasions aren't usually very big, right? We can fight together, as we should, as a Pair." She gulped, raised her chin. "Are our volarans able to handle battle?"

Marrec glanced at her. "You're the Volaran Exotique. You should know."

"You are more experienced. I don't want to hurt them,"

though when she probed she knew she wouldn't take Thunder, he was too tired.

Tilting his head as if he, too, did a mental sweep of their mounts, Marrec said, "Dark Lance is big and tough. The grooming has reenergized him sufficiently that he can handle the Distance Magic and battle. Thunder can't." He began reciting a list of volarans in the Castle stables—ones she'd flown with.

Exhaling slowly, Calli named one of Bastien's.

Prepare Sunray for battle, Marrec ordered their squires mentally. Through her link with Marrec and the men, Calli heard Sunray's excited trumpet. The volaran's mind brushed hers. *We will fly* well! His blood hummed with determination to protect, with hatred of the monsters invading the land, killing.

Thank you, Sunray.

Marrec wrenched open the wardrobe door and dressed quickly—the thin long underwear, his toughest leathers. He pulled out her second set of chain mail and his new chain-mail tunic, dreeth breeches and bespelled boots.

Calli dressed in silk undergarments and her second set of battle leathers.

Catching her fingers in his, Marrec brought them to his mouth, kissed them. "Are you sure you want to do this?"

"Ayes."

"Alyeka had much more training."

"I've learned a lot from you. I'll be a Shield, *and* I fly a volaran very well."

"Better than well. Exceptional." Expressions she couldn't read ran across his face.

"What?"

He grit his jaw, then answered, "I'm proud of you. As a Chevalier, I think you'd do fine. But I fear for you."

"I fear for you, too, and it will only get worse if you ride away and I don't." She helped him on with his chain mail.

Quick strumming came from the doorharp. It sounded much too innocent. A hard rapping or loud knocks would have been more appropriate to Calli—something that matched her heartbeat. She opened the door.

Seeva stood on the threshold, looking a little pale. "I didn't win my reins, so I can't fly to battle." Her shoulders straightened. "But I am still the head of staff of Horseshoe Hall and I know you don't have a servant yet and thought you might need help with your armor."

"She has me," Marrec said.

Expression strained, Seeva said, "Of course, but I meant both of you. It's faster when you have someone to help dress." She gestured to the window. "The first wave is already taking off for the battle."

Marrec glanced out the diamond panes. "Led by Bastien and Alyeka riding his primary stallion. Damn, the man's fast."

"All the Marshalls and noble Chevaliers have servants. You need some, too, but for now, can I help?"

Calli wanted to giggle. She didn't think Marrec had been referring to Bastien getting dressed, but Bastien getting Alexa. But then, hot monkey sex often went fast. She and Marrec might have made the fifteen-minute deadline to lunch. She cleared her throat. Humor, no matter how minor, always helped her before a competition. "Sure…" She gestured to the full mail that she'd only worn once. "Help me with this stuff."

Seeva looked Marrec over as if checking his fastenings and the strength of his armor, then picked up Calli's mail tunic and hurried toward her. The process was unexpectedly easy and quick, the mail lightened magically, only heavy with the duty of protecting Lladrana.

Seeva patted the shoulders and handed Calli her helm. "Chain mail is good, and so are protected leathers, but the best of all is dreeth skin. You'll have that soon, truly." She smiled, waves of excitement coming off her.

"Marrec!" Lady Hallard's shout accompanied her running bootsteps. She halted by the open door, glanced at them. "You've decided to fight."

It was stupid to feel a little left out of the bond between the Lady and her former household Chevalier.

"Don't you think I'm ready?" Calli's lips were cold now.

Lady Hallard squinted at her, considered for a couple of seconds, yanked her gauntlets from her belt and on. She nodded sharply. "Ayes." Then her smile flashed and she looked years younger. "I had three squires working to reenergize my volaran. Let's go."

"I helped dress Calli," Seeva said.

"Good. Find a maidservant for her, and a man for Marrec. Alyeka and Bastien will lead. They're the only ones with several seasoned battle volarans. Half of the older Marshalls refrained from training this morning just in case of this eventuality." That meant three pair. "All the younger Marshalls who didn't participate in training will go, too."

"Twenty-four," Marrec said. His shoulders seemed to ease. "Plenty to guard Calli."

The quiet was broken by the alarm clanging the call to

arms again. Seeva handed Calli her gauntlets and the battle helmet Calli disliked.

Marrec met her gaze, his face expressionless. He was fully helmed, gauntlets on. He held out a steady hand.

Knowing what he asked silently, feeling more than hearing the huge, overwhelming melody between them that twined with an undertone of partnership in the face of death, Calli put her hand in his. "We fight together."

In the yard, she mounted Sunray. He was a blond sorrel…with scars. His body was muscular under hers and she merged well with his mind. Thinking of mind-merging talent, she glanced left to where Marrec and Dark Lance flew in a bubble of Distance Magic. Sunray, too, was strong in this Power. He was fresh, and excited to be her partner to her first battle. Beneath that excitement she sensed determination to "blood" her—introduce her to combat as easily as possible.

Calli snorted. Like that wasn't going to be a culture shock. She set her back teeth. She'd get through this and only hoped that no one she knew fell. That would be the hardest, and that circled back to the question she wanted to ask about Marwey, the youngster best in mind-merging. Testing her bond with Marrec, she found him focused but not deeply entranced.

Marrec, she mind-whispered.

He turned his head, his deep brown eyes meeting hers. Serious.

Marwey won her reins this morning. Is she flying to battle, too?

He tilted his head, and she heard distant echoes of those who were linked with him and her in a loose net of Chevaliers who would work in a team. Not nearly as close as the Marshalls' ties.

Alyeka—everyone—wishes to protect Marwey as long as possible. She and Pascal remain at the Castle.

Nodding, Calli looked forward again at the curve of her own Distance Magic bubble that showed blurred blue sky and green land with hints of snow-topped mountains. She'd be the only one experiencing her first battle then. She let out her breath with a slow and easy exhalation. She'd be protected, too. Physically. She was pretty darn sure that this was going to take a toll emotionally. The Calli who flew back to the Castle would not be the same person as she was now.

She rolled her shoulders, shaking off the thought, and decided that there was too much thinking time. How did Alexa get through it? How did Bastien? Both were very action oriented.

Marrec's mental touch soothed Calli, as if he ran a hand down her back. *Trance. Follow our exercises.* All three of them—Marrec and Dark Lance and Sunray—began a measured human-equine chant that slowed her mind; panic kept her anticipation from turning into fear, lowered her energy level—for now. Everything was being tucked away, stored, so they could explode into action when the time came. Images of past fights came to her from the others and she let them drift and disappear without scrutinizing them. Only one thought stayed in the back of her mind. This was payment for her new life.

All too soon, Marrec and she banished the distance magic. Lush summer grass was shorter here up north, and white-capped mountains scraped the sky. The winged horses flew down to a patch of land that showed small forms fighting—Chevaliers, Marshalls and horrors. Adrenaline flooded her, the mist of her trance-thoughts vanished as if touched by the scorching sun of fear.

We outnumber them. Marrec's jaw was set. He loosened his sword in his scabbard.

Not by much. There must have been two dozen monsters down there. *Real* slayers and renders and soul-suckers.

Why don't we use arrows or throw spears? It wasn't something she'd thought of before, but looked like a real good option now.

They are bespelled against arrows. Have always been after the first invasion.

Calli's palms dampened inside her leather-lined gauntlets; she unsnapped the straps holding her sword immobile for traveling. Lady Hallard, now ahead of them and leading a second wave of Chevaliers, drew her sword and screamed a battle cry, sending her volaran slanting down at a large group of monsters. Faucon had taken the right side of the battlefield, Alexa and the Marshalls the center. Marrec followed Lady Hallard. They were only a few minutes behind the first attack.

The colors of carnage—red blood, yellow ichor, acid-green splotches, sluggish gray puddles from twitching severed tentacles—pooled on the ground.

Sing! commanded Sunray.

Shield! The defensive sphere snapped hard around Marrec and herself. He grinned, showing teeth, swinging his sword, decapitating a slayer. Swung to his left, fighting two renders and a soul-sucker. The soul-sucker's tentacles slid off Marrec's Shield.

Good. Good, Sunray sent, holding back, like other Shield volarans.

Calli struggled with horror, with terror, with nausea. She saw a horse-rider pair go down. Her throat closed.

Closest local lord, Sunray said, but his thoughts, too, edged with black fear. *We are too far into Lladrana.*

Calm! She sent the emotion…knew it was only the thin skim of her own surface emotion. Everything deeper was roiling—shock as she saw spines of a slayer nearly penetrate Marrec's shield. She used a spurt of pure fear to fling the darts away, killed a render with them and froze an instant. Only the quick reflexes of a man on the ground had saved him from *her* missiles!

She had to think, but panic bubbled up. This wasn't a thirteen-second ride. This was a long haul.

Sunray backwinged, banked. Wobbled. Her emotions were affecting him! She'd lost sight of Marrec.

Volarans were on each side of her—Marshall Shields—crowding her, crowding Sunray, turning them back to the fight where her husband risked his life.

He still attacked, killed two soul-suckers, sent chunks of them flying.

The Songs saved her. The strong one coming to her from Marrec, the Shields and their volarans brushing her mind like soft feathers. Fear diminished slightly and the trickle of notes became streams of fierce Power, merging into battle music. Brass harmonics rang in her head, steadied her. She would not run. She would stand—and fly.

There was a scream above her. A shadow fell on Marrec, on herself and the two Shields.

"Fire dreeth!" yelled the woman on her right…pulled away…drew her baton.

The long neck of the pterodactyl-like horror snaked. Beak with wicked teeth snapped. Marrec ducked. His shield took a hard hit that struck Calli on the chest. She sucked air. *Think!* She had to think. They'd practiced this.

Marrec cut a slayer in two. Dark Lance angled sideways.

Fire blackened the corpses around him, ashed a volaran-Chevalier pair.

Calli fought down a screech. Pushed back grief. Refused to let the last screams of the volaran and Chevalier echo in her head.

Anger trickled through her terror, and it was good, cleansing, supporting.

Two streams of Power—sapphire and gold—flashed from batons to the left and right of her, hit the fire dreeth. It cried in pain, in fury.

Face savage, Marrec and Dark Lance shot toward the dreeth's underbelly, dodged the spiny tail. Fire breath singed Dark Lance's outermost wingtip. He screamed, too, in pain, in defiance.

Showtime.

She wasn't thinking now, but listening to the surging Power fueled by the determination that ruled the battlefield. Calli *grabbed* the remnants of fire, twisted them, flung Power into them like gunpowder, sparking the flames like fireworks, turning them back on the dreeth. It shrieked in terror, tried to backwing.

Marrec, face grim, ducked under the fiery explosions and ripped the monster from throat to crotch. Gray-green guts pushed through the breach, glistening twists.

The dreeth went up like a torch, plummeted.

Other horrors were killed as it landed. The sound of the impact shuddered through the air.

Marrec and Dark Lance whirled, but there were no other dreeths.

Done! Huge relief poured from him to her. *Battle over.*

Calli tore her gaze from him, swept the land with a glance. Alexa and Bastien stood in the middle of the field, themselves surveying the remnants of battle. Alexa looked grim, but neither of them had wounds. Calli's breath escaped in little puffs. "It's over."

No Marshalls' batons rose from the land—none of them had died. Five swords showed where Chevaliers had perished, along with their volarans. A horrible ache throbbed through her entire body. One of her volaran partnering pairs was dead.

Sunray landed. Dark Lance did, too, but held his left wing awkwardly, away from his body.

One of the young Shieldmarshalls—the one with the golden baton—handed Calli a bag. "Volaran Burn Balm." Her smile was strained. "Recently developed by the Castle medicas."

This Calli could do. She stroked Sunray's neck, praising him. He stood calmly, a few twitches of his muscles showing the effects of battle, but mind serene.

She dismounted, wanting to fling herself in Marrec's arms, but reckoned that was too emotional for everyone else. Besides, he was on the far side of Dark Lance, examining the wing. She kept her show smile on and stiffened her legs, getting the feel of the uneven ground before she walked around to Dark Lance.

"Not too bad," Marrec said.

Dark Lance shifted and Calli smelled burnt feathers. Her heart pounded. It rose from the battlefield, too. Dead volarans. Hurt volarans. She'd never thought in her life that the smell of burnt feathers would forever mean grief.

She licked her lips, tried her voice as she opened the bag, which she realized was soul-sucker skin. She couldn't suppress the quick shudder.

"You all right?" Marrec's eyes were dark, in their depths was the lingering heat of fighting.

"Ayes." That was barely audible. She cleared her throat. "Ayes."

He nodded, then returned to examining Dark Lance's wing.

The bag was filled with a clear gel-like substance. She scooped some into her palm and onto her fingers.

With his right hand, Marrec held Dark Lance's wingtip steady. His left hand closed over hers. His fingers, too, trembled slightly from the aftermath of battle. "The feathers are gone, the bone a little scorched, but nothing permanent." He pulled his gaze from hers to look down at the wing. "This new stuff should heal it right up. Especially with a little Power from us."

Calli slathered on the ointment. Dark Lance's wing rippled under her fingers. She touched bone and they all flinched. She reached for more, but Marrec stayed her hand. "The cost is dear. Let's Sing."

A grunt came from Alexa as she strode up. Her lips had curved slightly. She jerked her head at the dreeth. "You are now a wealthy man."

Marrec's breath came out on a shudder.

Alexa tilted her head at the dreeth. "These don't burn as

well as the big ones, so you can harvest more. Of course, *my* first dreeth was bigger." She winked at Calli, but Calli got images from Alexa that the smaller woman had been just as scared as Calli was, and more—Alexa had been afoot and certain the dreeth would crush her to death.

Marrec's fingers touched the back of Calli's hand and the simple comfort of the gesture had bigger ripples of emotions washing through her. "Let's Sing," he said.

He led her into a simple healing chant. Calli raised her voice with his, steadied it, let the harmony of the music they made together sink into her. Dark Lance whuffled. The pain had greatly lessened for him until it was something he thought wasn't too bad. Calli reckoned that had Thunder been experiencing the hurt, he'd be stamping and giving voice to discomfort. But Dark Lance had been wounded before.

As had Marrec.

Both of them considered this injury light.

When Marrec and she were finished with the third round, they stopped.

People had gathered and the general murmur was that the wingtip was well tended. Marrec folded Dark Lance's wing against his barrel, then he and Calli wiped their hands on a towel and Calli gave the pouch back to the Shieldmarshall.

Alexa cleared her throat and something about the noise made Calli stiffen and meet her eyes, which showed a little regret. "The blooding," Alexa said.

Calli had forgotten the blooding. She straightened, every muscle tense. She did *not* want any horror's blood on her. Too bad.

Marrec stooped, rose. His hand whipped up, finger yellow

with ichor. He dabbed a bit above Calli's right eyebrow. It stank of death rotting. Calli swallowed bile, tightened her throat and stomach, refused the gag reflex.

A cheer rose, full of satisfaction and Song. It sounded nothing like a rodeo audience. Calli preferred clapping.

Marrec wiped his hand on a handkerchief then held her, and she leaned into his strength.

"How close are we to home?" she asked.

"We're east of the spur. And north." He whispered against her hair, stirring it until she tingled.

She heard what he didn't say. "Not far enough north."

"No, this is one of the southernmost incursions we've fought."

Alexa turned a little to stare at the white-peaked mountains rising high into the horizon, frowning. "I'd heard that the horrors could…um…'rise' from the ground the farthest they had penetrated Lladrana, but I'd never seen it before."

"Ayes," said Lady Hallard. "I think we fought in this place pretty soon after we discovered the fence posts were falling." Her expression hardened. "We must ensure that the horrors can never penetrate any farther south." After another sweeping study of the battlefield, she said, "As I recall, the previous invasion was worse, and we lost more people." She stared at the dreeth. "Though we didn't have any dreeths, let alone a fire dreeth." Slapping her gauntlets against her leg, she looked at Calli and Marrec and said, "I have a suspicion that the dreeth was for you. That all of this was for you."

Marrec seemed to turn to rock against her. "What do you mean?"

23

"Retrousse," Marrec said. "A place where the monsters were conjured *to,* not tramping over the border themselves."

Looking at the solid range of mountains to the north, Calli said, "No chance of that. No pass."

"No pass," Alexa said at the same time.

Thealia said, "This is the first retrousse ground battle— where the horrors were magically sent to a place that had been the stage of a previous battle—we've had since the first Exotique—" she nodded at Alexa "—came. That the dreeth—a horror we haven't seen lately—manifested over you, on the left wing of the battle, not in the middle of the field. And this invasion was within a few minutes of our Chevalier Exotique receiving her reins."

Calli turned to face everyone, Marrec warm and solid at

her back. "You think the…Dark…knew somehow that I might fly to fight?"

"That this was a trap like those inside the Castle?" asked Alexa, her green eyes very wide as she fixed her gaze on Lady Hallard.

The Lady shrugged. "Maybe."

"Another trap, sprung because someone in the Castle is in touch with the Dark forces," Alexa said. "To try and destroy Calli." She lifted her nose, sniffed. "Retrousse makes a place smell different."

"It would be interesting to know the history of this land," Marrec said. "How many battles were fought here throughout the ages."

"The landowner and most of her people are dead," said Faucon, joining them. "I was just speaking with the woman's page. Not even her squire survived." Marrec's arms tightened around Calli's waist, making her nausea worse. She struggled against him. He flinched, then let her go. Clammy sweat filmed her skin. She turned her head, strove not to vomit.

Alexa shoved an unstoppered canteen in her hand. "Drink this. Bespelled mint water. It'll help."

The liquid was cool down her tight throat, tasted good, but now she had the pale shakes.

"You don't look so good, girlfriend," Alexa said.

"Home." Calli backed closer to Marrec until his body was once again against hers as she looked up at his square jaw. "I want to go home. A coupla days ago the staff said the house would be ready by now. I want to go home."

Lady Hallard frowned. "We should have a war council on this."

Alexa and the rest of the Marshalls nodded.

"Do it without us. You can tell us of the results later." Last thing she wanted to do was fly back to the Castle to sit inside for an hours-long meeting.

"Bastien, can we keep Sunray overnight?" Marrec asked.

"Of course," Bastien said.

Sunray, would you fly with us to our new home?

Yes! Sunray lifted his wings in excitement.

"Burning dreeth is almost out," Bastien said. "Storm's coming in. The rain'll take care of the rest of the flames." He gestured to the clouds rolling in, big and puffy and dark gray.

"The local manor is available if we want to stay the night. War council there," Faucon said.

"Guess we'd better," Bastien said.

Lady Hallard snorted. "I hope they have minstrels who know the local history."

"Or Lorebooks," Alexa said. She reached out and grabbed Bastien's hand, her smile resigned. "I'd like to go home, too, but it looks like we're staying."

Marrec nodded shortly. "We'll be back midmorning tomorrow to harvest the dreeth, since only those who killed it can do so." He lifted Calli, waved at Dark Lance to back up, then set her atop Sunray. "Let's go."

He'd said those words earlier, to go to fight, and she'd agreed and followed him. She found his hands and squeezed, bringing his gaze to hers. He yearned for home, too, that Song rose from him. She replied as she thought she'd reply for the rest of her life. "We'll go together."

Raindrops splattered around them. The edge of the storm had reached them.

* * *

Calli entered their home. Marrec stared at it, disconcerted. A large three-story mansion of gray stone, it was far beyond what he'd ever aspired to and he wondered if he'd ever feel comfortable in it. He snorted. *He'd* feel more at home in the three-room shed off the stable that was the size of the cottage he grew up in.

But only he and she were here from the Castle. It was safe, and that was the most important thing.

Squaring his shoulders, he walked through the door with a trace of swagger that he borrowed from Bastien. He wouldn't let the imposing house erode his self-confidence. This was *his* home. If he hadn't been worthy of this place, Thunder wouldn't have pushed Calli and him to choose it. Those words came far too often to his mind. He'd soon have to shake off this doubt or others would see it. That could erode the respect he'd garnered just from being Pairbonded with Calli. He was a good Chevalier, now he needed to become a *great* Chevalier. Clenching his jaw, he vowed to be up to the task.

This time the door opened smoothly on oiled hinges. The entry hall was clean, though some of the stone squares making up the floor showed scars and pits. The wide stone banister was equally worn.

But the floor and banister were polished, the walls painted a soft cream color. He'd wanted whitewash, just to show how pristine his home was, no more living with stains. Calli had been right, there, too, the creamy color made the place more welcoming. The scent of mildew had been replaced by the aroma of fresh herbs.

Calli stood in the center of the hallway, hands on hips, turning around. He studied her aura, her stance, listened carefully to her Song that always murmured in his heart. She'd set the memories of the battle aside. He had no doubt they'd return, perhaps in nightmares as his did occasionally, but for now she was focused on the house. Their home.

The faint footfalls of a maid came from the second floor and Marrec frowned. He'd forgotten that they needed new rugs. Something to discuss with Calli. He'd begun to like their talk almost as much as their sex.

"Gina's freshening up the bedroom for us," Calli said, rolling her shoulders. "I'd love a bath."

He sighed. This manor, like many others, had been built on land with natural hot springs. To Calli's delight, a fussy glass house enclosed the bathing pool, which was surrounded by rough granite rock with green and orange lichen growing on it, like it was outdoors. Marrec suspected that this room itself would have sold her on the place. They'd ordered new panes to replace cracked and broken ones, and Marrec was glad it was summer.

"I'm sure that the shower in our suite has been repaired," he said.

"Bath."

"Since it's just the two of us."

She flushed a little, and that was as fascinating as usual. "Yes. Since it's just the two of us. I told my maid not to interrupt us." Her cheeks pinkened further and his body stirred.

"Good."

"There's stew for dinner."

"Good."

She sighed, glanced around again. "Not quite home yet, but we'll make it one."

"Yes."

Marrec lay in bed listening to Calli's even breathing. The house was quiet. He was used to the muted bustle of Horseshoe Hall, of Lady Hallard's manor, but since neither Calli nor he was accustomed to servants, they had kept their staff at a minimum. Only four lived in the house, and the aged caretaker in a gatehouse.

Calli had inspected the stables with space for both volarans and horses. Unlike the stables at the Marshalls' Castle, this one alternated large stalls for volaran and horse. That was the setup Marrec liked the best, and Calli had listened to his advice and agreed. If anything happened to the stables, the volarans might be able to save the horses if they were all together. He'd followed Calli as she scrutinized the work they'd paid for on the horse paddocks and arena, the volaran space, the other outbuildings. For both of them these had been the priority, even more than the house or hiring servants.

The long slow note of the mountains sifted into him. It had been a long time since he'd lived near mountains. Dread had clenched his gut when he'd seen that their valley was bordered on three sides with peaks. They weren't quite the size of the great northern range, of the peaks he'd loved as a child…before. Another thing he was determined to become accustomed to. He'd cherished the sight of sunrise and sunset colors on white-capped mountains once, he must not let the past continue to take that joy from him. He'd relearn it. And with another level of acceptance of his new future, he slid into sleep.

Something woke him. A sound, a Song, he thought. He strained to listen. The rain poured outside the window, splattered against the panes as the wind shifted, dripped from the eaves. No pings from frinks. That was good.

Gardpont. The mental call didn't tell him much—a rough male whisper edged with desperation. Marrec slid from the bed and pulled on his trousers, shrugged into a shirt and drew on his old boots, buckled his knife belt.

Dark Lance whinnied with fright, demanding reassurance from Marrec. *Someone comes.*

Easy. Sense him for me, check if you recognize his Song.

At Marrec's quiet tone, the volaran settled. Cocked his ears, sniffed. Marrec hurried from the suite. Stopped. Turned and locked the door. Shielded it with the best protection spell he had.

Now Sunray, closer to the stable doors, sent him jittery images. *I don't know him.*

I have heard this man's Song before, Dark Lance said. *But he is not happy...and there are two Songs.*

By this time Marrec was at the door nearest the stables, putting on a slicker cape, grabbing one of the new cowboy hats Calli had given him. He stepped into the rain, sending a widespread probe for danger. Vague movement, black against black, a man stumbling, a thin cry, made his belly tense. He fingered the hilt of his knife. Looking away from the stables, he hummed a lightball spell.

The other exclaimed in surprise. Hit the stable wall with his shoulder. Leaned there. "Gardpont?"

"I'm here." His eyes now accustomed to the dim light, Marrec saw the man huddled in a royal-blue cape, his arms full of a bundle. "Who are you?"

"Gentral."

The tension at the base of Marrec's spine eased. He'd flown into battle with the minor noble. "What are you doing here?"

"Got a baby for you."

"What!"

"Heard you and your bondmate—the new Exotique—were interested in adopting. My old mistress just told me I had a daughter…shook me down for blackmail. Hadn't seen her for more'n eighteen months, simply been sending her a stipend. She wanted more for the kid. Or didn't want the kid at all." His breaths were pants, more from anxiety than exertion, Marrec thought.

Gentral continued, "She has a farm just over the spur. Infant hasn't been treated well. I thought of you."

"We're not ready—"

"Can't take the youngster back, not good for her there. Can't take her home, my wife would gut me, harm the child." He laughed harshly. "I have a wife. A dynastic marriage, you know. Stuck with her. Not lucky like you. Won't ever be able to Pairbond. All I wanted was a little ease."

Marrec walked to where Gentral stood in the dark shadow from the roof overhanging the stables. The noble's eyes were wild, his face drawn with anger and distress. He held a bundle in stiff arms, then opened a smelly blanket to show the thin face of a young child with a dark bruise on one cheekbone. Her black hair stuck out in all directions. Marrec didn't know much about children, but enough to know this one was less than a year old and puny. He made no move to take her.

"I won't—"

"I saved your skin last year. This is payback. *I* won't take her. You want kids. You owe me. We all win."

"Marrec?" Calli called. Her squelching footsteps came toward them.

"Here! For the love of the Song, don't tell her who I am!" Gentral thrust the baby into Marrec's arms, turned and ran off with a ground-eating stride. Marrec stood helplessly, holding the babe, her big black eyes fixed on his face. He knew without a doubt that the moment Calli saw the child, heard her circumstances, he'd have a daughter. It was too soon to start a family, he hadn't even gotten the rhythm down of being a husband, a Pairling.

Merde.

"What's wrong? I see someone running. Dark red aura. Did we have an intruder?"

"Not exactly."

A volaran's whinny rose in the night, the beat of wings.

Calli scowled as she joined him, head tilted. "I don't think I know that volaran."

Marrec couldn't recall whether Gentral had been at the Castle when she'd been Summoned. He didn't think so.

The little girl coughed. Her tiny fingers flexed around the blanket edge. Calli froze beside him. Slowly she looked down at the small face. Her breath whooshed out as if from a blow.

"Who's this?"

"An acquaintance's bastard. Just abandoned to us. Was told she'd been mistreated."

"How terrible!" She glanced down, reached out to touch the little girl's cheek.

The child flinched, whimpering with fear, and struggled in Marrec's arms until he found it easier to hold her upright against him. The little girl's arms came around his neck. She set her face against his throat, sniffed him. Cuddled.

"Well," Calli said, looking dubiously at Marrec and the girl.

Marrec didn't know what to say.

"Do you think she's afraid of me because of my coloring?" She reached out to stroke the child's back.

The little girl shuddered. Calli jerked her hand away and met Marrec's gaze. Her eyes wide, her lips pressed together. "I heard a bit of Song. She's scared because I'm a woman."

Marrec had heard a short burst of panic notes, too. He nodded. He didn't think he'd be able to hand the little one over to Calli anytime soon.

"We'd better get her inside," Calli said brusquely.

"Good idea," Marrec said, following Calli as she walked back to the house. The little girl's cold fingers touched his collarbone, curled around the open edge of his shirt. He got the idea she was afraid to make a sound, that the strange woman would hurt her, that the child liked his scent.

Great.

"What's her name?" Calli asked over her shoulder.

"I don't know."

"Huh. And you're not going to tell me who dropped her off? Do you think we should keep her?"

Both thorny questions. "A Chevalier who saved my life in battle last year claimed payback."

Calli snorted.

"That's what I think, too. I never went around tallying lives I saved in battle," Marrec grumbled, shifting the child. Something squished beneath his hand. The little girl whimpered. "But since you don't know the person, I'd prefer to leave it that way."

"In case I hesitate to save the Chevalier's life in battle?"

Marrec grunted. Thunder rumbled and the little girl let out a wail. He found himself rocking her and muttering endearments that he dimly recalled from his own childhood and his younger brothers. He could almost see once more the faces of his family. He shut the door on the images. The baby's appearance seemed aristocratic, with a thin nose and large eyes and well-molded lips.

They hurried back to the house in the rain. Calli's excitement bubbled to Marrec.

"Do you think we can take care of her by ourselves tonight?" Calli stared at the blanket, looking for any wetness. There was a definite odor. "I, uh, don't know what are used for diapers here." Why hadn't she thought of that? "We aren't ready for a family yet!"

Marrec's smile held little humor. "No, we aren't. Help me with my gear."

She removed his hat, peeled the slicker off and hung them both on hooks, did the same for herself, all the while keeping her yearning hands from the little girl. He grunted a short spellsong and the mud disappeared from their boots. Nice. She hadn't learned that one yet, but it wasn't enough to distract her from the baby. A bone-deep feeling said nothing would distract her from claiming the child.

He didn't go up the stairs to their suite, but strolled down the left corridor and opened the door to the small parlor.

As they walked into the room, the fire flickered to life and a fuzzy yellow sunlike ball brightened the room. It was the warmest and homiest of the downstairs rooms, with good but shabby furniture. Marrec set the baby on the floor.

Before their startled eyes she whipped from the blanket and scrunched into a dim corner, crawling with an extra push of Power. They stared at each other.

Calli cleared her throat. "Is your friend Powerful?"

"He's not my friend." Marrec narrowed his eyes as if calling up an image of the man. "Powerful enough, I suppose. A wide streak of silver. He should have known better than to get into a fix like this."

"Ah. Huh," was all Calli could think of to say. She took a couple of steps toward the little girl who was only clothed in what looked like a long slip, and the child cringed, putting thin, bruised arms over her head. Hiding. "Oh, boy," Calli said, tamping down on anger. "I don't like your acquaintance much."

"No."

"She sure doesn't want me. Why don't you try?"

Marrec let out a sigh, lowered himself to the floor and inched toward the girl, who was peeping around her elbow. She trembled.

He stopped.

Song. Could a lullaby help? That might be a good idea, but Calli couldn't think of one offhand. She sure didn't recall anyone singing one to her. Shit.

She could hum, though. Hum something. To her surprise the first song that came to mind was "I Ride An Old Paint."

Now, she'd heard that sometimes as a kid. It was sort of slow. So she began to hum that.

Marrec tossed her a look, frowned. *Do we know any songs in common?*

Only our own.

He smiled at that, glanced at the little girl, crept forward a few steps on hands and knees. The child watched with wide eyes. Calli hummed a little louder. Marrec slowly walked forward. Finally when he was within the girl's reach, he stopped. They stared at each other.

Tentatively, the babe reached out and patted his nose.

Marrec smiled.

Gaze darting to Calli, then back to Marrec, the little girl's lips curved. She grabbed the strands of hair that fell around his face.

Good going, kid. That's nice, feeling stuff.

Minutes rolled by and both Calli and Marrec remained still, unthreatening. Finally the child squirmed a bit, held up her hands to Marrec.

He picked her up.

Calli exhaled slowly.

Marrec went to a two-person sofa and sat cradling the toddler.

"How's she feel?" asked Calli.

He smiled, slow and sweet. "Good. She feels good."

Swallowing, Calli sat next to them.

The little girl's face crumpled.

Calli scooted to the end of the small couch, not far, but it seemed to relieve the little girl. She stuck her thumb in her mouth and Calli thought about bacteria. Heaven knew what sort of dirt was on that thumb. She didn't have that much experience with kids. Yearned for them, yes, practical experience, no. Would the child still be on a bottle? Surely not. What did they use?

She sent the question…a montage of images from Earth about babies to Marrec.

The little girl blinked owlishly.

Calli decided to hum again. The child burrowed into Marrec, closing her eyes. Calli figured that was a good sign. She wondered what would happen if she sent the little girl Power as she had when the horses were frightened. Touching the toddler's mind might not be a good thing. Could she fashion something like a warm mood…an emotional blanket to reassure the girl?

Pairling, Marrec whispered in her mind.

Moving her gaze from the child to her husband's face, she saw his smile widen. *I recall when my younger brothers fell asleep so fast, so deeply.*

Yes, the girl was sound asleep. Marrec's vague childhood memories touched her.

If the little girl was helping Marrec remember the good of his past, then she was already a boon to them.

"I'll go to the kitchen and see what we might have for food. Pick up some soft cloths for diapers," he murmured, slowly shifting the girl.

"I can—"

He put the sleeping child into her arms. "Hold our child."

Calli looked up at him with suddenly swimming eyes. The warm little body filled her arms, lodged in her heart. She had a child now, one who would love her. Her dreams were coming true.

24

Their arrival at the manor near the previous day's battle with the baby caused a big commotion. Calli couldn't help herself from discreetly checking out male Chevaliers who might look like the child, but she knew everyone. Only what she'd come to think of as the core group remained and she already knew that neither Faucon nor Koz would give up a child...and neither was married. She'd gotten that much information from Marrec.

To her surprise, the rest of the older Marshalls had flown in, and so had Marwey, who organized everything for the little girl, including finding a former Chevalier of the place as a babysitter/guard. The feycoocus were there, too, and they Sang approval of the whole business. Marwey used the magical beings to send word to Seeva and have one of the bedrooms in Calli and Marrec's suite turned into a nursery.

The war council didn't take long and the only conclusion it came to was that more retrousse battles were probable.

Calli and Marrec had already decided that was likely, and had held each other through the night, dozing and thinking about what being fighting Chevaliers would be like with a family.

With more guts than she thought she had, Calli accompanied Marrec to the dreeth they'd killed. Marian and Jaquar, who had taken part in the discussion, were surveying the dead flying dinosaur. Marian looked a little pale.

The battlefield itself looked…serene. Calli'd known that the fallen humans were always quickly absorbed by the land and swallowed hard as she found the grass greener in certain spots…then shuddered as she saw the burnt areas. Yet, she sucked in a big breath as she walked to the dreeth.

As she drew near, anger and resolve burned within her. This monster had wanted to kill—Marrec, herself, anyone it could. That was the sole purpose of its life.

And its appearance matched its intention. It was ugly.

"Good," Jaquar said, "you're here." He gestured to the dreeth and green lines glowed on it. "I've designated the cuts for maximum skin."

Calli swallowed. "You want anything?"

"Teeth and claws are always good for spells," Marian said.

"Eyes—" Jaquar started.

Both women shuddered.

"My apologies." He cleared his throat. "I don't think we need eyes today."

Calli didn't even want to know what eyes might be useful for. She watched as Marrec took out a huge knife, set the point into the shoulder and drew it down. To her amazement, the skin cut easily, magically. More Power. Huh.

"A bespelled blade," Marian murmured.

Nodding, Marrec made short work of the butchering. Bracing herself, Calli unsheathed the knife Marrec had put on the Bonding Table and touched one to a tooth. Only a tap had them falling into her hand.

"Well done," Marrec said, folding the nearly bloodless—ichorless—skin and tucking it under his arm. He eyed the dreeth. "There's enough skin for leathers for you, a tunic for me and the rest can be sold as outer covering for hats."

"Hats?" asked Jaquar.

Marrec spared him a glance. "Dreeth hats are all the rage in the city-states. Carried, mostly, not worn." He lifted a shoulder. "To impress others."

"Conspicuous consumption," Marian said.

"I guess," Calli said. "It will pay the bills."

"For sure." Marian's smile gleamed. "You'll have plenty for that house of yours, and your new baby, Mama."

Warmth bloomed in Calli's heart, suffusing her, making her blush. Both men watched. She sniffed. "Thank you."

A shout came from the other end of the battlefield. Marwey hopped up and down, waving her arms.

Salutations, Calli, sent Thunder.

Having him here, too, was comforting. *Hello, Thunder.*

I have brought a carry sacque for The Daughter.

There was a loud snort, mental and physical, from Dark Lance. *I will carry The Daughter. She doesn't like Calli.*

"Thanks a lot," Calli muttered, the warmth of motherhood leaving her for harsh reality. Marrec's arm came around her waist as they walked with Jaquar and Marian to the manor house.

Once there, Calli checked Dark Lance's wound and energy level, while Marrec trotted into the house to collect the baby. Calli was standing outside the stables with the saddled and bridled volarans when Thealia strode up. The Swordmarshall's eyes flashed with a mixture of emotions. "What has gotten into you that you are adopting a young child after only a night with her?"

Calli had known Thealia could be blunt, but hadn't been on the receiving end before. She sent the woman a cool glance. "I have a husband. We want children. You fought when your children were young, didn't you?"

"The circumstances were not the same. There were occasional small incursions of the horrors. That was all." Her mouth folded into pinched lines.

"It's too bad that you Marshalls didn't prevent the current conditions," Calli said. "But that's past and Marrec and I deserve to shape the life we want, just as you and your bondmate did when you were young."

Marian, standing tall next to Calli, said, "Everyone knew that Calli and Marrec were going to adopt children."

"They should not adopt such a child, not when Calli's first duty lies with defending Lladrana."

"Who else will take the little girl?" demanded Calli.

Thealia's face set. "I will find someone."

"No, you won't," said Marrec, holding the clean toddler dressed in a linen shift and dark brown romper with buttons on a padded behind. At least the baby clothes looked like something Calli could handle.

"I don't want you distracted! We can't afford to lose you," Thealia said.

"Thealia," Jaquar said. "Look at the three of them. The child is bonding with Marrec as we speak."

Everyone fell silent, listening as Calli was, to the little girl's Song, harmonically weaving with Marrec's. Even last night the child's personal melody hadn't been like this—today it was stronger, more Powerful, as if being with Marrec, hearing him, taught her...something. Whatever fathers taught children, Calli thought, then winced inwardly as that led to her own father's lack of emotional support for her.

Every couple of bars, the child's Song included notes of Calli and Marrec's PairSong, and a little bit later, spiraled out to pick up a beat of Calli's own tune.

Thealia sighed. "You're right. But I am not pleased." She turned on her heel and went to the end of the stables where her husband and their flying steeds awaited.

"I think we should stay at the Castle for a while," Jaquar mused. He smiled at Calli. "Calli can teach us to properly partner with a volaran...more zhiv for her coffers." He nodded to Marrec. "Better formally bond with the little one as soon as possible."

Marrec inclined his torso, his large hand spread across the infant's back since she lay against his chest. "The ceremony will be this afternoon in the Temple. Luthan Vauxveau, as representative of the Singer and Song, will officiate."

Marian hummed approval. "That will be interesting to watch."

Calli glanced over to her. "Something new for you, too?"

"Oh, something new every day." She grinned.

"I was afraid of that."

That afternoon, after a ritual cleansing in the shower, Marrec carried the little girl to the Temple for the Bonding ceremony. Calli's heart pounded in anticipation as they walked slowly through the courtyards. She held hands with Marrec, and the infant turned her head away from Calli. People lingered to watch them, this new event having caused as much gossip as anything else that had happened since Calli had arrived.

Both she, Marrec and the toddler wore black robes edged with silver. From the Song that Sang between her and Marrec, she knew he was pleased and excited, too, though he was expressionless.

Luthan Vauxveau, Bastien's brother and the representative of the Singer, was already in the Temple. The ceremony would give the little girl a name and bloodbind the child to them in a simple manner. They'd all contribute a couple of drops of blood to a potion, then all would drink. Calli understood that this was the best way to bond with a baby.

Their squires opened the door for them and they entered the dim coolness of the Temple, redolent with incense rising from censers—an oddly fresh scent that seemed like new clover, fresh-mown grass and a mountain breeze. The little girl took her thumb from her mouth and raised her head, sniffing. Then she craned to look at the large space and smiled. She leaned back in Marrec's arms to clap her hands…and hum.

Everyone stared at her as her small voice matched one of the background tones of Power stored in the rafter crystals.

Luthan stood by an altar in the center of a shining golden star, and the rest of Calli's friends waited just outside a circle of the same color. He nodded to a wooden screen partitioning a portion of the room. "You may disrobe over there."

Calli tensed, she hadn't realized that this was going to be a nude ritual. She glanced at Marrec, but he only raised an eyebrow. But she was all too aware that this very first instruction tested her desire to adopt the baby. Marrec set the child on a padded leather table and she promptly stuck her thumb back in her mouth and watched as they undressed. Calli folded their good robes as Marrec freed the baby from her diaper and dress. Once again he lifted her and held out a hand for Calli. She linked fingers with him and breathed deeply. He looked aside from her, the trickle of his personal Song suppressed, his face stern.

"Marrec?" she whispered.

I do not want to display any...desire...for you.

Well, something about nudity they finally agreed upon, though the coolness of the Temple had already tightened her nipples. The first thing that sprang to Calli's mind was the simple "I love you." But she didn't know how he'd react and this was so not the time or place to say that. She scrambled for the phrase that had become the basic resonance between them. "We will do this together."

His gaze softened, then his mouth firmed and he jerked a nod, squeezed her hand and they left the privacy behind the screen with measured, matching steps.

Luthan beckoned them to enter the pentagram along one point of the star and they did. To Calli, their footfalls accompanied their bond Song.

"Place the baby on the altar," Luthan said. His voice boomed through the Temple, magically amplified.

Marrec had to pry the little girl's arms from around his neck, but soothed her...and Calli saw how he slid his mind against hers. Once on the altar the infant hunched into herself, watching everything with wide eyes, hands curled in front of her mouth. She'd stopped singing and that was a real pity.

"What are your intentions toward this child?" Luthan asked.

"To adopt this baby and make her part of our family," Marrec said.

Luthan turned to Calli. "You agree?"

"Yes."

He narrowed his eyes. "You are both fighting Chevaliers."

Marrec nodded. Calli thought everyone needed more explanations. "I am the Volaran Chevalier, and I will finish whatever the specific task I have been Summoned for, but I consider my true goals in life to be teaching volaran partnering to volarans and people." She inhaled, continued firmly, "My personal goals have always been to have a husband and family." She licked her lips. "The Song would not have Summoned me here if my priorities weren't...um...acceptable to...it."

A huge volaran Song comprising of all the winged horses in the Castle swept the room. *She is the Volaran Exotique. She is the Protector of the Flight. She will teach all what it means to fly with us.*

Luthan's well-formed lips lifted in a slight smile. "The Singer agrees and has blessed this adoption."

Calli shifted from foot to foot. That was quick. The Singer lived far to the south in an abbey. Had she sent instructions or was this an instance of one of her prophecies being fulfilled?

"Very well." Luthan sent a glance around the circle. Then held the naked baby high, spotlighted by a shaft of bright sunlight. She tensed, then eased, lifted her face to the sunshine, waved her hands and kicked, gurgling. "I charge everyone in the circle to examine this child. If anyone knows her and objects to her adoption by Callista and Marrec Gardpont, may they speak now or be denied forever!"

Stomach clenched, Calli kept sweeping her gaze around the group. She saw Bastien flinch, surprise come to his eyes, frown—and she knew he was in contact with someone. Then his expression hardened. He cleared his throat.

Luthan, his brother, stared at him.

Bastien said, "I have had…have touched the mind of the woman who birthed the child. She has no objection. Now or ever." His face turned grim.

Alexa scowled at him.

Luthan stiffened, cocked his head, as if he, too, listened to someone. "The sire of this child gives her up. Now and ever after."

A murmur went around the group. Calli mostly sensed anger in the room, especially now the bright light showed the bruises on the infant—little dark ones from pinching fingers, the fading one on her cheek. But other emotions were resignation and sheer haughtiness. She didn't know who radiated the last and felt spellbound in the ritual, so she couldn't search.

"It's done," Luthan said harshly. "The previous ties to the child are cut."

Now the baby was struggling, whimpering, stretching her arms out to Marrec. Calli's heart squeezed. In the quick, efficient actions of a prime warrior, Luthan nicked a vein in the little girl's arm and let a couple of droplets of blood fall into a silver goblet. Then he kissed the arm and she squealed surprise. The wound was healed…all her bruises healed.

"Nice," Calli heard Marian mutter. "Must be the ritual…"

Calli swallowed and stepped forward with Marrec, holding out her right wrist over the edge of the altar as he held out his left.

With equal swiftness and barely any pain, Luthan had three drops of her blood mixed into the liquid in the cup. Marrec dripped two.

Rustling came and she saw everyone link hands. A low hum, almost below her hearing, filled the room, reverberated.

Two big red birds flew *through* the small dome at the top of the Temple and alighted on the altar. They took turns stirring the potion with their beaks. Calli blinked, but the golden sparkles rising from the cup remained.

A wet beak touched her arm—Tuckerinal—and healed the small cut. Sinafinal had done the same for Marrec. The birds flew from the altar to sit on Marian's and Alexa's shoulders.

Luthan handed the brew to Marrec. "Drink, three swallows."

Nodding, Marrec did.

Calli *felt* bubbles slide through him, making him lightheaded. His Song reached for hers, she let it settle into her. They weren't quite as close as they'd been when their blood had run in each other's veins, but she welcomed the feeling, and him.

"Pass the cup to Callista," Luthan said.

Calli took the goblet from Marrec. Her fingers brushed his, they were warm and steady. She smiled at him and he smiled back.

"Three swallows," said Luthan.

She tipped the cool silver cup against her mouth, swallowed. Not a mimosa this time, more like effervescent mint water. When she was done, she gave the goblet back to Luthan. Pure joy spread throughout her. She grinned at Marrec, reached for him as he slid his arm around her waist. They stood together. She didn't think she'd ever felt Marrec so happy.

Luthan had set the baby down and she sat, black hair ruffled in all directions, holding her feet, watching…and listening. Slowly Luthan put the cup against her lips. She opened her mouth. He angled the cup. Her mouth formed a little "o," her tongue came out, she smiled and opened wide. Her hands went around Luthan's and she sipped once.

Marrec trembled, Calli, feeling dizzier, held on tighter to him. The baby's Song—mostly cheerful but with a lower tone of darkness—rippled through her, through them.

With blurred vision, she saw the little girl rock onto her back, wriggle around until she was sideways and stared at them with big serious eyes. She sucked on her fist.

Luthan propped her up in his arm, brought the cup to her mouth again. She made a face, but opened her lips. He poured a small amount into her mouth. She hummed. Grinned.

Love swirled from Calli to Marrec, to the child. Love. Yearning. Determination to nurture, to protect.

Marrec matched, exceeded, every emotion.

The little girl slithered out of Luthan's grasp, rolled onto her hands and knees, headed for them. Luthan caught her as she fell. Marrec and Calli jumped closer.

"One more time," Luthan said, putting the cup against the toddler's mouth.

She slurped loudly.

Marrec and Calli laughed. The Songs, the auras, of all three of them flared, merged.

The child sat, held out her arms.

They swooped on her together. Marrec held her to his chest with one arm, Calli sandwiched her between them.

"It is done," Luthan intoned. "The child is of the mind and heart and soul of Marrec and Callista Gardpont."

Music rose to the top of the room, a Song that Calli had never heard before but that spoke of love and belonging and spoke of the secrets of her heart.

Marrec kissed the top of the baby's head, pressed a kiss on Calli's lips. "We'll call her Diaminta," he said. "It was my grandmother's name. It means 'bright finch.' And we will teach her to Sing." His voice was husky, unsteady.

Calli twined her fingers with his. "We already are."

Calli immediately added a class in Lladranan child care, and began learning teaching Songs. Her voice was good but thin and she'd never trained it before. She and Marrec were always there in the morning to supervise the new nanny as she dressed Diaminta, and they took their breakfast together as a small family. It was the best part of the day for Calli. She spent an hour a day in the afternoon— between training her horses and giving classes on volaran partnership—sitting in the room while Marrec played with Diaminta. And every day he withdrew to sit behind Calli as she rolled a ball to Diaminta. Most of the time the little girl ignored her, and Calli would be forced to Sing the ball back into her hands, and roll it again. But the intimate

Song weaving between them, making them into a family, strengthened.

She cherished every moment that went without an alarm—a full six days—before the Klaxon sounded again, jolting fear into her, destroying her peace in an instant.

25

The sun was setting as they banished the orbs of Distance Magic. Calli hoped this would be quick. She wasn't nearly as good in night battles. At least in practice.

Marrec smiled reassuringly and unsheathed his sword. They descended through a wisp of icy cloud, weapons raised, ready to fight, Marrec in the lead with Alexa and Thealia, followed by another wave of Chevaliers, Calli and the other Shields dropping back. Then Marrec jerked straight, wavered in the saddle. Calli had already flung a Shield around him, couldn't understand what was going wrong—she linked with him and felt his every nerve ending fire with pain. What was happening? She swept a glance around, saw nothing threatening him. He pulled up. Dark Lance whinnied with fear. Marrec saw nothing, his emotions were in a turmoil. Nausea engulfed him and he leaned over to vomit.

Others dodged his spray and cursed him.

He slumped over Dark Lance, who faltered in flight, tipping from one side to another.

Swish! A slayer's spine missed Calli by inches. She strengthened her own Shield, found herself flying low into the middle of battle, a render leaping high at her with gleaming razor claws.

Thunder tucked up his legs, shot up and away in the nick of time. Calli kept his emotions cool, his mind steady, free of panic. Then she met Dark Lance's fearful Song with her own, drew him away from panic, from terror of monsters killing him. She *merged* with Marrec and felt his fright, his horror, his despair, cycling, cycling. Thunder's body rippled beneath her. She snapped her mind away, pulled her emotions from him. Kept control of her own feelings, and Thunder's.

There weren't many beasts—perhaps twenty—and the fight was quick. It took a few minutes to defeat them.

It took an eternity while Calli steadied Dark Lance and strove to reach Marrec, to make sense of the emotions racking him.

Thealia's usual shout of triumph rose through the air. She held her malachite baton aloft. "Victory! Return to the Castle."

One more tremor seized Marrec and he wheeled Dark Lance westward, to the sea. The other fighters flung bubbles of Distance Magic around themselves and headed southeast. Calli flew after Marrec. Her husband was hurting.

He didn't fly to the Castle, didn't fly toward home. Calli sent a mental demand to Alexa for her and Bastien to ensure Diaminta's well-being that night.

Sleepover! Alexa had replied, making Calli smile, knowing her child was in good hands.

A half hour passed before Marrec shook off his blinding emotions. He came to himself all at once, sat up straight in the saddle, sheathed his sword. He brushed her mind with his own, cool and logical as usual. Calli released the soft hold she had on Dark Lance.

Mouth grim, Marrec turned the winged horse back to where the battle had been. No one from the Castle had fallen, and the slain horrors still lay as heaps on the ground, being picked over by scavengers. Marrec angled slightly to the northeast to an area about a hundred yards from the battle.

Finally, they set down in the long evening shadows. Dark Lance dropped his head, his sides bellowed, his coat was beaded with sweat. Marrec swayed in the saddle, eyes closed, body stiff.

Calli dismounted, Sang a short, soothing tune and the tack removed itself from the winged horses, settled to the long grass growing in a large, lush square. The sun flung one last bright ray into the sky, then vanished. She walked to her Pairling in night. Stood beside Dark Lance and put her hand on Marrec's thigh. "What's wrong?"

He jerked his chin at a half wall covered in ivy. "I never wanted to remember, but since this afternoon, I can't forget. My…" His voice was hoarse, he licked his lips, turned his head to look down at her. "This land, this place was my old home."

She stilled, let her mind and heart reach out to him, experienced the flow of images. No pleasant ones this time, the battle had ensured that. The renders and the slayers of that day superimposed upon past images, the sounds of battle leached away until no slide of sword against claws was heard, no shouts of human triumph. Instead there was the ripping sounds of slaughtered humans, the screams of dying people. She laid her head in his lap, circled his lean waist with her arms. "Come away, we'll fly home."

"No. That's cowardly."

He lifted a hand as if it were heavy, set it on her head. More memories…colorful ones of blood and destruction—fabric, furniture, homes, people—flooded her. She bit her lip to keep her own cry of horror from escaping. "To…to the Castle then. We can bathe. Cuddle Diaminta."

Marrec flinched and she knew she'd made a mistake. He was too much in the past, with his parents, his brothers as children, to be reminded of another young one—so vulnerable to hurt and death.

But all he said was, "No. I must face the memories sometime."

The sky had lit with a nearly full moon. His features seemed sharper limned with silver, his face expressionless. His eyes glittered and Calli couldn't tell if it was with anger or grief. He'd shut his emotions away. He swung his opposite leg over Dark Lance's back and Calli retreated a few steps. When he was on the ground, he stroked his volaran's neck. "Good boy."

Dark Lance blew out a breath.

Marrec straightened his shoulders, walked slowly to the slightly curving wall before them. "This was the Temple. The only building made of stone." He reached out to touch it, then withdrew his hand. His neck tilted back as he looked at the stars. "Even the sky reminds me now. I know these patterns.

Mountain Moon, soon to be End of Summer Feast Day." Now
he rolled his shoulders. The burden of memory was hard for
him—hard to carry, hard to speak of. Calli kept quiet.

"I think…I think I would have left Gardpont. Gone south
to some town." His lips twitched up in a parody of a smile,
set again into a line. "I was restless…then."

She'd never met a man so entrenched in home, now. And
now she knew why.

Their bootsteps made no sound as they walked on the
verdant ground. Marrec circled around the temple, scuffed
a foot and revealed a threshold. He turned and situated
himself. "Nothing left of our wooden homes. The two shops.
My father was a cobbler." He lifted his boot and stared at the
sole. "He did work equal to this, though this leather was far
beyond his means."

"He was an excellent artisan, then," Calli said stiltedly. She
had to think hard for words, and the fancy ones were the
only ones that came. God, how was she going to help her
man? Especially when his memories flickered like broken
film in front of her eyes—a few frames of the round
temple—covered with roses in the summer, stark with snow
in the winter. The area in front of it had been wide and dusty,
a gathering place—then had been piled with half-seen
mangled bodies when the child Marrec stumbled from devastation to devastation after the monsters had left. His eyes
had been puffy with tears, his throat raw with the mewling
grunts that were the only sound he could make.

Her arm jingled with chain mail as she put it around his
waist. They both stopped for a moment, her thought
matching his. The townspeople had no armor, few weapons.

And now both he and she were battling the horrors. The killing had never ended for him.

Yet.

His head lifted, his nostrils flaring, and Calli herself could smell the rich land, the forgotten grain and vegetables and flowers gone wild. The stench of battle a few hours ago. All mixed up with the night wind carrying chill from the mountains. He shuddered and a snippet of his memory—of tying a rag around his face at the hideous scent of death as he went from door to door looking for survivors like him, finding no one. Seeing even the youngest torn...she whimpered. Couldn't help herself.

He didn't notice, but kept walking...down a street that was hard-packed dirt in his recollection, until they were about three hundred feet from the temple. He angled to the right, flung out an arm. "There. There was my home."

Nothing marked it.

He walked in, ducking as if the lintel was now too low for his adult height.

She stopped, then *saw* as he had last seen. His mother with a slayer's spine in her eye, his father raked open, insides gleaming through five deep slashes, staring at the ceiling, his two dead brothers... Calli turned aside, bent double, vomited. Was brought back to herself with his low groan, saw him fold to his knees, his back arch and a yell of anguish rip from him. She grabbed a big leaf and wiped her mouth, stumbled to him and fell to her own knees, grabbed him and held on as he once again screamed his throat raw.

Like him, she endured the memories.

Unlike him, she wept.

Finally they were too exhausted to grieve. Marrec held her close. "I have lived this, now faced this. It is…crippling. It is nothing I want inside me, to harm you or our children or myself." They toppled sideways to the cool earth, soft with fragrant grasses. "I *can't* remember! Not ever again."

Sweet darkness pinpointed with the light of stars enveloped them, then blackness rolled over them as if a heavy cloak comforted them, hid them. The cloak turned to fog in her mind, penetrating her, finding the memories she'd just shared with Marrec. Images disintegrated into nothingness. Calli hugged him tightly, knowing the same thing happened to him. He gave the memories up willingly to the planet of Amee, who absorbed them like the fallen dead.

When they reached the Castle early the next morning, Alexa and Bastien awaited them, Diaminta in Bastien's arms, her fingers twined in his black-and-white hair. Their squires took the flying steeds and led them with much praise back to the stables.

Diaminta stretched her hands out to Marrec. "Pa. Pa. Pa."

He took her, held her close. Calli came near and the little girl turned her head away, but watched her from the corner of her eyes. Calli kissed her soft golden cheek. Diaminta snuggled closer to Marrec.

"She hardly looked at me—Auntie Alexa—at all," Alexa grumbled. "Didn't even play with me. She likes the feycoocus, though."

"Fin. Fin. Fin!"

"I guess so," Calli said.

Marrec sniffed at Diaminta. "Smells like you need a change."

Bastien closed his eyes. "Again?" He opened his eyelids and cocked his head. "I think one of the new volarans that flew in last week is calling me." He took off at a trot toward an arena.

"I'll take her up to our rooms and meet you for breakfast in the dining hall." Marrec smiled at Calli easily, yet the lines around his eyes seemed a little deeper, the silver in his hair a little wider.

"Sure," she said. "I want to check in on my horses." She and Alexa strolled toward the horse pens.

Alexa said nothing until Marrec was out of earshot. "Lady Hallard knows Marrec's past. She told us yesterday's battle took place where Gardpont village was destroyed."

A shadow seemed to cross the sun, dimming the light. Calli rubbed her arms. "I don't recall. Not much. Just that Marrec lived through the massacre again that day, and I did, too."

Alexa shuddered. "Poor little boy."

"Yeah." Calli stretched, settling into the fact that she'd always be missing some memories. "I do recollect that what he saw was enough to cripple a person emotionally for the rest of his life." Like a wife abandoning a man and their daughter and a ranch, leaving the little girl in a locked room so she wouldn't wander. "And Marrec didn't want that," Calli continued softly. "He wants to be as whole as possible for us—and for himself. He let the land take the memories away. I did, too, I guess, since nothing vivid comes to mind, and I recall that there were...vivid...images." She swallowed, strode faster to the horse pen and held out a hand to welcome her horses. Solid friends that she knew. "I didn't know Amee could do that."

"I didn't, either." Alexa stroked a horse nose shoved in her hand. "Relinquished memories. Huh." She frowned. "That's stronger than I would be. I'd never let such memories go, and maybe my heart would shrivel. And as my beloved Bastien would say, 'Not much comes out of a shriveled heart.'" She smiled. "I can just hear him saying it."

She looked around, but Bastien was nowhere in sight. Her gaze went back to Marrec. "He's had a tough enough life as it is." Shrugging, she gave a half smile. "He was an orphan here. I was an orphan in Colorado. I listened when they talked of him."

"You didn't put it in your Lorebook of Exotiques."

Alexa lifted her nose. "Of course not. I think those books should end with the Snap."

A little chill coated Calli's stomach. "I don't want the Snap."

"I can't see it taking you," Alexa agreed. She grinned, nudged Calli in the ribs. "Still got your task, and your training to do, Volaran Exotique."

"Speaking of which, I think it may be time for another lesson."

"I'm doing well. I ride my own volaran in practice now! I *do* miss Bastien behind me when we fight, but am glad I'm off horses on the battlefield."

"And so you should be. A battlefield is no place for horses." She tangled her fingers in the mare's stiff mane. No one would know, now, that this beautiful animal had been abused, and she sure wouldn't ever let anyone ride her into battle.

Alexa said, "It's no place for anyone. Your man, there—" she nodded as Marrec and Diaminta disappeared around the edge of the stables, Diaminta babbling and waving her arms "—he's filled out. Not quite so lean as he was. Finally getting enough food, I'd say. Your coming has been the best thing that's ever happened to him."

Tears prickled behind Calli's eyelids. "Thank you."

Alexa's smile was gentle. "I've noticed that you have a great deal of patience. You had to in order to get me flying on a volaran, to work with others and the volarans themselves. Your daughter will love you, just wait and see."

Calli hugged her. "Thanks. But compliments won't get you out of a lesson."

That afternoon when Calli and Marrec were playing with Diaminta, the siren screeched. Calli heard the new additional bell mixed in the alarm that was added. Retrousse. The Dark was sending monsters to an old battlefield. She listened hard, heard the modality of notes that indicated the place. The same as the day before. Gardpont. Her shoulders tensed. Diaminta flung herself at Marrec and held on hard. "Pa. Pa. Pa." She knew they left when the siren wailed.

His jaw grim, Marrec shook his head. "We're off rotation until tomorrow." A hint of relief showed in his eyes. Calli heard the shouts of Marshalls and Chevaliers, the jangle of armor, the swish of volaran wings as they rose to the sky.

She was relieved, too. No one had said anything, but she was sure she wasn't the only one who thought that the call to arms the day before to Gardpont was part of the ongoing campaign to harm her. Remove or cripple or kill Marrec when battling inner and outer demons and she would die, too.

But the relief didn't last long.

Every day after that, at varying times during the day, the

siren sounded. Retrousse. And always to the same place, the battle plain that had once held the town of Gardpont. Additional alarms rang, too, along the northwestern border, near Gardpont.

Retrousse here, too, monsters being sent where greater battles had been fought, in larger numbers.

Marrec grew strained, paler. The fact that his memories were gone should have been a boon. But every day he faced that his town had once been here, that the ground showed where his family had fallen, in the house that had disintegrated around them. That the village itself was gone forever.

Calli was sure that if they had had to fight time and again here with total recall of Marrec's experiences, they'd have gone mad. And again she wondered if that was the point.

As it was, Marrec became more somber, withdrew from her emotionally. It was slight but noticeable to Calli and she yearned to help. So she insisted that when they could, they return home and worked on their estate—the volaran areas, the horse paddocks, the arenas. He threw himself into the reconstruction, becoming an ideal landowner.

After visiting the village on their land his Song was more cheerful, as if he carried the image of this village close to his heart to replace the one he'd lost.

He, too, learned—of ranching methods here in the north, of crops and trade. Of what the villagers needed from them, and how he and Calli could help the people who welcomed them. They certainly won enough money fighting to build whatever they pleased.

For three weeks as summer grew less hot, and fall drew near, battle-weary Marshalls and Chevaliers fought, flying in shifts from the Castle, returning. Those who survived. Attrition took a toll. The next oldest Marshall Pair died, as did the newest, and the Castle grieved. One or two Chevaliers, usually the lowest of the low—like Marrec had been—fell in every fight, and this haunted the man.

The loss of every volaran haunted Calli. Some would perish with their fliers, if they'd been good partners. Some had broken wings and bones and minds that couldn't be easily mended and flew to the sanctuary that Bastien offered—and land she'd set aside for them on her and Marrec's new ranch, too.

Pascal and Marwey earned their batons, but Seeva tried and failed to win her reins.

Battle debriefings grew shorter, not much to mull over than what had been said before. One afternoon the fighters of the morning sat in the grand entry hall of Horseshoe Hall. Once again most of the force had had to turn out because they'd fought on an ancient battlefield in the northeast where a mass of horrors had invaded.

An idea that had been floating around in the back of Calli's brain bloomed. From the corner of her eye, she watched Marrec, with his usual serious expression. He didn't like these meetings, no matter how short. He'd much rather be doing his duty, or following his passion—managing the estate. With his natural business savvy and her talent for teaching and training, they'd be wealthy if they ever got a chance to truly settle down.

She coughed to attract attention, then stood. "We're always flying to the same area."

Swordmarshall Thealia raised her eyebrows but said nothing about Calli stating the obvious.

"I know the Distance Magic isn't a great energy-sapping spell, but it does bleed everyone of Power. We haven't battled the Dark anywhere except the northeast in a month—"

Marian spoke, "I think it's because the Dark doesn't have a human master to control the horrors. To order them and move them to wherever they were kept to invade. Instead the Dark must *send* them itself. I think retrousse battles are easier for the Dark." Marian stood, too. She and Jaquar, and a couple of other Circlets, had come and gone through the deadly weeks.

"If you say so," Calli said. She sucked in a breath. "Why don't we…uh…make an encampment a little ways south of the general area where we always fly. I've read that this was done before." She licked her lips, not looking at Marrec, who had stiffened from a slouch beside her. "If even one life is saved because our fighters have more energy, it would be worth it."

People talked over each other, discussing, as she sat down. Marrec continued not to look at her. He didn't say a word. After Thealia called in household experts—the Castle Head of Staff and Seeva—appointing them as liaisons to the Lord who held land near where'd they'd been fighting, she adjourned the meeting.

The Marshalls and Chevaliers left the hall with new purpose. Simply introducing another option had lifted morale.

Calli felt Marrec's simmering anger at her. He headed toward their suite, but instead of going to the rooms, he took the stairway to the Castle walls. She accompanied him, and a bit of recollection from their bloodbonding came to mind. When Marrec was very upset he walked the walls.

His previous room had been tiny, about twelve-by-twelve

feet and no good for pacing. He liked the space without high walls, and the perspective of looking out on the land he fought for, and the fact that he could walk. He usually paced the length of the wall between Horseshoe Hall and the keep and back. He didn't fly on Dark Lance, as she would have Thunder, because he'd never known when they would fight again and he would not endanger his volaran by tiring him.

With that knowledge, she learned that he hadn't walked the walls since they had bonded. He'd never been perturbed enough. Not liking his mood, but not wanting to leave him, Calli accompanied him. The ramparts were wide enough for three abreast.

They'd strode to the keep wall next to Alexa's tower and halfway back before he spoke.

"A baby should not be kept in an armed encampment."

She swallowed hard. "I know." She kept her eyes level with his. "Sometimes a greater need must be served at the cost of personal desires." She hardly believed she was saying this. Always, always, she'd done whatever needed to be done with the single goal of making her home better.

His expression set. He was such a quiet man, such a controlled one, it took real observation to know what he felt…or a bond. She put her hand on his forearm and he jerked it away. When he spoke, his tone was soft and mild, more evidence of his control and completely opposite what she knew he really felt. "Our primary goal has been to make a home for our child—and children to come. We have been in accord, and focused on that. It should remain our single purpose."

Oh, this was going to be rough. This was going to be big.

26

Inhaling deeply, Calli let her breath out on a rough *whoosh*, then said, "The best way to ensure our children's future is to defeat the Dark. I want this *over*. Over before our children are of age to become Chevaliers or Marshalls. Over before Diaminta wants to fight."

"You plan on staying at the encampment?"

"I...it depends."

He glanced at her. "This will take zhiv, too. Tents for y— us, for our squires. Camping equipment."

She wanted to apologize but wouldn't. Instead she lifted her chin. "This will save us energy, too."

He laughed harshly. "It will add tension, being away from our child." Turning, he looked out at the rolling landscape to the west of the Castle, but Calli didn't think he saw it. She stepped closer, not quite brushing against him.

"I don't want to keep Diaminta here at the Castle when everyone else is gone," he said.

"I'm sure we'll be on rotation in the camp, too—"

"Doesn't matter." His hands flexed. "Our estate is close enough for us to go home between rotations."

Calli licked her lips. "If we will be traveling between our estate and the camp, it will defeat the purpose of being less tired."

He seared her with a look. "But it will keep our child safe. Will you not travel back and forth with me?"

She couldn't answer.

His expression hardened. "I see. You leave your child."

"I am not abandoning my daughter!" she cried. Far too out of control. She breathed deeply. Looking at Marrec from behind a film of tears, she said, "I must be there. People depend upon me, will expect me to be there all the time. I am the *Chevalier* Exotique. I fight. That's my definition."

Another big breath. "I can't split my concentration between here and my home, like you do. I'm not so good a fighter that I can just turn off battle scenes in my head. I don't want to get us killed."

He sat next to her and put his arm around her, but he was still stiff with his own anger. "You are strong enough to do whatever you must. That means putting your child first."

"She doesn't even want me!" Another cry that tore from her heart. She'd loved her mother, wanted her. She wasn't abandoning her daughter for another man, a richer lifestyle. Gulping, she dried her eyes and wiped her nose. "I know I have to be there for her to learn to love. But I'll come home once a week or so. Why is that not enough?"

"Because she needs you more often. You owe us as much attention as the Chevaliers and Marshalls. Fall is coming on, and winter. Our estate must be readied for it. There's much to do."

She really looked at him, the man. He carried himself differently—like a man who is certain of his future, a man of property and responsibility. Not quite the noble...yet.

"I will be spending more time at our home," he said.

"I understand, and that's...that's the way it should be." Again she wanted to touch him. Again she didn't. It was hard reaching for someone and being rejected.

By the end of the week, arrangements had been made for a cantonment to the north. The distance between the Castle and the encampment seemed less than the emotional gulf between herself and Marrec. And there was no magical spell to breach it.

They talked little, *at* each other more than *with* each other. Marrec had done his duty as a Chevalier, flying to battle, buying a two-room tent and bivouac equipment. They flew to the place with the last wave of Marshalls and Chevaliers one evening, arriving to see the tent city still going up later than scheduled. Marrec would ensure their camp quarters were acceptable, then fly back to the Castle in the morning and transfer Diaminta and their household goods to their home. He'd stay on their estate until the morning of their every-third-day shift.

Calli would stay behind, learning, training, meeting. She loathed it, but felt that was *her* duty. Unable to stay with Marrec as he worked with his squires, she walked the perimeter of the large camp, finally stopping on a low ridge to the northwest of the rising city, still pondering her decisions. Like it or not, she felt she owed the volarans, the Exotiques, the Chevaliers for giving her their trust.

She stood on the hill for a while, and when she looked down, she blinked. Though Calli hadn't known what to expect, the colorful tents surprised her. The Lladranan forces may not have lived in the field for some time, but they knew what they were doing. Seeva and Marwey had been the primary designers of the city.

The camp had been set up, with tents in angled lines—of a star, a pentagram. At the end of the points were fires—common areas. The walkways were along the points, down to a center pentagon where large canvas pavilions stood. Between the arms and upper point were volaran areas. Interesting.

With that thought, she looked for Marian and Jaquar's pavilion, with a flag showing a whirlwind casting off light-ning bolts. Their tent marked the entrance to the southeast-ern point, slightly outside the cluster of the Marshalls' pavilions in the middle of the pentagon.

In the exact center of everything was the largest pavilion of several rooms. It shone as if it were truly made of mala-chite—Thealia Germaine's and her Shield's tent. It might even have an inside fire, though that sounded scary to Calli. She supposed Power would handle any fire.

The smallest pup tents, standard issue for the lowest of Chevaliers, were near the end of the points. The size got larger as they approached the middle...generally. Calli noticed a big tent ruining the symmetry near the top of the northern point. Since a flag—with red trident, a Maserati trident—waved, she figured it was Koz's and snorted.

Narrowing her eyes, she could see the black and silver of her new tent, with a flag sporting a flying volaran, on the opening to the east point. Their pavilion had two rooms. One for sleeping and one for gathering. She glanced at the evening sky and sniffed the air. No sign of rain, and that was good.

Seeva called up to her. "Calli, I have someone I want you to meet!" She and her companion, a middle-aged man only a little overweight, climbed the hill. Calli cursed inwardly, slapped a smile on her face. She'd seen the guy in passing, the owner of this land, a noble. "Sleaze" alarm bells went off inside her.

Calli wasn't used to slick opportunists in Lladrana. She'd run across the revulsion reaction, of course, had been condescended to by the rich, arrogant and haughty, but hadn't met anyone where she'd wanted to shower after being in their presence. Probably because the folk she associated with were dedicated—obsessed—with defeating the invading Dark. Landowners that *didn't* fight with the Marshalls and Chevaliers she didn't meet.

By the time they'd arrived, Calli had set her personal Shields high and wrapped her Song tight. Seeva had linked arms with the man, her attitude one of pleasure with a hint of seduction. "Calli Gardpont, may I present Threo Veenlit, the lord of this land. He's generously offering it for our encampment."

Not that generously. Calli herself had handed over three prime dreeth claws, and both Lady Hallard and Swordmarshall Thealia had exited the "negotiations" with pinched mouths.

Calli inclined her torso. Seeva frowned at her and Calli reluctantly offered her hand.

"Ah, another Exotique." Lord Veenlit took her fingers in

his soft, damp hand, tried a mindprobe and, when that didn't work, slithered his own Song along hers to read. Natural enough, Calli supposed, after all they were on his land, but it felt rude.

Even with a physical connection, she heard little of his Song—some brassy notes that actually sounded like a donkey braying. She smiled genuinely.

His heavy features returned the smile. "Quite, quite unusual coloring. Stunning," he said, eyelids lowered but still showing a gleam of sexual calculation.

Withdrawing her hand, Calli said. "I thank you again."

"Not at all, not at all." He waved her words away. "I met your husband, a very excellent Chevalier."

"Yes, he is."

Veenlit chuckled. "He was looking for Lord Faucon Creusse, but I don't think that one has arrived yet."

Veenlit would make it his business to know when one of the wealthiest Lords of Lladrana arrived. "I still don't see Creusse's pavilion." His eyes glittered avid satisfaction as he surveyed the small village below. Then he scowled. "What's that?"

"Exotique Circlet Marian Harasta Dumont's pavilion," Calli said.

"I authorized no Circlets on my land!"

Sounded as if Marian would have to do her work of integrating Circlets with nobles again.

Well, surely there was one thing the man respected. "I'm sure you can negotiate with the Circlets for rent," Calli said.

He jerked straight as if he were a puppet on a string, rubbed his hands. "Quite true, quite true." Absentmindedly he bowed to Calli, his gaze still on Marian and Jaquar's tent.

"Honored," he said. "You will see me and my chief Chevalier, Raoul Lebeau, in camp." He pointed to a gaudy pavilion of red and yellow just inside the entrance to the northern star point. His sigil was a dagger.

"You're going to stay here?"

He nodded. "My manor is quite a ways from here, alas." Making a quick bow, he said, "Until later," then descended the hill.

Seeva started after him, but Calli stopped her with a hand to her arm. "Seeva, how could you associate with him? He's greedy, only after what he can get."

The younger woman lifted her chin. "At least he's honest about that. He's not being a savior. He sees his Chevaliers as *people,* not counters on a game board, not expendable. And for me, that's refreshing."

The man was sleazy. Calli didn't know "sleazy," in Lladranan.

But Seeva was on a roll. "And he listens to me. That's damn refreshing, too."

"You're Head of Staff of Horseshoe Hall."

Her face fell into dissatisfied lines. "When I wasn't shaping up to be an extraordinary Chevalier and disappointing my mother, I turned to what I did better, which was managing the household." She grimaced again. "Not even the whole estate, like you and Marrec do, just the *household.* Then there was an opening in Horseshoe Hall and Mother brought me in over everyone else." Her arms crossed. "Which made a lot of people dislike me, and my job a hundred times worse. I haven't even won my reins, I may never have it in me to win my reins. I've been a Chevalier in name only. People hate me."

Calli had seen no evidence of that—but she'd been living in a little sheltered world of her own.

Seeva sniffed, met Calli's gaze. "I have never been able to do exactly what I want."

Well, who had? Calli fumbled for words. "And how does being with Lord Veenlit change that?"

Lip curling, Seeva said, "My skills have brought me here, and he can give me what I want."

"Which is?"

"A home of my own, if I work it right." Her laugh was bitter. "One thing that Mother has given me—prominence in the noble circles. I may even be able to get some sort of dowry like my sisters."

"Seeva!" Veenlit called, hovering outside the Circlets' tent. Obviously he wanted her to smooth any transaction.

She turned on her heel and went toward him, leaving Calli in the dying daylight.

A tremor of fear shivered through Calli at the thought that this could be Diaminta in twenty years as she herself focused on the continuing fight for Lladrana, ignoring her daughter. Her fingers clenched. No, that would not happen. She would not let that happen.

Not then and not now. Her small progress with Diaminta was disenheartening, but she'd continue. Slow and easy. She would not physically abandon her daughter as her own mother had her. She would not emotionally abandon her daughter as her father had her.

There had to come a time when she believed her duty to the volarans and Chevaliers was done—except for training. Then she'd put her family first. And why did that echo so hollowly?

By the time she walked down the hill, Veenlit was exiting the Circlets' pavilion, a small leather bag firmly in his grasp. Seeva murmured goodbyes, then both of them angled toward Calli. She stifled a sigh. When they met, another man joined them, wearing red and yellow. Calli blinked and blinked again at him. His was the most exquisite male face she'd seen on Lladrana, including Luthan Vauxveau and Faucon Creusse, both handsome men.

"Raoul Lebeau," Lord Veenlit said, smiling.

The Chevalier bowed gracefully before Calli. "Welcome to my Lord's lands, Bella Dama," he said in a well-modulated voice.

She could do nothing but let him brush a kiss on her fingers, though she was getting bad vibes from him, too.

"Raoul, we part ways here. Walk the Lady Exotique to her pavilion."

"My pleasure."

Calli said good-night to Seeva and Veenlit, ignoring the fact that he and Seeva went into his tent together, and said nothing when Raoul tried to amuse with his comments on others. The Chevalier wasn't snide or malicious, and might well have made her smile if she'd been in a better mood. She managed a polite dismissal when they reached her tent, and stepped back before he could do anything more.

Lifting the flap, she entered and stopped when she saw a huge, foot-long hamster sitting on her weapons chest. She cleared her throat. *Salutations, Tuckerinal.*

"Salutations, Calli," he squeaked in perfect Lladranan.

"Why are you here?"

He smiled and it warmed her heart. "To sing you to sleep."

She stared at him. "Sing me to sleep?"

"Ayes."

"Oh-kay." She went into the bedroom and undressed. When she turned down the covers of the mattress and slipped onto the bed, feeling all the aches of her body as she settled, he opened his mouth. "Shenandoah" rolled out, played by a full orchestra, that melded into a hauntingly beautiful tune that had tears stinging her eyes. She was so far from ho—Earth, caught in an alien land.

Thunder's mind touched hers, content and supportive, and she sensed more volarans, too. She swallowed. She loved the volarans. Loved Lladrana.

Loved Marrec and her child. Perhaps she should abandon the camp and go home—to her true home, here in the Lladranan mountains.

It is not yet time for you to only *teach and train,* Tuckerinal said, even as his rounded mouth poured out a slow country waltz. She turned her head and saw his big, protuberant eyes gleaming, yet they held wisdom and sadness. *Not yet time.*

Not yet time, whispered Thunder in her mind.

Not yet time, said Sinafinal.

Her heart ached, and sleep claimed her.

Marrec came to her. He slipped in, his skin cool with night, and she turned to him and warmed him.

His steady, caressing touch on her, stroking her to arousal, brought futile tears. She touched him, too, telling him with her fingers, with the rising notes of her personal Song that melded with his, that she loved him, though she couldn't say the words. The deep richness of their Song echoed long in her mind after he'd fallen asleep in her arms.

* * *

The next morning when the tent filled with the tension of their disagreement and low, angry voices, it was as if the tender night had never been.

"This new tent is another expense." He locked his hands behind his back.

She started to apologize, stopped. Just for a moment he reminded her of her father. "We are needed here."

"Alexa is needed here. She's a fighter first and foremost, that's why she was Summoned."

She turned to him, wanted to touch him, wanted the affection that had flowed between them. God help her, she'd become addicted to that, and now it was gone. "It's not for long, just until we find out why the horrors are targeting this area."

"To draw us in—you and me—to kill us."

"We don't know that for sure."

He shrugged. "Don't you think I've noticed the miasma that has surrounded us at the Castle, on the battlefield? No open attacks, just…an evil pressure."

"What?"

"You haven't realized that?"

"I…no." She was shaken and it came out as stiffness in her voice, an obvious accent. "I don't always recognize nuances of Power."

He took her hands, his eyes shadowed. "The Dark *wants* us here. I don't like that we've accommodated it."

She went cold—hands, lips, gut. "The Marshalls and Alexa and Marian asked us to come."

"And we're here. We can only hope we won't leave our daughter an orphan."

There was nothing she could say to that. The silence stretched, for the first time since they'd bonded, uncomfortable.

"If you insist that I come with you, I'll forsake my duty."

27

He dropped her hands, lifted a tent flap for a moment to watch the bustle of the camp. More than his face was inscrutable. She could barely hear his Song through the rush of her own blood.

"That's your main fault, Calli. You want to please everyone."

It was like a slap, she took a step back, couldn't figure out what to say, settled on what might cause the deepest hurt but would be the deepest truth. "Do you regret bonding with me?"

Again his gaze met hers, hooded. "No."

She wondered if that was because he'd received what he'd wanted all his life.

"Do you want me at our estate or not?"

"I always want you."

And that might annoy him. But the Pairbond between

them could not be broken. He could withdraw, she could step back in pain, but they were linked together.

He made a rough sound. "I see Marian and Jaquar are here. I wonder if they will take the field."

"Jaquar has fought before."

"But not the Exotique Circlet."

"She battled the Dark in its nest." Calli frowned. "And she fought when she came back—" Calli realized the points he was making.

"She completed her task and she returned after the Snap. You haven't completed your task, whatever it might be, and this present endeavor may lead to our deaths before that is done. Will you stay on Earth when your Snap comes?"

A cry ripped from her. She stumbled toward him, put her arms around him, but he didn't return her embrace. Still his heart beat faster, his Song enveloped her now she was against him.

"I am Pairbonded to you and bloodbonded to *our daughter.* I won't return to Earth." Any love she'd ever found was here.

His hand brushed her hair, just once. "You must know your priorities, Calli."

"You. You and Diaminta."

"So you say, but you don't fly with me home today," he said.

She hesitated.

His face hardened.

"No, I'm not flying home. Perhaps you're right, I want to please people. I want people's trust." She wanted to be loved.

Because she needed to pace and carry on, she kept very still. She put her fist on her heart. "I feel that I must be here now, though I want to be with you more than I can say."

There was one thing she *could* do. "Diaminta must be fully protected. I'd like to accept some new Chevaliers into our service, set them on rotation, too, here with u— me, and at home."

He frowned. "Good idea." Then he surveyed the field of tents one more time. "Four more would be best, and that will delay construction of the indoor arena until spring."

Calli nodded. The indoor arena was her main dream as a trainer, but it was also the most costly outbuilding.

Without looking at her, he asked, "Will you fly as Shield to someone else during the times I am gone and battle is engaged?"

Shock flooded her and she knew he had the answer to his question through their link before she managed to answer. "No. Never." *I'm a lover, not a fighter.*

He nodded. "What will you do?" His gaze had focused on the large training ring going up near their tent.

She cleared her voice. "In my Power lessons I have been crafting spellsongs to kill dreeths in battle, especially the little ones."

A pulse of surprise came from him to her and he looked at her again, this time his face less expressionless, interest gleaming in his eyes. "Yes?"

"Yes." She licked her lips. "It's more Shield Power than fighting."

Did his gaze soften a little? Was there pride in it? She hoped so. "Dreeths have focused on us the last three battles. And we've killed all three." His eyebrows came down. "In different ways."

"I know. I don't get caught up in the fighting—lust—as

you do. I've been experimenting." Anything to keep deep panic from freezing her. "If…when…you must go and I must stay, I will train others."

"Marrec!" The shout came from Koz. He peeked inside the tent. "I have the man here," Koz elbowed Faucon, "who will answer some estate management questions for us."

Marrec's attention immediately veered from her, fastened on the men outside, on his priority of tending their estate. Calli couldn't fault him for it.

"I'll be right there," he said, then whispered, "I'll see you later."

He was gone before she could reply.

An hour and a half later, she stood in a landing area and watched her husband fly away.

"Hey, pretty lady." The words were Lladranan but lilted in an English accent. She turned to see Koz.

"Hey, Koz."

He jerked his head toward the main camp. "Wanna beer?"

Sensing nothing but sympathetic companionship coming from him, she smiled and kept her mouth from trembling, sniffed back tears. "Sounds great." She walked with him along an angle to his pavilion, realizing it was made of the best materials and had several rooms, was actually larger than her and Marrec's tent.

A man sat on a stool outside the pavilion with a whetstone, sharpening a sword. He had a number of weapons beside him, including a long fancy dagger that seemed to glow. She blinked, tilted her head to try and hear what sort of Song emanated from it. Not Lladranan.

"Medieval Damascene," he said. "I—uh—brought it with me. Marian didn't know." A flow of embarrassment came from Koz. Now that she'd spent more than a few minutes alone in his company, she realized she could sense his emotions easier than any true Lladranan's.

Even Calli had heard of Damascus steel. "Wow," she said.

"Yeah, I'm the envy of all." His smile flashed as they entered his pavilion. "I was lucky enough to bring plenty of jewels and some gold with me from Earth. I've got a nice rich estate now." He nodded to the man outside. "But only one Chevalier to fly under my banner."

"Your Maserati banner," she said.

He grinned. "Guilty." A hint of wistfulness shadowed his eyes. "I could never drive on Earth."

He'd had multiple sclerosis there, she knew, when he was Andrew. Here he had a healthy body. "Volarans are better than cars any day."

Laughing, he said, "You got that right." Then he went to a chest and hummed a couple of bars of "I Can't Get No Satisfaction," to release a lock, she realized. He held up a bottle of beer and she gasped, was pulled to the small chest.

"My last one."

"Don't waste—"

But she was too late, he'd snapped off the top. He offered the bottle to her. Just the scent of it took her back to dusty rodeo days. Man. She couldn't refuse. She should. Couldn't. Tipping the bottle, she let cool beer trickle into her mouth, coat her tongue. Oh, yeah! The taste was all Earth, and for that she closed her suddenly damp eyes and savored. But she only took a swallow, then handed the bottle back to him.

He was still grinning.

"I like the ale better, here, too," she said.

He wiped the top of the bottle on his shirt, and guzzled, smacked his lips, then shrugged. "I do, too."

They laughed together. Gesturing with the bottle, he pointed to fat pillows made of plush rugs on the floor. "Nice," she said.

"I remember my Arabian Nights." He struck a pose. "I think I've already started a trend. Faucon was in here, took one look and left to commission some."

Calli sighed and sank onto one of the pillows. "Really nice."

"Thanks." He sat, too, stretched out his legs and crossed them at the ankle. "I've got it lucky."

"I don't think so," she said.

Once more he smiled, eyes crinkling. "Maybe not at first, but now, yeah." He angled the bottle to her, then toward the encampment outside the door. "I wasn't really Summoned, so I don't have to worry about fulfilling any quest."

The taste in her mouth turned bitter. She stood.

He did, too. "Don't let all this stuff get you down, Calli. You're doing great."

She forced a smile. She didn't think so.

"Really." He turned around and swiped a water bladder. "Here. I set up a little brewery on my estate. Finest ale you'll find on Lladrana."

"Different people have different tastes."

He cocked his head. "Very true. But by any standard, you, Calli Torcher Gardpont, have made the grade."

Her smile felt strained. She didn't think so. Her husband had left her, her daughter avoided her. All she'd wanted was love, and that still escaped her. "Thanks for the ale."

With an inclination of his head, Koz opened the pavilion's flap so she could leave. "You're very welcome."

As she walked back to her own three-room tent, she kept her smile in place and returned greetings, both human and volaran. Still, emptiness was a big hole in her chest. Their squires weren't near her tent, though other guards were and she nodded to them and went inside to an equally empty place.

What the hell, she uncapped the bota and swigged. The ale was perfect.

Marrec would have thought so, too. But he wasn't there to share the drink or conversation, stories of the day. Or love.

As Marrec flew toward home, he noticed he was…lonely. He kept peering through the Distance Magic bubble, looking for Calli. This was the first time they'd be apart for any appreciable time. They'd just developed their partnership…which seemed a little shaky right now. Because they disagreed.

He was right. He didn't like leaving Diaminta more than a day and a night alone without her parents, and those damn nobles were keeping Calli, at least, tied down with their demands. He wasn't used to being high status and he had little tolerance for their interminable meetings. If he had to fly to battle, they could direct him as they always had. He didn't want to learn strategy.

He wanted to learn ranching. To make sure he was equal with Calli in that. She'd had a ranch on Exotique Terre, but she wouldn't know Lladranan methods. He wanted to learn farming, how to ensure their estate produced enough to feed them and the people who lived on it. And it was best to do this before winter. But Calli's sad Song…he shook his head. Someone had to take care of their child. He had to prepare for the future.

Now that he was sure he had a future. He was doing this for Calli, too. But Dark Lance did not speak to him all the way home, kept his equine thoughts distant—except for one time when the volaran wondered what was happening at the camp.

When Marrec landed and strode up to the door of his home, and his daughter held out her arms in welcome and said, "Pa. Pa. Pa," he knew he'd made the only choice he could have. Even though her little face wrinkled and she looked around, searching for Calli. Who wasn't with him.

That afternoon the alarms rang. Calli knew these bells now. A large retrousse rising in an area where they'd fought more than a half-dozen times over the last few weeks. She ran for her tent. Her squire and maid blocked the opening, arms crossed.

Her squire lifted an eyebrow. "You aren't thinking of fighting, are you? Of being Shield to someone other than Marrec?"

It all came rushing back and hurt, hurt, hurt. Marrec wasn't just somewhere else in the camp. He was gone.

She pushed her voice past her clogged throat. "No."

Shouts came as volarans soared, flying to battle.

"No," she repeated. She turned away from the tent. "Some new volarans flew in last night from Volaran Valley. I'll go work with them, teach them the basics of partnering, determine what sort of person each would fit well with."

She reached the large corral that was set aside for wild volarans—they always knew to land here rather than into other areas where the partnered volarans had formed their own herd. She blinked as she saw Lord Veenlit and his Chevalier, Raoul Lebeau, leaning on the fence. Veenlit pointed to a pretty buckskin mare.

"I thought you'd be fighting," she said.

"Not our rotation." Veenlit smiled.

He lied. The fact was that he didn't intend to fight, seemed to think that renting space to the Marshalls and Chevaliers was his contribution to the effort to free Lladrana from the Dark. For a northern lord, he was offhand about protecting his lands, but this portion was miles away from his manor in a rich, secure mountain valley.

After she'd walked a few yards away from them along the fence, the volarans came over to her, pushing each other to greet her.

Hello, Volaran Exotique, the buckskin said.

Hello, Calli! said a bay stallion.

Hello, whispered the third, a black, smaller than the other two, ducking her head, then bringing it up to look at her with large, dark eyes. This one was a sweetheart, too gentle to fly to battle.

Salutations, winged ones, she said.

They liked that, and she took turns palming their lips, stroking their faces and necks. To Calli's disgust, the two men sauntered up to her.

"You have a way with volarans," Veenlit said, reaching out to stroke the buckskin's nose. She backed away.

Calli lifted her eyebrows. "Probably why I'm called the Volaran Exotique."

A spark of annoyance showed in his eyes before he suppressed it and smiled—too widely. "I could use a couple of fresh volarans."

She played ignorant. "I thought if you wanted to increase your volaran herd all you had to do was Sing them from the wild." Like any volaran would come to his call.

He shrugged heavy shoulders. "Hadn't thought much about it until you all came camping. One of these…"

"These?" She widened her eyes as if in surprise. "But these have come to be trained as war volarans." Then she smiled warmly. "Of *course,* I'll work with you and them in the fighting patterns." Now she lifted and dropped a shoulder. "I'm not on rotation to fight. We can begin immediately." With a sweeping glance up and down them, she said, "I bet I could have you two in the thick of battle and slaughtering horrors within a week."

They'd backed away from the corral. She followed. "So, I've never asked, do either of you speak telepathically to your volarans?" She hadn't made time to visit with the local volarans, something she noted she'd have to do.

They both stared at her blankly. "What are you talking about?"

Letting surprise creep into her voice, Calli said, "We've found that about ten percent of the Marshalls and Chevaliers can mind-speak with volarans. We call their language Equine."

Veenlit grunted. "Thought that was only crazy black-and-white Power, like that Bastien has." His nostrils flared. "Castle matters. We don't hold with that weird new stuff here."

"Hmm," Calli said. "As the volaran trainer, I'm not sure I want to send any of the winged steeds into battle with someone who isn't strong in Equine. I don't think I've seen either of you fly, either."

"Volarans shouldn't be just for battle. The beasts have other uses around a manor, too. You don't know anything about how life is lived outside the Castle."

Anger rose. "That's pretty much right. All my experience has been in training volarans for partnering Marshalls and Chevaliers in battle and fighting the horrors. I haven't seen much peace here." Even now her husband was taking care of their estate and she was dealing with these sleazeballs who thought posturing was as important as fighting.

Turning her back on them, she went into the corral, smoothed a hand over the buckskin. The mare bent her neck around Calli in a volaran embrace, looked at her with big brown eyes. *I will be an excellent battlemare.* Her ears twitched nervously, but determination radiated from her.

I will find you the right partner.

The bay pushed forward. *I will be an excellent battle stallion.*

Calli moved to him, ran her hand down his strong neck, tested the flavor of his Song. Yes. *Fly to the Castle and speak to the Chevalier trainer there.*

The black dipped her head. *And me?*

If you wish to stay with people—

I do! Good food. Warm stables. She licked her lips, then sent a sideways glance. *Strong stallions.*

Calli laughed. *Then wait for Bastien to return from battle. He would cherish you and welcome you on his estate.*

I came for you.

The simple statement had Calli fighting back tears. So

teary today. Too many raw emotions. Here was someone who wanted her. Just her. No demands.

Thunder trumpeted. *I am here, too!*

Keeping her face in the black mare's fragrant neck, Calli said, *This is no place for a gentle soul like yourself. I will take you with me when I next go to my manor.*

With a nicker and a lift of the wings, the bay flew away to the Castle.

Both men had watched in narrow-eyed, cross-armed silence.

"As you say, I'm most concerned with fighting the Dark." She frowned, honestly curious. "Tell me, Lord Veenlit, when was the last time you lost people to the Dark?"

Again his fake sad expression. "I lost a village last year. Terrible, terrible."

His Song pulsed and she caught a strain of terrified notes and the fact that after he'd heard of the massacre, he'd reinforced the walls of his castle.

"The land will be very fertile after this is done," he said.

He seemed to realize he'd shocked her and set his face in sorrowful lines. "I grieve for all the lives we've lost."

Yeah, right.

That night, Marian visited Calli in her tent. Did the Circlet know she missed Marrec so much her bones ached?

Marian tilted her head as if listening to the Songs in the tent. "You are very bonded to Marrec. Perhaps *too* bonded."

"You mean I'm holding on too tightly to him."

"Yes, and your daughter."

Calli had wondered about that, whether her need for Diaminta scared the little girl.

"Loosen up the reins." Marian tilted her head. "You love the volarans, but you aren't binding them so closely to you and don't accept very tight bonds from them. Maybe you can do the same with your family."

Calli's smile was small and tight. "I've never had someone love me...or a child that *could* love me. I want it too badly." In the shadows, she could say this.

Marian sighed. "One of those 'easy to say, hard to do' things."

"Guess so."

Her smile rueful, Marian said, "Then I wonder about bringing up one of the subjects I came to talk to you about—bloodbonding with me and Alexa."

28

Pulse skittering, Calli said, "Too much for me right now." These women would know her failures intimately. She couldn't bear that, she just couldn't spread her focus now...all right, that was a rationalization...but would she tie the other Exotiques to her as strongly as she had Marrec? That would be wrong.

Marian dropped to a small chair, watching her with silent sympathy. "You've read Alexa and my Lorebooks of Exotiques. You know it wasn't easy for us, either."

Calli made a noncommittal noise. Even scrupulous Marian probably hadn't included all her doubts and fears and failures. Who would? Though the visual "recording" of her time in the Dark nest embedded in the book was enough to give anyone the cold grue. "Don't you think I'd make the same mistake with you?"

Chuckling, Marian said, "Alexa and I are strong, I think we'd erect mind shields, if necessary. And I think we'd all benefit."

"I can't," Calli said.

"Okay." Marian smiled as she switched to English. "Not yet." Her eyes turned wistful, "Though it would be good to have another female friend I could depend upon implicitly."

Calli jerked a nod. She'd like the women as sisters, too, but not...right...now. She had too many people to deal with on a personal basis as it was. Crossing to the small liquor cabinet, she opened a side of the split top. Despite the pressure, the four large bottles of alcohol were nearly full. Neither she nor Marrec were big drinkers. A little unusual in both the world of rodeo competition and the fighters of Lladrana. She shrugged off the little insight. Which reminded her of what they had in common. "White wine, right?"

"You have it?" Marian sounded pleased.

"Yes. White wine, the mead you like, the ale I like and the ale Marrec prefers." Their squires had done well. She saw the gleam of metal and squinted, reached into the cavity and pulled out a purple tin chased with silver, opened it and smiled at Marian. "And tea."

Marian chuckled. "Alexa isn't here, but I'm sure she appreciates the thought."

Raising her eyebrows, Calli said, "Why isn't Alexa here? You don't want to intimidate me by double-teaming?"

"One of the reasons. Also, she's just plumb tuckered out from today's battle. One of the dreeths got too close." Marian's gaze slanted at Calli, back. "It couldn't hurt if she was bonded to another Shield."

Calli's hand trembled as she clinked bottle against wine-glass. She finished pouring and stoppered the bottle, set it deliberately down and poured ale for herself. With equal care, she handed Marian the wine. "Not fair."

"No." Marian sipped.

"Every Shieldmarshall looks out for Alexa."

"It's not the same. They can't possibly anticipate her."

Calli laughed. "And you think I could?"

Marian shrugged. "Better than they."

Sitting on a camp stool and stretching her legs, Calli said, "Topic closed."

"Okay." Marian circled her finger around the rim of her glass. "Second issue. The Snap."

Calli choked, coughed. Marian put a hand on her back and hummed two notes and everything was fine. Nifty trick.

"Jaquar and I have learned more about it from studying the very meager information we've gathered from *everyone,* including the Friends of the Singer's Library."

"But not the Singer herself?"

Marian frowned. "Not her, nor her personal library."

"Bet that's like a burr under the saddle, and collecting all that info musta plumb tuckered you out, Prof."

Grinning, Marian lifted her glass. "I can't help it, sometimes. I was born in Colorado, too, ya know, and something about you just brings out the ol' western slang."

"Whatever meager western slang you ever knew."

Marian laughed. "Got me there." She took another swallow of wine and when she looked up, her expression was serious. "But you can't deter me from speaking about the Snap, either. Sorry to ruffle your delicate sensibilities."

"Yeah, sure." Calli shifted, brought in and extended her legs again. "What's it like?" she whispered.

"Like those old-time cartoons where someone hooks a performer onstage and yanks them behind the curtain. You know, time's up."

Calli exhaled slowly. "Oh-kay." She put grit in her words. "But Alexa didn't actually go into the dimensional corridor, and you went back."

"I had my brother, whom I love."

"And managed to get him and return. Good going."

A corner of Marian's mouth kicked up. "Thanks. But it sure didn't work out like I thought it would."

"Got that. But I study, too. You weren't *quite* as bonded to people here as I am."

"No. But the Snap *will* come, Calli. Don't think you can duck it. It's Mother Earth's call, the primal Song of your home planet."

"I won't go back."

"No beloved relatives?"

Calli shrugged. "I only have my father." Her laugh was uglier than she'd intended.

Marian frowned. "Careful, I think unresolved issues can haul your ass back, too." She smiled with an edge. "I speak from experience."

Sighing, Calli said, "Lucky Alexa. No unresolved issues."

"Yes."

They shared a moment of silence. Both of them drank and this time Calli actually tasted the mellow ale. It was good, and the small warm path it took down her throat and into her belly was plenty nice, too. The small gaps in the tent flap showed white. The moon had risen and was painting the space outside her door silver. "So what's the deal with the Snap?"

"As we all know, we have previously had no idea when the Snap will occur."

Calli perked up. "You think you can predict when it happens? That would be *big* progress."

"We think we might have deduced one component."

"And that is?"

"The Snap happens after you have completed your task."

Muscles tensed. "I thought the task was something the Marshalls gave Alexa."

"Apparently not. There has been a specific requirement that an Exotique must fulfill."

"Like Alexa finding the way to make new fence posts."

"And the Exotique before us teaching the Singer good English."

"Huh."

"We extrapolate that the task is set by—" Marian coughed "—the need of the planet Amee herself."

"Wow."

"Yes."

"And though there might be one major duty, Amee, shall we say, is not averse to getting as much as she can for the Power expended to bring us here."

As much bang for her buck as she could. "So something big is still waiting for me." She'd felt it all along.

"Yes."

The first night and day home kept Marrec too busy to think of anything but work around the estate, presenting him with problems he had to solve—or at least consider before he figured out the right thing to do. He told himself that Calli was surrounded by excellent guards and good friends in the Exotiques. Many more Powerful than he would protect her.

But by the time evening had fallen on the second day, he'd caught up on all pressing matters and fallen into the slower rhythm of country life.

Marrec sang Diaminta to sleep, then ate a light meal and went to his bedroom—the master suite. Empty of his Pairling. He hurt. Why had he done this to them? But it was the *right* thing to do. No matter how safe behind the lines the encampment was, it was no place for a child, let alone an infant.

He stripped and showered, firmly closing the images of Calli and the hot spring in the conservatory from his mind. Though he preferred bathing, he didn't see himself using the pool anytime soon. Not without her.

His body yearned for hers. For sex. He'd gotten spoiled. As an independent Chevalier, sex had been irregular for him, with long periods of celibacy. He preferred to save his money than pay for sex, and other female Chevaliers only occasionally indicated that they'd care to spend a night with him. Now he wanted more. He wanted Calli.

Restless, he dressed and wandered the large and echoing house. They still had only a few servants, though he wanted to hire more guards, especially for when he was away.

Before he'd had time to settle, a knocking came on the front door of the house. Stretching his senses, he felt a surprising spurt of pleasure when he realized that Jaquar and Marian were visiting. He hurried to the door. "Salutations," he said.

Jaquar bowed and Marian curtsied, dazing Marrec's wits
a little. He still wasn't used to Powerful people treating him
with respect.

They entered and Marian looked around with approval.
"You've done wonders here."

Heat flushed under his skin. "Thank you."

"And on the estate as well," Jaquar said. "I can sense
when land is tended and nurtured, and the Songs of the
people are cheerful." They'd reached the one good parlor
now and Marrec issued them in, poured brandy for himself
and Jaquar and wine for Marian. He knew what drink they
preferred and that pleased him. He, too, was making new
and Powerful friends, finding the rich and noble weren't so
different after all. Though he sipped his brandy much
slower than Jaquar. Marrec wasn't used to strong, expensive
drink either.

Marian sat on a new love seat, her robes arranging themselves around her. "Yes, this estate is obviously prospering
under your hands—and Calli's."

Marrec stiffened. He should have remembered that they
would be Calli's friends more than his own. "We have a
child, and a battle encampment is no place for her." He
swept his hand around them, irritated that he was defending himself. "And responsibilities to our home."

"I know what it is to protect a beloved one, while loving
something else, too. It tears you apart."

He hadn't wanted to think of that, had shut his emotions
down with regard to himself and Calli.

"Calli has responsibilities to all of Lladrana, to Amee
itself. Don't you think it hurt her for you to choose your

child and your land over helping your Pairling? She has a problem believing that people can love her."

Marrec had never thought of that. His gut burned. So did his eyes. "I'm not going to talk to you about Calli. But you are welcome to spend the night."

"Ahem." Jaquar cleared his throat. "We didn't come to discuss responsibilities. You and Calli gave us several dreeth teeth and claws to commission into magical objects that would sell for a high price. We have deducted our price and now return the rest for you to trade." He waved a hand and a bulging saddlebag appeared on a table. "I suggest you take them to Troque City near the escarpment to the City States." He drank, then finished. "I mentioned them to a colleague of mine and the merchants there are expecting them." He glanced at the bag. "The objects should command a very high price. Enough for you to hire a short-term caretaker and nanny."

So much for not lecturing about responsibilities. "A child needs a parent. Diaminta is accustomed to having Calli and me near, seeing us each day, which would not be the case were I to stay at the camp. We are on four-day rotation."

"A wife needs her husband," Marian said gently.

That ripped at his heart. At least they didn't point out that without Calli, he'd never have had an estate.

"Wrong," Jaquar said.

Marrec blinked.

Marian rose and put her glass back on the liquor cabinet. "We are linked with Calli in some measure because we participated in the Summoning and the Healing, and that means we hear your Song better than most."

"You are a very determined man," Jaquar said. "You would have earned land of your own."

But not an estate like this, and Marrec loved this place fiercely, as fiercely as his daughter.

As fiercely as he loved his wife. But his daughter and the land needed him more.

Both Circlets' gazes were fixed on his face. He thought his expression was as impassive as always, but they *could* hear his Song.

Finally, Jaquar said, "Since you wish to spare your daughter the knowledge of the absence of her parents as much as possible, I suggest we travel to Troque tonight—a merchant will be available to bargain for our wares. We can return at dawn, before she awakes."

It was sensible.

"I'll watch Diaminta," Marian said, her face lighting in the way of women thinking of babes. "After all, you and Calli intend to ask us to be godparents, um, *parenties* for her, don't you?"

"Ayes. I didn't know that Calli had told you."

Marian's smile was warm. "She mentioned it in passing, though it's only logical. We're the least likely of all your friends to be harmed in this battle with the Dark." Her expression turned serious and she reached for Jaquar's hand. "We assure you that...that..."

Jaquar said, "Should Diaminta come to us, we will always put her welfare before anything else."

Cold touched the base of Marrec's spine. "Thank you."

Marian smiled. "Now, you two go take care of your business."

29

A couple of hours later, a dazed Marrec stood in the Troque Guildhall's Landing Area, Dark Lance's reins in his hand. The master merchant himself had negotiated with them, and they'd gotten a staggering price for their items. Marrec was stunned at the amount he received for magical amulets, had to dismiss himself behind a screen so he could place the rare jewels in a money belt wrapped close to his body. They wouldn't go in pouch or pockets. His wits hadn't quite grasped the wealth he now had or exactly what he could do with it.

Jaquar leaned on the open gate of the paddock. His volaran was the only steed within. "I have a colleague here. I'm sure you'd be welcome to stay overnight."

The last thing Marrec wanted to do was to spend time in a Sorcerer's home and be bored by talk of various obscure spellsongs that had little use to a Chevalier.

"Thank you," he said, "but, no. I've traded in this town before, I know the Chevalier places."

"Very well. My colleague's tower is some ways outside of town. I'll meet you at your estate tomorrow morning."

"Good." Marrec hesitated, then offered his hand. He'd enjoyed Jaquar's company, the way they'd worked well together to bring the price of their goods up. The evening had been the most pleasurable he'd had with another man in a long time.

Grasping his hand, Jaquar gave it a firm squeeze. "I enjoyed our bargaining."

"Me, too."

Jaquar adjusted his dreeth-skin hat. "I'll see you tomorrow."

"Yes." Marrec eyed the hat. He'd like one, too.

Jaquar opened his mouth, then shut it, shook his head. "Women are a puzzle, even for Sorcerers. I'll not give you any advice."

Marrec was thankful for that. He nodded and walked away, leading Dark Lance. The inn he usually patronized was shabbier than he remembered, but still close to the more expensive tavern and inn that most Chevaliers frequented when they were in town. At least he knew the prices and services here, so he got a room to himself and stabling for Dark Lance.

But once he was in his room, he was restless again. He definitely was unaccustomed to being alone now that he'd wed, and being solitary was different than being lonely. So he clumped down the stairs and headed toward the tavern.

This place, too, wasn't quite as he recalled, but narrowing his eyes, Marrec figured the change was in him more than the inn. Raucous laughter came from a table, one voice lifted, demanding more ale. Marrec recognized the voice and saw three Chevaliers, all men, sitting and drinking, with a deck of cards on the table. They were all independents, as he'd been, and he hadn't spoken with any of them for a while. He wended his way to the table.

"Ay, Marrec!" Zhardon, an affable moon-faced Chevalier, stood and pounded Marrec on the back, grinning. "Long time since we've had a drink together." He nudged Marrec in the ribs with his elbow and winked. "Got a whole lot better to be doing than hanging with us, eh? Beautiful new wife, rich new estate."

"A kid, even," Luc said, finishing his drink and wiping his sleeve across his mouth. He smiled. He'd lost a tooth since Marrec had sat with them last. But Marrec had seen the flash of bitterness in his eyes.

"Guess you're here for the same reason we are. To get a better price for our portion of horror kills?" Gentry asked smoothly. He was better educated than them all, but his Song held resentment, too.

Marrec wasn't about to tell them that he'd traded with the master merchant himself, that he'd received a fortune for his kills—his and Calli's. Odd how fortunes begat when you had a big stake. He dropped into the open chair.

"Barkeep, an ale for my friend, here, and another round for us," Zhardon ordered, grinned at Marrec and winked again. "You can pay for it."

"Looks like he can," Gentry said. "Nice leathers."

The others checked out what Marrec was wearing. It was one of his dreeth-skin leather sets and didn't show wear, and he had *two* sets now, and two of regular cowhide. When he'd once only had one very mended set, the same as these men.

Zhardon leaned closer, his breath warm and smelling of ale. "So, tell us of the beautiful new Volaran Exotique."

"Lucky dog." Luc finished his drink and belched. "Damn lucky, to get that woman." His stare fixed on Marrec as he lowered his voice. "Strange-looking woman."

"But in a fascinating sort of way." Gentry lounged back, arm across the top rung of his chair. "They *say* that she has fascinating ways in bed, too."

"Calli?" Marrec stiffened, grabbed the wooden handle of his mug and downed a gulp, the rawness of the brew lay on his tongue.

Zhardon chuckled, drank, too. "All the Exotiques. Beautifully strange or strangely beautiful. That Circlet..." He shook his head. "Hair with colors of deep fire."

The pretty lady who was now watching over Marrec's child, whose eyes had gone soft with pleasure at the thought of being a *parentie* to his daughter.

"Is it true?" Gentry's smile sharpened.

Almost, Marrec wished that he'd taken Jaquar up on his offer. And why was he now wanting to be bored out of his skull with the Circlet and his sorcerous colleague? No, that wasn't where he wanted to be either. Home, with Calli and Diaminta. Simply, home.

He looked at these faces around the table, men he'd spent hours with, men who'd mirrored his own station and beliefs...once. "A woman's a woman."

"'Cept you're bonded with this one. Just think, loving every night." Zhardon sighed, saw his new mug of ale and his expression lightened.

"A plum estate," Gentry said.

"Zhiv," Luc said at the same time. He riffled the grimy deck of cards with his thumbnail. "Care to play?"

"No, thanks," Marrec said. "I was lucky Calli chose me."

"Very true, and a good thing you bonded with her," Gentry said, gesturing Luc to deal.

A note in his voice sent Marrec on alert. "Ayes?"

Luc finished laying out the cards. "Heard you planned on taking four-day rotation, lucky bastard to be able to do that, I'm on two." He fanned his cards. "We all are, to make more zhiv. But you're leaving your lady at camp." He shook his head, at the cards or Marrec's foolishness.

"Some of my zhiv will have to go to a better tent," Gentry grumbled, his gaze flashed up to Marrec. "So I can entertain. Camp's good that way, keeping the women on-site. They get bored, too."

Looking up from his cards, Zhardon met Marrec's eyes with a warning in his. "Saw that Raoul guy, that local Chevalier who didn't never come to the Castle and fly with us, move in on your lady, better watch out for that."

Marrec stood, put a few coins on the table. "I'll leave you to your game."

"Ayes, strut right out of here the way you came, my lord noble rich landowner. Don't think we'll be seeing much of you again," Luc said. He didn't even look up from his hand.

He didn't sleep well. The bed was lumpy and had a funny scent, though no fleas or lice or bedbugs. The sign outside the inn creaked in rising wind. Sometime in the early morning a light rain came—with frinks. The sound of the metallic worms skittering against the roof made Marrec's hair rise. He'd gotten accustomed to living in areas where no frinks sent by the Dark fell with the rain. If any Exotique had visited Troque, none of them had been near this section.

His mind nagged at what the Chevaliers had implied about Calli and other men and jealousy gnawed. But nothing had changed. Calli and he were bonded. She wouldn't, couldn't betray him with another man. Could she?

But she wouldn't be disloyal. No. One of the qualities that rose from every Exotique like perfume from their skin was their absolute loyalty.

That was the knot between Calli and himself, her loyalty to Lladrana, his loyalty to their child and their home.

Finally he dozed near dawn and didn't wake until bright sunlight bore in through the window. He swore. He'd wanted to be gone by now. No doubt Jaquar had left at dawn as they'd agreed.

After a tasteless but filling meal, he paid his shot and walked toward the stables, looking around the courtyard one last time. He wouldn't stay here again. Or at the inn where he'd met Zhardon, Luc and Gentry. He could afford better.

He grunted and stretched. *Good morning, Dark Lance.*

The volaran shifted in his stall. *Good morning, Marrec. We are late. I should have awakened you earlier.*

Probably.

But you needed the sleep. Been an eventful week. His tone dropped to a lower note. The volaran, of course, disapproved of Marrec's decision.

Your feed was good? He'd paid for the best the inn could offer. Dark Lance deserved better.

The volaran snorted. *Adequate. I am the only volaran here. All the rest are horses. You must find better lodgings next time.*

Marrec gritted his teeth. *Understood. We'll leave as soon as possible.*

Perhaps.

I didn't think you wanted to stay here any longer. Outside the stables, warm, volaran-scented air wafted to him, comfortingly usual, so he allowed himself to consider that last ego-pricking remark of Luc's. Had he been filled with hubris at becoming a landowner, strutting around as accused? He winced.

"P-p-please, L-l-lord G-g-g-gard-d-p-p-p-pont," a whispery, young voice said.

Marrec was so stunned by the title applied to *him,* and not sarcastically, that he stopped before entering the stables. A small, thin boy of about eight dressed in worn clothes too big for him watched tensely from the dimness inside. He'd placed himself so that there were several avenues of escape. Marrec stopped the impatient words he was ready to snap because his brooding had been disturbed.

"Yes?"

The boy swallowed, licked his lips, said something so fast and brokenly that Marrec didn't understand. "Can you repeat that?"

"I-I-I h-heard you and the Ex-exot-exotique w-w-were l-l-l-looking f-for ch-children t-t-to ad-d-d-dopt. T-t-take m-m-me!" He shut his mouth, looking deeply disappointed at himself. Pitiful. His body trembled. He clenched his fists and stood straight as if to deny the shivers of fright or excitement.

Marrec stared. This had probably cost the boy all his courage, guts Marrec could only admire. There was something about the aspect of the boy… "Come out in the light so I can see you."

"I-I-I m-m-must d-d-d-d—"

"Spit it out, lad!"

"D-d-duties!"

Marrec nodded, stepped inside and glanced around the stable. It was painstakingly clean. The horses looked well cared for. "I'll help you with whatever needs to be done."

The boy's mouth fell open and he stared.

Marrec raised a hand to draw the boy out into the sunlit courtyard and the child flinched. A low burn began in Marrec's belly. The situation of this boy, alone when everyone else was eating, no doubt living in an empty stall when there was one available, echoed Marrec's own memories. But Marrec thought that he, himself, might have had it better than this youngster.

With his hand open and flat, Marrec walked out to the courtyard, gestured to the boy for him to come. Phrasing questions to keep the boy's responses short to avoid his terrible stutter would be a challenge. Marrec inclined his head, touched fingers to his heart. "I promise to help you. There's a bench right here, in the warm sunlight. Come on out." Marrec sat and waited.

The youngster's face set in lines of resigned despair. He sidled to the edge of the threshold, standing in the sunlight, but still looked as if he might bolt. Across the yard and into the inn or into the town. Back into the stables to a hidey-hole Marrec was sure the boy had, or scrambling up a ladder to the loft.

Again Marrec stared. The lad's skin was paler than a true

Lladranan. His face was shaped more like northeastern Llad-ranans, more like the folk that Marrec grew up with than the people here in central Lladrana. Something else was differ-ent. He had dark hair, but not quite the black of a Lladranan. More like a dark brown. His eyes were a lighter brown, too.

"What are you?" Marrec said, and grimaced at the rudeness.

The boy swallowed, as if he'd heard such a question all too often in his brief life. He curved in on himself, ducking his head and hunching his shoulders as if he expected a blow—or more than one, a beating.

"I-I-I'm a b-b-bastard. M-m-mother was f-f-from S-s-sill Est-t-tate, c-c-came h-here t-t-to w-work, s-s-said s-s-sire f-f-from B-b-biod-d-dono."

Biodono was one of the City States to the east of Lladrana. It was easy to understand what had happened. A merchant guest visiting the inn lay with a woman, got her pregnant, then returned to his home, unknowing or uncaring that he'd left a child.

Lladranans weren't often kind to children of mixed blood. Not even Exotique children—unless the blood was noble and several generations had passed to make the family acceptable.

"Where are your parents?"

"M-m-mother's d-d-dead. F-f-f—"

"Wait." Marrec raised a hand to halt him. "Why don't you nod or shake your head."

Looking sad, again as if this was an all too common request, the child nodded.

Best get the brutal questions done first. "Did you ever know your father?"

The boy shook his head.

"Do you know his name, station or direction?"

A hunch of the shoulder and a shake of the head.

"Your mother never told you anything?"

His mouth twisted. "S-s-she l-left a p-p-paper."

Marrec sighed. "What kind of paper...wait, an official paper?"

A head shake. "F-f-father's n-name and c-city."

"What's your name?"

"J-j-jet-t-t-y-yer D-d-d-e-s-s-sill-p-p."

"Jetyer Desillp."

Jetyer nodded.

Desillp must have been the name his mother had used, coming from the Sill Estate where she'd been a peasant. At least Marrec had the name of his town. His lost town. "And you'd rather be Jetyer Gardpont?" Marrec asked softly.

A strong nod now.

"I see." A couple of moments passed as he gazed at the boy, his lighter skin, hair and eyes. A notion bloomed inside Marrec. This is what a child born of himself and Calli might look like. Maybe. His heart clenched. Here was a youngster who could be a son.

A boy with the guts to approach a complete stranger with a huge request. A request, not a plea. A boy with the determination to get ahead in life. A boy quick enough to dodge the odd blow, smart enough to have escape routes and hidey-holes.

And perhaps Marrec was doing too much looking and not enough anything else. "Can you take my hand, please, to see how our Songs merge? I promise I won't hurt you."

30

Fear and hope warred in Jetyer's eyes. Marrec vowed that he'd see the boy well set whatever happened.

Jetyer threw back his shoulders, stepped out of the stables and into the bright light. His hair showed an even lighter reddish tint. He had a few little spots of brown on his nose and cheeks. Squinting, Marrec saw that there were even a few hairs of silver at each temple. From what he knew of the City States, their Power wasn't so openly shown on their head as in Lladrana. The strength of the boy's Power wouldn't be obvious.

Once again Marrec held out his hand, leaned out on the bench until he was slightly off balance and no threat to the boy. Jetyer set his grubby fingers in Marrec's palm. At his touch, Marrec closed his eyes and listened to the youngster's Song.

It was subtle, as if tightly reined in. Jetyer's shields—mental and emotional—were strong enough that Marrec would alert and hurt the child if he pushed past them. Shields Marrec was all too familiar with himself. Had he been closing himself off from Calli, trying to ignore the too-intimate Pairbond? Maybe, but this wasn't the time to think of that.

He sank into himself, *stretched* with his own Power to hear the beat and tune of Jetyer's Song. The melody lilted, deeper, darker than Marrec expected, and more complex. The clipping rhythm of horses wound in, the soul-yearning to experience wingbeats—volarans. Marrec smiled. It was a rare Lladranan child that didn't want to fly. But this was more, almost a *need* to fly, and that Marrec recognized as being much like himself, like Calli, like all the best Chevaliers.

Marrec listened and heard a faint lilting twist, the Song of the blood. Foreign blood. Calli had some counterpoints in her Song. Could Jetyer's fit with hers? With theirs?

The boy started to slide his fingers away. Marrec squeezed with his thumb. "One moment, please," he murmured. "Try to relax."

"W-we'r-re b-being w-w-w-watched!"

No doubt they looked strange, but any person with Power would realize what was going on—Marrec gauging a boy's Song. Still...*Dark Lance, here!* That should give busybodies something to think about.

I heard you! A high-toned, nonstuttering mental exclamation from Jetyer!

Good. Try to relax.

But the child couldn't. Dark Lance had exited the volaran stall and stable and come to stand near them. Jetyer's pulse skittered, his Song pulsed with awe, excitement, shattered into individual strident notes. Marrec released the young-ster's fingers, observing Dark Lance lowering his head to a frozen Jetyer and whuffling his hair. They'd drawn a small crowd in the courtyard, which would increase when word got round that a volaran was there to be admired.

Dark Lance stretched out a wing and there were "oohs." The volaran smirked.

Marrec sighed. He should have gone somewhere more upscale, more used to Chevalier and volarans—and nobles. He didn't have to watch his coins now, and he—and Jetyer—could have done without all the attention.

But since Dark Lance was here, checking out the boy, Marrec might as well consider the volaran's opinion. He looked into one large, dark eye. *What do you think of the boy as an addition to our family?* He really wasn't ready for more children, didn't think it wise, but he couldn't reject Jetyer, especially if the child's Song matched well with Calli's.

Dark Lance seemed to hear that last bit of Marrec's thought. *The boy would be good with Calli. Please her. You need to please her more.*

Marrec grunted, watched Jetyer raise a tentative hand to stroke Dark Lance's nose. The kid had guts and smarts and determination—and a well of more Power than Marrec would have thought. Like Marrec himself, the youngster could develop more, and perhaps his silver marks would widen. A lot about this boy reminded Marrec of himself. And would that mean that Calli would love the child? How much did she really "love" Marrec, and how much of her feeling of him was because of the Pairbond? His jaw clenched. Dis-tracted again by thoughts of his Pairling.

Looking around the courtyard, Marrec started to rise, to lead Jetyer someplace private where they could discuss the matter further, when he saw one of the tavern wenches wiping her hands on her stained apron and watching him with an eagle-eyed stare.

That made him think of something else. *Sinafinal, Tuckerinal!* he called with his mind, wondering if either being would answer him, where they might be—at the Castle, the Circlet Island Alf, or the camp....

We are here. The phrase echoed in his mind. Two hawks circled around the inn yard then settled on Dark Lance's back. The volaran sidestepped and grumbled.

With a half bow of his torso, Marrec mentally sent, *Salutations, feycoocus. This child has asked to become a son to Calli and me. Should I accept him?*

Sinafinal lifted a foot and used her beak to clean her claws. *Why do you ask us a question you already know the answer to?* But Tuckerinal flew down to land at the boy's feet and circle him, walking under Dark Lance's belly, causing another rumble of irritation from the volaran.

Jetyer had gone pale, eyeing the birds warily. Turning to meet Marrec's eyes, he said. "Wh-what are th-they?"

Feycoocus, Marrec replied in a loud mental voice.

The youngster jumped.

He will do well, Tuckerinal said.

He has acceptable Power for the child of an Exotique. You will teach him and raise him right.

I suppose, Marrec said.

Dark Lance snorted.

Turning her head to pin him with a narrowed gaze, Sinafinal said, *You will raise him to be a fine man.* Was that a prophecy? Or an order?

He didn't much like the latter, but these were magical beings and he'd called them. *Thank you.*

Sinafinal swept a look around the yard, stepped close to Tuckerinal when he flew from the ground to alight beside her. Dark Lance's back rippled. *We will stay to witness the adoption.*

By the Song, Marrec wasn't quite ready to move so quickly. Too late now. He gestured Jetyer to stand in front of him.

Lips pressed together, but with a long, sure stride, the boy did so.

Keeping his voice low, Marrec said, "The most important thing a son of mine must do is love his mother, Callista Mae Torcher Gardpont, the Volaran Exotique. Can you do that?" He hoped to the Song that this child wasn't one of those unfortunates that instinctively loathed Exotiques. Surely Dark Lance and the feycoocus wouldn't have approved the boy if he had been.

The child's breathing went ragged, he blinked rapidly and his lips trembled. "Ay-y-yes."

Marrec considered him, the rising Song. "We'll have to consult the medicas about your stammer."

Jetyer flinched.

The adoption, prompted Sinafinal.

After a deep breath, Marrec projected his voice. "It is my intention to adopt this boy, Jetyer Desillp as the son of myself, Marrec Gardpont and my wife, Callista Mae Torcher Gardpont. To show my good faith and assure you all, I will seal my oath with blood." He took out his new knife and made a slight cut in a vein of his right arm, flicked a few drops on the cobblestones near his feet where they dried quickly and remained bright red.

"Do you agree to be our son, to take the name Jetyer Gardpont?" he asked Jetyer.

"I ag-g-g-gree!"

Jetyer's eyes were wide, the rim of iris looking lighter than ever.

Marrec said, "I am willing to participate in a surface bloodbond with Jetyer, to bind him to myself and my Pairling, my Shield." With a touch of his mind, he searched for Calli, found her with Alexa in their tent. Good enough.

Calli, Pairling? he sent.

Marrec? What's happening? Your Song is so...so different!

He wanted to ask "different how?" but time was short and the way Jetyer was shaking, Marrec needed to get the bonding done quickly. He cleared the static from his mind, calmed his tone. *I have found a son for us.* His words rang like destiny between them.

Her Song dipped, soared, exploded into a thousand shards of tinkling notes, and he knew her eyes had filled with tears. *A son? Really?*

Yes.

Her next sending was tentative, as if she whispered. *We should not.*

Dark Lance and the feycoocus agree the boy is ours.

Boy?

Jetyer is his name, a bastard orphan of a Lladranan woman and a foreign man.

The boy flinched. How much was he hearing?

I cannot reject him, said Marrec.

Of course not. There was that spinning melody of her soft heart, her staunch loyalty. Her trust in him and his judgment.

Her need to be loved.

All harmonized in yearning, in acceptance.

Again Marrec focused on the boy, knew instinctively that the pale child quivering before him would love Calli.

Keep your mind with mine as I participate in a surface bloodbond.

Yes. She, too, was quivering. He sensed her sitting atop their bed, Alexa's arm steadying her. The Swordmarshall's Song came, too, excited and happy. *Do it!* Calli said.

He returned his awareness to Jetyer. "Do you agree to a surface bloodbond?" asked Marrec.

Standing tall, Jetyer held out his right wrist, his dominant hand. "I ag-gree!"

Marrec unrolled the boy's sleeve until the too-large cuff flopped over Jetyer's hand, then shoved the cuff up to expose an arm a shade paler than the child's hand. He met Jetyer's steady gaze. "Ready?"

Jetyer nodded.

Glad the knifepoint was sharp and that the cut would be relatively painless for Jetyer, Marrec nicked the boy's vein, swiped his own cut over the child's.

Memory images flashed before his eyes, Jetyer's, Calli's, his own, even one or two of Alexa's. His gut dipped, steadied, the boy stumbled, Marrec caught him close with one arm circling the child. "Easy," he said, frowning. The youngster's eyes had dampened.

The feycoocus cried out, shot into the sky, disappeared. Dark Lance trumpeted.

Jetyer continued to lean heavily against Marrec.

The tavern wench who'd been watching intently bustled forward. "Best get ya both up to your room. Get some good nourishing broth into ya."

"Good idea." Marrec frowned as he picked up the boy, who closed his eyes and went limp in his arms.

"He was mightly 'fraid of askin' ya to be his folk," the woman said. "Don' think he et much last night nor nuthin' t'day."

Marrec hoped that was the reason for the youngster's weakness, and not any memories of his own that the child had picked up or any images from Calli's strange land. They'd have to be careful of a full bloodbond. Something else to consult the medicas about.

Dark Lance whuffled comfortingly. *We should stay.*

Yes, Marrec agreed, minding his step up the steep stairs to the room he'd just vacated.

Marrec, what is wrong? Calli sounded nervous.

Overexcitement on our son's part, I think. He fainted.

He felt her touch on his mind, steadying him, warming him, then she reached further. *You are right. He is healthy.*

We'll stay here today and tonight. Jaquar and Marian are at our estate.

Alexa says they know what's going on.

Huh. More bonds of friendship. He assured himself that was good.

I'm coming! Give me exact directions—

No! Marrec settled the boy on the truckle bed that slid out from under his own. *Jetyer is resting. We don't know how long it will take for him to recover from the small bond.* From long-ago experience of a life Marrec had left behind him, Marrec eyed the boy. *I'll probably get some stew down him then he'll sleep all night.*

Oh. Her tone was stilted. Marrec reached for her Song, felt it tumbling with need—for him or the boy?—disappointment, traces of the previous anticipation. There *was* a slight emotional distance there, a wary note to her tune, a missing beat in their shared Song. *Alexa is joyful, too. We have agreed that I will meet you at home tomorrow morning.*

Did Alexa offer, or did you request leave? he asked.

Her hesitation answered him, but he already regretted bringing up her need to please.

I would have requested, but Alexa made the offer when I was still stunned by our small bonding ceremony. I am *going to request that Luthan Vauxveau and a Castle medica accompany me. Luthan can perform another bloodbond ceremony in our own village temple.*

Marrec blinked. He'd never have thought of that. Delight and...affection for Calli pulsed through their bond. He bowed his head as if she stood before him. *Good thinking, thank you.*

I must make the arrangements now. I will ask Luthan how much time off we all need for the bloodbond and recovery. Then I will inform the Lady Knight Swordmarshall.

He could imagine Thealia Germaine's reaction to the Volaran Exotique adopting another child while the rest of the world needed her. *Good luck. And thank you for bringing a medica, too.*

I have a feeling that both Luthan and the medica will be curious, as always, in Exotique affairs. Bide well, Pairling.

And you.

Midmorning the next day, Marrec stood in the town square, holding Jetyer's hand. Jaquar stood next to them, holding Diaminta. The boy looked paler than before—both from a scrubbing and renewed anxiety. He'd barely said a word, and once again a fine trembling coursed through his body. Marrec had brushed his mind with a reassuring touch, but it hadn't helped much to calm Jetyer.

He'd been fascinated with Diaminta, who had crawled over to him and climbed into his lap upon introduction, with the sure sense of being accepted. Jetyer had encircled the baby with both arms and raised a damp gaze to Marrec. "I will protect her always." Marrec hadn't thought that his son had realized he hadn't stammered. The moment had been precious and had made Marrec's heart ache that Calli hadn't been there to share it.

Diaminta's emotional hurts were healing well, to the point that she was being spoiled...by the males of the staff. She'd dimpled at Jaquar, but had ignored Marian all morning. Diaminta needed to have more women around her and spend more time with them. Still, it was better this morning for her to be held by a man.

When Marrec sensed Calli and Thunder nearing, he'd led a procession of most of his staff to the village, carrying a quiet Diaminta and walking hand in hand with Jetyer to the village. He was unsurprised to see that most of the town had turned out, dressed in their best, ringing the square. News traveled fast in villages.

Now they gasped as Thunder and Calli appeared, flying far ahead of four other volarans. Luthan Vauxveau and a medica—a man—and Alexa and Bastien. Marrec frowned.

Alexa and Bastien are additional witnesses, Calli said. She waved. *Good. Marian and Jaquar are there. You agree that they should be—um—parenties, just in case?*

He'd thought on it and since she felt strongly about this and he couldn't think of anyone he'd prefer—certainly not Lady Hallard or the folk who raised him, he answered, *Ayes*.

Good! She and Thunder descended in a landing more efficiently beautiful than any Marrec had seen. Thunder walked up to Jaquar. Diaminta squealed and patted his neck, tugged on his mane. "Thud! Thud!" The volaran winked at her but didn't nuzzle. Diaminta pouted.

Calli dismounted, greeted Marian and Jaquar, and brushed a kiss—and a loving mind-touch—on Diaminta. Their daughter's face crumpled and Calli circled around to face Marrec and Jetyer. A shock of deep attraction went through Marrec when he saw her fully. She was wearing a dark blue mage-gown that flowed from a split wide-legged skirt to full dress as he watched. Gold embroidery wound around the hem and up the sleeves, showing flying volarans. The robe emphasized the blue of her eyes and the gold of her hair. How had he kept himself away from her? Why?

Jetyer rippled with a shock from beside him, small fingers clamping hard around Marrec's. The boy was dazzled by Calli, and he *needed*. He yearned for the soft touch of a mother more than Marrec ever had.

31

Calli pressed a smiling kiss on Marrec's lips and their Songs met and knit and their Pair Song rose and it was sweet, sweet. Damn. He should have had her come to the inn last night, rented the adjoining room for them. He didn't know if he could last through a long ritual.

Then her smile widened—he wondered if he looked love struck—and she stepped back, moved in front of Jetyer and knelt until her eyes were level with the child's.

"I am Callista Gardpont," she said, her voice accented. "I will be your mother, if you please." With a slow gesture, she reached for his head, gleaming brown-red in the sun, stroked his hair. *Calm, dear boy,* Marrec heard her say, including him and Diaminta in the mind-speak. She sent comfort and approval to Jetyer and he released Marrec's hand, flung himself at Calli.

She held his thin body, stroked his back. Tears trickled

down her cheeks. *Their* Song billowed, shadowy visions of uncaring men in both their pasts merged, vanished in the knowing of like to like.

"Well," said another voice. "This shouldn't be difficult."

Marrec hadn't noticed Luthan Vauxveau landing, but the noble Chevalier stood in pristine white flying leathers before them. Marrec wondered what Luthan saw. He'd never known the cool nobleman well, but since the man had become the representative of the Singer, even more depth lingered behind his dark eyes and his streak of silver had widened. Marrec supposed that the Singer had chosen Luthan because he had prophetic moments.

Luthan gestured to the medica.

Calli tensed, sheltered the boy. "Shouldn't we be private—"

But the medica had already touched Jetyer's temple, sent a mind probe. The healer frowned. Luthan set a hand on the medica's shoulder and all of them connected mentally— Marrec and Calli and Diaminta and Jetyer and the medica and Luthan. The medica sucked in a harsh breath, dropped his hand and stepped back, shaking his hands and his head, flicking the Power that had risen and cycled through all of them from his fingertips.

"Interesting," Marian commented lightly.

Marrec blinked, noticing that she was dressed like Calli, in a dress identical except for the embroidered gold lightning bolts. He thought she was considering joining the connection and Jaquar clasped her around the elbow, holding her back.

Luthan stepped aside. He looked at the medica and spoke coolly. "It is my understanding that when the bloodbond is forged, Jetyer will have the mental and emotional support of the rest of his family in diminishing his stammer."

The medica nodded. "That's my reading of the situation, too. As the boy's life stabilizes, he will lose his affliction."

Calli stiffened.

"Shh," Marrec said.

"Release your soon-to-be-mother and we will proceed with the ritual," Luthan said.

"Oh, good," Marian said, rubbing her hands. Jaquar smiled and slipped his free arm around her waist.

Jetyer snuffled and let go of Calli. Marrec reached into a pocket and handed his son a fine linen handkerchief. The boy fingered the quality of it for a moment, then blew his nose and smiled up at Marrec with a brilliance that shot straight through him.

"That Temple is far too small for all of us." Luthan stood with hands on his hips, surveying the village, the manor staff, the resplendent Circlets and Marshalls, and their family.

We witness, too! Thunder and Dark Lance and the other volarans whinnied in unison. Marrec hadn't seen Dark Lance arrive.

Luthan cocked his head. He didn't speak mental Equine. An excellent, patient Chevalier and fierce fighter, but not one blessed with the talent to hear the winged horses.

"The volarans insist on witnessing the ceremony," Marrec said.

Nodding, Luthan said, "Then I think we can do this outside, here. It will please the Song and Amee equally. We will need the traveling altar from the Temple." A man hurried away to fetch it and Luthan gestured Marrec and

Calli and the others to move to the center of the square, the volarans to go to the edge.

"I will continue to hold Diaminta since I will be her and Jetyer's *parentie*," Jaquar said smugly.

Marian sniffed. "I'll be part of the ritual, too."

Luthan said, "Best form a bond between you and the children, too."

The volarans called.

"They want to participate in the ritual," Marrec said.

"No," said Luthan. "Humans only in the pentacle."

The townsman returned with the light traveling altar and implements and set it in the middle of the square where a faint pentagram showed as a trampling of the grass.

A horrible screeching arose. Luthan's shoulders tensed. Jaquar and Marian smiled.

"It only needed this to complicate the ritual further," Luthan muttered.

Two peacocks, feathers fully spread, pranced toward them.

"The feycoocus." Luthan sighed.

All around the square people nudged each other, commented excitedly.

Marian clapped her hands and a rumble of thunder reverberated around the square. Everyone fell silent.

"Everyone is welcome to witness the Gardponts adopt their new son, and the designation of the Circlets as *parenties*." Luthan projected his voice. "Family and *parenties*, enter the pentagram with me. Volarans, stand outside the circle at even intervals. Townspeople and well-wishers, circle around and link hands."

The ritual was slow and stately. Luthan spoke in a loud,

clear voice so all could hear. The binding this time was more complex but fully as potent as the one when they'd adopted Diaminta in the Castle's Great Temple. Though they didn't have the impressive resonance of Power used and stored, the different atmosphere of tree-dappled light, blue sky and land underfoot that had been the gathering place of simple people for ages touched Marrec more.

Baby Diaminta and Jetyer were bound first, and Jaquar and Marian formally linked to the family as *parenties* to the children with a few drops of blood. Even that small amount of Circlet blood made Marrec dizzy and Calli helped him and Diaminta and Jetyer stay conscious. Then came the blood-bonding—the cutting and binding of arms, Jetyer between Calli and Marrec himself. Luthan had judged that they should all be bound for only four hours and Marrec was grateful.

They walked from the green a family. Then there was a disturbance among the volarans.

One comes, Dark Lance said mentally. *A mount for the children.* He snorted and Marrec got the impression that he didn't think much of the volaran.

The other winged horses parted to show a bluish-gray mare, one of the smallest Marrec had seen. The volarans were getting smaller, seemed to be breeding for daintiness. Not too good for big Chevaliers. He'd mention the notion to Calli, see if she could encourage the herds to breed for larger mounts.

Like me, said Dark Lance.

Jetyer let out a breath, then his eyes focused on the bluish-gray mare. "Sh-she's b-b-beautif-ful."

She was, in the manner that volarans prized, but she was

too small for anyone to ride but a youngster—or an equally small woman like Alexa.

I am Sapphire.

Sapphire, said Jetyer, easy in Equine.

Calli slanted Marrec a glance. "Think we can put Jetyer on for a try?" She didn't wait for him to answer, but spoke Equine with her body, and reassured the little winged horse as she moved behind the mare.

The volaran stood still, turned her neck to look at them. Marrec thought he was the only one of them to realize that Calli had complete control of the winged steed's mind. The mare could not kick. He and Calli lifted Jetyer to sit bareback.

Jetyer shouted in joy.

A flood of memories tangled between them—Calli on her first horse, Marrec his volaran. Calli and Thunder, Marrec and Dark Lance.

"Me and Sapphire!" cried Jetyer.

"She's so intelligent and quick," Calli said, beaming as Jetyer leaned forward and stroked the mare's neck.

I am intelligent and quick, Dark Lance said.

Not as quick as this one, Marrec said. "Beautiful lady," he said aloud.

Yes, Sapphire replied in Equine, lifting her head and tilting her ears. *I flew in for the boy.*

"Me, me!" screamed Diaminta, waving little fists.

"Jetyer?" asked Calli.

"She can sit ahead of me."

"Good boy," Marrec said.

"That's kind of you," Calli said.

Jaquar placed Diaminta on the volaran and stepped away. He shook his head. "Truly, the Volaran Exotique."

They let the children sit a while on Sapphire's back, then Jaquar took Diaminta, and Marrec and Jetyer and Calli walked slowly back to the manor. The blood traveling through them caused their minds to daze, as usual.

Sometimes the boy's blood and memories were more familiar than Calli's, sometimes the events Marrec had shared with Calli were easier to accept and understand than Jetyer's ideas.

Calli's and Jetyer's Songs harmonized amazingly. So well that Marrec was almost jealous of his new son.

Once again emotionally bound with Calli, Marrec understood she'd been hurt by his withdrawal, yet his logical side continued to insist that what he was doing was right, for the best of them all. It was true that Calli still had a great need to be loved and to please others, but he saw her strong determination that their child—children—not be forced into the Chevalier life that was expected of both her and Marrec.

Once they reached the manor, they lay on three side-by-side pallets in one of the parlors. Diaminta's crib was close so that she'd experience their binding Song. The room didn't get direct sunlight and was cool and shady, and Marrec's mind drifted away on music until voices rang around him and the cloth bonds of he and his Pairling and his new son were cut away.

They all embraced—with Diaminta—and then spent the evening in celebration. Jetyer kept close to Calli, and Marrec got the idea that he was spilling all his hopes and dreams— in only slightly stuttering language.

Later in the night, he and Calli loved with desperate tenderness.

The next morning breakfast was cheerful and lively. Afterward, Calli took Jetyer to the arena and she and Marrec gave him his first volaran-partnering lesson. The grin on his face made Calli's eyes sting.

Finally, though, it was time to wash and change for her flight back to the encampment. Her steps dragged, her movements slowed.

She had just dressed when there was a quick, hard rapping on the door.

Marrec and she shared a strained glance, both knowing Jetyer was outside their door. Marrec strode and opened it.

"Mama?" Jetyer said, shifting from foot to foot on the threshold.

"Yes?"

"I...I...h-heard about the S-s-snap. W-will you b-be l-l-l-leaving?"

"Oh, honey." She opened her arms and he ran into them, burrowed close, and she shut her eyes as she heard the pretty strains of his boy Song, smelled his scent. "I love you very much, and the more an Exotique is bound to Lladrana and its people, the easier it is for her to stay. I'm bound to you and your father and baby Diaminta. They say the Snap is a *choice,* and I choose to stay here with you and the rest of our family."

"Are you sure?" The words were muffled against her body, but they were clear.

"Very sure. I won't go back."

"Son, *I've* heard from Shieldmarshall Bastien that I can help Calli during the Snap by hanging on to her. When it comes, why don't we both hang on to her."

The boy released her to look at Marrec. "T-truly?"

"Ayes."

"And baby Diaminta, too? M-mama could hold her."

"Well, you know Diaminta still prefers you and your papa," Calli said.

Jetyer shook his head. "I th-think you should hold her."

Smiling, Calli brushed his hair from his forehead, pretended not to see his wet eyes. "We'll do that. Feel better now?"

"Ayes." But there was a little frown between his brows.

Calli went to the love seat and sat down, patted the cushion beside her. "You know you can ask me anything, right?"

"Ayes." He shrugged a shoulder. "I just don't like this S-snap idea."

"We won't let it concern us. I don't want to go back to the Exotique Land." Like Alexa and Marian, she never thought of Earth or Colorado as home anymore.

Marrec sat next to her, draping an arm around her shoulders and now the fragrance of his skin teased her. Man. Lover.

"Calli isn't going anywhere."

She tensed a little at his words, kept a smile aimed at her boy. "I have to go back to the encampment, but your father will stay here with you. Flying lessons every day, and I'll come back as often as I can."

"Maybe I should go with y-you, so you'll stay safe." He nodded.

Oh, the dear child. "I like thinking about you here, at our home."

Jetyer stood straight, looked Marrec in the eye. "Th-then Papa should go with you. I will look after Diaminta and…here. Someone m-must be with you."

Just that easily the huge, black canyon of their differences opened between them. Marrec stiffened.

"You should go," Jetyer insisted.

Calli rubbed her temples. "Jetyer, I haven't finished my duties to Lladrana yet, and your father and I love you. We want you and Diaminta to have *good* lives. And both parents."

"B-but that c-can't happen just yet, can it?"

Why couldn't Marrec help her out? She swallowed. "No, not quite yet, but soon, within a month, I hope."

Marrec frowned at her.

"I feel it…that everything will be settled in a month." Calli put her hand on her chest. Just for that instant she had *known.* She only hoped she could hold on to the memory of the feeling in hard times.

After a quiet lunch, she kissed her children and husband and walked with back straight to the Landing Field and they went to an arena for another flying lesson. She waved then soared high and sent Thunder toward the camp. Her volaran's sympathy eased her rigid seat, made her concentrate on what was ahead, not behind her.

Calli fretted through the next couple of days, giving volaran-partnering lessons, teaching Equine, flying patterns. She even helped with the final testing of a Chevalier class and handed out newly won reins. Nothing fulfilled her. The only place she wanted to be was home—continuing to learn about her new family, bringing *them* together as a unit.

Raoul Lebeau had appointed himself her companion and was occasionally amusing, but it didn't take the calculation in his eyes for Calli to know he kept her company because he wanted to get ahead. She also reckoned that he was a spy for Lord Veenlit, who was courting a happy Seeva. That woman seemed much more content in managing the camp than she'd ever been in attempting to become a Chevalier.

The battles continued, and though Calli didn't fight without Marrec, she spent hours with the Marshalls and noble Chevaliers over battle maps, listening to strategic plans and planning warfare, which she loathed.

Chevaliers and volarans were lost and Calli grieved—more, she took the suffering of volarans who'd lost their fliers upon herself, serving as a counselor. This depressed her spirits even more, though she won praise from Bastien and the other volaran mind-speakers for being able to save three that would have pined to death at the loss of their human partners. She even determined where those volarans would survive best—one went to her estate, one to Bastien's and the third returned to the great herd in Volaran Valley.

When Marrec showed up for his rotation the fourth day, he was still remote, their PairSong suppressed, unhappy that they were not together. Calli watched his every gesture, drank in his stories of their children, but did not apologize for doing what she thought was right.

No battle alarms sounded, but midafternoon Thealia Germaine's Head of Chevaliers strode up to them. "There's a meeting in the Lady Knight Marshall's tent. Now."

Calli and Marrec looked at each other. He reached for her hand, the first time he'd touched her.

* * *

Thealia glanced up from an unrolled map on the table in her magnificent tent. Her face looked pale, her eyes set deep in worn skin. At first Calli thought it must be the dim light, but then understood that it wasn't. This campaign was grinding on all of them. She made a tiny sound in her throat and Marrec's arm came around her waist. She savored the feel of it. Strong. Reliable.

Then she noticed Marian and Jaquar and stilled. They'd been absent from camp for the last couple of days. Something was definitely up.

Thealia nodded at the two Chevaliers at the tent flaps. "Close the entrance." They did and a thick atmosphere darkened, gloom draping the space. A potent spell of secrecy.

With a short whistle, Thealia lit the lamps until light glowed. It might have been cheery and comfortable if everyone wasn't so tense. Gesturing to Jaquar, Thealia said, "Report."

Jaquar cleared his throat. "The Dark has been more vicious, more active because it is searching for a new human Sorcerer or Sorceress to become a new Master of its horrors. We believe the attacks on you must be an attempt by someone great in evil Power to prove himself or herself to the Dark."

Alexa blinked. "Are you telling us that the Dark might be *less* aggressive if it gets another Master?" She sounded incredulous.

Shrugging, Jaquar said, "Perhaps, for a short amount of time. It *is* less organized." He waved a hand. "The continual retrousse of monsters here instead of spreading them across the northern border where other fence posts remain fallen—and we can't raise fence posts without killing horrors—the spending of a lot of dreeths—" He shared a glance with his wife. "We think the fire-breathing ones are all gone."

"That's good news," Marrec said.

"All point to some *thing* that is not human, clumsy with detail," Jaquar ended.

"We must carry this battle to the Dark before it finds another Powerful minion," Thealia said, her voice harsh.

Silence throbbed in the tent. Calli found herself licking her lips as everyone stared at her. "I thought there was no way to get to the Dark."

Marian said, "The Circlets have endeavored to penetrate the maw of the Dark's nest on all other planes. To no avail."

"So now we must carry the battle—or at least survey the nest here on this physical plane. Marian gave us the location," Thealia said. She gestured them around the table, then stabbed at the map with her finger. "Here, Funeej Island."

It was far to the northwest.

Marian stepped closer to Calli. "From old Lorebooks, it's one large volcano."

"Great," Calli said. "Active?"

Shrugging, Marian said, "We don't know."

"It's a long distance. It will take the strongest and most Powerful volaran and flier to scout for us." Thealia met Calli's eyes unflinchingly.

"Calli will not go alone!" Marrec insisted.

Thealia's eyelids hooded her gaze. "It's probable that on this physical plane, as in many, only an Exotique can penetrate whatever Powerful Shield the Dark has placed."

"Neither Alexa nor Marian can go. They have been here on Lladrana long enough that the Dark knows them and has Shields against them," Jaquar said.

Well, that was that. Calli's stomach clenched.

"And while she scouts, she may have a chance to harm or destroy it. That fancy, blood-red knot you found, Marian, the weapon knot—" Thealia said.

"Calli doesn't have a four-octave voice," Marian said. "It needs a trained Singer to use the weapon knot."

Thealia scowled. "I thought the requirement was perfect pitch. From what I've heard, Calli has perfect pitch."

Calli just stared at the two women. She'd never had singing lessons, never much sang before reaching Lladrana, so how would she know if she had perfect pitch or not?

"A mistranslation," Marian said stiffly. "I made a mistake."

"Did that admission hurt?" asked Bastien.

Marian smiled. "A little, but I have rationalizations all prepared." The tension in the room lessened. "Besides, I think that more than one person must release the knot."

"Some other weapon, then. A bomb," Thealia said.

"Ever think what the backlash might be to a volaran Pair from a bomb against the Dark so Powerful it sucks the life from our very planet?" Marrec's arm tightened around Calli until she could barely breathe—at least that's what she thought was causing her panting. Not sheer terror.

"Calli doesn't go alone," Marrec repeated. He stared at Jaquar and Marian, swung his gaze to Thealia. "This is all speculation. We don't know what Shields the Dark might have. We mount a *large* force."

Sometimes a sacrifice of one must be made for the good

of all. Calli opened her mouth to say so, when Alexa punched her shoulder.

Alexa said, "We should also consider the fact that the Dark would love to get Calli in its clutches. To destroy an Exotique that has great potential to make the partnership between volaran and flier so Powerful that it threatens the Dark." She smiled fiercely. "Like all of us Exotiques, Calli is more important in the long run than using her as an expendable sacrifice. We of the Marshalls *will not* consider Calli disposable. Absolutely *no* bomb." She shot a glance at Marian. "That weapon knot. How many people does it need to Untie it with Power?"

"Six."

Alexa jerked a nod, set her hand on the hilt of her baton, angling it forward. "And that's the number of times an Exotique can be Summoned in the next couple of years, right? Coincidental? I don't *think* so."

32

Mingled Songs surged in unspoken consideration, agreement.

"We'll mount an expedition to survey the island and find an entrance where we can invade," Thealia said.

"Great," Calli whispered.

That evening, as Marrec was once more mining Faucon's brain for experience in running an estate, Calli reluctantly accepted Marian's invitation for some after-dinner wine.

She'd gotten into the habit of spending time with Alexa or Marian or both in the evenings when they were in the encampment.

Alexa and others had flown to battle. Calli and Marrec had been relieved from their fighting shifts until the scouting trip was over.

Though Marian, too, had adopted lush Arabian Night

decor, Calli couldn't get comfortable. Kept having to unclench her jaw to drink ale. Jaquar was nowhere to be seen.

"I suppose you want to talk about my task," Calli grumbled. Her ale sat sour in her stomach. "You think this flyover of the Dark's nest is my task."

"It rang true to me, Calli," Marian said, and Calli knew that was the simple truth. When they'd spoken of it earlier, Marian had heard the same sound of Rightness as she had. Damn.

Calli rubbed the back of her neck, met Marian's sympathetic eyes. "Yeah, I heard it, too."

"Calli…" Marian's voice was almost a whisper. "I thought I'd remind you that both Alexa and I had to fulfill our tasks alone."

There were several heartbeats of hard silence. "Alexa was in battle!"

"But she'd lost her Shield, all her other support."

"So you believe I'll have to do the scouting alone." Her chin lifted. "I can do it if I must."

Marian set her empty glass aside and came over to kneel by Calli, took her in soft arms and hugged her tight. "I'm sorry."

Just before dawn, Marrec slipped away from their bedroll, dressed and left the tent quietly. Even the rise of Dark Lance's wings into the sky as they flew away home was nearly silent.

And Calli hurt. He'd thought he'd left her sleeping, and she supposed she was grateful that he tried to come back at night as often as possible. Of course, that might just be for the great, driving sex. Now that they didn't discuss things as often, that they kept their feelings to themselves and were apart as much as they were together, the passion between them had taken on a dark sensuality that ravaged Calli. She'd never done such things with a man before, been taken to so many edges, had returned the exploration of sexuality.

She should have been exhausted, but she always knew the instant he left their bed. She rose and put on a loose gown, went to a nearby pool and dunked, efficiently bathing. The sun was just sending the first shafts of light into the sky from behind the hillocks by the time she returned to her tent. To see Thunder standing in front of the flap, waiting for her, fully caparisoned in his fanciest black-and-silver tack. *Time to go,* he sent mentally.

Her nape tingled. *Go where?*

The lead stallion and mare of the wild volarans in Volaran Valley Summon.

She hesitated, then nodded. *I'll be right with you.*

The Valley is on the far side of Lladrana, we fly over mountains, much Distance Magic will be used.

Right. I'll leave a note….

Not necessary, said another voice, light and chirping.

Calli glanced down to see a peacock dragging its long, colorful tail come around her tent. Despite the fact that it was a peacock, Calli recognized Sinafinal. She tilted her head and the comb fluffed in the wind. *I have not been to Volaran Valley for a while.*

Thunder looked down his nose at her. You *are not invited.*

She clicked her beak, beady eyes glittering. *No?*

Thunder moderated his tone. *I was told volarans and the Volaran Exotique only.* His hide rippled. *If you want to come, you must ask for an invitation yourself.*

Sinafinal spread her tail, and it was more brilliant than the dawn. *I will tell Alexa and others of Calli's absence.*

"Thank you," Calli said. "I need to dress." She hurried into the tent and inspected her clothes. She'd left her blue gown at home. Rubbing her fingers over the stains on her least battered leathers, she gave up and took new dreeth leathers that she'd never worn from a pegged clothing stand. Sliding the tunic and pants over her silk underthings, she found the skin unusually comfortable. Pliant. And she knew it was nearly indestructible. Though the color was a drab brown, there was a slight sheen to the clothes. She wished for a mirror, then shrugged and gave up. Wearing dreeth skin made a statement in itself.

When she stepped out of the tent, Sinafinal was gone and Thunder greeted her with a flick of his ears and a nuzzle. She stroked his nose, then mounted. Small sounds came of servants rising to tend fires and start breakfast.

Raoul, who now slept in a little guard tent between hers and another wealthy landowner's, exited the tent wearing only breeches. He sent her a smile and stretched. "You're sure taking off early."

Calli nodded and swung onto Thunder, who ruffled his feathers.

Making a noise of disgust, Raoul curled his lip and said, "That man of yours is crazy to leave you alone for anything."

"He's watching our children."

Raoul snorted, opened his mouth, then shut it. Calli knew what he'd stopped himself from saying. She'd heard him calling her children "orphaned brat bastards" when gossiping with others. "Good fighting," she said. *Let's go,* to Thunder.

"I hope not. Good journey. Where are you going?"

Thunder rose with a loud beating of wings, leaving the question unanswered.

As the sun rose, painting the sky in pastels, and the winds whispered to them of bright skies and sunny days, Calli's mood lifted, too. Excitement fizzed in her blood. As far as she knew, she was the only person in hundreds of years to visit Volaran Valley.

She and Thunder stole precious time to do a couple of loop-de-loops and other aerial tricks, just for fun. No reason to worry about the cost of Distance Magic. Whatever the cost to their Pairling relationship, the dark night sex always energized her the next day, and did the same to Marrec.

As she passed over noble estates, volarans flew to join her in a colorful stream, wind caressing roan and white and gray and brown manes. *This* was the kind of flight she liked to lead, not trailing with other Shielded Pairs onto a battlefield.

They flew over her estate…and all the volarans, including Dark Lance, rose to accompany her…. *Calli?* came Marrec's startled mindcall at the sight.

I am Summoned to Volaran Valley.

She felt surprise from him, a flash of envy, and she was human enough to smile. *I'll be home tonight.*

They don't need you for the expedition planning?

No.

I'll see you later.

Volaran Valley was gigantic, an oval crater-like depression in the continent, ringed with mountains and showing a rich verdancy of grasses and flowers. The wild herd, though, was smaller than she expected. She circled down, sighing as the kiss of volaran Power—a magical shield—slid against her skin.

When she landed, a young mare trotted up, stared at her, swiveled her ears and dipped her head in greeting.

Salutations, Calli said in Equine.

Welcome.

She dismounted from Thunder and staggered. The beauty of the valley itself was near perfection. She was drunk on volaran Song.

The herd circled her. No, not as large as expected…especially if this was *all* of them. Narrowing her eyes, she scrutinized them. The younger ones seemed smaller than the older ones and there were slight signs of inbreeding—color, conformation, the closeness of one Song to another.

The alpha stallion, a compact, muscular black, came up to her and she felt the strongest mental probe she'd ever had from him.

You were brought here to tell us of this Flight to the Dark's nest, as the stallion projected the concept in Equine—a huge black hole with a writhing tangle of snakes—a shudder ran through the mass of the herd. Younger volarans flung their heads back, rolling their eyes, and galloped away. When they came back, they stood at the edge of the crowd around her, protected from her and the dire news she brought by their elders.

The young ones have not fought any horrors yet, a calmer, more resonant mind-tone said. Calli sensed it was from a mare, the alpha probably, but she didn't step forward. She left Calli to the one running on testosterone.

The people believe this is your task, the stallion said.

Calli unfastened her waterskin from her side, unplugged it, swigged a little cool, minty water, then said, "Yes."

The stallion nodded, a larger gesture than Calli expected. As if he spoke loudly to someone who didn't know his language well. It irritated her, but perhaps her mastery of Equine *wasn't* as good as she thought it was. And perhaps she should get over her nerves at the beauty of the scene and pay attention to the visual cues he was giving her. Concentrate on the alpha male. Yeah, that might be good if she didn't want to get kicked.

Ears flicking, the stallion eyed her. *We, too, believe this is your task.*

Her mouth dried. She bowed. *Thank you for that information. How can I do it?*

Trust yourself and Thunder and the Song.

In other words, he didn't know or wasn't telling.

There is something else... said the female voice.

Yes?

The Song has been unclear, but you smell so good and look so good. A small, older white mare came forward, extended a long tongue and licked Calli's arm. *Taste good.* She tilted her head one way, then the other. *Your Song...it makes me want to Sing.*

Calli simply closed her eyes.

The ambience of the valley sank into her, ancient Songs imbuing the mountainsides, the vitality of the winged horses. When she opened her eyelids, only the mare remained with her, and Thunder was eating and watching a few feet away.

Stay as long as you want, return whenever you want, the mare said.

Thank you.

The mare fluttered her black-etched wings. *We would all like to greet you. To smell. To touch and be touched.*

Ayes.

Some would like to fly with you.

Calli pulled her handkerchief out of her pocket and wiped her eyes.

She spent the day with the volarans. This was the one essential task that she must fulfill, she thought, to bond with each of the wild ones, know their character. Sing with them. Fly with them.

It was after dark before she left. Wholly content.

Her pleasant mood was shattered as she began the descent to her home. *Don't bother to land,* Marrec said. *The Marshalls want you back at camp. The expedition to the Dark's island leaves at dawn.*

She hesitated, but before she could insist Thunder alight, he shot off toward the encampment.

33

Calli shared tea with Alexa before dawn, letting her squire pack for her. Since her eyes felt rolled in dirt from sleeplessness, she was glad for his help.

"Everyone wants to survey the island." Alexa grinned.

Calli's heart jumped. She didn't. This was not a beautiful flight with her volaran. This was a flyover of the enemy's headquarters. An enemy that had been sending unlimited monsters across the borders of Lladrana for centuries.

"Good. That's good," she mumbled.

"But we're limiting it to twenty. The strongest Marshalls and Chevaliers. We had trials while you were gone yesterday." Alexa slid a look at her. "Volaran Valley pretty cool?"

"Nothing in two worlds is as cool as Volaran Valley," Calli said sincerely.

Alexa sniffed, looked at her from the corner of her eye.

"If you'd been here yesterday, we could've put up some barrels. You'd have won."

Calli laughed. "I guess so."

Sobering, Alexa said, "Marian and Jaquar are coming, too. I don't know how many others of the Tower Community might show up—probably a few now and then along the way, bringing and taking reports and suchlike."

The interlude of peace was over. Calli glanced around the camp. "We're leaving this here?"

"Yes. Packing lightweight camping equipment only." She pulled a face. "I never cared for camping. Hiking, yes. Camping, no. I hate bugs."

"I can do that. I traveled more than one rodeo circuit. Did about sixty-five rodeos one year."

Alexa stared. "You must have been on the road all the time."

"Yes." And she wouldn't do it again.

Clearing her throat, Alexa said, "Will Marrec be coming?"

Calli's smile was bitter. "Despite his shocked and loving attitude a couple of days ago, we are currently not speaking. I don't think so."

Alexa rubbed her face. "The, um, orders to be here this morning, huh?"

"I'd say that was the last straw, yes."

"It's only for a little while. One task."

"One more task. One *big* task. That could kill me, and he'd die, too, right?"

"Oh. Yeah. I'm sorry." Since Alexa's hair stood straight out from her head with Power and tension, Calli guessed she meant it. Alexa shook her head. "It's like riding a tiger. And

I don't guess I ever knew what that really meant 'til I came here. Rare that you get any breaks."

"Ayes." Calli put her teacup down and stretched her aching body. She'd flown with about twenty wild volarans in the valley the day before and every muscle ached. Concentrating on her breathing, she let her mind rest. "But even though Marrec and I aren't getting along, I have him, a wonderful—sometimes—jerk of my own."

Alexa snorted a laugh.

"And beautiful land of my own."

"And great children," Alexa said quietly.

Calli stared at her. "Do you mind not—"

Alexa shook her head. "No, not really. I'm pretty much obsessed with fighting the Dark. And Bastien. Well, not fighting Bastien, but being with Bastien. You know what I mean."

"Yeah."

"Leaving in ten minutes!" Thealia's Powerful voice rolled over the camp.

"Guess we'd better get along," Alexa said.

"Guess so."

Even with Distance Magic, it took the Chevaliers and volarans time to fly northward. Marrec did not accompany them. Oh, he made the first couple of camps—as many as four, and Calli went home to visit after the first couple of camps—then the distance was too far. The skies outside Lladrana seemed heavier, as if Amee kept most of the magic in the world concentrated in Lladrana. And the Dark's existence and its use of the area—breeding camps for the horrors—layered an additional danger.

Three weeks later the expedition camped on a gentle sweep of land that curved closest to the island. They weren't in Lladrana anymore, hadn't been since the first couple of days, but this land had always been claimed by the Dark. No one lived here.

Though it was cool so far north—maybe like Greenland or Iceland—the freshwater inland sea could have been dotted with settlements. All was barren of human life, and had very skittish, very limited animal life. The Chevaliers and Marshalls mostly subsisted on food they brought with them. No way could an army come this route. Not even all the Marshalls and Chevaliers who partnered with volarans.

A small strike force, maybe, and Calli nearly choked on her dry bread as she reckoned who'd be the main part of that strike force. Exotiques. Six in the next two years. It made sense.

The passage of time had crept up on her, the plans she tried to forget, and the next day was the flyover of the island.

Her mouth flattened. Even with the strongest steed, the greatest merged will of man and volaran, Marrec wouldn't be able to reach her—them—in time to join her. All that concern of his for her back at the camp, and he was not here to support her. It was like a festering sliver. Nevertheless, she requested Tuckerinal take a message to him. Maybe with feycoocu magic, Marrec could arrive in time.

He'd want to know if she was putting her life in danger, if he was going to die at the same time. Morbidly she wondered how that worked, if fate caused an accident to happen, like a beam falling on him, or he just gave out of heart failure or something.

And didn't that sound whiny and self-pitying and depressing? But all the time they were on the journey, her skin had itched. Actually, *under* her skin had itched, as if her nerves were tweaked every moment or so.

Sleep had been elusive. Often the most she got was when she grabbed some in the saddle in flight, but she, like everyone, bedded down early and quietly tonight.

Once again they rose before dawn. Calli shivered as her squire helped her on with her dreeth leathers and mail. They could only pray that whatever the Dark's nest threw at them would not be lethal. They hoped for stealth. Whether they would succeed in that, she didn't know.

Expression serious, Alexa walked over to Calli. "You aren't going with us."

"What!"

Alexa let out a breath. "We—" she gestured to Bastien and Marian and Jaquar who were clumped together a few feet away "—don't think that this expedition will be successful. We think the Dark knows us all, has a force field that none of us can penetrate. You're our secret weapon. So we want you to stay back, just in case."

"Why don't I ride with you and just go on if the rest of you can't?"

"Because we'll attract attention. They might mobilize, we don't want you going in alone after we've alerted the nest as a sitting duck—volaran Pair."

Calli gulped. "Good thinking."

"We can save you for later, send you in alone as a surprise. Tomorrow morning. Just as the sun rises." She appeared as dubious as Calli felt about that statement.

"Okay, I'll stay." She drew off her gauntlets.

Alexa smiled. "Right. Keep the home fires burning." She grinned. "Or make breakfast for our return, or something."

"I'm sure I'll occupy myself. Maybe rereading the Lorebook of Exotique Alexa."

"It's very entertaining." Alexa smiled. "Can't go wrong."

"And the Lorebook of Exotique Marian."

"Not at all as fun." Alexa kissed her cheek. "See you later."

"Bye." Calli sat under a stunted tree and watched them fly away.

A couple of hours later, the Marshalls and Chevaliers straggled in and fed the campfires. Calli knew from their faces that they'd had no luck—not the Marshalls, nor the Circlets, nor anyone else. Alexa was the only one who showed any emotion beyond weariness. She strode into the circle around the largest bonfire where they all congregated. "It was just like everyone said," she grumbled. "I couldn't get through."

Marian frowned. "They must be able to set specific spells against us." She shivered a little. "I was there, so they know my...let's say DNA pattern...for simplicity."

Alexa folded down to a cross-legged position, grabbed a spitted bird they'd saved for this meal, swore at the heat and munched. Around a bite, she said, "Yeah, I've always considered DNA the utmost in simplicity."

"Smart-ass," Calli said. That phrase meant the same in Lladranan and English. She tried to keep the tone light, as if it wasn't a problem that she'd be the only one flying over the island tomorrow morning.

"But where would they have gotten your pattern, Alexa?" Marian asked.

"Dunno." Alexa frowned. "Maybe the sangvile that attacked me. But, no, we killed that one."

"We've been operating with the belief that the horrors aren't telepathic, but have a group mind—what one knows, all know," Marian said.

"Scary thought," Calli said.

"Yes," Marian agreed, "but I think it's right." She stared at Alexa. "They have your pattern somehow."

"Looks like." Alexa shrugged. "I've been here longer than you two. Fought in many battles. If one of the beasts or something was on the battlefield to, uh, take samples from me, not a problem. If the Dark bases its pattern on a DNA level, only a drop or two of blood would be needed." She ran her forefinger down the scar on her cheek.

"Blood magic," Calli murmured. "Sounds Powerful."

"It is." Marian glanced away from the fire and into the sky where the sun had just set.

"I've fought, too," Calli said.

"But you haven't lost as much blood or bone."

"None of us have lost bone, thank the Song," Alexa said.

Calli leaned forward to tap her fist on the end of a log.

Marian stared at her.

Her face warmer than just from the heat of the fire, Calli said, "Superstitious, knock on wood."

"Huh," Alexa said and did the same. "Never know what magic works here, do you?" She aimed a smile at Marian. "Simple charms might work, couldn't they?"

"A simple protective charm to ward off danger. Maybe," Marian said, and rapped a piece of wood near her. "The old Master probably got some blood from me, too."

"Old Master?" Calli asked.

Marian cleared her throat. "There is a definite power struggle for the position as intermediary between the Dark and the invading monsters."

"Not exactly a job I'd want," Alexa said. Then scowled at Marian and Calli. "And no lawyer jokes."

"That never occurred to me," Calli said.

Marian kept silent.

"Huh," Alexa said, then turned her attention back to the food. "I really could go for some coal-baked potatoes."

Groaning, Marian said, "Why did you remind me? I *love* potatoes. There are none here."

"'Cause you were thinking of lawyer jokes," Alexa said.

Calli stifled a chuckle.

They ate and grew quiet. Whatever bravado they'd mustered until now vanished.

Thealia stalked around the camp. "We are tired, our plan futile. But there must be something we can do to help Calli."

Her Shield leaned on his quarterstaff and whispered in her ear. Her face cleared, eyes brightened and she nodded sharply. "Ayes. Listen." Her voice projected over the camp and everyone turned to her. "We will place Calli in the center of the camp, then initiate a Ritual. Of Security. Of Peace. We—and especially Calli—will rest in a strengthening trance all day. The feycoocus will guard us." She bent a hard look at them. "They assure us that we will be safe."

Murmurs and nods followed the pronouncement.

Almost reluctantly, Calli took her place in the center of the circle, as did Thunder, watched as people joined hands, and the volarans clumped behind the humans.

Then she slept.

Alexa shook her awake. "Time to get up."

The knowledge of what she had to do chilled Calli. She dressed in dreeth leathers and armor, helmet and gauntlets as she had done the day before. Took crystal recording stars. She didn't eat.

Far too soon she was mounting Thunder for the flight.

34

They lifted off and soared, rising ever higher, and even though Calli knew she flew into certain danger to scout the island and map it, the tension she'd felt at camp dropped away.

She was flying.

She was free.

She had all the magic of a dawning day surrounding her.

Let's go, she said to Thunder, firmly inside his mind, holding fear at bay.

He sent her a wave of love.

Truly, she was blessed.

They flew over the sea between the continent and the island. The enormous island of only one mountain.

The island that was really the nest, the home of the Dark that preyed upon Lladrana. Calli rolled her shoulders, set her teeth, this was it. Her true task. Once this was over, no more pressure.

Just do it, get it done, go back to her real life with Marrec and her children. Raising and training horses and volarans, making a family.

Even though her real life included incredible things that she'd never imagined.

They drew closer to the great mountain spearing out of the sea, snow and ice near the bottom, rising to black-encrusted lava and glowing red around the lip. Light and heat pulsed from it in ghastly intervals as if it was the Dark itself.

All the hair on her body prickled, her skin quivered. A susurration rose like water dripping on a red-hot surface and Calli's heart lurched. The Dark's heart? The sound liquefied her bowels.

She concentrated on viewing the mountain. The crags showed folds and crevices where Calli was sure evil horrors lurked. Dreeths, small and fire breathing, or large and vicious. Farther down the mountain black mixed with the white of snow and ice.

A miasma of danger enveloped them.

Her breath came short and ragged, matching the irregular rhythm of Thunder's wingbeats. They both shivered. She'd have liked to pretend it was simply the result of the thin, cold northern air, but it was more.

Panic was not allowed, especially in a volaran flier responsible for her mount. Hadn't she taught that every day?

So she sucked in a large breath, aware of the ice crystals, the chill penetrating her lungs. She *reached* for Thunder's innermost mind, and merged, past thought and feeling, until there was an incredible brightness in her own mind. Living in the moment, living in the very stream of the Song.

She felt as light and as thin as a cloud, and so did Thunder. They'd reached the edge of the mountain now and Calli glanced down.

And saw nothing of herself or Thunder.

They were transparent! Invisible. A cry escaped her and she saw the lines of her legs, of Thunder's barrel forming, taking on color. No!

Another slow, deep inhalation, a lightening of her mind and spirit, a casting off of all worry and keeping Thunder with her, doing the same.

They were a wisp of cloud, a feather floating on the air. They were unseen, and it was so.

Awe whirled inside her. *What a wonderful talent you have.*

Slowly words formed in Thunder's mind, as if solidifying through the bright Song and drifting down. *I do not know this talent.*

But you have it.

Then you have shown me what I did not know, and now teach me how to master it.

And you can teach all the other volarans.

Yes. You have demonstrated how we can protect ourselves. I will tell the alphas, they will consider it.

Ayes, now let's do our duty.

They spent a long hour spiraling around the peak, from the bottom up, Calli memorizing the landscape, marking the fissures and lava domes, hoping the many-faceted crystal stars were transmitting. There was no harbor to speak of, nothing that would hold a fleet, but cliffs on the north. Any landing on the base of the island would be immediately noticed—visually, if by no other sense.

She saw no level place large enough to hold more than a couple of volarans, and no obvious entrance to the nest.

They passed over the caldera and reached the round, open vent. Calli looked down at bubbling molten rock, orange and red and awesome. No opening there. Other ethereal planes might indicate a maw, but not here before physical eyes.

As terror nibbled on the edges of her consciousness along with exhaustion—they must be expending a huge amount of energy staying invisible—Calli closed her eyes and let her senses rule, feeling an unholy pull of evil more like a putrid stench than anything else. She nudged Thunder's slowing wings toward the spots that made her heart pound, her mouth dry, her body tremble with atavistic knowledge of torturous death. Opening to the evil core.

Three places, deep in slitted canyons so that she couldn't truly see them, only sense they were there. She marked them on her internal map, and noticed her dreeth trousers were no longer transparent but turning their usual brown.

Boom! The air shuddered around them, heated instantly. A liquid fountain of magma missed them by inches.

Home! she screamed to Thunder. No time to stop and soak up energy. If she were Marian she could leach it from the lava, but she was not a master of fire.

Her specialty was air. Air. Heat, ash, lived in the air. Trembling, she squeezed the energy of heat from the air around her, did her best to filter it, transmute it to Power she poured into Thunder and herself.

Thunder surged forward, dodging more fiery spurts.

Dreeths screamed battle cries.

Go!

She thought of lava, of rock, and croaked a Shield spell.

Their invisibility spell vanished.

Leaning down against Thunder's neck, she urged him on, sent him all the Power she could spare, even prayed to the Song for a tailwind.

In the distance she saw tiny volarans speeding toward her, faintly colored Shields indicating the Marshall Pairs, heading to guard and defend her, battle horrors here at their home. All she had to do was pass the nest's Shield, which she hadn't even noticed on her way in.

Grinning, she urged Thunder faster. As fire—dreeth and volcanic—rained down on them, she drew the energy from them into her Shield.

And she stuck to Thunder as he dipped and dodged in the air.

Wham. Wind struck them hard from behind, ripped at Thunder's wings, sent them cartwheeling. The dark blue sea advanced.

Thunder screamed.

Easy. Easy.

She checked him over. No major wounds. Keep him calm though the sky and clouds spin, the waves' reach…. Closing her eyes, she drained herself of Power, sent it all to him. Water splashed around them, icy. Her eyelids popped open. They were facing the island. A tidal wave bore down on them.

Wind and wave, flame and earth, by the Song hear me! Help us!

Another gust of wind swept under Thunder's wings; he angled them and rode it upward in a long spiral, heading toward the continental shoreline.

Alexa and Bastien bracketed them. Bastien flashed a grin.

You got through the Dark's Shield. You did it! Alexa sent mentally.

Marian and Jaquar waved, then dived under Thunder. He squealed as more wind, a warmer breeze, lifted them farther, bathed them in energy.

Calli eased the clamp she had on his emotions. He was fine. Out of danger, and fine.

Alexa looked back. Calli did, too. Fire and steam still plumed from the mountain. The tsunami rolled below.

I hope the camp is packed up, Alexa said telepathically. Her smile flashed. *Woman, you really caused a ruckus.*

I doubt it is unaware of me anymore, Calli said, smiling, conscious of the cool air drying her sweat. *Can't go back there anytime soon.*

Ttho, Bastien said. He shook his head. *You were lucky.*

Luckier than they thought, learning of the volaran's invisibility talent.

You Exotiques. Always exciting to be around, Bastien said.

Like you wild magic users, Calli retorted.

He flung back his head and laughed.

Thealia Germaine flew around them, outstripped them to take point. *Did you get the information?*

Lady Swordmarshall, Exotiques always deliver, Alexa said.

Good, we'll debrief Calli as soon as we make camp again. Some new Chevaliers have arrived to help us on our way back. Apparently, the feycoocus spread the word that we are returning. I'll see to the arrangements. She flew ahead. Her husband and Shield winked and saluted Calli.

Breath coming more steadily, Calli asked, *Did Marrec come?*

No answer.

Jaquar rose to take Thealia's place. *He has not arrived yet.*

Surely he'd gotten her message. Calli forced a smile, though seeing these loving couples hurt. She blinked rapidly. *Good to see you all, and together.*

We all had our differences, Marian reminded drily.

He'd better come around soon, Alexa grumbled.

When they landed in an area they'd camped a few days before, Alexa and Marian hugged her, then stepped aside so the men could do the same. Calli liked the male affection, their solidity, though it reminded her how long it had been since Marrec had held her.

Expression set, Alexa said, *I'll inform Thealia that she should go easy.* She fingered her baton, pivoted and marched off.

Bastien patted Calli on the shoulder. "Well done."

"That reminds me." Calli plucked the recording stars from both her shoulders and Thunder and handed them to him. He didn't even glance at them before flicking them magically away.

Calli sighed long, her shoulders slumped. She thought the tension rolled from her in waves. Maybe as big as the tsunami.

Jaquar lifted one of her limp hands and kissed it. "You have done us all a great service."

"Yes, you have," Marian said.

Sniffing, Calli smelled frying eggs, onions, bacon and salivated. One glance at the sky showed her it was still midmorning, though it felt like an eternity of days had passed. "I'm hungry. I'm gonna nab something to eat. I know you two want to look at those stars." Calli flapped her hand. "Go."

Marian smiled. "One of the stars is with Thealia. We'll see you in the command tent."

Calli nodded, realized she'd been leaning against Thunder, who had his head down. His feet occasionally scuffed in the earth, drawing Power from Amee, something volarans rarely did unless they were near the last of their strength. She rubbed him in his favorite spot. "I need food. I'll make sure you get prime feed, too."

Thunder swiveled an ear in agreement. *Do not speak of the volaran invisibility to others,* he asked softly. *Marshalls and Chevaliers would want us to use the skill all the time, and it is a volaran secret, something a volaran should decide to use.*

"I won't talk of it, but you can tell the alphas that the talent is very, very costly in terms of Power—at least, when newly learned and for a Human-Volaran Pair. You volarans may be able to wink in and out by yourselves easier. Also it is mutually exclusive of the Shield spell." I think.

Thunder tilted his head, a lock of his mane fell between his eyes. *Perhaps only you can use it.* He glanced at the others walking toward Thealia's tent, being stopped by Chevaliers asking for news of the mission.

Or only an extremely few can merge with a volaran to Sing such a skill, like Bastien with wild magic. Swinging his neck around, he stared at Marwey. *Or the one best in mind-merging. Or a good mind-speaker like Marrec.*

It had been like an altered state. She grinned. She bet if anyone knew about altered states it was Marian. *And Marian and Alexa, too.*

Of course, all our Exotiques.

He sounded like himself. She took in an easy breath. A great weight she hadn't realized she was carrying lifted from her heart.

"Chevalier Callista," called Thealia impatiently, standing at the entrance to her pavilion. "We await you."

Calli's squire hovered. *I wish I could stay and groom you.* Her stomach grumbled.

Thunder rolled an eye, smirked. *I will be pampered.*

"I guess so." She walked to the campfire where the food was, had the cook stuff a pocket of bread with eggs and onions and cheese and began eating as she went to Thealia's tent. She gulped the food down, then regretted it when she entered and everyone's eyes turned to her and her stomach tightened.

"The stars are useless," Thealia said. Her lips set into a tight line.

Jaquar stared at one in his hand. "Now, Swordmarshall, it's true the Dark may have superficially blocked our devices—"

Thealia snorted. "More like they never recorded at all."

"But several Circlets created each star. That took plenty of Power. We'll find a way through the Dark's defensive spells."

"Meanwhile, Calli's memory is our primary hope," Marian said with a commiserating look at Calli. Marian gestured to a large table with blank parchment spread on it. "The parchment is magic, Calli. All you have to do is touch it and remember everything you learned during the flyover. We have a stack." She looked eager, as always, to observe something new.

"Huh," Calli said. "Water, please." Her throat was dry.

Marian handed her an open bota and Calli drank. As she did so, her body absorbed the innate Power of the water. Interesting. Somehow during the ride, she'd bonded with another element of Amee, water, and could pull that energy into herself easily and naturally.

Her stomach settled, she twitched her lips in a polite smile and went over to the table.

Setting both hands on the parchment—render skin, because it took ink best—spread out on Thealia's desk, Calli closed her eyes, gathered her best memories of the nest, sent them down to the waiting sheet. She opened her eyes and saw a precise topographical map with circular lines going up and up and up to the black open mouth of the volcano. Waiting. Waiting. Waiting for her, for them, the other Exotiques.

She pushed the large page aside. "More!"

A man's hands shoved a stack of parchment onto the desk. Jaquar. These sheets were smaller, but still useful. Again she leaned over and let what she saw drain out of her...a geographical map of the island. A climatological. The volcano itself. The boulders, the fissures seething with steamy miasma. The domes and crevices.

Again and again and again until her knees gave out and her memory finally blurred and she crumpled.

Bastien caught her, his vibrant, vital Song sloughing away some of the grimy film the Dark had left on her. He helped her to a chair. Someone shoved a goblet into her hand and the fragrance of the potion cleared her mind. Everyone else gathered around the table, talking over each other.

"Merde!" Thealia's voice was hard. "No good harbor. A few flat spots for volarans, but all in the open. How will we invade?"

She looked at Calli. "Good work." Then the Swordmarshall turned back to the maps, flipped through them, her forehead wrinkled. "We'll find some way."

Calli's stomach rolled. Sending volarans...people...

Pairs…into that place. Her mind couldn't grasp it. Her feelings rebelled. She chugged the potion, rose.

She couldn't stay and listen to the endless discussion about strategy. The nest had worked its evil on her. She knew they wouldn't be attacking it anytime soon. Too much bad mojo. Cold, she rubbed her arms, even though the day had been unusually hot for the north. She left the tent, ignoring calls after her. What she needed was her bondmate.

But Marrec wasn't here.

She'd never forget that ride, the sight of the festering boil of evil, for the rest of her life. The shakes had started again in her toes and would spread upward. She wanted to get out of the camp, where she could fall apart alone. She wanted to ride in the sun. Fly high—higher than over the Dark's place—feel the heated caress of sunlight, the embrace of the cleansing wind.

Thunder had been as affected as she, and in the back of her mind she heard her squire and others coddling him—and getting information about the flight and the nest. She'd have to ask Bastien to write down Thunder's impressions, too. Marrec would have been the best person to do that, of course, and she'd hoped that he would have been waiting for her return. She'd been certain he'd be here. But he wasn't and she set aside the disappointment. She was tired, that's why she was so emotional, so wanted him.

Concentrating on the freshness of the air, she strolled to the corral, knowing that there would be no shortage of volarans volunteering for a high, fast, fun flight with her. Her mouth curved in a half smile.

"Ah, a pretty lady, dreaming. What are you thinking?"

Raoul's voice was nearly a purr, yet it pulled her from a slight daze and she stumbled. He caught her arm to steady her, linked his with hers. What was he doing here? One of the new arrivals. She should have known. Sleaze oozed everywhere.

"I'm flying."

He raised his eyebrows. "You just came back from a long flight."

This confirmed her judgment that he wasn't a good Chevalier. She shifted her shoulders...those muscles were still tense and one of the reasons she wanted to fly. Sex would be better. "That was a mission. Now I want to indulge in pleasure." As soon as she said it, she knew she'd given him an opening she'd never wanted him to have.

"Pleasure." He smiled, slowly. Some woman must have told him he had a killer smile. It was nice enough, especially combined with twinkling eyes and handsome features, but it had no effect on Calli. "I would be honored to provide you with pleasure."

She pulled her arm from his. Didn't look his way when she replied. "I'm Pairbonded." Though she still wanted to amble, she picked up the pace.

"I've never heard that Pairbonding was completely exclusive. And your Pairling leaves you so long, so often."

Widening her eyes, she said, "No? Exclusivity is definite. It said so in the Lorebook of Pairbonding." She didn't even know if there was such a book.

His totally blank look amused her. "There's a book on it? And you *read* it?"

The exchange was beginning to energize her, or the rapid

walk. "Of course I read it. We Exotiques are given *lots* to read, and since I wanted to know about the Choosing and Bonding—the ritual and all." Sounded good to her.

Within sight of the corral, she quickly scanned what volarans idled there, reaching out with her mind to discover which one would best match her mood. Her squire's volaran was fresh. *May I fly your volaran,* she sent to man and steed. Her squire bowed, the volaran neighed in delight. So she walked up to the young stallion and smoothed his neck, noticing her hand shook. *Let's fly high and free and play!*

The volaran lifted his head, twitched his ears, then eyed her companion. Pulling his top lip up in a smirk, he made a short hop to just in front of them, kicking up dust. Calli had had just enough warning to hold her breath.

Raoul doubled over coughing.

They were off and into the blue, soon away from the camp. Her body shook in reaction. She'd managed to fend it off as long as she had duties to perform, but now... Now shudders ripped through her. The volaran murmured in her mind, more than one, Singing, soothing. On one turn, he said, *Look,* angling his head.

Marrec and Dark Lance zoomed toward them.

Tears, pulled deep from her heart, flooded her eyes until she could barely see her Pairling. *Marrec,* she whispered mind to mind.

I mounted within minutes of receiving your message from the feycoocu.

He hadn't known. She hiccupped, slumped in the saddle, reached in her pocket for a handkerchief.

The blow hit her hard, toppled her forward, sideways.

Darkness edged her vision. The volaran screamed, dropped. He'd been hurt, too! Another hit, backed by malevolent hatred, and pain exploded in her head. She fell. Saw thin mist below her, the gray tossing sea.

She was going to die.

Marrec and Dark Lance were there. He Sang, leaned far out from Dark Lance's saddle. Grabbed her.

Air whipped around them, plucked Marrec from his volaran. The winged horses screamed but were lost from sight.

He and she fell together. She wrapped herself around him. So this was how bondmates died. Together. Complete and utter despair shrouded her. They were orphaning their children. *I love you.*

I love you. His arms wrapped tighter.

They didn't plunge into the sea.

Another wind sucked them, buffeted them, into a gray place of mighty winds.

The dimensional corridor.

The Snap had come.

35

Holding each other, they spun to a portal on the far side of the corridor and hung suspended. In the wide, wide door, the Rocking Bar T spread before her with all the lush richness of summer. Her heart tore. She loved that place. If she could have transported it back to Lladrana, she would have. The view telescoped and she saw her father near the corral. He was smiling, whistling, talking to a handsome younger man who had more city on him than cowboy.

Calli thought she whimpered, but the screaming tornadoes around her took her voice. She knew she trembled because Marrec squeezed tighter, nearly stopping her breath. At least that's why she thought her chest constricted so. The only time she'd seen her father smile in recent years was when she won a race and when she handed over money. He looked happy.

That she was gone? He sure wasn't grieving. She blinked her

eyes, sent her gaze away from the man and back to the land, the fields and pastures, the trees, the gorgeous mountains, not nearly as threatening as those north of Lladrana. Then she turned her head into Marrec's shoulder. She loved the place, but she loved him, their children and Lladrana more.

The winds seemed to calm and they drifted back to a closing window on the other side of the corridor, down to where a new portal was opening…ground level near the encampment.

A high-pitched note and glass shattering hit her ears. The whirlwind picked up again, took them. Thrust them toward Earth, through the door.

She saw where they were coming out. "Cliff!" she screamed, sent mentally with all her might, *Side by side! Narrow path.*

Calli stumbled out first, staggered to the side and kept her fingers linked tightly with Marrec's and her body angled so that when he plunged through, she slowed his forward momentum. She grabbed him and forced him back against the wall of the hillside, away from the cliff. The ledge was pretty wide here, over a yard, but for a tall man running that was only a pace.

Trembling at the quick succession of danger, her breath rasped in and out in shudders. "Shit, I'm home," she said in English and her eyes stung. That was so wrong. Her home was on Lladrana. A more verdant, older ranch than this one.

But seeing the land, the beauty of her native home, made her throat burn with unshed tears.

Then he was steadying her—and standing perfectly still, as if probing for danger with all his senses. "This is not Lladrana," he said flatly.

"No." She gulped in one last shaky breath, determined to get ahold of herself. "This is—was—my home on...on—" The scents were so familiar, the colors of mountains and sky and ground achingly beloved. Once. All her emotions tumbled inside her at being...here.

"Exotique Terre," he ended for her.

"Yes."

Slowly his gaze encompassed the panorama.

The clashing of wants, of needs, stopped in Calli. She loved this ranch, but not as much as she loved Diaminta and Jetyer. She flung herself at the crystal, pounded on it. "Let us in. Let us *in*." She thought she screamed it...in Lladranan. Frantically, she peered into the depths of the shadowed layers, and saw nothing. No sign of the world she'd fallen into.

Marrec covered her fists with his hands, pulled them away. Her hands were red and scratched, but that didn't matter. She gasped out words. "I came through here. Right here. That morning. I came through *here!* Why can't I get back?"

"It was the Snap."

"I know what it was! But I didn't want to return. I didn't." To her horror, tears dribbled from her eyes, her nose started running. "And even...even...if I ha-had come back, it shouldn't have t-taken you, should it have? I was *sup-posed* to stay. *We* were s'posed to stay." Fear fluttered like a panicked bird inside her chest. "Why are we here? Why aren't we *there?*"

"I don't know."

"How are we going to get back?"

"I don't know."

"Jetyer!" she screamed. "Diaminta!"

He shook her. "Calli. Stop. Stop this now!"

Wildness beat inside her, then she focused on his face. His golden-skinned, Lladranan face, alien to Earth. "Oh, God," she moaned in English, dropping her head. "I've lost it."

"Calli?"

She was too ashamed to meet his eyes. All these emotions rolling through her like a freight train. An English comparison. She switched to Lladranan. "I panicked. I'm sorry. I've never been so scared." And now, in the cool shade of the mountains, she was cold. Shivering. Shock.

He gave her a handkerchief and she wiped her face, buried her nose in it to catch the scent of Lladrana, the faint odor of their children was on that piece of linen. She clutched it close. He set her back against the rough hillside, then stepped in front of the crystal. Tested it himself with large, firm hands. "Whatever doorway was here is now closed."

Calli hiccupped. "Can you see any shades of Lladrana, any volarans?"

"No. It is but crystal to me. Would you have returned without me?" Marrec said conversationally.

That shocked her out of her grief. "Of course not. You shouldn't have come," she said and knew she was speaking Lladranan again.

"Shouldn't I?" His tone was that mild one he used to hide deep hurt. Their Songs were only a whisper.

She looked up at him, gulped and pressed her lips together hard to keep from breaking into deep sobs. She wanted to be home, in Lladrana. She wanted to be here. If it had been at all possible to transport this slice of land to

Lladrana, she'd have done it, swapped the place in Lladrana for this one. Foolishness. Despite all the strange and wonderful magic she'd experienced in the last couple of months, that could never be.

But most of all, she wanted this man and her children, her beloved children.

She framed his face in her hands. When she could speak, she said, "I would not have torn you from your home. From your children."

"It is our home and our children."

Her chin wobbled. She set it. "Yes."

Once again, he turned to survey her old home, hands on hips. Every movement of his was outwardly casual, but very, very deliberate. She couldn't hear much of his Song here. Hell, she couldn't hear any of her own, but she sensed he was using the skills he'd developed over a hard life to keep himself from giving in to the panic she'd already succumbed to. He glanced at the clouds gathering over the mountains. "I don't think we will be able to stay here on this ledge indefinitely."

She cleared her throat. "No." She patted her face on one small corner of the handkerchief, knowing she wouldn't want to wash any scent of Diaminta away.

He stared at her, and she couldn't tell what he was thinking. Their bond had all but vanished. She cast aside gibbering fear. That sure wouldn't help anything.

"Neither of us are Circlets, with knowledge as to how to open any portal between worlds."

"The dimensional corridor," she said and couldn't prevent one last, racking shudder.

"Ayes. I read Alexa's and Marian's stories."

She hadn't known that. She tried for a watery smile. "Then you know as much as I do, which isn't very much."

A rumble of thunder punctuated that remark and made her feel even more helpless. "We have to get off the mountain."

"Ayes."

She steeled herself. "It's 'yes' here. Ayes. Yes. How good are you at languages?"

His eyes were dark, fathomless. "Good, I think, with dialects at least, and once I went to Krache in northern Shud. I know some of that language. But Calli, you forget, we bloodbonded. I think I will pick up your Ang-lish quickly." He smiled but it had no humor. "It's in my blood."

"I suppose so." With a deep inhalation that told her once again she was back in Colorado, she held out her hand to him. "Let's go."

"Together." He nodded.

That started her eyes swimming with tears again. Her lips quivered as she smiled. "At least we *are* together."

He grasped her fingers and lifted them to his lips and she heard the faintest wisp of Song. "I would not let you leave without me."

She closed her eyes, opened her lids slowly. "Thank you."

"Say that in Ang-lish."

"*English*. Thank you."

This time she tried to wipe her eyes on her leathers, but they were dreeth and useless for absorbing anything.

"Why aren't you using my handkerchief?"

She gulped, whispered. "It smells of Diaminta."

He flinched.

"Still, wouldn't you rather be alone in Lladrana with our children instead of with me?" she asked.

"We have grown apart."

She opened her mouth, but he raised a hand. "Both our faults. I would rather we *both* be on Lladrana. But we are a Pair. Pairbonded. We will always belong together." His breath jerked out. "We can only hope our children will be cared for."

"Alexa and Marian would never let our children be abandoned." That was one thing she was sure of. "Never. They will raise Diaminta and Jetyer themselves, if necessary."

He stared at her. "You trust them."

"Yes."

The wind spattered them with fat raindrops. Calli set her shoulders. "We'd better go on down."

"Yes," he said in English.

They were halfway down the hill when her gaze automatically swept the ranch. She noted that it had been a good year. The fields were green, the cattle fat. Something odd registered and she stiffened, fixed her scrutiny on the house. It had been painted. She could only stare.

As long as she could remember, it had been brown fading more into drabness every year, with darker, dustier trim. Now it was white and blue.

She stopped in her tracks.

"What is it?"

"The house. It's been painted."

"Then there have been some changes."

"More than small changes, believe you me." With force of will, she kept her body from trembling. "My father hasn't painted that house since…since…never."

Her scrutiny jumped from the house to the arena. It was in good shape, too, better than what she'd had time to fix up. Her father still stood with the younger man whom she'd seen when she'd been in the dimensional corridor. The men talked and gestured at four horses. Calli recognized none of them.

As soon as they reached the bottom of the path, Marrec took her hand, and she held tight. She and Marrec were only a few yards from the corral when her dad looked up. He stiffened and his expression went cold.

Marrec squeezed her fingers and she glanced at him. He looked equally impassive, but she sensed alert wariness from him.

The wind came up, more raindrops pattered around them as they stopped beside her father and the young man.

"So you're back," her father said.

"Yes," she said.

"Will?" asked the young man.

"This is my stepson, Roy. Roy, this is Calli. You've heard of her," her father said.

The emotional blow that he'd *married* was like a sock to her stomach, but it wasn't quite as hard as it should have been. Her subconscious had put all the clues together. She lifted her chin, met her father's eyes—the same color as her own. "This is my husband, Marrec Gardpont. Marrec, my father, Will Torcher."

Her father looked Marrec up and down. Though he said nothing, Calli knew prejudice was kicking in. He nodded at Marrec. A nod of acknowledgment of someone standing before him, not approval, not respect, not even acceptance that Marrec was worthy of a handshake. Marrec stiffened beside her. She pressed his arm.

Her father's smile had long gone. He was thin lipped now. "You back for good?"

She was pretty sure that everyone here thought her being back wasn't good. Though Roy looked less tense than anyone else.

"I'll fight you for the ranch." They were months-old words that shot out of her mouth, filled with anger and bitterness, which she already sensed were futile.

"You won't win," he said, and turned away.

"I've put plenty into this place, and everyone knows it." She kept step with him.

"Calli," Marrec said.

36

She stopped the anger and humiliation and bitterness from bursting out in more hurtful words. Who knew all that was still inside her, as strong as it had been before she'd been Summoned to Lladrana?

Her father's gaze swept the land and for the first time in her memory, she saw love for the ranch on his face. "Calli, you won't win."

"We'll see." Maybe not the ranch, but she'd get a stake.

"I'll tell Dora you're here." He lengthened his stride.

Calli would have had to run to keep up with him, and that she refused to do.

"Will." Roy's smile was strained. "He's a tough guy."

"Yeah," said Calli.

Roy held out his hand, "Roy Etrang."

His grip was firm. Calli asked, "Aren't you upset?"

"The ranch isn't mine." A brief smile, but flickering sadness in his eyes. "I won't lie and say I don't want it. But the ranch is Will's."

"And mine," Calli said, then spoke another truth. "And Dora's."

Roy nodded, sympathy in his gaze. "And Dora's. I'll take you in." He didn't say, but Calli figured he knew, that her name wasn't officially on any papers, and Dora's was.

They circled the house to enter through the side door and the mudroom. Marrec was silent and Calli knew he was soaking everything in. She was glad now, for herself and him, that he'd had a rough life. He'd know to be quiet until he could adapt. He'd fight with her and for her.

Since she and Marrec wore no outer gear, she only brushed her feet on the mat, keeping her gaze from shooting up the narrow back stairs to her old room.

The rumble of her father's voice came, along with high, shrill protests. She stopped at the open door to the kitchen. Marrec put his arm around her shoulders. Briefly, she laid her head against his arm. Felt the dreeth-skin leathers.

How things had changed.

"I won't have her here!" a woman's voice spiked.

"Then she'll go stay in town," her dad said expressionlessly. "Better to keep this here."

Well, things wouldn't be getting any better by lingering in the mudroom. Calli stepped into the kitchen, and color—pastels—burst upon her vision as if they'd been bold carnival hues, they were so different than the dingy white she'd left. The walls were newly painted in pale green, with pretty flowered curtains at the window matching a cloth on an equally new table with polished curvy legs.

A woman whirled to her. Calli's eyes went wide. Her father's new wife was a plump woman about his age with carefully tended colored blond hair, a slight sheen of makeup and bright blue eyes holding anger and greed. "You aren't welcome here."

"Mom," Roy protested.

Dora tossed her head; no hair flew from its ordered place in the sprayed bob.

"I'm Calli *Torcher* Gardpont, this is my husband, Marrec." She shut up. Nothing she could say would sound believable. She'd left without taking anything and had now reappeared, with a husband but nothing else. Her dad might not have noticed or cared and she could only hope Dora was too selfish and Roy too preoccupied to ask piercing questions.

Dora's lips pushed in and out. Finally she said, "How long are you going to stay in the area?"

"As long as it takes to resolve things. And if we leave, it won't be empty handed."

"We'll see about that."

"Yes, we will. I poured a lot of money into this ranch."

"Hmmph!" Dora huffed.

"Mom."

"Your room is pretty much the way you left it when you ran off." Dora's eyes slid to Will to see if he would defend Calli from the jab. Calli could have told her that he hadn't even noticed the slight. "You and your husband—" she stared at Calli's ringless left hand "—can bunk there until we figure this out." She turned to Roy. "I hope you're happy now."

He'd reddened, but jerked a nod. "It's the right thing to do."

"Doubt it," Dora said. "Supper's at five. That gives you about an hour to clean up."

"Right," Calli said. She'd always prepared supper at five. Discreetly tugging Marrec's hand, she led him back to the side entrance. She needed to get somewhere private where she could have a quiet breakdown.

She climbed the narrow stairs to the attic, to her room, and opened the door. How small it was. How sterile. She stumbled in, no tears now, but continuing shock after shock, folded onto the double bed.

Marrec sat beside her and the old mattress pitched her into him. He circled his arm around her, drew her close. He was the only warmth in the universe. And his strong chest against her, the beating of his heart, was the only thing that mattered.

This wasn't home anymore.

Probably hadn't been "home" for a long time, but she'd defined it that way.

She—they—were torn from their real home, the one they'd built together.

"I am receiving flashes from your past," Marrec said evenly. "So I know this is the house you grew to adulthood in."

"Yes." Her throat felt dry, but she didn't have the energy to go to the tiny half bath for a drink of water. She scanned the room. It was relatively clean but smelled musty, and the heat would be too much for her if she weren't shivering so.

"I recall when you were Summoned."

That had tears flooding back and down her cheeks. Marrec swept a pillow from its case and handed her the cloth. She sniffed and wiped her eyes. "I remember, too," she said thickly.

"You were injured."

She flinched. "Yes."

"Had been very hurt, for a long time."

She nodded.

"Your father did not ask about your injuries."

A strangled noise came from her and she turned into him. "I don't think he even noticed that I am fully healed." She held out her hands to him. "This is not our home. Can we link and try to project our thoughts to Lladrana?"

"Good idea." He took her hands.

Love, hope, fear cycled between them.

Alexa! Calli shouted, sending all her Power in a burst toward the first Exotique. She thought the scream got lost in whistling winds.

Marrec squeezed her hands. *Try visualizing Marian. She's a Circlet. Has a Powerful Song.*

Telepathy didn't work as easily here. Calli formed an image of Marian, and she was leaning back against Jaquar.

Good, Marrec said. He took her image and layered it with his own—Marian's dress against her full figure, refined the shape of her breasts and hips, added shades of color to her hair. Calli chuckled. Then she concentrated on Jaquar, the blue, blue of his eyes, the line of his jaw—and his shoulders. When she glanced up, one side of Marrec's mouth had quirked up and his eyes gleamed amusement.

She closed her eyes, gathered her Power, felt Marrec's Song and Power join her own. *Mar-i-an!* The yell echoed through her head. She thought it might have circled the world. Her shoulders slumped and she opened damp eyes to look at Marrec. His expression was somber. He shook his head slightly. "Ttho. I did not reach her, either."

Her lips had been pressed tightly together as she'd sent everything with her mind. "We'll try again."

He nodded, but she felt no hope from him.

They walked down the stairs and heard bustling from behind the kitchen door that was open a crack. Roy was saying, "But how did they get here? Looked like they *walked* in. They sure didn't drive the truck Calli won last year. We've been using that. Put a lotta miles on it."

Calli stopped in the mudroom. Luckily, neither Roy nor her father had seen her and Marrec descend the hillside path.

"Her fault if she left the truck for our use." Her dad snorted. "Bert, next door."

The next ranch over was about five miles away, if you rode.

"Huh?" said Roy.

"The Honorable Trent Philbert next door," her dad said patiently. Calli had never heard that tone from him in her life. Something niggled at her mind as she heard Bert's name, but she lost it as her dad continued.

"The guy with those fancy horses? He's a big shot in Denver. The Philberts have had the spread down the road for the last eighty years, but mostly live in Denver and use the place a coupla times for vacation. Damn shame. He and that new flaky wife of his and those horses came down the day before Calli left. Bert's always had a soft spot for Calli." He grunted. "She gave him some money to invest from her winnings."

"Really?" asked Dora. "How much?"

"Dunno," her dad said.

Neither did Calli. She'd given Bert five percent of her first year's winnings, and a little more every year when she'd seen him at the National Western Stock Show in Denver. Wonder how much she had. A soft sigh escaped her at the recollection of that money. If nothing else, it would give her and Marrec a stake. She hadn't known Bert had arrived, with or without fancy horses.

"But their clothes!" Dora tsked.

"Yeah, those looked weird," Roy said.

Marrec met her eyes, looked down at himself in his dreeth leathers. Calli had changed into some of her old clothes.

"Probably came from onna those theme parks," her dad said indifferently. "Guy had been callin' Calli to persuade her to work for him—Renaissance Past, or somethin' like that."

Calli blinked. That was true. Interesting how her dad spun a story. How easily he'd accepted and explained her disappearance. She bit her lip as anger spurted through her.

The clock in the living room bonged five.

"It's suppertime and they're lat—" Dora started.

Pulling the door open, Calli went into the kitchen. All places were set. With flowered paper napkins, too.

"Good evening, folks," she said.

"Good evening, folks," Marrec echoed.

After dinner, Calli showed Marrec around the ranch, helped with the evening chores and introduced herself and Marrec to the new horses—cutting horses, appropriate for a cattle ranch.

If...if they couldn't get back to Lladrana...nerves jumped

in her stomach…but she shoved that thought into a little box and locked it away, because otherwise she teetered on the edge of panic. Continued to plan for a future here on Earth. Had to. Keep moving forward.

But there was no way she'd get the ranch now that Dora had taken possession. Everyone in the area would favor her dad and his new wife over Calli. Calli was younger, would be expected to make her own way, live at her husband's home. She swallowed hard. How she wanted that.

She'd fight, but didn't expect it would take long. Only the time to talk to the bankers, negotiate with her dad, probably three weeks at the most. Three weeks to find a way back through the crystal to Lladrana…after that, the best Calli could do would be to walk away with money in her pocket to find a new place, another Power point to reach her home.

Time and again, Calli touched Marrec—more often than she ever had since those first few days in Lladrana. And each time, he returned her affection…even if it was only a warm look in his eyes.

Her fears calmed. She wasn't alone with people who disliked her, had no use for her.

She gave Marrec the penny tour of the house, too, noting with wide eyes that the place now had *three* computers. The one she'd installed for the ranch business was replaced by a much newer, fancier model, and the desk papers looked arranged in a different pattern than her dad used—Roy, or Dora. Another, smaller desk made an L and sported another new computer.

Roy had a computer in his room, the spare room on the second floor. From what she could see at a glance, he had a stack of college texts—mostly on agriculture and ranch management.

As soon as it was dark and the others had gone to the living room and switched on TV, Calli took Marrec up to her room. She wasn't up to explaining television, and Marrec, who'd been doing pretty well around the ranch, showed strain lines dug in near his eyes. He'd spoken little but observed everything. She got the impression that he was learning English quickly.

They showered, bumping bodies and making love, then went to bed after another try to contact Alexa and Marian, and a language lesson, with Marrec asking questions.

There, in the dark, Calli could whisper her real concerns. "Do you think we'll be able to get back through the crystal? Do you think they'll be able to Summon us back? Do you think they'll even try?"

He didn't answer her for long minutes. "The survey of the island must have been your task. You completed it. And have trained people to partner with volarans. It will depend upon the volarans, if they leave like they did before."

She cleared her throat. "There was something else. Something I showed the volarans—how to turn invisible."

He jerked beside her. "What?"

So she told him of the flight over the Dark's nest, how she'd triggered an instinctive response in Thunder—for invisibility. She even took Marrec's hand and tried to enter the same state of consciousness, but was too disturbed and tense. She almost laughed. She could manage to enter a different mindset above an evil that gnawed at a planet, yet couldn't throw off her own fears in a house that she'd known all her life.

She gave a watery sniff, rolled close to him, welcoming his hard body against hers, his arms around her. "Surely they wouldn't think that I'd, *we'd,* abandon our children, would succumb to the Snap. They *must* know something went wrong."

He stroked her hair. "I don't know, Calli."

That night, after Calli was asleep, Marrec lay in the small, lumpy bed and felt the tension they'd released explosively in lovemaking claim him once again. He was petrified down to his toenails and trying hard not to think that they were stuck in this very strange world. Yet he had little hope. The Marshalls didn't consider Calli essential. They had their own Exotique. Calli had fulfilled her task, and her techniques for training volarans had been taught to others.

She'd even shown the volarans how they could protect themselves. Whatever her task had been, she'd fulfilled it. Them. Exceptionally well, of course. Would they want her back? The Chevaliers were still an independent force and he didn't believe they would muster the desire and the zhiv to pay the fee the Marshalls would want *again* to return Calli. If the volarans left again...but would they? They loved Calli, but she'd given them something new, too, would they consider that enough?

Did anyone even realize that the Snap had gone wrong? That Calli hadn't left of her own free will?

He, of course, was of no importance whatsoever and wondered how much Power it would take to open the crystal in the mountain from Lladrana. He knew enough from the time he'd spent this day to understand his Power—and Calli's—was much less here.

He tried not to think of his children, of how Jetyer would feel abandoned. Nothing he could do there. He'd tried on his own to contact his son, to no avail, and was hesitant to ask Calli to send to Jetyer. Would people believe the boy if he said he'd heard his father and mother? Somehow Marrec didn't think so. They'd put it down to grief.

Marrec pulled Calli closer, closed his eyes as they prickled when she snuggled close, threw a leg over his, as if to keep him near. He was glad he was with Calli. Despite the way it appeared, with him knowing little of the language and nothing of the society, he sensed she needed him more than ever.

This little trip had certainly unblocked his hearing in some ways. The air here was different, with an odd metallic tang he didn't like. The sky was not quite the correct color blue, and the *machines* he'd seen were frightening. He hadn't much cared for the food, and had listened hard to the quiet Song between himself and Calli to sense what was going on. Just from the abrupt and sharp tones others used with her, he'd known she was fighting battles where he could only stand beside her and offer support, not even understanding.

All this time, he hadn't fully comprehended how hard it must have been for Calli on Lladrana. She'd seemed to fit into life—his lifestyle—so easily. He was smart enough to figure that the Song would Summon only those people who *could* adapt to Lladrana, but still it was a major accomplishment that he hadn't given her credit for.

When they'd had that argument, he'd been right. Their priorities should have been with their children, and Calli wanted to please everyone. He could see why that was, now, with that hard old man who didn't care a brass coin for such a lovely daughter. But she'd also felt as if there were other duties she had to fulfill—which he hadn't truly realized.

He had been the one most at fault. He'd embraced his new life, wanted to be the best landowner in Lladrana. Wanted his estate to be considered a model for others. Wanted to implement every good idea he'd dreamed of over the years.

Underneath everything, he'd still been looking for status. His motives hadn't changed, only the means—which Calli had given him when she'd chosen him. He'd drawn away from Calli—as much as a Pairbonded person could—and now he regretted it.

Now he could make amends. His life had changed once more, for the worse, riding down the wheel of fortune instead of up, and he *knew* he'd be lost forever on his own. But Calli would never leave him. The idea wouldn't even enter her mind and he Sang a quiet prayer for that blessing. If they had to, once again, they would make another start together.

He slept little that night, woke as soon as he heard stirrings below, yet he didn't get up. He wasn't ready to face this world on his own, not even to stride across a room that wasn't too different from those at home. Calli opened blurry eyes and smiled when she saw him. "Marrec." She rolled a little closer, her gaze sharpened and he saw the joy drain from her.

No, this was not a good place for her, either.

She rolled back and stared at the ceiling. He'd studied those cracks himself.

"I'd forgotten." She blinked hard and he saw tears on her lashes. "We aren't home."

She awoke and it all came rushing back. Her children had been torn from her. Curling up in a ball, she moaned. He held her as she cried, sobs shuddering through her body. He let her weep for them both. Wiped her tears with a handful of funny soft cloth from a box on the bed, and kept her close, stroking her back, making soothing noises.

Finally, she sat up and rubbed her eyes, glanced at a flat circular thing on the wall. "I want to know where I stand, and don't want to take anyone's word for it. We need to visit town—Bellem—to look at land records and go to the bank." Her words were a mixture of Lladranan and English, but he got the drift.

He was glad she'd said "we." He picked up her fingers and pressed a kiss on them. "Pairling."

That made her face soften, a smile curve her lips.

"I'll follow you, just as you followed me."

She looked stricken, her gaze fell. "I didn't. I didn't follow you on Lladrana."

He cleared his throat. Brushed his lips to her fingers again. "You did those first days."

She snorted. "We were bound together."

Brushing hair back from her face, he said, "True, but later you followed your Song, and did what was needful."

"As you did."

"Calli, I'm sorry. I should have been less demanding."

Sighing, she said, "There weren't any good answers, once we adopted the children. But now it's different. If—when—" Her lips quivered. "We've done enough and we have a family. We can contribute by training, on our estate, not by fighting."

"I'm glad you see it that way." He kissed her, long and slow and deep. His body readied. So did hers as he tested it.

"Breakfast, Roy!" called Dora.

Calli flinched.

Marrec gritted his teeth and accepted that he'd find himself in a cold shower shortly. Still, he wanted her happy. So he kissed her brow tenderly. "We will go into this Bellem, then check the crystal again."

She rolled out of bed, all business. "Yes, Koz transferred money for gems and brought them to Lladrana. I can do the same, but I need to know how much I have…and…" Her eyes were too bright when she rushed into the little bathroom.

He knew what she meant. If they couldn't get back to Lladrana.

37

Marian knocked on Alexa's door in her Castle tower.

"Entre!" shouted Alexa.

Opening the door, Marian saw Alexa pacing. The Sword-marshall hadn't been still since Calli's and Marrec's volarans had returned to the northern camp without them.

"How're the children?" Alexa asked.

"As well as can be expected. Settled here in the Circlet Apartments with us. Thank the Song the feycoocus used major magic to bring us back, and you and Bastien, too."

"I tell you, she'd never leave those kids of hers. And wouldn't take Marrec, either."

"Marrec had to go, he's Pairbonded," Marian said.

Scowling, Alexa said, "And how does that happen? I thought a Pairbond was a pretty damn good guarantee that an Exotique stays."

"We know hardly anything about the Snap."

"Don't give me that shit."

With a weary sigh, Marian sank into a plush chair. "It's true. I've gathered journals, letters, other papers and items from previous Exotiques."

"Really?" Alexa looked a little distracted from her worry.

Marian smiled. "Yes, I'll let you have them as soon as I'm finished."

Alexa scuffed the carpet with her foot. "I still don't read Lladranan well, especially handwritten cursive. What's with the Pairbond Exotique thing, though?"

"You're right, as far as I can tell, no Exotique, male or female, who was bonded to a Lladranan returned to Earth."

"There's something screwy going on here," Alexa said, fiddling with her jade baton.

"There's always something strange going on." Marian sighed again, clasped her hands, unclasped them. "Every day something new happens that I'm not prepared for."

Alexa grunted. "Got down to every few days with me, 'til lately." She walked to the curved windows of her suite, staring to the west, where shadows still draped the land. "She wouldn't leave the children." Her face set in stern lines of determination. "I want her back. Her and Marrec."

"The volarans didn't abandon the Castle like they did before she came."

"Yet." She shot a glance at Marian. "I can feel the wrongness of her not being here in my bones. Can't you?"

"It's as if a major theme is missing from the melody."

"Got that right," Alexa said. "I can't settle." A brief grin flashed. "Bastien has liked that—for now, more active sex."

But I want Calli back." She looked up at Marian, eyes shadowed. "I don't think we can win this war without her. This could be the work of her enemy. Or the Dark. Or both. Tell me we can get her back."

Pain swirled through Marian. She felt it all, Calli's children's anguish, the volarans' shock and distress, the Chevaliers' wariness, the Tower Community's deep unease. She promised something she didn't know she could deliver. "We'll get her back."

Marrec had learned early in life that it was near-fatal to show fear, so he kept his locked down around the men and the older woman. And with Calli, too, since he didn't want her to know how extremely disturbed he was.

He was being very, very careful, like the first weeks on the noble's estate after he'd been orphaned. For the first time in his life he'd realized the three great streams of luck he'd had. When he'd claimed the trained volaran on the battlefield, which led to being taken with the winged steed to the estate, when Calli had claimed him, and now, surviving once more in a place completely alien to him—with Calli as his guide.

Seeing, *feeling* her home, was illuminating. The land rejoiced that she'd returned, Sang of her—as did the house and the barn and the stables. As her father did not. The man was a dry stick, whatever emotion he had focused on his new wife. A woman that was a small flickering candle flame to Calli's incandescent star.

What was the most incredible thing was that Calli needed him. Here at her home as much as, or more than, in Lladrana. The man and woman stared at his different skin and hair and features, and he finally recognized the small hum of wariness that had been in Calli's Song from the moment they'd met. She was not Lladranan and every person there—except Alexa and Marian—had stared at her. No wonder she strove to please. No wonder she cherished the other two Exotiques.

After breakfast, they went back up to her room and she headed straight to a low wooden cabinet and opened it, pulling out a small brown tooled-leather bag. She flipped through it, face pale. Then she just shook her head and met Marrec's eyes. She lifted the bag. "This is a purse. It's a standard joke of our culture that no woman leaves her home without her purse." Her smile trembled on her lips. "But here it is. And though I think Dora went through it and took my money, everything else is still here." She shook her head. "My father…" She lapsed into silence, but Marrec knew her thought. Her father had not cared enough about her disappearance to wonder about the bag.

She opened a panel in the back of the cabinet door and took out a white paper envelope, looked at a stack of green pieces of paper. Dividing it in half, she gave him some and told him it was zhiv and explained the denominations. Then she studied him, hard, before asking again in simple English whether he wanted to ride to town.

He had agreed, but thought she meant they'd ride horses. Instead, it was in a wheeled metal vehicle that sent any Song he could hear of nature or even between himself and his mate into random notes. With white knuckles and stiffened body he suffered through the minutes until they arrived. He was out of the "car" in an instant. Mastering the door handle had been easy.

There weren't a lot of people on the white walks near the buildings or in the streets.

"It's still early yet, but the mercantile will be open," Calli said, then repeated the phrase in English.

Yet everyone in town stared—at his clothes, at his face. Calli had told him that this was a small town but the center of local government, "county seat." It was as large as Castleton, but appeared much, much stranger. The first thing they did was go into a shop and buy clothes for him. That morning Calli dressed in some of her old clothes. He changed behind a curtain and Calli bundled his dreeth leathers into a bag of thin, slick, noisy composition.

The only thing he liked was the hat and boots. He'd admired Roy's and Will's hats and boots and was glad to get his own. The hat was gray and sturdy, the boots black with intricate white stitching.

They walked down the street. But Calli stopped at a huge glass shop window. "This is new."

Inside showed a multitude of colorful items, all glittery and colorful except for a thin, white scarflike wrap with gleaming silver beads and silky fringe at the ends of the sleeves and the hem.

Calli sighed, shook her head. "Who would put a world import shop in Bellem?"

Her gaze once again shifted to the scarf-robe, pristine amongst the bold reds, blues and gold.

Marrec gestured at the door. "In."

"No." She met his gaze steadily. "We don't know what the future will bring. We may need all our assets."

His jaw clenched. Just as in Lladranan, here the assets

were Calli's assets. That fact had gnawed at him, even though she'd let him handle the zhiv.

But she read him like no one else, and stepped closer to him. "Marrec, I'm so glad you're with me. I'm so glad you've always been with me. I couldn't have— You have helped me so much and continue to do so." She brushed his cheek with a kiss. They stood there for a while, and people walked around them, giving them curious glances.

The moment crystallized for him, the look of her and everything else in this strange world, the smells, the way the breeze slid against him, the underlying Song. He knew that somehow if he was trapped on this place forever, he could survive.

Then they went to an imposing building where Calli wanted to check on the ownership of the ranch.

Marrec decided to wait in the corridor. The more he heard the language, and from a variety of throats, the more he understood it. Many concepts might be lacking, but if the people were talking about something simple, "kids," "lunch," "horses," Marrec could winkle out the meaning.

A young couple came in holding hands. The man wore strange black-and-white garb, the woman a long white dress. Smiles greeted and followed the couple as they walked along the hall. Marrec frowned. An image tickled his memory and he patiently tracked it down to something he'd seen in Calli's mind during the first few minutes of the heady rush of the bloodbond. It wasn't a real recollection of hers, but a dream, a visualization. Of herself wearing such a gown. The image had had a lot of yearning associated with it. She'd wanted it badly.

He rose and sauntered after the couple. They turned into

a doorway, and he heard the young man's excited voice. "We have an appointment with the Honorable Judge James." The woman giggled nervously and said, "He's going to marry us!"

Marrec walked closer, until he could see into the doorway. A gray-haired woman stood behind a desk, smiling. "I can see that," she said and looked down at a book with very white pages, little lines and handwriting. "You're his second couple today. John Anderson and Rebecca Schmitt, right?"

"Yes."

"Did you bring anyone else?"

"Witnesses? Uh, no!" the man said. He shared an anxious glance with the woman, who clutched the little bunch of flowers so tightly that Marrec saw a drop of green juice hit the floor.

"You aren't required witnesses for the marriage," the woman soothed. "But it's nice to share the occasion, and we have a lovely marriage certificate as a memento in that case. No charge." The young man swallowed and sent glances all around, then caught sight of Marrec.

"Uh, sir, could you…uh, we'd 'preciate you joining us to witness the marriage, I mean, see us married."

The repeated word of "marriage" made the definition finally sound in his mind. Bonding. Pairbonding. The man was wearing two sets of long sleeves, so Marrec didn't think that it would be a bloodbond. This might be interesting. He used one of the few words he knew. "Yes."

The door to another chamber opened and they went in. A man Marrec's age glanced at the couple, and stared a few seconds at him as the older woman closed the door behind them. Then the man inclined his head. Marrec already knew people of authority didn't have streaks in their hair to show it here, but he sensed the man's status all the same.

The ceremony was interesting. And short. It only took a few minutes and Marrec listened hard to the vows, trying to set every word in his memory. This is what he and Calli would have done if they'd both been of this world.

Marrec didn't know how to sign his name in English. Something he'd have to ask Calli. So he took the writing instrument awkwardly in his hand and signed in Lladranan. The young man shook the judge's hand, then held his out to Marrec. Marrec did the same. The young woman threw her arms around him and stood on tiptoe to kiss his cheek. "Thank you. Thank you!"

He said what the others had. "You're very welcome."

"This doesn't look like Japanese or Chinese or Korean," the older woman said, studying the official parchment.

"No," said the judge. "More like Arabic, but not that, either."

The bride shifted. "Can we have it now?"

"Of course." The judge handed her the paper. She grabbed her *husband's* hand and they hurried out.

The older man studied Marrec. Uneasiness pricked his nerves and he said what Calli had told him. "I'm with Calli Torcher."

"The Rocking Bar T? I hadn't heard she was back," said the woman.

"Yes," Marrec said.

The man considered him another moment, offered his hand. "Good job."

Marrec shook his hand and said, "Thank you," then bowed and left.

Calli was waiting for him outside the room she'd gone in. When she saw him, her expression eased. "There you are. Is everything okay?"

Since he'd heard the latter English sentence even on Lladrana, Marrec said, "Yes."

She linked arms with him, as if to make sure he wouldn't stray. "Good."

"Yes."

Her manner was restrained. He sensed she didn't have nearly as nice a time as he'd had. Must have been the distressing news she'd anticipated. But they didn't go back to the ranch. Instead, they sat on a bench in a well-groomed green area that looked like the squares townsfolk made in Castleton.

"Dora moved in fast. From what I heard from Roy, she'd only been in town a couple of weeks before she met Dad. They were married—and she was named co-owner of the ranch—after another two weeks." Calli made a disgusted noise, then blinked hard. "I never would have thought he'd fall for a gold digger."

"Gold digger?"

"A greedy woman only out for what she can get."

Marrec put his arm around Calli, scooted her close. "There seems to be affection between them. I don't think she will run out on him." He'd heard violent whispers between Calli's father and his new wife—all about how Calli's mother had left and then how Calli had "run out."

"No. Her life isn't too hard. Beautiful land. Adoring husband. Future for her son. *After* I get out of the way."

Marrec stroked her hair, her lovely, lovely hair, more common here than in Lladrana but still unexpected to him.

He touched her face, turned it so he could see her eyes. Damp blue eyes. "You have an adoring man."

Her chin wobbled. Her eyes closed, then opened, and tears trailed down her cheeks. "Thank you. Thank you for being here with me. It would have been so hard on my own." She brushed his lips with hers. "Thank you for being you."

He frowned.

She smiled. "Thank you for being the kind of man you are. Strong. Supportive."

"Adoring."

Again she closed her eyes, shook her head, then settled into the curve of his arm. They sat together, thigh by thigh, and Marrec made no suggestion to leave this place. Instead, he closed his eyes, too, and listened. He heard the babble of English, footsteps slow and brisk, but beyond that, he could hear the Song of this world. So rich. So vibrant. So strong. Unlike Amee's.

He was glad Calli hadn't said they'd had the same simple life that Dora had found. That they would have it again—somewhere, somehow. They'd fight and fight again to return to Lladrana, but what happened when years passed? Would they adopt more children, different children? A shaft of pain so deep lanced him at the whisper of the thought that he cast it aside. Calli wrapped her arm around his waist.

They sat for a while, until the peace of the land infused them and their own human problems diminished. Calli sniffed and disentangled herself from him.

He asked what he'd wanted to know all morning. "Calli, am I your husband?"

Her smile was slow and beautiful. "Yes. Yes, you definitely are."

They sat for a few minutes in silence and he found the world beautiful.

She straightened and kissed him on the cheek. Determination was back in her eyes. "The bank is opening. I want to check on my money, see how much I have and get records for the last few years." Her lips twisted. "For my personal account and the ranch's. It will be interesting to see if my father took me off the ranch's account." She took a deep breath. "If he did—well, I'll leave it for now, but will come back if we don't get what we want. Will you wait here?"

He sensed her roiling emotions. She didn't want to believe that they would have to stay in this world, but she was planning as if they had to.

"Yes," he said, tried more words. "I'll wait here."

With a smile and a nod, she walked to another stone building. He waited until she was inside before he hurried to the shop with the white robe.

That afternoon, Calli and Marrec stood on the hillside, hands joined. She smiled up at him and took a deep breath. "Here goes."

Together they placed the palms of their opposite hands to the crystal. A jolt of electricity sizzled through her. She hissed out a breath and kept her hand flat.

38

"Alexa!" Calli and Marrec shouted in unison, mind and heart and Song.

Nothing.

"Marian!"

No response.

Calli clunked her head against the crystal. The hard, unyielding crystal. "I guess this proves that it only opens when the Marshalls do a Summoning ritual." Her voice was thick.

"I guess so."

"How will we ever know? If we go away—and we'll have to—how will we—"

"Shh." He took her in his arms. "Let's not worry about that now."

She snuffled, cleared her throat. "All right. Let's not cross that bridge until we come to it."

"A good saying. We're Chevaliers. We won't quit fighting for the life we want." His lips twitched up in a smile. "We're Chevaliers, though I haven't spent as much time as I wanted with those fascinating horses here. They are much more intelligent and sensitive than the ones on Lladrana. English I am beginning to understand. Equine I still know." He took her hand and led her down the path. "Earth Equine has additional nuances not known to their kind on Lladrana, and not used by volarans. Another, quite beautiful, language."

That notion distracted her. "You're right."

"I also now know why you use so much body language and cues—the effort to speak mind to mind is considerable."

"Also true. I wonder if it will get easier, or if there's some way to boost it."

"A question worthy of Marian."

She tensed behind him, realized she couldn't go on ignoring references to their life *then*. "Thank you." But they both lapsed into silence until they reached the corral where Will and Roy were with the horses. To Calli's amazement, she actually thought she saw relief in Will's eyes. The horses were greener than he'd anticipated when he'd bought them, and neither one of the men were good trainers.

Between herself and Marrec, they had the horses trusting them within an hour.

"Looks like Calli's been teaching you that natural horsemanship deal," Will said.

"Yes. She is an exceptional woman."

Roy narrowed his eyes. "I've heard of that natural stuff. Never paid much attention to it, but you guys…" He shook his head. "What a display of horsemanship. Horsewoman-ship. Those horses actually follow you around now."

Marrec bowed and said, "Thank you."

Calli said, "These are the basics. I'll have to brush up on my skills to work them to be cutters." Then she heard what she'd said, caught the glance Roy and her dad exchanged, and rushed on, "Just for a little while." And felt stupid.

Taking her hand, Marrec lifted her fingers—which smelled like horse—and kissed them. "Until we move on. I need a shower."

"Yes," Calli said.

While they cleaned up and changed for supper, clouds rolled in, the wind whipped up and the sky darkened to leaden gray. Summertime in the Rockies.

Dinner was a stiff and silent meal. Dora had poked and poked at Calli until Roy turned red and refused to look at Calli or Marrec, clearly unsettled by his mother's rude behavior. The older woman finally asked point-blank of Marrec what his and Calli's plans were. He looked at her coolly, then replied that they were still considering.

At that point, Calli pulled out Marrec's new wallet from his equally new jeans and put a hundred-dollar bill on the table. "This is for our room and board for the rest of the week." Surely they'd be back on Lladrana by then.

Roy choked on a bite of food, her dad's expression went stony, that she was paying for hospitality that should have been free. It was an insult, but Calli reckoned they'd be mer-cenary enough to take the money and ignore any hurt feelings. Dora burst into tears and fled upstairs. Calli and Marrec remained behind but didn't speak.

When the storm rolled over them, she could almost think it was there to relieve her own tension. The sky was darker, the network of lightning huger than she'd ever seen. She'd heard of boiling clouds, but had never believed in the phrase until now. The wild wind puffed up curves of black clouds then tore them apart. She shouldn't be standing at the large plate-glass windows of the living room.

Beside her, Marrec said, "Beautiful."

"Yes." She frowned. Both her father and Roy were upstairs—with the hundred bucks—soothing Dora. "I think we should check the stables. Let's make sure the horses are fine." She pulled the curtains to protect the room from flying glass if the window broke. She'd look in the storage shed to see if her dad still had large pieces of plywood there.

A crack of thunder, the pelleting of rain against the window, had her hurrying to the mudroom. She pulled on her slicker and boots in record time, while Marrec took her father's coat.

They ran through a pummeling deluge to the stable, grinned at each other when they were dry. Together, they checked each stall. The horses were nervous, but a touch of the hand, a murmured word soothed them.

Calli opened the door wide enough for her and Marrec to look out at the downpour.

"Let's wait a little!" he shouted over the pounding rain.

She nodded, then glanced up at the hillside. Lightning struck the hill again and again as if *drawn* to it.

The crystal! Their way back home!

Calli plunged from the stable, slipping and sliding in the mud of the yard, running toward the hill, wordlessly screaming her fear.

Marrec tackled her. Held her down under his body as she fought and bucked to get away, run to her hope of returning to Lladrana.

Finally he pressed hard on her, every muscle of his body subduing hers. His wet hands wiped hair and rain from her eyes, framed her face. "Look at me!"

She blinked and did. His face was hard and impassive, as it always was when he felt the most. Instinctively she listened for his Song and found it fast, like his heartbeat, yet he wasn't frightened—at least not about the crystal.

"It's dangerous there! You're not going up."

She wriggled a little under his weight. He didn't budge. "Promise me. We're going back into the house."

Calli realized he was speaking Lladranan. "The crystal!"

"We cannot prevent whatever happens."

She didn't want to believe that. "Our return home!"

Still expressionless, he said, "We'll discuss that later, *inside*."

Hope crumpled inside her. She'd once loved this land more than anything else in the world, more than her father, even, but now it was no longer her home. Everything she cherished was not in this world, her children, her friends— except for this man, her husband.

Marrec's eyes, dark brown and steady—he was so steady—held hers, calmed her. He'd help her get through this. They'd help each other. Their Songs surged and twined together and all she could hear was *their* Song. The Song of the Chevalier Exotique Pair.

He leaned down and brushed her lips with his own. His warm tongue swept across her mouth and she opened it. The kiss was warm and comforting, reminding her of their bond, all the things they'd accomplished together. Now she put her hands on his face and gave, letting her fears go. With her stroking fingers, her mouth nibbling at his, she told this man she trusted him, she loved him. They would find whatever they needed together.

It was right.

He ended the kiss, then rolled off her and pulled her to her feet in one quick and easy move. They ran for the front door, opened it and stepped inside to drip on the small linoleum square entryway.

Her father, Dora and Roy looked at them.

"We checked on the horses," she said.

Roy chuckled. "Looks to me like that wasn't the only thing you did."

She stared at him, this interloper, this young man who would have everything she'd ever wanted, the ranch, her father's affection and respect. His aura showed he was a good man, one who would take care of what once she'd considered hers.

Her time here had passed, and she could give over her dreams of the ranch to Roy—letting him make of the place whatever he wanted—in peace. She nodded to him and smiled. "Maybe we copped a feel or two."

He cocked his head as if sensing her change in attitude. Then he grinned. "What's a good storm if it doesn't stir us up?"

Since it was exactly her opinion, she grinned back.

Dora made a disapproving noise. "You're dripping all over the floor. You should have come in by way of the mudroom."

But the front door had been closest.

"Go dry off and change," Dora said.

Marrec helped Calli off with her coat, then hung his

slicker on the hook beside hers. She turned away from her father and helped Marrec off with his beautiful boots.

When she and Marrec entered their bedroom, neither of them turned on the light. Calli went to the bathroom and pulled towels from the rack, drying herself, then going to her husband and wiping him down, so their clothes would be easier to take off. Though it was the end of summer and hot, being downstairs in her wet clothes had chilled her. Up here was better. She handed him a couple of towels and they both skinned out of their clothes, dried off and started dressing again.

"The crystal had been tuned. Maybe that's why the lightning was attracted to it."

She blinked. "What do you mean?"

"The crystal had been tuned. I have heard of Mirror Magic. Someone tuned the crystal to be able to watch this place as well to be a portal on the Lladrana side of the corridor."

"Who?"

"I don't know. Someone Powerful."

"But, but I looked in the crystal all of my life, why didn't it break before?"

He frowned. "You must not have felt it when we came through, since you are part of both Lladranan and Earthen Power, but I did. The crystal had been tuned on *this* side, too, more recently."

Her mouth dropped open. She definitely needed to suck in more air to make her brain consider Earth Power. She'd read Marian's story, but supposed she'd disregarded the parts that didn't make sense, like magic here on Earth. Calli hadn't tried to do much magic, only used what came naturally, like her "gift" with horses. Marian was the type who'd consider experimentation.

"Been tuned recently?" Her voice was high. "How recently?"

Marrec shrugged. "I'm not a Circlet, I don't know."

"Before I left or after?"

His brows dipped deeper. "I think both."

"Oh, wow." She dropped to sit on the bed in her underwear. "What does that mean?"

"You've seen Lladrana through that crystal for years. I can only think that's the Singer's doing." He shrugged but it was more of a shudder, then he dragged on a T-shirt and covered it with a chambray shirt. "That the crystal was tuned recently...I don't know if someone from Singer's Abbey came through then went back, or..."

"Or what?"

"Or there is someone here."

It was Calli's turn to shiver. "Oh, I can't think that's right."

"Okay." He sat down next to her and scooped her up and put her on his lap. They sat there a moment. Calli wanted to relax against him, to hear the steady beat of his heart, but she just couldn't.

"But I wish it were so." She sniffed, wiped her face with the towel. "That someone here knew how to get us back. What are we going to do?"

"I don't know."

"I can't do a ritual like Marian. I've never made one up. Have you?"

"I don't know how to return us to Lladrana." That sounded torn from him. She circled him with her arms. Calli bit her lip, hard.

His body was tense, he held her tight. When he let out a breath some of his fear went with it. "We *will* teach ourselves. Find a place of Power."

She thought a minute. "There's Marian's apartment." She grimaced. "Though she never wrote of the actual address, and it's probably rented."

"Perhaps."

"I won't give up," she said fiercely. "We may be forced into some sort of normal life, but I won't give up. If I have to study to be a damn Circlet."

"We will never give up," he agreed. "But for now, there's only one thing we can do. Proceed with plans here."

"As if we'll stay forever?" She could barely say the words.

"Aye— Yes. And plan for the next few weeks."

She licked her lips. "The next few weeks... You don't know how to get us back, and I don't either. So we'll have to hope they want us..." She tried not to think of her father, of rejection, of circles and cycles in life. "And Summon us home."

"Best not to hope too much."

They loved, then slept.

Alexa called a meeting midmorning the next day. They gathered in the shady cloister, in the corner where the keep wall met the round wall of the northeast tower. The men weren't yet concerned about Calli and Marrec going to Earth, so the group was all women. Alexa herself, Marian, Lady Knight Swordmarshall Thealia and Lady Hallard.

Tea and cookies were served, and like the fighters that most of them were, they ate when they got a chance. After inhaling two cookies—they were snickerdoodles, which weren't her favorite—Alexa brought up the topic. "How are we going to get them back?"

"I'm not sure that is the correct question," Thealia said. "The question can very well be, 'Should we bring her back?'"

"That's cold," Marian said.

Thealia merely raised her eyebrows. "She is an excellent trainer, but some of us now know her techniques—"

"I wouldn't bet on that." Alexa stuck out her chin.

"And she has already found and surveyed the Dark's location for you, hasn't she?" Marian's voice was soft with disgust.

"For us all," Thealia said evenly. "And since she has left we've had no threats within the Castle to anyone, and no battles of any kind."

"I think that's significant in itself," Marian said.

Lady Hallard snorted. "So, Swordmarshall, it doesn't look as if the Marshalls will try a Summoning."

Thealia's nostrils flared before she answered. "The last 'return' Summoning of you, Marian, was made possible because you were performing a ritual yourself. That effort included Marshalls, Chevaliers and Circlets. And we paid for it."

"And I paid for it, too. Both before and after. In full." Marian sat with straight and perfect posture in her chair. She blinked, then a little frown line formed between her brows. "But I've read the notes Calli has been keeping for her Lorebook of Exotiques. She came through a crystal. A portal to the dimensional corridor, perhaps."

"That's something you Sorcerers and Sorceresses can work on," Lady Hallard said.

"We will!"

"But in what time frame?" Hallard stretched, crossed her

legs at her ankles. "We Chevaliers don't have the teamwork, experience or Power to Summon Calli on our own."

"And Marrec!" Alexa snapped.

"Calli *and* Marrec," Lady Hallard agreed. A small smile played about her lips. "But every single day that Calli was here, we heard how she was the *Volaran Exotique.* Let *them* bring her back."

Alexa's mouth dropped open. She glanced at Marian to see her rapidly blinking, considering all sorts of plans, options, spells, *Songs,* but she seemed surprised, too.

Rapid hoofbeats sounded and they turned to see Thunder trotting down the cloister walk. Even Thealia's eyes went wide.

He stopped and snorted, his head going up and fixing his dark gaze on them all. *And so we shall. Perhaps. At the proper time. We, too, can form a Circle. We, too, can Summon.*

"Then why didn't you before?" Lady Hallard jerked from her slouch.

Humans had to want her, too. Chevaliers. To work with us. To work with the Marshalls and the Tower. He beat a little tattoo on the flagstones, causing sparks, then ran and jumped out the next open cloister window.

Mouth twitching, Alexa said, "Guess that told us." She turned to the others. "Marian, are the children still with you?"

"For the moment."

"Good." A touch of glee spritzed through her as she stood. "It will be interesting to see when and how the volarans bring our Volaran Exotique and her bondmate back. But then, we might not *see* it at all. Now the matter is completely out of our hands. Thealia and Lady Hallard, you might want to remember in the future that *no* Exotique is ever without options…or friends. Whether here or on Exotique Terre." When a thought occurred to her, she spoke to Marian. "Exotique Circlet, what number of us Exotiques do you think it would take to Summon another?"

"How many Exotiques does it take to screw in a light-bulb?" Marian murmured in English.

Alexa choked a laugh.

Marian lifted a shoulder. "I don't know," she replied in Lladranan. Then she lifted her brows. "But I will definitely figure that out."

Nodding, Alexa shoved her hands in her pockets. "You might want to draft a Summoning Song for us."

"Ayes, ayes." Marian was already scribbling on parchment. "Songs for groups of three, four, five of us. I don't think just the two of us could do it now, without more connection." She glanced up at Alexa, eyes serious. "It's too bad Calli didn't bond with us, too, before she left."

"Uh-huh," Alexa said—an English phrase she'd introduced into Lladranan and was now well known. "I bet Calli is thinking that, too."

39

That same idea had occurred to Calli late that afternoon and she cursed.

"What?" asked Marrec.

"How many people are you bloodbonded to?" she asked. They were up on the hillside. Only shards of the crystal remained, none of them larger than three inches. Nevertheless, they'd tried reaching out to Lladrana again.

Marrec rolled his shoulders in a shrug. "Some bloodbonding occurs when you fight on a battlefield and you and another share a kill, or drip blood on each other. That's the least amount of connection. In that way, quite a few. I swore an oath to Lady Hallard, but did not actually bloodbond with her."

"Were you ever an apprentice?"

"Stable boy," he said shortly. "Never noble enough or well connected enough to be a squire. My master is long dead."

"Oh-kay." She shook her head. "I should have bonded with Alexa and Marian. With that bond…"

Marrec placed his hand around the nape of her neck. "You gave of yourself to many."

"To too many, you thought," she said gruffly.

"True. Had I but known…"

"Yeah." She kicked some of the crystal off the cliff. "Well, no use hanging around here, do you think?"

"No." He squinted into the distance. "They will either Summon us or not."

"Let's settle everything about the ranch tonight, then."

He turned to her, cradled her face in his hands. "Are you sure?"

"Yes. We've talked about…about how much we want from Dad. I called Bert yesterday and the investments have done well." A long sigh emptied her breath. She put her hands on his wrists. "We should have enough to buy a ranch, start a training program." Stepping back, she scanned the land she loved. "Not here. Not in Colorado. Montana. Idaho, maybe." She managed a smile. "We can look for properties on the Internet tonight. Wait 'til you see *that*."

Waiting got on Alexa's nerves—and it showed in her work with the horses and volarans. They were all pretty much irritated with her by midafternoon. She sat alone in the indoor arena and watched the mare teach the only filly in the Castle some flying patterns. Since the filly was learning just like her, and since the little volaran was supposed to be her destined steed, Alexa figured that she provided moral support to the youngster. And it was cool in the arena. And private.

Clip-clip-clip. Alexa didn't have to look to know who was coming. Of course, their sister bloodbond preceded Marian, too, but Alexa recognized her from her footsteps. Only Marian could make soft slippers sound like professional high heels.

"Ayes?" she asked when Marian stopped next to her.

"I think we should fly to Volaran Valley."

Alexa felt waves of curiosity and anticipation emanating from Marian. "You think so?"

"You're impatient."

"Tell me about it."

"So am I."

Standing, Alexa said, "You think we should get this show on the road?"

"I think events need a little prodding."

"Okay."

"And," Marian said, "since we're the only ones who are concerned, I think just we two should visit the valley."

A laugh bubbled up from Alexa. "No guys allowed."

Marian sniffed. "They don't seem to be taking this seriously."

"I'll meet you in the Landing Field in half an hour."

Alexa waited for Marian in the deepest shadows of the Landing Field. Their winged horses stood quiet, with a lot less tack on them than usual. Since this was what Calli had considered best for rider and volaran, and since they were going to the home of the volarans, Alexa deemed it politic to follow Calli's instructions.

Marian arrived without notice, touched Alexa's arm, and she jumped. "I'm ready," Marian said.

"Me, too. Jaquar?"

Marian's smile gleamed. "Sleeping the sleep of the very well satisfied."

"Great minds think alike. So's Bastien."

"Shall we go?"

"Let's ride."

Even using Distance Magic, they didn't drop through the Volaran Valley security shield until a half hour before sunset. The place was breathtaking, shades of green dotted with colorful flowers. The herd of volarans—all ages—looked incredible.

Their descent was very slow, made of ever-narrowing circles. Providing the maximum visibility, Alexa thought, and knew her mount was speaking telepathically to the others—maybe one, maybe many, but Alexa wasn't conversant enough in Equine to catch the stream of thought. She looked over to Marian, who shrugged.

They lit in the middle of the field. As soon as they dismounted, their steeds deserted them, and the rest of the herd turned toward them.

They stood alone.

Alexa wasn't entirely sure, but she thought that Marian's knees trembled just as much as her own. Well, maybe not. Marian had owned horses, after all. Or her mother had. Duh. She, herself, was dithering.

But she didn't think she'd ever seen such an awe-inspiring sight in her life as a herd of volarans closing in on her from all sides.

Marian reached out and fumbled for Alexa's fingers. "Thanks," Alexa muttered from the corner of her mouth. "I'm glad I'm not the only one who's nervous."

"Not at all," Marian said, her voice higher than usual.

Alexa swallowed. "Volarans are littler than regular horses, right?"

"Mostly. Dark Lance is larger— They're galloping straight toward us!" She ended on a squeak.

"I see that." Alexa herself had nearly lost her voice as her mouth dried.

"What should we do? We *can't* be aggressive!"

"Shut our eyes?"

Marian snorted, caught dust, coughed. "Impressive, oh, Exotique Swordmarshall."

"Yup. 'Zactly what I'm going to do. Shut my eyes. Good decision." She did, and immediately noticed Marian's personal Song spiraling high, wide and *loud*. Alexa clung to Marian's fingers and kept her other hand from her jade baton.

The thunder of hooves came closer and closer.

Then stopped.

Her eyelids flew open. A volaran was inches from her— face-to-face. She stumbled back and was shoved to her feet by a long head hard in her back. "Uhn!"

All around her volarans *laughed*, mentally, rolling their eyes, and making noises that had bubbles coming from their noses and drool dripping from their mouths. Disgusting.

Marian laughed, too.

Alexa was about to huff out some comment, when the horses parted in front of her, forming an aisle for a small gray mare to glide toward them. The mare lowered, then raised her head. *Well done, Exotiques. Standing your ground.*

"I guess she's the alpha. They have alphas, don't they?" Alexa squeezed Marian's hand.

I am Lead flier, the mare said, coming up a little too close. Alexa figured volaran personal space and American-woman personal space was different.

"Right," she said. "Good."

You are concerned that we are not Summoning the Volaran Exotique and the Lead Mind-speaker back.

"Lead Mind-speaker is Marrec," Marian clarified.

The mare nodded. *Indeed.*

Alexa wanted to put her hand on her baton, but instead she lifted her chin. "Ayes. We are concerned that you do not Summon Calli and Marrec."

And you spread that concern to Gray-Clouds-That-May-Rain-Or-Thunder-Or-Clear and One-Who-Will-Be-The-Dark-Lance-At-Evil and other younglings. She bent her neck back and forth around the circle, scolding in her gaze. Some of the volarans rustled their wings and sidled back.

The names made Alexa realize just how out of her element she was. "Oh, boy."

I will answer your questions.

Marian cleared her throat, and when she spoke it was with words and mind. "We know that Calli had a…portal to and from Exotique Terre."

The mare swished her tail. *The crystal mountain. The Singer's crystal. It has been destroyed—from Exotique Terre.*

Alexa stepped forward into the mare's space, narrowed her predator eyes on the front of her face and looked at the prey eyes on the side of the head. "Destroyed! Is Calli—"

We would know if the Volaran Exotique and the Lead Mind-speaker were harmed, even on such a backward place as Exotique Terre. They are well.

"Backward?" murmured Marian.

Exotique Terre has no volarans.

Now Alexa cleared her throat. "Good point."

"You know of the crystal portal?" asked Marian.

Of course. The crystal portal shaped the one who would become the Volaran Exotique.

Alexa knew that the crystal had been on Calli's ranch. How many others could it have worked upon? How did it work? She decided to let Marian consider those questions. For her, this was getting way too mystical.

"And you said it's destroyed." Marian turned in place and Alexa followed her, looking at the herd. "It's my understanding that when the Snap comes, a person is returned if they are not willing to live in Lladrana."

The mare lifted her lips to show her gums. It looked like a smile—sort of—to Alexa. Maybe a snide one.

Exotique Circlet, you proved that wrong yourself. Or did you? You found a way back…if the yearning and the need is great enough…

"Back to ruby slipper time," Alexa muttered. "Just give us the bottom line. Are you folks…uh…volarans going to Summon them back or not?"

Perhaps at the proper time we will form a circle and Sing.

"When—" Marian started.

With a quick turn, the mare reversed. She kicked up clods of dirt that landed on their boots, then cantered away. The volaran circle surrounding them broke up into clumps. Alexa waited until she thought they were all out of earshot before saying, "Well, this was a futile trip."

"Not necessarily," Marian said. Alexa thought she meant

to sound calm, but a tightness around her eyes gave away her irritation. "Negative data can always be informative."

"Huh. Sounded more like a 'Patience, grasshopper' situation to me."

Marian laughed, flung her arm around Alexa's shoulders and hugged. "Good one."

"Thanks." Alexa let out a relieved sigh, stroked her baton and looked around. "But it wasn't a total waste of time. This place is absolutely beautiful. Think we can squeeze out a little more time to walk and observe, maybe talk to the anim—volarans? There are a lot more here, appearing a little different than those at the Castle." She took off at a good clip to the sunny side of the valley toward a bunch of volarans who raised their wings, then moved off. Marian kept up.

"I think it depends upon the volarans," Marian said.

Pounding hooves attracted Alexa's attention. Their mounts were running toward them. "Doesn't look like we're real welcome." A wistful sigh escaped her. "Calli said in her notes that she was invited to stay as long as she wanted, right? And to return whenever she wished?"

"Correct. But neither of us are Calli."

"Got that right." Still, just because, and just for fun, Alexa unsnapped her baton sheath, took out the jade baton and threw it up into the sky. She watched it sparkle as it tumbled end over end, the symbol of her life, herself, here in Lladrana. Caught it with a light smack in her palm. "You got that right. But we have our own places."

"Indeed we do."

"And if they don't get Calli back, *we* will. Somehow."

"That's right."

* * *

Bastien and Jaquar were waiting for them when they descended toward the Landing Field. Actually, the men were two figures separate from a large group. Alexa noticed the colors of no less than twenty Marshall Pairs, and high-ranking Chevaliers such as Lady Hallard and Faucon Creusse. Oddly enough, Luthan wasn't there. Alexa reckoned that was significant, but decided to let Marian deduce the significance. The Singer already knew the results? Had known before they'd left? Closemouthed old biddy.

Bastien had a certain tilt to his head. "Oh, man, he's gonna make me *pay*," she said to Marian.

Marian sighed. "Jaquar's not too happy with me, either."

"I'll offer him a sex game. One sex game."

Marian sent her a startled glance. "A sex game?"

"Beats long, long minutes of tickling."

"Is that so?" She looked thoughtful. "Sex-game payment works for you."

Melty heat warmed Alexa. "Oh, yeah."

Marian nodded decisively, a smile hovering on her mouth. "I think I'll give it a try."

They touched down. Bastien lifted her from the saddle, kept his hands on her waist. "What did you learn?"

"Not much." Alexa rubbed her butt. "It's been a long ride. Marian will lay it all out better than I can."

"Thanks, *former lawyer*," Marian said. Definitely a long ride if Marian was being sarcastic.

"*Alexa…*" Bastien started.

She tapped her forefinger three times over his heart. *One sex game of your choice.*

He was suitably distracted and began lowering his mouth to hers, when Jaquar's superior tone cut through Alexa's haze of desire.

"While you were gone, Bastien and I worked a few spell-songs of our own."

"So?" Marian had crossed her arms under her breasts. Jaquar looked at them with a twinkle in his eyes, but said, "We found out that Calli and Marrec were 'helped' a little back to Exotique Terre during her Snap, by Power. 'Magic' as you would say, of the highest order."

Marian's eyes widened, her lips parted, Jaquar basked in her fascinated attention. "What magic?"

Bastien chuckled and squeezed Alexa as she waited for the punch line.

"Singer's magic."

That was a punch, all right.

After they cleared up the supper dishes and before her dad and Dora and Roy left the kitchen, Marrec said, "We wish to speak with you about the future of the ranch." His English was careful, lightly accented.

40

Dread swirled around the room, tightening faces. No one wanted the confrontation, but it, like the storm last night, could not be avoided and the land would be better for it after it passed.

Roy tensed. His shoulders tight, he shrugged, tried a half smile that was just a mask. "Not my business. I'll be upstairs, studying."

"All right…" Her dad's voice was rusty and he reached for Dora's hand. They stood together.

"In the living room, then," Dora said.

Calli looked at them, understood that if she had faced this unit of her father and another woman months ago, she might have been emotionally damaged beyond repair. She was stronger now.

Dora and her dad left first, then Marrec pulled her into

his arms and kissed her soundly. She leaned against him, felt the tensile strength of him, glad of the physical support that so mirrored his emotional backing. Then they went into the living room.

Her dad and Dora sat on the new love seat, Calli and Marrec went to the sagging couch set at a right angle.

Calli looked at her father steadily. Though he sat holding his new wife's hand, his aura and hers mingled with love, there was nothing of love for Calli in his eyes. She wondered why. Because she was too much like her mother? Too much like him? Had given him all her love freely? She didn't know, and she was coming not to care and that was good.

Dora's mouth tightened. "Give her a check for a quarter of the place, Will, then let them be on their way."

"Half," Marrec said in his careful English. "Calli and I went over the figures last night. She gave a lot of money to her father. Worth half the ranch."

Not quite, and Dad had done all the upkeep, all the work.

Gasping, Dora put her hand to her plump bosom. "You can't believe that!"

Marrec nodded. "Yes."

"You're nothin' but a greedy—" She stopped her bitter words when Will looked down on her. She clutched his arm, simpered up at him. "Oh, Will, all your hard work. You love the land so!"

Did he? A shadow dimmed the bright blueness of his eyes. He did. He might have not known when he'd taken out the reverse mortgage, might have only discovered it when Dora and her son had come into his life, but he knew now.

Calli stood. "I have tallies of the rodeos I competed in, and my winnings. I've spoken a little to Jim at the bank. He knows the value of the place better than I do, but wants to talk to all of us if we disagree on what my fair share is."

Dora frowned. Calli bet she knew the worth of the ranch down to the last penny, had known it before she'd married Will. She wouldn't want fair. She'd want more.

"I'd like to keep this between us. Quick and clean." And get somewhere they might be able to go back to Lladrana. "I don't really want everyone else in town to know that I mean to fight you for this place."

Dora wouldn't like that. Right now the town had a favorable opinion of her and her son. It was pretty evident that Calli and Marrec would leave, and Dora, Roy and her dad would live with whatever gossip came of this whole thing.

"Give Calli what she put in and we will go," Marrec said. "This place will be yours." He laid his hand on her thigh in support. He knew she loved the land, would want it more than money, would have fought for it. This was her concession. She linked fingers with his.

Will grunted and named a figure. It was a lot less than half, not as much as Calli had put into the place, but higher than the final price she and Marrec had decided to accept, still they would need as much as they could get to start their own ranch.

Marrec leaned forward. "Let's talk about this."

Calli wanted to shift in her seat, to squirm, but knew that would be showing a weakness and like it or not, she couldn't be weak in front of her dad and Dora. There was only one person in this world she thought she could be vulnerable before.

The bargaining lasted a whole lot longer than she was

comfortable with, but the men were involved and Dora sharply followed the discussion. Calli kept her teeth gritted and her mouth shut. Marrec fumbled, pretended less comprehension of the language than he had.

Finally, finally a price was agreed to. Something she wouldn't have been able to reach with her dad. She leaned back against the couch and Marrec's arm draped around her shoulders as she watched her dad, still expressionless, walk stiffly across to the desk, pull out the ranch checkbook and write out a draft.

Still silent, he returned to them and handed Marrec the check. Calli was glad to see her dad's hand didn't tremble.

Marrec glanced at it and passed it to Calli. She read the figure and her eyes stung. She'd never wanted money for this place.

But her home here was gone and any claim she had to the land was past. She nodded and stood, slipping the check into her jeans pocket. "Good." Clearing her throat, she angled her head toward the computers on the desk, and said, "Marrec and I would like to take a look at real estate on the Web."

With a tight-lipped smile, Dora said, "Of course."

Calli and Marrec settled in front of the computer, while Dora turned on the TV.

Calli's skills were a little rusty, so she went slow, explaining to Marrec as she went along in a mixture of English and Lladranan. With a glance at her father and Dora, who were engrossed in TV, Calli pulled up Web sites on Boulder, where Marian had lived and had been Summoned to, returned from and went once more to Lladrana. Marrec stared at the photos, going so far as to touch the screen showing the university campus and the Flatirons in the background. "I don't think…" He frowned, exhaled. "A place of Power, yes, but not for us. It…it…has few notes in common with the crystal on the hillside."

"You remember that melody?" Calli stared at him.

He rolled a shoulder. "Well enough."

She let her breath out. "Oh-kay."

They looked at Berthoud Pass. Alexa had been Summoned from that area, but, again, they didn't know specifics. Calli frowned, something teased at her memory, but it faded away. Dammit! If they ever got back, Calli would make sure the women damn well added directions of where they'd been Summoned from.

Touching her hand on the mouse, Marrec said, "It's time we look for land. We can't stay here for long."

She bit her lip and went to a horse properties Web site. Marrec looked to her dad and Dora and back, then ran his fingers over the small images on the screen, shook his head.

Calli nodded and tried another site. On the sixth Web site, Marrec tapped the computer. "Here." His voice was low and strained. "Here is our best chance." His lips pressed together tightly, then he gazed at Calli. "It resonates a little like the crystal, a few notes of my own Song, a little of Diaminta's. But much of you…and Jetyer the most of all."

Her heart gave a hard thump in her chest. "You think we could form a good ritual there?"

His gaze stayed firm, calm. "I think it's our best chance."

Sighing, Calli pulled up the particulars, winced. "A big piece of property, just a trailer for housing, stables for six horses. It's costly."

"Beautiful mountains."

"Yes." She clicked on various views of the place. The scenery *did* call to her. It wasn't here and it wasn't Lladrana, but...

"Yes."

The rain came in the night, clouds opening with huge washes of fat, pounding raindrops and rolling thunder. Alexa sat in the tiny pavilion of the Brithenwood Garden at the Castle, watching the storm, cradling a cup of hot tea in her hands.

A huge crack of sound smacked her. Lightning struck two feet from her, then Marian stood where the blue-white light had seared the ground. Alexa choked on her tea, coughed.

Marian strode into the small structure and thumped her on the back.

Alexa gasped, "Some way to travel. You really will have to teach me how sometime."

"How about now?"

A squeak escaped Alexa as second thoughts rushed into her head. She noticed Marian's grim expression, reached for the teapot on the table.

"Actually, I'd rather have brandy." Marian lifted a window seat and pulled out a decanter and snifter and went about pouring herself a stiff drink.

"What's wrong?" Alexa's hand went to her baton.

"The children are gone."

"What!"

"Calli's. Children. Are. Gone."

"Ohmygod!"

Marian slugged down some liquor, shivered. "We were all

at Bossgond's Tower. Bossgond and Jaquar and I were trying to locate Calli's ranch through the cross-dimensional telescope. The children were only a floor below."

Still stunned, Alexa blinked rapidly, trying to wring some sense to this story. "But…but Bossgond has Powerful Shields around his Tower. No one of evil intent can enter. At least I didn't think so…."

"Exactly right." Marian's mouth went flat. "There was no sound from the kidnapper. No outcry by the children. Naturally, as soon as we discovered they were gone we did a 'Find' Song. To no avail. Then we did a 'Who Was Here Songspell.'" She pulled up a chair and sat.

"And you found out?"

"Luthan took the children."

Alexa hopped to her feet. More and more fantastic. "Luthan!"

Marian's lip curled. "We couldn't reach him. He's at the Singer's Abbey. Jaquar's at home, still trying to contact the Singer."

"Luthan took the kids to the Singer's Abbey?"

"We think so."

"Why?"

Shrugging, Marian said, "Who knows."

"That damn sneaky old bitch of a Singer." Alexa paced. She wanted to hop on the nearest volaran, take to the stormy skies and fly to the Singer's Abbey. But the oracle of Lladrana scared her spitless. "Hell." She glanced out at the sky full of wind and sleeting rain and distant shards of lightning. "You really want me to ride the lightning with you?"

"We're—Bossgond and Jaquar and I—aren't sure what to

do. We thought we had a line on Calli's ranch. But someone should go to the Abbey tomorrow."

Alexa cleared her throat. "I guess that means you want to stay and keep looking while *I* confront the Singer."

Grimacing, Marian said, "Ayes. We really are close to finding Calli's ranch. I think. One more day…"

"Your idea of close and mine aren't the same." Alexa huffed out a sigh. "I'll go." Then she smiled. "With luck, I can guilt Bastien into going with me, though he's as nervous about the woman as I am."

Marian joined Alexa in her pacing. "This whole business, Calli's strange Snap, the volarans' reluctance to Summon her and Marrec back—it all indicates great Power at work— the Song or Amee or the Singer or all three. I don't like it."

"I don't, either." Alexa licked her dry lips. "But I'll go see what I can get out of the Singer…"

"Merci." Marian went back out into the rain, and the droplets didn't seem to touch her. A whirlwind of air scooped her up and she disappeared.

She hadn't finished her brandy. Alexa poured it into her tea.

Calli couldn't sleep. Her time here at the ranch grew shorter, and that was a concern…going somewhere new…but she'd had dreams of her children crying and awoke, tears on her cheeks. Marrec slept on and she was glad. She went downstairs for some milk. When she opened the door to the kitchen she saw Will sitting at the table. He looked up at her, stilled.

"Hi, D—" She'd almost said "Daddy." "Hi, uh, Will."

He didn't look at her. "Calli."

No comfort from him. Never had been. Never. All her night fears and old angers coalesced. She could do nothing about her children, but she could finally face her father. "You sold my horse that I loved!" burst from her. That last rankling betrayal.

Will glanced away. "I'm sorry for that now. Sorry for a lot of things."

Calli's knees trembled, weakened. She leaned back against the refrigerator. She blinked until the dizziness went away, then stared at him. She launched herself at him, hugged him tight. He stood stiff, touched her shoulder.

And Calli knew. Despite that she'd loved him all her life, that he'd been the only man in her heart before Marrec, Will's heart had been scoured of emotion before Dora. He had a limited capacity to love and only his wife touched him. He felt affection for Roy, but nothing for Calli.

Nothing at all.

She stepped back, swallowed the last lingering hurt that she would inflict upon herself over this man, forced the pain from her gut into the earth, away from her, out of her forever. She wanted no bitterness in her life. She kept her eyes wide so the tears wouldn't fall, hoped her dad—Will—wouldn't see them. "We'll be out of your way in a couple of days, as soon as we figure out our plans."

"Calli, come back to bed," Marrec said softly from the shadowed doorway. Calli turned on her heel and went to him. His arm came around her.

Will looked at them, held out his hand to Marrec. "Interestin' meeting you."

Marrec shook. "And you. Calli and I are thinking we will go to Montana."

Relief passed through Will's eyes. He nodded. "Plenty of pretty places in Montana."

With a return nod, Marrec ended the conversation, and they walked to the door to the steep stairs up to their room. When it closed, Marrec handed Calli a bandana. She blew her nose and wiped her eyes.

"I love you," he said.

She flung her arms around him, pressed herself to him. He held her tight, his body young and strong and vibrant against her. His sex hardened.

Their loving was hard and fast and quiet...and near violent, from an excess of feelings. Her hands roamed, aroused him ruthlessly, accepted no mercy from him. They joined and their bodies slicked and their mouths fused and they rode to staggering climax together. Pretending they were ready for another great change in their lives.

Calli woke to find Marrec gone and her heart lurched. He hadn't ever left the room before. Straining all her senses, she found him riding to the north. *Wait!* She flung everything into the one Lladranan word. Wait. Please. Whatever had gone wrong with them, they'd been mending it. Yet now he was leaving—for good, oh, no, she didn't think that. Not her practical husband who knew he'd need her to navigate the outside world, but he was on some errand of his own.

I wait.

Calli slipped on her clothes, ran down to the fence around the house acreage and the cattle grate. There he sat, a dim figure in the dawn. Dressed in cowboy hat and boots and jeans, he should have looked like a cowboy. He didn't. Something about the way he held himself would always be Llad-ranan. Had she looked that foreign on Lladrana? She supposed so, but she'd defend him fiercely.

She strode up to him, he tipped his hat and she almost smiled. "Where are you going?"

A touch of color came to his golden cheeks. Looking peachlike. She'd never tell him that.

"I heard a call. It comes from that 'spread' next door."

"Bert's place."

"Yes, the Honorable Bert who has the fancy horses. I think it is the horse herd Song that is Calling me."

Calli rubbed her eyes. "You're dressed in dreeth leather."

"I wish to impress him." His gaze met hers with a darkly puzzled look. He stood straight. "I think I will want the horses. Now."

"We hadn't planned on buying horses yet. We need the property first. At that place, we might be able to return to Lladrana, we shouldn't buy horses yet—"

"The horses Sing."

She scrutinized him. He was the most pragmatic, logical man she'd ever known. "All right, then. I'll go back to our room and get the check. We can sign it over to him if we want the horses, and he'll deposit any overage to our account. We can trust him with the money."

"Because he is an Honorable."

Blinking, she said, "Yes, that's his title. He's a judge." Once again something tugged at her memory. Something in Alexa's book?

But Marrec was speaking. "A judge was in the building where you went to look at the land records."

"The county courthouse. Several, I'm sure."

"Judge James."

Her brows went up. "You got around."

He nodded.

"Okay, I'll be right back."

Smiling, he shifted and sent his horse back toward the stable. "I'll ready your horse."

She ran back to the house, her own lips curved. So many things to be grateful for. Marrec. To be able to see this place again. To be free emotionally of her father. As quietly as possible she hurried up the stairs. Her Pairling had shot their plans to hell. If they bought horses, it was almost certain they couldn't afford the land. Snapping the hidden panel of the cabinet open, she jammed the check into her pocket. She trusted Marrec's instincts. Somehow they'd make it work. Maybe they could rent-to-own the land. Maybe they'd find another place.

She grabbed the check, decided she wanted to show solidarity with Marrec and undressed, then yanked on her own Lladranan dreeth leathers.

Her horse was saddled by the time she came back.

"Thank you, Calli."

They reached Bert's ranch in about a half hour. The sun had risen, but the day was cloudy and gray. His arena had been repaired with new fencing freshly painted and the paddocks showed some electronic fencing. That was the last thing she noticed about Bert's ranch.

The horses were absolutely gorgeous. No high-strung, high-bred Arabians these—what most folks thought of as "fancy horses," but a breed that was more compact, powerful. More baroque.

Lipizzaners. Four mares and a gelding moved around the arena. Separate from them were two stallions. *Two stallions!*

One was in a large paddock, close to the arena, flirting with the mares. The other stallion was in a big stall.

How on earth had Bert gotten ahold of these magnificent animals? Why? Calli'd never heard that he was interested in the breed. He must be breeding them. Had to be. Dazed, she stopped, just watching the horses. They weren't the warm-bloods and the quarter horses she was accustomed to.

Marrec continued on.

By the time Calli clucked to her mount to continue to the corral, Marrec stood laconically against the fence, with three mares' noses waiting to be scratched.

She dismounted, tied her horse to a nearby tree and joined him—to feel tension humming in his body. Singing from him.

He wanted these horses.

41

Listen to their Equine, he said.

Clear mind speech, again more intelligent, more curious than she was used to, whispered liquidly in her head. *Good-smelling man. Fine. Fine. Beautiful woman. Very fine smell, but whiff of something scary.*

They were wearing dreeth leathers.

Strange images. Winged equines. Flying us. Wings. Wings. Wings, whispered from many mind voices.

Calli blinked. The Lladranan leathers must give off a subtle scent of *otherworldliness.*

"Howdy," said Bert.

Calli jumped. He walked quietly, an elegant man of middle age, still handsome, wearing ranch clothes, hat, boots. "Good to see you again," he said to Calli.

Gesturing to Marrec, Calli said, "My husband, Marrec Gardpont."

Marrec bowed stiffly.

"Pleased to meet you." Bert opened the gate and entered the corral. "Come on in."

Calli and Marrec went inside and the horses crowded around them, curious.

Easy, little ones, Marrec soothed.

A couple tossed their heads, whinnied, sidled backward. They weren't used to hearing such perfect Equine.

They were fabulous. Now they kept a courteous distance from the humans as if they already accepted them as alphas, due to telepathic Equine and regular physical cues.

"Thanks for talking with me about my finances—and the great investments you made with my money," Calli said stiltedly. She was finding it difficult to keep her eyes and mind and hands off the horses. The nearest stallion was rolling a come-hither eye.

"Like my babies?" Bert asked.

"Gorgeous. Are they for sale?"

He rubbed his chin, glanced up at the low-slung ranch house. Calli thought it had been spruced up, too. A lacy curtain fluttered. He hadn't had lace at the windows before, had he?

Come say hello, cooed a mare.

She did, stroking the horse from top to tail, loving the animal's conformation. Compact. Powerful. Fluid. Intelligent.

"Yes, they're for sale," Bert said.

Calli was jolted back to the here and now. His smile was easy, but his eyes sharp.

She calculated their expenses. They *might* be able to talk the Montana ranch owner into renting, or selling a portion of the land—the part that might lead back to Lladrana and their children. If they lived in that pitiful trailer and did a lot of the work themselves…and Calli pulled in every favor she might have in Montana, and spread word she was setting up as a trainer…

Sidling casually over to Marrec, she brushed her shoulder against his. He glanced down, face expressionless.

She quoted a figure. "That should buy them all," she said in Lladranan.

His dark eyes lit, softened. "I thought only two."

Her smile was easy. "You want them all."

His glance flicked to the horses, back to her. "Ayes."

"We'll put our money in the horses. Less house."

He nodded.

"Now you bargain. You're better at it."

The smile she loved formed slowly on his face. "We'll do it together." Once again he glanced at the horses. "I think we'll have to walk away, then come back. You can nail him down at the end."

Bert said, "You really interested in buying them? They're all registered and I have official pedigrees."

That sounded like an opening to negotiate to her.

Marrec stepped forward, eyes gleaming. He kept his voice slow, but as the men dickered, Calli realized that Marrec had changed his strategy…and showed much more respect for the man than he had her father. Her Pairling did indeed gesture her to leave and she let out a long breath and drooped a little as she untied her mount, Marrec walking slowly to the arena gate before Bert impatiently called them back.

Finally, Bert pushed his hat back on his head, took a straw

and twirled it. Though he was a big-city guy, there was just enough rancher in him not to make him look too stupid doing that. "We'll even throw in the fancy saddles. Millana and Pluto won't be ridden without them." He gestured to saddles resting on the top fence rail. The tack was the strangest and fanciest getup Calli had ever seen and she stared from one to the other. The stallion's saddle was midnight-blue leather worked in gold, with edgings of scarlet. Squinting, she thought she saw suns, moons, stars and...the spiral of a tornado? The mare's saddle reversed the colors, being mostly scarlet and gold with blue facings—and symbols of musical notes? Her heart picked up a beat and she couldn't tear her gaze away from the tooling that *almost* made sense, until she heard the slap of hands and she looked over to see the two men shaking on the deal.

"Why don't you ride 'em back to the Rocking Bar T, try 'em out. Take the rest on a line. Looks like they'll follow you. I'll keep Will's horses here until you can pick them back up," Bert said.

Calli looked at the Lipizzaners. They were gorgeous. Her whole body *itched* to get on one.

"Yes," said Marrec. She sensed he wanted to put her past—and Will—behind them and ride out on their future. Then he cleared his throat. "One moment," Marrec said. He strode over and picked Calli up, brought her back to the arena and set her down before Bert.

"What?"

Patting her on the shoulder, he went to the horse he'd ridden and opened the saddlebag, withdrew the fabulous white beaded scarf she'd seen in the store window and draped it over her shoulders. He jumped over the fence and stood by her side, taking her hands.

Marrec stared at Bert. "I've heard that you are one who can listen to marriage vows."

Calli's heart beat hard.

Bert's brows rose. He straightened, his voice deepened. "In Colorado you can exchange your vows yourself."

"I do not have the papers, but I would like to say the vows with Calli before you."

"You have any objection to this, Calli?"

"No, he's my husband." Her breathing came a little ragged. Acknowledging that was a step toward common law marriage, too.

"We have shared a Bonding ritual in my land," Marrec stated, "but I want Calli to have a—some sort of—a ceremony, here, too, again."

He'd never been so inarticulate. Calli bit her lip. A wedding. The man was trying his best to give her a wedding. The pretty, long scarf that draped over her, glittering like shards of the crystal, hanging to her calves. She blinked and smiled at her Pairling. "Thank you."

"You're very welcome." He smiled.

Bert rocked back on his heels. "I think I've conducted enough civil ceremonies to know the words pretty much by heart."

Calli didn't doubt it a bit.

"We are here to unite Marrec Gardpont and Callista Mae Torcher in marriage, which is held in honor among all people. As they pledge their constant and abiding love to each other…"

The old words, so familiar, spoken by an authoritative,

honorable man. The scarf as her wedding dress. More, the sturdy, reliable man standing in front of her with love in his eyes, his Song rising loud to her ears, merging with the heart rhythm of her own personal Song, twining together, now on Earth as it was on Lladrana—a perfect wedding.

Marrec said his vows strongly and clearly.

Calli's were a little rushed, a little loud.

"Here is where I'd say something like 'by the authority vested in me by the state of Colorado,' but I'll just say, 'You are husband and wife, blessings upon you.'" Bert winked at Marrec. "You may kiss the bride."

Her husband's mouth brushed her own.

"Right," Bert said, "that's done. The horses are restless."

They weren't really, they'd observed with some curiosity, even hearing part of the Songs, Calli thought. She should take off and fold the scarf, wrap it in the tissue paper stuffed in Marrec's saddlebags. She didn't.

Marrec kissed her again, harder. Calli slid her arms around his neck and kissed him back.

Bert carefully stepped away from the bunch, folded the check Marrec had given him and stuck it in his back pocket, then grinned. "Good doing business with you. I'll make sure the excess is invested for you."

"No, thanks. Please deposit it in my account. You know the number." Calli was caught for an instant by his smile. For an older guy, he sure was attractive.

A head butt brought her back to the here and now, and the group of horses—a small herd—that was the basis of her new life. She swallowed. She could almost *see* Jetyer and Diaminta mounted on these lovely beasts. She had to look away and swipe her sleeve across her eyes.

Marrec murmured, "Marian and Jaquar, Alexa and Bastien will care for them like their own, until we find a way back." Their rote comforting phrase, but his voice broke. He set his shoulders, made one corner of his mouth turn up. "These are our children for the moment."

Calli still wanted children but didn't know if her heart could take the strain. How long would it be before they gave up hope? If they adopted in the future, would that be giving up on their intention to return to Lladrana? Could they possibly take children back with them? Would more lost orphans break her heart further? Ease it slightly? No other children could replace her own.

But Marrec was ordering the horses so that they could ride back to the Rocking Bar T. Bert saddled the alpha stallion and Calli hurried over to saddle the mare. There were leads to tie the rest so they would follow...though Calli sensed their fascination with her and Marrec would make the task much easier.

Marrec swung onto the stallion. His face scrunched a little. "What?" Calli asked.

He just shrugged, gathered up the lead lines and looked back at his string of three. "I like this type of saddle," he said, tapping the horn.

Calli hadn't introduced the western saddle to Lladrana. She wondered if that might have been a mistake. Her mare's pretty ears flicked forward. She licked her lips. Calli smiled. The saddle was western and she put her foot in the stirrup, grabbed the horn and swung up. Her butt tingled all over when she settled into it, and it was warm, especially for being outside in this cloudy gray morning.

Bert finished tying the rest of her line, dodging a kick from the smallest mare, who matched Thunder in size. Then he went to the gate and held it open, nodded at Marrec. "Montana, eh?"

"Ayes," Marrec said.

The older man cocked his head.

"Yes," Calli said.

Bert nodded. "Good country. Let me know where you settle. Good luck to you."

"Thanks." Calli shifted the tiniest bit in her seat, as she would have on Thunder or a horse she'd trained for years. Millana moved out, smooth and easy.

"Good luck to you, too," she said to Bert.

He grinned again. "I've had plenty of it, but am always happy for more."

"Fare well," said Marrec. His stallion caught up with the mare and Calli.

The gate was wide enough for them to leave side by side, with slight mind control from Marrec and Calli, suppressing urges. The road beyond was much wider. More clouds darkened the day and Calli shivered. She should have brought a heavier jacket. Fall was approaching. It would come even earlier in Montana. She let her gaze travel over her beloved mountains, the view not much different from her own ranch's.

No, not hers.

Despite the fact that she'd returned to Colorado, had been ready to fight and claim her ranch, it truly was no longer her home. She swallowed.

Riding with the ease of a top cowboy, or an Equine-speaking Chevalier of Lladrana, Marrec held the reins in one hand and reached out to her with the other.

She gave him a watery smile and took it. The silence of the cool day was impressive. No cars, only the clopping of the horses' unshod hooves on the dirt of Bert's drive. Even the sounds of his place had faded since they'd made the first turn around a stand of evergreens.

Calli looked at Marrec and her heart simply turned over. His eyes were serious, and shadowed, and soft.

"I love you," he said, then, "J'adora," in Lladranan.

Her throat clogged. She glanced down at her white scarf, sniffed, nodded. "J'adora. I love you."

The day winked out. Colorado was gone—green and gray. Gray fog enveloped them, whistling winds. Their entwined fingers grabbed tighter.

The Snap! Marrec said.

Snap? Calli was beyond confused.

My *Snap!* he shouted with joy. *I never thought it could happen.*

She hadn't, either.

The horses screamed. Marrec's and Calli's minds meshed as they worked to calm them. The mist parted to show the portal across from them closing.

42

Calli bit her lip to prevent her own scream, angled downstream. The winds settled into a definite current.

Marrec jerked his chin at a wide portal, afternoon sunlight pouring into the corridor.

"Ayes!" Calli shouted, yelled again. The Lladranan "yes." "Ayes!"

Then they were through the door and on a road.

Calli blinked at the bright sunshine, the heavy scent of worked fields around her.

Marrec whooped with joy, pointed off to the right where intricate and fancy buildings shone white in the sun.

"The Singer's Abbey," he said.

"Oh, my God," Calli said in English, then switched gears and forced her voice through a throat thick as realization spread through her. They were back! "By the Song."

"Well," Alexa said, looking startled, baton out and ready, standing in a copse by the side of the road. Then she sagged against the tree at her back, shook her head hard and shut her eyes. Popped her eyelids up again and stared more. Her breath whooshed out as she looked past them at the horses. She gulped, cleared her throat, and her voice was cleared when she said, "I guess you guys are the only ones to ever bring a string of horses to Lladrana." She spoke Lladranan.

Tears trickled down Calli's cheeks.

Marrec stroked her palm with his thumb, dropped her hand. "How are our children?"

Alexa straightened to her full height. "Good enough. They're up at the Abbey. I guess now I know why the Singer had Luthan kidnap them."

"Kidnapped!" Calli exclaimed.

"That's right," Alexa snorted. "Took them right from under Jaquar's and Marian's *and* Bossgond's noses."

"Come help us with these horses. We need to secure them, then we'll talk to the Singer." Marrec's tone was sharp as steel.

Alexa heaved a breath. "I don't like that woman, but after I help you, I'll go and tell her you're here. For formality's sake. She probably already knows. I'll wait for you there." Alexa walked slowly to them. "There're stables up ahead, and separate paddocks for horses and volarans." A few feet away, she stopped, tilted her head. "Those horses obviously came from Earth, but they look...different...than what I'm used to seeing. More like an antique strain or something."

"They're Lipizzaners."

For an instant, Alexa's mouth hung open. "Wow," she

breathed. "The ones trained for war. The kind that can do those fabulous jumps."

"That's right." Sometimes Alexa surprised Calli with her knowledge. She'd expect Marian to know about Lipizzaners, but not Alexa.

"Wow." The small woman stared at them. "They start out brown and turn white, don't they?"

"Gray."

"All right." She stepped forward, Calli could hear her wrangle her mind into Equine-speak. *Beautiful.* "Can I have one?"

"You'll have to ask Marrec."

Marrec shrugged.

Alexa grinned. "I'll have Bastien do the dealing. Wait 'til he gets a load of these!" She rubbed her hands. "He'll go wild with greed." She tilted her head and her eyes widened, squeezed shut, then opened again as she flushed. "By the Song, I didn't even notice your scarf-thingie—just saw you and Marrec and those horses." She stopped, tried to look casual. "Nice robe."

Beaming, Calli said, "We got married this morning." Sort of. Memory prodded her and her smiled turned to frown. "By Bert. The Honorable Trenton Philbert the Third."

"Congratulations." Alexa stepped forward and stood on tiptoe to kiss Marrec, then hugged and kissed Calli. When done, she said, "Judge Philbert, I know him slightly." She frowned, too. "Didn't Marian meet him and his wife at some party or other?"

"Yes! That's what I was trying to remember."

At that moment a Powerful Song hit Calli. Marrec stumbled back.

I am the Singer and I await you. Come, An old woman's mental tone ordered.

Alexa shook her head as if righting herself after the command. Her lips pressed together, then she said, "I'll go prepare the stable hands for you, then head on to the Singer. You take the time you need." She jogged off.

"We're back," Calli whispered, looking at Marrec.

"Ayes. We're home." He rolled the words as if savoring them.

She swallowed tears, glanced up at the Abbey. "Not quite. Have you ever had—whatchamacallit—a Song Quest? That's why most Chevaliers and Marshalls go to the Abbey, right?"

He sent her a laconic look. "Never could afford one." His shoulders rolled. "Don't think I'd want one anyway."

"I don't either. Alexa—"

"Marshalls *must* submit to a Song Quest. Part of the deal. With luck, we won't have to talk to the Singer."

Calli stared at him. She didn't believe that for an instant.

A corner of Marrec's mouth lifted. "You're right. Not much chance of escaping an interview." He turned in his saddle, frowning as he considered their strings of horses. "What say you to trying a little experiment?"

"Such as?"

He dropped the lead. "I bet we could ride up to the Abbey without any lines on the horses and these fabulous beasts would follow."

She relaxed in her seat, closed her eyes, tested the minds of the horses. "I think you're right."

"It would be an impressive sight."

"May give us some maneuvering room…in our own lives."

"Maybe."

As they reached the volaran area, a black-winged steed lifted, flew toward them, then landed a yard in front of them.

"Dark Lance!" Marrec choked. He sprang off his mount, ran to the volaran, threw his arms around the stallion's neck and leaned against his companion.

Calli heard the joyful mingling of thoughts and Songs from where she stood. She waited until the first rush of emotion had decreased to a strong tune between them before clearing her throat. Marrec stepped back, his face flushed more than she'd ever seen, blinking fast.

Dark Lance whinnied at her. *I stayed with the children,* he said, full of pride. *That Thunder, he been all over everywhere.*

Wisely, Calli kept her mouth shut, watched Dark Lance's eyes widen when he saw the horses, which were about his own size. He took to the air in instinctive, pleased surprise, circled over the wingless ones. *These! These are why you went to Exotique Terre. To bring back more mates for us. Breed larger.* His mind brushed hers, then the horses'. *Smarter than the horses here. They will enrich our lines.* He flew over to the rest of the volarans, chattering excitedly in Equine.

Marrec joined her and they organized the horses once more, with soft touches on their minds.

The stable workers' mouths dropped in awe as Calli and Marrec led the horses into a large, empty corral without any lines or reins. "Be careful of the tack, especially the saddles," he said.

A woman bowed low. "It will be done, my lord."

Again Calli sensed relief from Marrec. He was back where he belonged, where he knew his place and the rules.

At that moment there was a great, trumpeting cry from

the air. *Our Exotique has returned,* screamed Bastien's stallion, Sunray. Immediately the winged steeds flew from their arena to light near Calli, pushing at her and Marrec.

He opened his arms wide and threw back his head and laughed, deep and full, and it was the best sound Calli had heard in weeks.

Her whole body was stroked by volarans brushing by her, nuzzling her head, thrusting their muzzles at her to be caressed.

Then a frightened whinny came. Checking mentally, Calli discovered that the horses had bunched together at the far side of the paddock, stallions out, on the verge of panic. She pushed through the volarans and clapped her hands, making it echo.

Apologize to the horses for scaring them, she ordered Sunray, the volaran with the most status.

He snorted.

I mean it. Apologize or I won't ride you for a long time.

Glancing at her, he said slyly, *What is a long time? A day?*

Bad choice of words. The volarans didn't experience, nor count, time, as people did. *For a whole season.*

His nostrils flared. He stamped a hoof, then he glanced over to the horses.

She'd never seen a volaran do a double take. His neck came up, his eyes brightened, ears perked. *Beautiful Exotique mares.*

"Ayes," she said.

Large beautiful Exotique mares. He trotted over.

It was fascinating to watch a volaran communicate in Equine with Earth horses. Luckily, neither of the herds considered the others mutants, and, of course, just like Lladranan horses, the Earth animals were charmed by their incredible cousins. The Lipizzaner stallions were disposed to guard their females...until a young volaran mare trotted up to them, fluttering a wingtip.

Someone cleared his throat. A group of six Singer's Friends stood just outside the fence, observing, all dressed in different-colored robes from midnight blue to pale yellow.

Calli knew the Singer was the oracle and prophetess of Lladrana, like a high priestess. The Friends were nuns or monks or priests or priestesses or something.

Marrec tore his gaze away from the volarans and horses. He strolled to Calli and took her hand, then they both walked from the corral. The stable hands hardly noticed them leave, still engrossed in the horse-volaran meeting.

"Salutations, Chevalier Marrec and Exotique Chevalier Callista." The man in pale yellow bowed.

"Salutations," they replied in unison. Marrec squeezed her fingers.

"The Singer awaits you."

Raising his brows, Marrec said, "Already?"

The man gave a discreet cough. "The Singer anticipated your arrival."

Though Marrec appeared expressionless, subtle tension ran through his muscles. He took a while to consider that, then said, "We aren't prepared for Song Quests."

"There will be no Song Quests. Merely an interview."

A woman in a purple robe frowned, and Calli blinked at the disconcerting thought that the horse-volaran meeting was being replayed here with people. A Friends-Chevaliers meet. Or a Friends-Exotiques meet. She definitely considered her husband and herself of higher status...and Lladranans *did* put great emphasis on status.

"Very well." Marrec scowled at the white buildings that covered the low hill. "In which one does the Singer await us? And how do we get there?"

The Friend inclined his torso, his expression smug. "Just let your feet and your heart guide you."

Calli didn't like his tone. She adjusted her white wedding-scarf robe, let her fingers linger on the soft cloth, the glass beads, then grasped Marrec's hand. Since they'd returned, Power had gathered around her, suffused her, as if Amee itself had wrapped her in a thick down comforter. She stared at the man until he met her eyes. This Singer who scared Alexa wasn't the only one with Power. Calli was a Paired Exotique who'd traveled through two Snaps, both herself and her husband fulfilling tasks for Lladrana and Amee. "We'll follow the Song, won't we, Marrec?"

Pulling the most intricate strain toward her like a thread, she let it touch her mind. She sent one to Marrec, who let it twine around his shoulder, then she wrapped the Song around the pompous man and smiled. She and Marrec strolled in the lovely Lladranan sunlight toward the spires and towers of the Abbey. Back home and together. Nothing could subdue her quiet joy.

The Friend took a step, his expression went comically surprised as he realized he was tangled in the great Song of the place and hadn't even known it. He fell.

She tilted her head and looked at him. "One of the texts of the Song in my land says, 'A haughty spirit goes before a fall, and pride goes before destruction.'"

The other Friends stepped aside as she and Marrec took a humming path up the gentle hill.

After a couple of minutes, Calli realized that Marrec matched her steps. His Song, even and with burgeoning Power, radiated from him, encompassing her, supporting her. As her own Song went to him. Their melded Pair Song was stronger than ever, and she let a breath out at the thought.

He glanced at her. "No other person could have kept me sane and functioning in a world like yours." His voice was rough and she realized that he'd kept his words short, until now. His emotions swirled around them—released fear, dreadful confusion, incipient despair. He'd kept them all pent up on Earth.

She stopped and wrapped her arms around him and stood with him, not caring who watched. They'd survived. Stroking his cheek, she said, "You could have lived on Earth. You're strong and adaptable enough. We would have made a good life there." But they'd always have had holes in themselves. She was so glad to be back, she ached. She'd hold her children in her arms soon.

Tilting back her head, she welcomed his kiss. He pulled her tight, swept his tongue across her lips, then thrust it inside her mouth to explore. She gave herself up to sensation, sweet knowledge that she belonged here, with this man, on this world.

When the heat had risen between them, he stepped back, fire in his eyes. "We'll celebrate tonight." His rare grin flashed and he took her hand again. "Now let's retrieve our children and talk to the Singer."

There was an edge in his voice as he mentioned the prophetess. Sharp images ran from his mind to hers. The milky crystal in the hillside of her ranch on Earth…throbbing with

Power that had been "tuned." The same crystal in shards so they couldn't return to Lladrana that way no matter how they tried. The recollection of the "push" that had spun them through to Earth when Calli would have stayed on Lladrana with the Snap.

His anger fueled her own. Oh, yeah, she had things to say to this Singer.

At the top of the hill was a rust-colored curlicued iron gate, which a woman held open for them. They walked through without stopping, though both Marrec and she thanked the gatekeeper. Calli didn't hear it shut behind her.

Marrec's grip tightened on her fingers. *Let us probe for the children.* He sent his mind, his heart, his Song out.

"They're here!" Her heart found them first. "Playing in a garden."

One side of Marrec's mouth quirked. "Quarreling."

She chuckled. "Yes." Then she leaned her head against his arm. This time he stopped and they stood in a small cul-de-sac of green. "I want to hold my children."

His jaw flexed. "I do, too. But I have a feeling that the Singer isn't going to release them to us until after this 'interview.'"

"Well, she'd better not think she can keep Diaminta and Jetyer. I'll lead an army of volarans against her!"

He lifted her fingers to his lips and kissed them. "You'd do that, go against the most Powerful person in Lladrana, perhaps on all of Amee?"

"Yes, and Alexa and Marian and their men would join me."

Again he kissed her fingers, then said, "A high standard, me being cast in with Shieldmarshall Bastien Vauxveau and Circlet Sorcerer Jaquar Dumont."

She kissed his cheek. "You're their equal."

He stilled. "I'm glad you think so."

"I *know* so."

There came a screech, and a peacock paraded around the edge of the building and up to them.

"Which feycoocu?" Marrec murmured.

Calli squinted. "Though it's male…I'd say Alexa's companion."

Sinafinal shut and opened her tail feathers, then turned as if to lead.

After sharing a glance, they followed the stately peacock. It actually walked slower than they'd been, so they earned a few more minutes to acclimate. As Calli recalled Alexa's tale of the Singer, and from the buzzing Power surrounding them, she began to think that she'd need all her wits.

All the buildings were fanciful, mixing spires and onion domes with round and square towers in a jumble that still twinged Calli's heart at the beauty. As they walked, heavy spells of protection and Songs pulsed from the walls. The pretty pathways included cobbles and greenery and stepping stones and live thyme. None of the paths were long and they often curved, branched, came to a dead end at a wall. It didn't take long to realize that they were threading a maze— and unlike the Castle's, this one was of stone.

At the end of the last twisting path was a high pointed arch doorway set in a jewel of a chapel. Another Friend waited on the threshold of the open door. "The Singer awaits," he said.

43

The Friend stepped aside as they entered, waved toward the end of the gracefully arched stone building. "Just walk straight through all the rooms."

Calli once again adjusted her wedding robe over her dreeth leathers. Both reminded her who she was. The feycoocu chirped and stayed behind.

A few steps in, all her tension drained and she stumbled. Marrec caught her elbow and smiled at her with an easy curve of his lips.

Calli frowned and glanced at the Friend behind them, who stood with placid expression and folded hands. "This entryway suppresses negative emotions."

Of course.

Marrec shifted his shoulders. "The Abbey is lovely."

The light inside was wonderful, painting the white stone

walls golden from the windows set in arches on the bottom and huge towering rectangular windows above them. The space was relatively narrow compared to the height. They were the only people in this chamber, though the soft hum of voices and Songs rose from elsewhere.

A small line appeared between Marrec's brows as if he heard his own words whisper in an echo back to him. His fingers closed harder on Calli's arm and that helped focus her thoughts, though she didn't get her suspicions back.

"Is this where Song Quests are done?" Marrec stood solidly in place.

"No," said the Friend.

"Guess we're relatively safe then," Calli said.

"Safety is always relative," Marrec said.

About a third of the way down was a beautifully carved wooden wall about sixteen feet high that blocked the rest of the space and emphasized the austerity of the tall creamy stone walls and glass. The wooden screen held a small door they'd have to go through single file.

Their steps were muffled and Calli noticed that some areas had thick rugs and others were bare stone in patterned squares of dark red and blue marble.

They walked fast through three chambers, nodding to Singer's Friends who stood or talked or worked at desks, then entered the last, smallest space. The walls were paneled with gleaming dark oak, the floor layered with rugs. A couple of steps led to a dais where a chair that looked like a throne stood. Behind the chair a tall velvet curtain of royal blue rippled and Calli was sure there was more space and at least one door behind it.

Alexa hovered at the door, waiting for them, as she'd promised.

Sitting up straight in the chair, her feet placed on an embroidered footstool, was a very small and very old lady whose eyes pierced Calli.

Marrec's hand unlinked with hers and he put his arm in a loose circle about her waist, again matching step with her. Alexa kept pace with them. When they reached the steps up to the platform, Marrec gave a half bow, so Calli did, too.

With a graceful gesture the Singer indicated some chairs on the dais that Calli hadn't noticed.

"Welcome to Singer's Abbey. I am the nine-hundred-and-ninety-ninth Singer." That stopped Calli in her tracks. She looked over at Alexa, who was looking right back at her.

The Singer chuckled, the rich timbre of it sank right into Calli's bones. This was a woman who *breathed* Power. Someone deeply trained in magic over a very long period of time. Every sound she uttered would carry spells.

Calli and Marrec went to chairs on the Singer's left. Marrec hesitated, then put her between himself and the Singer—protecting her more from whatever might burst through the door than the old woman. Well, strange things had happened to Calli in the last couple of months, she wouldn't bet that more unusual events couldn't occur, like an attack in the seat of Power in Lladrana. She sat, arranging her scarf.

Alexa took a chair to the Singer's right, legs dangling. She was nearly as small as the old woman. With a sniff, Alexa settled back and crossed her legs on the chair seat. The Singer raised a hand and a man dressed in midnight blue separated himself from the shadows and put a little footstool near Alexa's chair. She smiled up at him, with teeth. Her wariness was sharp enough to overcome the smothering spells in the walls. "Thank you. I'm fine."

"Swordmarshall, your boots on the chair and cushion—"

"Consequences of you not being prepared," Alexa said. "Cost of doing business."

Calli listened in admiration, but then Alexa was a woman used to being aggressive.

Cocking her head, Alexa said, "Tell me, Lady Singer, does your vocal range include four octaves?"

Everyone looked surprised at Alexa's question, the servant horrified.

The Singer laughed, once again tickling nerves deep inside Calli.

"Ayes, dear, it does."

Alexa met Calli's eyes. "Marian would have wanted me to ask."

Calli was clueless.

"The weapon knot," Alexa said. "It can only be used by someone who has a singing range of four octaves."

"Ah, the Circlet Marian Harasta," said the Singer. Her words lilted and Calli figured she could listen to the woman all day and that if the Singer actually Sang she might fall out of her chair in a blissful faint.

"Thou mayst tell Marian that she is most welcome to visit me," the Singer said in English, in a Boston accent.

Marrec sat up straight. He was listening hard. Still protective of herself and Alexa. What a man. "You hold our children?" He spoke English, too.

The Singer made a moue. "They are safe and healthy,

enjoying the Abbey." She'd switched back to Lladranan and Calli didn't know if she liked it. The Singer's voice was much more a subtle weapon of infinite meanings and tone when speaking Lladranan.

Calli caught the sound of the far outside door opening and voices coming from the end of the hall, which were silenced by an authoritative command. No one said anything as they heard quick boot heels in long strides snapping on stone and muffled on rugs. No one else tried to stop the man, though there were murmurs as he passed through the other rooms. Finally the door opened and Luthan Vauxveau in his white leathers entered. When he reached the bottom of the dais, he made a sweeping bow to the Singer. "Lady."

The Friend hastily placed a chair to the outside of Alexa, though Calli would have bet her manor that Luthan treated antique furniture with care, no matter what the circumstances. He took the chair, then sent a less than respectful glance toward the Singer. "I just heard that Calli and Marrec are back. All the volarans are Singing with gladness. You didn't inform me that Calli and Marrec would return today."

"It is time you trained your own prophetic Power," she said.

His head jerked back as if from a blow.

"And that leads me to why I wanted this interview." The Singer turned to Calli. "You have brought new understanding between volarans and people, fulfilling that task. You have mended the rift between the Chevaliers and the Marshalls, which has fulfilled the Chevaliers' task. You have found and surveyed the Dark's nest here on Amee, another task." She tapped the wooden arm of her chair with her fingernails and even that sound echoed through the room.

Incredible acoustics. Incredible woman.

The Singer looked at Marrec. "And Callista brought you, the finest Volaran Speaker, into your true Power. You also completed your task on Exotique Terre. You brought the horses to breed with the volarans. I do not travel well anymore, and I wanted to meet you here in my home." Her smile held an edge. "I was sure that Alyeka would come, too, as she did, and hoped to see Marian also. Three Exotiques." See them together and study them and their interactions, Calli got that. "And their Pairlings."

Calli's stomach clutched. "You have our children."

The Singer nodded. "The only children adopted by Exotiques in centuries. They have been very informative."

"You took the children away from Marian and Jaquar." Alexa aimed a laser glance at Luthan. "*You* took them."

His face somber, he made a sitting bow. "I apologize once again."

Alexa sniffed. "I'll never let you forget it, brother of my Pairling." Then she stared at the old woman. "And you ordered it."

"I wanted to see the children, learn their potential, and know of their bonds to their adopted parents."

Alexa hopped down from her chair and paced across the dais and back. "Not fair."

"And you still think that life should be fair, Alyeka," the Singer said.

Doves flew through the upper windows. Alexa raised an arm automatically and Sinafinal lit on it. The other circled around Calli and Marrec then landed on Marrec's shoulder. He looked pleased.

"Ayes, everyone manipulates the Exotiques—except the other Exotiques." Alexa came over and stood by Calli, but continued to gaze at the Powerful woman. "So, my lady Singer. Is it true that you had a magic mirror that connected to a crystal on Calli's mountain?"

The shock of that revelation jolted all the way to Calli's toes, sharpened her concentration until she could feel the faint stirring of a draft over her skin. "Is that true?" she asked. Her hand went to Marrec's, they linked fingers again, always. Once again she saw the lost crystal hillface in her mind. Something that had been special to her since childhood, that she hadn't even realized until now. It *had* been a portal. She *had* seen images of Lladrana through it. Because of the crystal, or the Singer?

Outrage pulled Calli to her feet. "Did you destroy my crystal?"

The woman lowered eyelids puffy with age and Calli knew something with deep certainty. "You pushed us through to Earth, didn't you? Broke the crystal on my mountain." The little old lady's eyelids flicked, but she didn't meet Calli's eyes. Yet she sensed that what she'd accused wasn't the whole truth.

"Why?" asked Marrec, cold and softly.

The Singer tilted her head. "Surely you know the reasons."

When they stood and let the silence grow, a silence that sent furious waves of sound through the atmosphere, she waved a hand and banished the negativity. Then she met their stares in turn and her musical voice came once more. "I will not answer your charge, but I will admit that there was a need for you, *both* of you, to visit Exotique Terre and return here. Bringing the horses was one reason, the only one I'll tell."

Marrec grunted. "Calli wouldn't have gone back in the Snap."

"Ttho," said the Singer. "She would have stayed."

"Right," Alexa said, fingering her baton.

"You made me break a promise to my son." Calli's voice quivered with pain and anger.

The Singer's mouth turned down. "I discovered that too late. I am sorry for the hurt that was caused."

"But you don't admit responsibility for the deeds," Marrec's voice grated. "And I don't want to probe these mysteries. I want recompense. No. I *demand* recompense."

"Ah." The Singer gave a little cough. She stared at each of them in turn. None of them dropped their eyes. Then her mouth rounded and liquid notes of pure beauty came from her throat. A servant hustled up with two sheets of paper and a bar of soft gold. The Singer put her lips to each sheet of paper. Before Calli's eyes, words appeared as if written in ink on the paper. Then the page was folded over and the end of the gold liquefied and dripped onto the paper, then spread out like a seal.

Calli goggled.

When it was done, the Singer handed the two sheets to Marrec. "These are my recommendations to Lady Knight Swordmarshall Thealia Germaine and Lady Hilaire Hallard that you, Marrec and Callista Gardpont, have fulfilled all your duties and should be allowed a normal life upon your estate. That all my listening to the Song says this is best." Her lips firmed, then she said, "That much is the truth *at this time.* But I will consult with the Song at moonrise, and that truth may change. So these letters are only in effect for two hours, after that the spell ink will vanish. You will find the Swordmarshall and Chevalier at the encampment."

Alexa squeaked. "Two hours! That's barely enough time to use Distance Magic to reach the encampment."

"Sufficient time," Luthan disagreed.

"We can't even visit with the children for a few minutes!" Calli said.

Marrec cast a hard look to the Singer, set Tuckerinal aside, put the letters in his belt pouch and took Calli's hand. "We'd better go. The sooner we leave, the sooner we can return and claim our children. We'll be back."

They left the room without another word, though Calli heard Alexa mutter something to the Singer and Luthan, then her short strides sounded behind them.

Alexa caught up to them near the entryway. In a cheery tone, she said, "I think that went pretty well, don't you?"

Marrec snorted.

Alexa raised her eyebrows. "Hey, at least she didn't grab you and send your mind spinning into alternative futures here and on Earth."

"No, and we guilted her into helping us with this bonus." Calli tapped her finger on Marrec's belt pouch. "In two hours we'll be free to raise a family." Then she wished she'd bitten her tongue. Alexa was a warrior, she'd continue to fight.

As if discerning her thought, Alexa smiled. "These battles won't go on forever, you know. We'll beat the Dark, and in the next two years." She opened the large door and after-noon sunlight painted a bright square on the stone floor.

"And here's my cowardly Pairling, waiting for us *outside* the Singer's lair."

Bastien immediately began to strip.

"No!" Alexa nearly shouted. "We *don't* need to see all your scars."

He smirked. "I proved my courage in my Marshall Testing that way."

"Not necessary," Alexa repeated.

Turning to Calli, he widened his eyes. "Calli may wish to appreciate me."

"I've seen you naked in the baths," she said drily.

Marrec stared down at her. "You noticed another man?"

She touched his fingers wrapped around her waist. "Only vaguely. And he compares poorly to you. You fill my senses with your Song."

Bastien clutched at his chest. "Oh, the terrible wounds a woman's words can inflict."

Alexa snickered, then her expression froze as Luthan joined them. He bowed stiffly to Marrec and Calli. "My apologies for any concern I caused you."

Alexa punched him on the arm. "You should apologize to Bastien and me, too. We were worried. And you owe Marian and Jaquar *more* than a verbal apology for what you put them through."

Luthan winced. "I will discuss that with them," he said stiffly. "The Singer has *requested* you and Bastien join her for dinner." He turned to Calli and Marrec. "Your volarans are saddled and ready to go. Thunder came with me from the Castle."

Since Marrec kept quiet, Calli said, "Thank you."

"You'll be fine," Alexa said. "The camp is perfectly safe.

Actually, since you were gone, there have been no battles, and the camp is still a fair way behind the line of previous fighting."

"Good to know," Marrec said.

"This is Thealia and Lady Hallard's regular inspection day."

"Ah."

"Excellent. It'll be efficient, catching them together," Calli said.

"Try and arrange that you confront them outside a tent, in public," Bastien advised. "Then they can't manipulate you as easily."

"Good idea," said Marrec.

Bastien smiled and bowed, waving them on their way. "I try my best."

Luthan hooked his arms with his brother and Alexa. "The Singer's private dining room is in this direction."

"Private," muttered Alexa. "*Private.* I don't want to be private with her."

With a sigh, Calli took off her wedding robe and carefully folded it, handing it to Alexa. "Will you find a bag and keep this for me?"

"Of course." Steps dragging, Alexa followed Bastien and Luthan.

A hawk cawed and they looked up to see Sinafinal perched on a gargoyle-laden drainpipe attached to a building a few yards to their left.

This way. Faster. Tuckerinal will lead you inside, through buildings. I will lead you outside.

The small greyhound standing in front of the entrance barked. Tuckerinal.

They hurried to the door.

A few dizzying minutes later, they were approaching the gate. Calli glanced back in the direction where she sensed their children.

44

"We can't see them now. There's no time for greetings, let alone explanations and goodbyes," Marrec said.

She swallowed. That was the very reason she kept her link to them very quiet, so they wouldn't notice she and Marrec were back and become overexcited. It would be only a couple of hours before they'd all be together and at home.

Marrec was keeping his bond with the children low and thin, too. She nodded. "Jetyer's Song contains a darkness. He thinks we betrayed him, abandoned him."

Marrec took time to stroke her back. "By the end of this night we'll be home together."

"Ayes."

The gatekeeper opened the gate and watched them jog through.

Following Marrec, Calli moved fast. Her greetings to the

equines were brief, her reunion with Thunder abbreviated. Within fifteen minutes they were rising to the sky.

Calli, you're back? Marian's voice came strong and clear in Calli's mind.

Ayes!

Marian laughed with her.

Jaquar and I attended a meeting on Parteger Island and we want to see you!

Fly to our home. Too much to explain about the Singer and everything else, though Calli sensed Marian's curiosity.

Marian sent, *All right, we'll leave immediately. See you later.*

All too soon, Marrec was gesturing for Calli and Thunder to engage a Distance Magic bubble. She sighed, she'd barely gotten a taste of true flying.

Marrec glanced at her. *I feel the yearning in your heart. Soar and play, Pairling. I will go ahead.*

I should not. But she yearned to fly.

His chuckle came to her mind. *I will give you an excuse. All the volarans are linking with Thunder, to hear whether their Volaran Exotique has taken any harm from her days away. How she has changed. Give them the reassurance they need.*

Calli found herself grinning. *Very well. We'll catch up.* She watched Marrec and Dark Lance waver as the Distance Magic orb engulfed them, then set Thunder climbing steeply into the sky.

The sheer delight of being back, being *home* and *flying* was something she wanted to savor with her entire body, feel the movement of the volaran beneath her as his wings flapped, the amber scent of him. It felt good to stretch muscles used in flying, her mind in telepathic communication, her Power.

Thunder whinnied, matching her joy. He paused to do some spirals upward, catching rising thermals. She shrieked in glee, leaned close and said, *Loop de loop!*

Tucking his legs in he soared, whipped over, extended his wings on the downward circle to catch the wind at just the right angle to glide.

She saw the first star wink into the evening sky.

Perfect.

Since she was alone, she raised her voice in Song. She sang an old Chevalier flying song, enjoying the Power that buzzed around her, the deepening blue of the sky bowl around them.

She grew cool, and added this observation to the rest—the seasons were changing. They'd reached the edge of summer and would soon be into fall. Autumn would have its own Song—*Songs*—and she relished learning them.

She'd just finished a breathless dive and spin when she caught sight of a small blue-gray volaran coming her way—with two even smaller forms mounted on it.

Her heart lurched in her chest. *Marrec!* she called.

What!

The children are here!

The children?

They're riding Sapphire.

He cursed. *I will return.*

No, you go on.

I will return. Nothing is more important at this moment than the children.

He reached her just before the children flew the last few lengths up to them.

Pa! Pa! Pa! Diaminta squealed both mentally and audibly,

waving her arms. She was strapped to Jetyer, and they were both strongly bespelled to the small mare.

Jetyer's face was set and a little pale. Calli could see a few of his freckles. He looked a lot like Marrec, with that expression. His gaze was bruised. He'd thought they'd abandoned them. He had paid the most for the Singer's little jaunt. Calli *hated* that.

So she opened her heart and her mind and let her joy at seeing him, at being home, her *love* for him bubble forth. Her Song brushed her children, enveloped them, sank into them—and not her Song alone, but Marrec's, too. And their shared Song. All the bonds between them opened to exchange feelings, brief images of the last few days. Jetyer's tense body eased, his lips curved and his eyes shone with dampness. He *knew* that she'd—they'd—been forced away from their children.

And then there wasn't much need for words at all.

Marrec jerked his chin southward. "Can't send them back by themselves, and since we don't know what the Singer put in her letters, I think we'd better both confront Swordmarshall Germaine and Lady Hallard." One side of his mouth lifted. "They aren't going to be happy that we're retiring. I'd just as soon have all my family with me."

Jetyer cheered. Diaminta screeched joyfully.

Dark Lance circled the children's mare, sandwiching her between the two stallions.

Drawing Power from her joy at seeing her children again, Calli helped Marrec settle a Distance Magic bubble around the mare and headed onward toward the encampment.

About a half hour later, Calli realized Thunder was faltering.

What's wrong?

His neck bent and he rolled an eye at her, blinked in embarrassment. *I was at our home last night, then went to the encampment this morning, then to the Castle....*

Then came to the Singer's Abbey and we played and now we are off to the encampment. A lot of Power usage.

He blew out a soft breath. *Ayes.*

She sighed. She should not have taken the time and strength to play.

Calli? questioned Marrec.

Thunder is tired.... I am, too. I think I must try pulling those replenishing energy spells from the sky and land. The ones she'd just learned before she left.

She sensed Marrec's hesitation.

Go on! Get us the life we deserve. Care for the children. I'll be along as soon as I can. The ladies can both link with me, if they need to, understand that I'm on the way.

Very well. Do what you must.

She'd spent some time playing and now it was time to...not work, because none of the time spent here on Lladrana except when she fought was work...but definitely time to pay attention to important matters.

And events had swept over her with relentless force again. Her lips twitched up in a rueful smile. Only here a few hours and they'd been packed with strange and unusual occurrences. That almost felt normal now. And she'd had Marrec this time.

God—by the Song—she loved him. She couldn't think of her life without him. If she'd kept him from panicking and sane on Earth, he'd been invaluable to her, too, given her someone solid to lean on, kept her grounded in what was important—not winning her father's love, which was something she'd never be able to do, but planning their future.

Now they *had* a future, and it was definitely time for her to implement it. Thunder had said nothing to interrupt her musings. She sensed he'd been content to be in her company. Their current speed and energy outlay gave him time to recover. She frowned in consideration. She seemed more *aware* of sunlit motes of Power around her, as if they were drawn to her—or sent to her. Same difference, she supposed. Anyway, Thunder was using that to strengthen himself, as she should be.

You know the Live in the Song Spell, she said.

Of course. The flick of his wingtip was smug. *Volarans always Live in the Song. It is only unaware people who cannot master it.*

Enough with the insults. I've only been back a few hours!

He shook his head as if brushing off insects. *I did not like you gone.*

I didn't like being gone, but it wasn't my choice.

A long breath escaped him, as if he'd needed that reassurance as much as her children had.

They wouldn't let me Call to you, try and get you and Marrec back.

They?

His head came up and pointed to the left. Two hawks flew near them. *The feycoocus?*

A ripple of Thunder's irritation shivered his muscles. *Everyone. Only the Exotiques tried to get you back.*

"Huh."

Everyone else said you and Marrec were where you were supposed to be, he grumbled, and Calli got images of the head volarans, of Thealia and Lady Hallard.

Marrec's voice came. *The children and I are above the camp and going down now. Everything looks very calm. Dark Lance says there have been no night battles in months.*

Startled from her thoughts, she looked around to see the sun setting quickly, and they were still quite a ways from the encampment. Distance Magic would rectify that, but she had to move *now*. She'd been thinking too much and not doing— or perhaps putting off the time when she'd have to try a spell that had always been hard for her to master.

All right, she sent to Marrec and Thunder and reinforced her own confidence. She could do this, *would* do this.

She heard her magic teacher and Marian's previous instructions in her head. "Open yourself to all the elements, to the land of Lladrana and the whole planet of Amee." But that didn't seem right to Calli, so instead of opening herself, she tried something different, she imagined sluffing off layers of protective shields—around her mind and heart.

Not *opening*.

Letting go.

Releasing her fears, her expectations, living in the moment. Living in the Song.

The air around her held the last warmth of day. She drew it into her, felt as if sparks traveled up and down her muscles. The wispy clouds above, tinting pink with sunset, held cool ice crystals, with the Power of mountain wind and sky water. That, too, she brought into her, and the Power was like silk slipping along her skin. She kept a little and sent most of it to Thunder and his wingbeats grew stronger. She *felt* him revitalize, gathering and storing energy for use in spells.

She lifted her hands from her saddle, held her arms away

from herself to find the waves of energy from the land below. The rich, heavy feel of earth, the pulsing planet. This was harder than fire and wind and water. Hard to feel, hard to harness. She thought of landing but brushed the idea aside. No time. And she wouldn't let the tension of a deadline distract her. She settled deeply into her seat. Closed her eyes. Yes, the last touches of the sun and the water suspended in the air and the wind itself was easier to feel than the land. She let her mind flow down with a breeze, play with leaves, ruffle grasses, sift into the ground, and through that connection, she pulled the land's Song into herself, let it sink, rich and coating, into her bones.

Then there was simply the Song of existence itself—of life and space and time. Something Calli had rarely heard but now knew. The Song of her new home and a future shaped the way she yearned for. Deep down, she'd been afraid to believe in it, so hadn't been able to accept the Song and the Power. It caressed her now, poured through her, like thunder rolling in her veins.

One last deep inhalation, one last expelling of breath.

Our Song. She sent the energy to Thunder, for him to use, felt refreshed and full of vitality herself. With a hummed couplet she formed an orb of Distance Magic around them, and they flew fast and far with Power.

A moment later she saw something ahead. A horrible yellow-green-gray cloudy smudge against the horizon, blocking starshine. If she didn't know better, she'd have thought it was smog. She sniffed, smelled only a trace of a noxious odor. *What's that? Can we avoid it to reach the encampment?*

That is *the encampment,* Thunder said.

What is that cloud?

What cloud?

Calli scowled. She didn't want to go down there. All her instincts warned her that evil lurked ahead. *Marrec!* she called.

Ayes? he asked with his customary calm.

What's going on? Why is the camp so foul?

What are you talking about?

It's not bad down there?

Humor came through their bond. *We are still being cheered. Everyone gathered to greet us, and all the volarans want to say hello. I gave the letters to Swordmarshall Germaine and Lady Hallard. They are not pleased but cannot deny the Singer. They want to see you before they release us.*

He sighed and his exhaustion came through. *The children are tired. We will wait for you in our tent.* Pride suffused his thoughts. *Jetyer has cared for his volaran. He flew well, has done everything well.*

Everything's okay? she persisted.

Fine. We only wait for you before we fly home.

I'll see you soon, she sent to him, but aloud she grumbled to Thunder, "I don't like this." The smog trailed upward in wisps and hugged the ground close. Her man and her children were down below. She had no choice. *Keep your senses open.*

Thunder snorted.

They entered the wisps of cloud. Now they were in it, it seemed unthreatening, insubstantial. There was no nasty smell. Yet Calli had to keep herself from shifting in unease, which would give Thunder wrong cues.

By the time they reached the ground, the events of the day

weighed upon her, like a burden of weariness. Only a couple of volarans lifted their heads and gave her a whicker of greeting. That disappointed her a little since she hadn't seen many of them for what seemed like ages and she'd expected them to crowd around her. None of the other Chevaliers or Marshalls had waited for her to land, either.

She dismounted, shrugged and stretched, trying to work out kinks she hadn't noticed before. Using more Power than ordinarily, she did a quick groom of Thunder so he'd be ready to leave again shortly. He folded his wings and dropped his head. *I am very tired and want to sleep.* The volarans around them were all dozing.

She stumbled through the gate and kicked over an empty metal feed bin. The sound shook her. She felt it reverberate through her foot to her legs, her chest, ringing in her ears. Her wits sharpened a little, and she kicked it again.

Clang! It echoed subliminally, like the very gong that had been used to Summon her here.

Amazed, she slipped against the fence and some bridles hanging over the top rail clinked. Sort of like the chimes. Again she felt the noise.

Something was wrong.

No.

Everything was wrong.

Marrec! she shouted with her mind. Then realized what she'd done. She'd kept her mouth shut, hadn't yelled for him with breath from her lungs.

No answer.

Thunder!

She got an Equine grumble. *Sleeping, here.*

Don't sleep too deep, we're getting out of here as quick as can be.

She left the volaran area fast and quietly. The fug of the camp staggered her, no longer benign to her senses but a gray, filthy atmosphere that rasped into her lungs. She wrapped a bandana around her face that still held the sweet scents of the Colorado Rockies and managed a little smile as she recalled that she'd cherished Marrec's handkerchief at the ranch for the opposite reason. She blinked and blinked again as her wits fuddled. Walking was like pulling a boot out of thick mud, taking a step and sinking knee high, and repeating the process.

She saw no one, and that tinkled an alarm in her mind. She had to get to their tent, had to get to Marrec. *Had to reach her babies.* That fear was strong enough to dissipate cotton-headedness, have her picking up her feet faster, holding the cloth closer to her nose and mouth. Hum a protective Shield and watch it form around her. Yep. The Volaran Exotique was back.

Inside the Shield, she still swayed. It wasn't enough. Closing her eyes, she *pulled* at her energy, her Power, deep inside her, yanked it up sluggishly through her body, stalled somewhere around her heart. Her eyes didn't want to open, she wanted to crumple where she was into the arms of sleep. Though she'd prefer Marrec's arms. She sighed. *Marrec!* Her brain was definitely half a bar slower. That wouldn't do.

Oddly enough, a commercial came to mind. Some cleaning jingle. She gathered her power and *whisked* the sleepiness and complacency away. Spun the muggy effect of another spell from the inside of her egg-shaped Shield.

And came back to her senses, shivering in the cold, crisp air inside her Shield. She narrowed her eyes, surveyed the camp. No one stirred.

This was bad. Very, very bad.

Why hadn't anyone told them that the camp was bad?

Because the dark spell had worked slowly, incrementally, like poison...and the Circlets hadn't been living at the camp since they'd taken the children for protection. And another layer—the final trap—had been sprung when Marrec and the kids had landed.

By her secret enemy within the ranks of the Chevaliers and Marshalls.

This time she could feel the evil.

The evil one who had wanted to kill her.

The evil one who had bespelled the camp and everyone in it—including Calli's children and husband.

The evil one with great Power linked to the Dark itself.

She found Jetyer in their tent sleeping on a cot, but not Marrec or Diaminta.

45

Forcing her hand shaking with fear to write, she penned
a note to Marian, struggled to form words, write them. She
lifted the boy, ran from the tent, casting her mind about for
any volaran patterns. Sapphire was sleeping just a row away.

With drunken strides, Calli found the volaran, strapped
Jetyer in as if he'd been a wounded Chevalier…and he was.
Wounded already in this battle with evil that shrouded
Lladrana and not yet nine. She vowed this would *not* happen
again while she lived.

Shouting in Equine, Calli sent enough fear spurting into
the volaran to rouse her. The mare tossed her head, rolled
her eyes, backed.

Calli infused Sapphire with steely determination to leave
the camp and fly to Marian and Jaquar. The winged horse
remembered the Circlets. She could find Marian's and

Jaquar's Songs, especially aloft and flying. Marian had been kind. Jaquar had had an interesting smell. She would find them. She would deliver Jetyer to them…and the warning about the bespelled encampment. She would save herself and bring help! Sapphire, the hero.

Heart thumping hard, Calli watched her soar, disappear too soon into the sky. A spell definitely lay upon this place like smog.

She'd rescued Jetyer, done the best to warn others.

But her husband and baby were missing. Her blood pumped sluggishly in her veins, cold with terror. The camp was so unnaturally quiet, Calli thought she'd run into the Dark lurking around the next tent corner.

She could feel the evil one—and accomplices—like a burning on her skin, against her Shield. The closer she got to them, the more her skin heated to bubbling. She gritted her teeth and pressed on.

At the break of a row, Calli stopped in horror. Before her was an open gathering space around a fire. The flames flickered cheerfully against the darkness—and illuminated the three people all too well.

Seeva bent over a sleeping form, framed the woman's face, inhaled and *drew* the life, the Power from her. Calli could see it sparkle like bedewed diamonds from the noble Chevalier to Seeva. She'd never known that could be done. She shuddered. Of course she wouldn't. She hadn't been taught how to recognize or battle evil in human form.

Horror kept her still as she watched Raoul Lebeau strip the body of a jeweled necklace and rings. Then he speared the woman casually, as if making sure of the kill. He stepped back to observe her body sink into the ground to be embraced by Amee.

Lord Veenlit joined them, his face aged—by evil?— heavily jowled and ruddy in the firelight, holding a beautifully jeweled sword, stroking the hilt.

Seeva glanced at him. "You finally got what you wanted."

"My enemy's sword, yes. And riches." He gloated.

Calli forced her gorge down. Stepped back in the shadows to look for a weapon, ducked into the nearest tent, and shivered with relief as she found it to be Koz's. Anything she chose here would work for her, with her, on several levels. She saw the chest, ran over and hummed the keycode. It opened to show her the Damascene dagger, wickedly sharp, strong and Singing of the skill and magic of two worlds.

Grabbing it, she sped back out, just in time to see three more bodies vanish into the soil, the men pocketing more gems, and Seeva moving on toward her next victim—Koz. She set her hands on him, frowned.

"Another of those strong in Power and determination against the Dark?" Raoul mocked, but he sounded drunk. "So much harder to drain them, ain't it?"

"Stop!" Calli shouted.

All three jerked to stand before her. Calli swallowed as she met Seeva's eyes. Eyes living with evil, a smile all viciousness. "You," Calli said, then. "Why?"

Seeva rubbed her hands. "Finally you come." She glided forward a couple of steps.

Calli stood her ground. "Why?"

"The Dark needs a new servant, a Master of the horrors, that we might win dominion of Lladranan, of Amee."

Calli's mouth threatened to drop right open. "You wish to be the—the—" She couldn't seem to get her brain around the thought.

Lifting her chin, Seeva said, "The new Master. She who rules the horror. She, who, after the Dark entity itself, is the most Powerful person on Amee."

"The Singer—"

"Bah! A weak old woman."

Before Calli's eyes, the air around Seeva began to glow, lighting her brilliantly, with the brightness and abundance of her Power. The Power she'd stolen from others.

"Always and ever I had Power. Wanted to apprentice to a Circlet, but that wasn't what people of our family did. So said my father when he was alive, and mother, and my sisters and brothers. None of them listened. None of them understood."

"Why didn't you just leave? Do it on your own?"

Seeva's lip curled. "Live like a servant for years while I apprenticed to some arrogant Circlet who was lesser than me in nobility? Precious few Circlets come from the noble class. I petitioned the one I thought would be the most useful and she rejected me. Me! Sent me a note that she couldn't be bothered with a girl who'd struggle to raise her Tower." Seeva whirled and Calli looked for an opening, but the men watched her narrowly.

"That was then," Seeva crooned. "But see me now, see how much Power I've taken, how much I will keep."

"Enough magic from others that it has made you mad. You have little personal Song of your own left." Calli licked her lips. "And the silver streak in your hair is no larger." Maybe they all were wrong. Maybe Seeva couldn't keep the Power she'd ripped from others.

Seeva snorted. "The silver is so easy to hide if you want to, and my mother preferred it." She shoved back her locks and when her fingers released her hair, her whole head glowed silver—as silver as Alexa's.

"You want my Power," Calli said, gripping the hilt of Koz's dagger hard.

With a glittering smile, Seeva nodded. "Ayes. From the moment you arrived—from *before* you arrived."

"Alexa is too strong a warrior." Calli was figuring it out. "Marian too strong a Circlet."

Shrugging, Seeva said, "A matter of convenience. A Chevalier's Power is closest to my ancestral family Power, and you are still untrained in the greatest uses, concentrating on your stupid volaran speak. You command weak animals. I will command potent monsters."

She had a point in that Calli knew few purely Powerful offensive spells.

"But I will weaken you first."

"You can't use me like that." She looked at Marrec lying on the ground. He appeared to be sleeping, but looked as tough and strong as usual. "And you couldn't use Marrec, could you?"

Seeva laughed and it was ugly. Made *her* ugly. "Many are stupid and excellent sources. They're too lazy to use their considerable Power, so I drain it off them just…like…this." She put a hand on Raoul's upper arm and *sucked*. He went up like a torch.

"Now, Seeva," Veenlit scolded.

Seeva turned around and Calli's blood froze in an instant. Seeva, the *evil, crazy* woman had a limp Diaminta in a backpack on her back. A cry tore from Calli.

Laughing, Seeva said, "She's Powerful—a gift for the Dark."

Calli leaped, fell far short.

Seeva gestured to Lord Veenlit. "Kill her."

Calli had to be smart and accurate and fast. She rolled and lunged, butting her head hard in his solar plexus. He went down. Rolled and rolled again as Seeva stared. The woman had never been athletic. Calli came up behind her, fast. Power was making her fast. Desperation was making her fast.

Praying for accuracy, she slipped the dagger between Seeva's back and the backpack, cut the straps cleanly, dropped the weapon to catch Diaminta. Thankfully the baby was still alive and asleep.

Marrec! she shrieked.

He shook his head, rocked to hands and knees.

Catch Diaminta! She made sure she met his gaze; he appeared dizzy but determined. He reared back to his heels and she tossed the baby to him. He caught her close, staggered to his feet.

Screaming fury, spittle flying, Seeva flung herself on Calli, fingernails ripping cheek and neck.

The pain steadied her, gave her something to focus on. She'd won. She'd saved her family. Now to kill the evil bitch who'd sold her soul to Darkness. They rolled. In mud. In blood. Calli pummeled the woman, gasping, hit her on both temples.

Thunder! she called.

I...I come. The sound of hooves echoed in her head, she thought she could hear the whir of wings.

Seeva was jerked away.

Calli fell back, saw Marrec's enraged face. He held Seeva by the neck of her robe, had the dagger in his other hand.

He plunged it into her.

She arched, gurgled a cry, died.

Marrec fell, too.

Lord Veenlit had regained consciousness, grabbed the dagger, kicked Marrec in the ribs and staggered toward Calli. "You ruined it all!" He threw the knife. It flashed toward her, hideous pain speared her as it pinned her shoulder to the ground.

"You. Will. Pay," Veenlit panted.

She couldn't feel either of her hands, writhed and only made the wound worse. Desperate, she *reached* for Thunder's mind.

Sweeping down, he kicked Veenlit in the head, followed him down to trample him into a bloody pulp in pure fear.

Calli fought through Thunder's violent terror, clamped her will upon his to calm. But as he realized what he stood on, he shuddered, threw off her hold, began to panic.

The pain was a tearing ache, but helping Thunder distracted her. She could handle volaran panic. Once again she imposed her steady mind upon his. "Calm. Look at me and step sideways."

Wiggling a foot the volaran could focus on, and biting her lip to stifle her scream, she drew Thunder's attention.

With delicate steps, he shook each hoof and set it outside Veenlit's body. Dropped his head, barrel heaving. Veenlit's corpse sank into the ground.

Marrec was there, whispering tender words, removing the dagger with one clean stroke. He set his hands on both sides of the shoulder wound and pulled Power from Amee, from other minds now throwing off the enervating sleep. He healed her, banished her pain.

She gaped at him. He sagged beside her.

"How did you do that?"

"A once-in-a-lifetime gift from Amee, I think." He rubbed his left temple. The silver streak there was wider than ever.

"Why aren't you with our children?" Her voice rose.

He pulled her into his arms, cradling her close. "They are safe. Koz watches them."

Calli turned her head to where she'd last seen Koz's body. He wasn't there.

"Why aren't you with our children?" she repeated.

"Because you needed me more, beloved."

In the sky, thunder rolled. Lightning struck in three forks, on the two darkened spots where Raoul's and Veenlit's corpses had lain, and incinerating Seeva's body. It had not sunk into the ground. Seeva had been as evil as the horrors and Amee had not accepted her.

Alexa, Jaquar holding Jetyer, and Marian stood where the lightning hit. Jaquar let go of Jetyer and the boy ran to Calli and Marrec, sandwiching himself between them.

Marian and Jaquar linked hands and minds and swept their staffs around the encampment, chanting. Alexa looked shell-shocked. Her hair stood straight out from her head. She fumbled to sheath her baton, stared down at Seeva's crisped remains.

"Eeww."

More thunder, lightning.

Rain pummeled down, washing away the smog, cleansing everything, then stopped as suddenly as it came, and a dry, hot wind followed. Jaquar smiled.

Alexa shook her head. "Bad show."

"Yes," Calli said.

"I felt you," Marian said. "Both Jaquar and I did. We all are linked enough for that. We met Alexa and landed, then rode lightning here." She shook her head, glanced around at the sluggish camp. "The sleepiness wouldn't have alarmed me." She grimaced. "I think your death would have jolted me, but by then it would have been too late."

"Far too late." Calli coughed.

At that moment, Luthan arrived.

Calli jerked to her feet, glaring. "Your Singer set us up."

He closed his eyes and sighed. "All three Exotiques live." When he opened his lashes, he said, "Did Koz live?"

"Right here." Koz exited his tent with Diaminta.

"Thank the Song, the best future won." Luthan glanced down at Seeva. "She's dead, good." Then he met Calli's gaze, face grim. "Only you could make everything turn out as it should. She would have been the best Master for the Dark. That has been prevented."

Jaquar tilted his head. "I've just been notified that another Master to oversee the management and the invasion of the horrors has been chosen."

"But it is not Seeva. *That* battle we won," Luthan said.

"And it isn't someone from us, from the Castle or the Chevaliers, who know us well," Alexa said.

Silence.

"What?" asked Alexa.

"It's someone from Castleton," Jaquar said.

Calli gritted her teeth. "Still not quite as bad."

"One of Townmaster Sevair Masif's assistants," Jaquar added.

"Ouch." Calli winced.

Alexa tapped her baton. "The Community of the Cities and Towns have approached us to Summon the next Exotique."

Sighing, Calli said, "And so it continues."

"And so it continues."

Then Diaminta began to yell. She wriggled and Koz put her down on her feet. She rocked a little, held out her arms to Calli. "Ma. Ma. Ma." And staggered to her.

Marrec grinned. "Her first steps."

Calli scooped up Diaminta. Her daughter nuzzled her, set her face against her and sighed a warm, good, baby breath onto her neck. Standing, she settled the little girl on one hip, stretched out her arm for Marrec. He moved in and put his solid arm around her waist, kissed her cheek. Jetyer joined them, grasping Marrec's other arm and standing in front of them both. It would have made a perfect picture back home. Too bad they had no cameras on Lladrana.

"We'll hire a painter this very month," Marrec said. "To image us so our children's children will know how we made a family. And we'll trade services for a musician to set our Songs into the canvas with our images. Song willing, strains of us will live for a long, long time."

Calli swallowed, pressed close to her husband as he shifted toward her. They'd survived. Through everything that had happened, on Lladrana and on Earth. They'd done more than survive, they'd triumphed, fulfilling the dreams of their own and their children, their children to come.

Volarans circled them, running around them, wings slightly lifted, in some ritual blessing of their own that flowed out and covered her and her family with sparkling Power, and Calli heard for the first time, the Song of the Volarans for their Exotique. Tears filled her eyes and she didn't stop them as they meandered down her cheeks.

She kissed Diaminta's soft black hair. "I love you, Diaminta."

"Ma. Ma." Her daughter snuggled closer.

Calli bent and made a loud smacking noise as she kissed Jetyer's temple. He grinned up at her and she noticed he had a dimple. Like his father. "I love you, Jetyer."

"I love you, Mama." His eyes, too, sheened.

When she turned to kiss Marrec, his lips were there, a little open. Their mouths melded, his tongue caressed hers and sent Power through her. They withdrew from the kiss at the same time. His eyes were as deep and rich and soft as melted chocolate. "I love you, Calli."

"I love you."

The volarans stopped running and fanned around the family.

Alexa and Bastien, Marian and Jaquar faced them, all in attitudes reflecting their character.

"A real Hallmark moment," Alexa said, hand on hip.

"You look a picture," Marian said at the same time.

"Of a happy family," Bastien said.

"We are a happy family," Marrec said.

Content, Calli smiled.

"Let's go make a home and a family and a life," Marrec said.

"We'll make a family," Calli agreed. She glanced around the now-busy camp, bustling with Power and energy and life. The stars were bright against a black sky, and she felt like one of them, as the people around her were stars, too. Bright and burning. "But there will be a last battle."

Marrec's arm tightened like steel around her waist. His gaze had gone tough and hard. He nodded. "We'll be there for that, too."

"Together," they said.

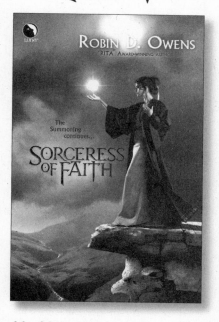